ASHES AND FLAME

A Two Part Story

KIMBERLY M. RINGER

Note from Author

PART 1, **SAPPHIRE ASHES** was originally published as a YA novella. There have been major additions to include vulgar language, adult content, dark themes, expansion on back stories, and additional points of view from the 2014 release.

Part 2, **Eternity's Flame**, is the completion of Tiberius' story.

CONTENT CONSIDERATIONS

Please be aware of the following throughout Part 1 and Part 2. These items are not all-encompassing, and while I tried to do them realistically, please remember this book is at its heart, a romance with a happily ever after.

Abuse
Non-Consensual BDSM
Explicit Sexual Assault
Torture
Kidnapping
Mature Language
Family Death
Sexual Situations
Abuse of Power
Attempted Self-Harm
Misogyny
Off-page Domestic Abuse
Talk of Trafficking

If you or someone you know may be struggling with suicidal thoughts, you can call the U.S. National Suicide Prevention Lifeline by simply dialing 988 or the full phone number 800-273-TALK (8255) any time, day or night, or chat online. Crisis Text Line also provides free, 24/7, confidential support via text message to people in crisis when they dial 741741.

DEDICATION

To all the dreamers who make your dreams a reality.

To all those who fight their own brain demons and still get up each and every day and conquer that day. This book was written during a time when the brain demons were attacking in force. Every day that you continue to get up is a win.

Finally, **Elisabeth Garner and Tara Tappin.** From the moment you two read this book you have been huge cheerleaders for this project. Thank you for all the spaghetti sessions, the laughs, and the times you have literally talked me off the ledge.

Copyright

Contact Information: www.kimberlymringer.com
ISBN Hardback: 978-1-7373358-7-0
ISBN Paperback: 978-1-957447-22-3
ISBN E-Book: 978-1-7373358-9-4
Second Edition: February 2021
Re-edited: April 2023

Contents

Sapphire Ashes

Part One

CHAPTER 1

PROLOGUE

FIRE FROM THE EARTH SHALL RENEW THEE LIFE

TIBERIUS

I DUCKED THE PUNCH, but the wire-haired drunk jabbed me with his other fist in the small of my back. That punch to the right side sent a sharp pain down my leg.

"Damn Romans. Think they can just take whatever they want. No regard for what we have worked hard for. What our families have *died* for!" he said through his teeth, throwing his ale down the front of me as I stumbled back.

"I'm not Roman," I said, trying to get my footing. "I'm only an advisor to the Empire. My name is Tiberius—"

"So what? You just parade around the lands and report to them who hasn't bent to their will?" He lunged for me, and when his fist landed squarely on my jaw, I thought I felt something crack. Pain shot through my face and I stumbled back a few steps, falling against the bar.

What was wrong with me? I was a better fighter than this. I should be able to handle him with no problem. I've only had two ales. My world spun again. *Seriously, what the fuck is wrong with me?* I saw an older woman, at least I was fairly sure it was a woman, walk up to the drunk and hand him some coins.

"He's all yours," the man said to her as he walked away, but then he paused, turned on his heel, strode back to me, and spit in my hair. "Filthy Roman scum."

The woman pushed him away and immediately blew something in my face. I choked on the spicy wood taste, but whatever it was had an instant effect. One moment, I felt as if I were flying above the clouds, and the next, I was plummeting from the sky. Just before I hit the earth, everything went black.

There was a loud pounding in my ears as I came to. In the distance, I heard a raspy woman's voice in a language I didn't understand. The harsh way she uttered the words led me to believe she was dictating orders. As the other two answered her in the same foreign tongue, it sounded mischievous and excited. There was something familiar about its cadence. I've been all over the Empire and heard many variations of languages spoken, but this . . . this I couldn't quite place.

I shook my head, and it pounded violently. The gag in my mouth pressed on my jaw and sent a sharp pain through my skull as I tried to talk. I reached to remove the gag, but they had tied my arms around a pole that reached far above my head. Slowly, I opened my eyes and looked down to find my feet were bound and tethered to the wood base I was standing on. Twitching my wrists, I tried to dislocate one of them, like I had done many times before, but the binding was too tight. When I closed my eyes and tried again, the world spun, sending my stomach flipping. My eyes flew open. Leaning my head back against the pole, I focused on a tree branch above me and waited for the world to right itself again. Slowly, it was getting better, but everything was still muddled.

The moon was high in the night sky, and the only other light came from a tiny fire with three women huddled around it. I blinked hard a few times, and my eyes adjusted to the darkness just enough to see that I was in a small clearing in the forest. Only the Gods knew where, though.

"Ah. He's awake," one of the women hissed loud enough from the fire in the common tongue. She moved her head almost all the way around in a completely unnatural way. My eyes widened when I realized it was the same woman I had seen at the tavern. As she faced me, she smiled, showing her rotten black and green teeth. My stomach twisted and bile rose high in my throat. It took all my concentration not to throw up from the sight of it.

"It is time, sisters," one of the other women hissed, looking up at the moon.

Standing in unison, they turned and strode toward me, shoulder to shoulder. The one on the right had her dark hair completely covering her face, and through the dark curtain of hair, I could just make out a cloth tied around her head and covering her eyes. She was splattering something on the ground that landed with a thick, wet slosh.

The one on the left, however, the one from the tavern, had blonde hair, soft features, and none of the creepy looks of the other two. Dressed in what appeared to be a newer dress than the others, I imagined she would have been beautiful, until you looked at her eyes, which were as black as the night surrounding her. She was looking up at the moon and never once blinked the entire time.

The most wrinkly of the three was the size of the other two put together and stood in the middle. She had long, thin, stringy gray hair and a huge wart on her forehead right at the hairline. When she spoke, you couldn't see any teeth, just a black void of a mouth.

Together, they took slow, careful steps toward me, chanting in a dark tongue that shot through the haze in my head. Some part of my brain finally identified that tongue, and fear swept through me. My heart dropped to my stomach, and all the blood drained from my face. It couldn't be. *The Dark Moesia Witches?* I had heard only bits and pieces about them through hushed whispers and stories shared over late-night pints of ale. No one knew what the words meant, but the cadence was one that most knew enough to fear those who spoke it.

Legend was that the Dark Moesia Witches could make you cry in terror with a single word. They were the stuff of nightmares and horrors and the basis for every scary story in history. According to the stories he had heard, they were the start of the bloodsucker and shapeshifter myths, and these particular witches were rumored to be immortal. For a split second, I wondered why they were so far west in Vendelicia, but when the full picture began to form, fear overtook me again.

These witches were leaving a trail of bodies all across the Empire. Men and women had been found tied to poles, just as I was in that moment, but their necks had been slit open. Little was known about the witches' beliefs or rituals. It was only known that if you encountered one, you were not likely to survive it. Death was all the Dark Moesia Witches knew.

When they reached me, the one to the right sprinkled a putrid substance on my chest, and my stomach once again lurched. I could only describe the smell as rotten eggs crossed with three-month-old vegetables and horse manure that had been left out for days in the heat of summer. It was a smell even the pigs would have turned their snouts up at. She poured the remaining goo over my feet, threw the bowl to the side, and peered up at me with a wicked, crooked smile. I was so distracted by what she was doing, I didn't notice that the eldest one had unsheathed a knife and brought it to my chest.

I stopped breathing.

I didn't dare to move a muscle.

There was no way to fight my way out of it. I was going to die. The eldest witch chanted the words again, and with the last sentence, she and the other two witches spoke in my native tongue. "Fire from the Earth shall renew thee life." They elongated their last word as all three of the witches took hold of the hilt of the blade and, as one, slit my throat.

I jerked awake, feeling the sun on my face and the cool earth at my back. My heart was racing, so I concentrated on slowing my breathing. Lifting my hand to my neck, I was relieved to feel it was in one piece, fully expecting to have a slit throat like the others who had been found across the lands. After taking a few more deep breaths, I mumbled, "What a dream."

I lay there longer than I usually would, taking in the sun's warmth and the cool, fresh breeze. My head was pounding, and I didn't dare open my eyes. The sun coming through the trees was already too bright through my eyelids as it was. Massive hangovers weren't something I wasn't used to, but I was very glad that there was no need to rush to get up. I didn't have to report to the new commander for a few more days.

Pain continued to ricochet through my head like a hammer striking an anvil. I remembered the brawl in the tavern, and I gingerly ran my hand along my jaw. It zinged with pain, but it didn't feel broken. It would hurt to eat breakfast this morning.

As a breeze blew by, my nose filled with something foul in the air. My eyes flew open, and I instantly regretted it as the world spun a moment. Blinking rapidly, I let my eyes adjust and willed myself to see straight.

Finally, I looked to my feet. "Oh, Gods! What did I tromp through last night?" Sighing heavily, I stared at the goo that covered my boots. "I need to find somewhere to bathe and wash out these clothes."

Examining the rest of my attire, I realized there was a lot of blood on me. Too much blood for anything to have lived through. Past experience would say a broken nose, but mine didn't feel as if it had been. I didn't remember killing anyone last night.

Studying my boots, I realized they weren't fully on my feet. Reaching down and pulling them on all the way, I shook my head at the smell that blew back into my face again. Between the blood and whatever it was on my boots, I decided that new clothes were needed at the very least.

As I got up and gathered the rest of my things from where they were neatly piled against a nearby tree, I added new boots to my list of things to buy. There was no way I was getting the smell out of them. Bending down to grab my pack, I thought how odd it was that I would have neatly placed my things before crashing by the fire last night.

I had been exceptionally drunk, which usually meant everything was sprawled everywhere the next morning. I double-checked to make sure the fire was completely out by stomping on the flames, and the warmth from the still burning embers only made the smell of the boots that much worse.

"Yes. New boots are a must," I grumbled, heading into the forest.

As the breeze wafted around me once again, the awful smell invaded my nose. "Whew," I said, waving the air around my face. "And a bath. I really need a bath."

CHAPTER 2

TIBERIUS

YEARS LATER

I HAD BEEN ON this mountain for a few days. Herculaneum was only a short hike from here, but I had held back, not ready to go back to being a proper person yet. I had spent years in the Empire under the rules and expectations of my commanders, under the weight of all the people I'd killed. Whether or not they deserved it, it still weighed heavily on me. In Herculaneum, there were going to be more rules, business pressures, and, most of all, the pressure to marry now that I was back and willing to help my father run his business.

It was nice to just hunt, sleep, and be by myself while on the mountain. No armies or battalions to coddle. No sneaking around, gathering information. No more hiding in the shadows to eavesdrop on those having secret and not-so-secret meetings. No commanders to give me orders.

No. Never again. Commander Suilius had ensured that.

It had been nine months since that day. Nine months since I had turned over information that condemned an entire colony. The next morning, Commander Suilius and all those under his command raped and pillaged the little colony in the middle of Macedonia.

I will never forget the women lying in their homes, brutally abused, after their husbands and children were killed in front of them. The smell of vomit, blood, and feces was everywhere. The colony had only housed some insurgents a few months before, but the town was otherwise clean and had been since they had left. Only Commander Suilius thought they should be taught a lesson, and that the punishment for helping insurgents was the complete destruction of the colony. I couldn't stomach watching innocents being abused and murdered any longer. I had fulfilled my minimum time, and if I wanted out, it was then or never.

The next morning, I turned my armor over, signed the documents, and submitted them to be sent to the Emperor. I received the release papers two months ago while going through one of the larger settlements on the way back here. Never again would I allow information gathered by me to be used to slaughter men, women, and children.

Today was hot, blisteringly so. One more day and I'd head down to see my family. I had just finished stuffing my blankets into my pack that held what few personal items I owned when there was a soft, musical voice that flowed over the hill near my campsite. The hill protected me from anyone's view who might look up the mountain. No one would see me during the day, and only the light from the fire at night would give any indication that anyone was there at all. It was a couple hours after the sun had broken the horizon, so I wasn't too worried about firelight causing me to be discovered. No one would know I was there. No one *should* know I was there.

I crawled up the hill on my stomach, peered over the edge, and stopped.

There, standing just far enough away that she couldn't hear or see me, was the most beautiful woman I had ever seen in my life. She looked to be several inches shorter than me, with long brown hair and a body that proved she took care of herself. She was strong, and I loved that she was not dainty in the slightest. She was built like a storm and radiated something powerful, but I couldn't place my finger on what that power was.

Big, round brown eyes, soft cheeks, and a button nose graced a face that punched the air out of my lungs as she turned in my direction, and I hardened, painfully so. My mouth watered at the thought of tasting her. By the Gods, she was stunning.

I pressed myself into the ground to stay unseen. As she moved a little closer, picking through the plants, plucking them meticulously, and carefully setting them in the basket she was carrying, I just stared at her. The woman was humming a soft song that reminded me of one that a woman in an apothecary shop in Dalmatia had been humming a few months ago while I was there.

Wrap thy in grass shall it brass,
Flowing, growing,
Heal thy wounds,
Flowing, growing,
Earth to Earth to keep us safe
Mother, may thy guide

How had I even remembered that? I had continued to mouth it for days after it had become stuck in my head. I studied the woman for a long moment. She froze just for a heartbeat before plucking another piece of grass and placing it in the basket.

She looked around quickly before calling out, "Lars? I'm ready to head back."

There was no one else there. I closed my eyes and strained to hear where this Lars could be, but I didn't hear anyone. I smirked, recognizing she wasn't a stupid woman. She had only called out to make it sound as though she were accompanied. *Why was she unaccompanied?*

Staying perfectly still, I waited until she was far enough away that I could move without being heard. After throwing what few belongings I had left out back into my pack, I trailed down the hill after her. I had to know who she was.

The entire way down the mountain, she kept looking over her shoulder, like she could tell she was being followed but wasn't really sure by whom. The closer we got to Herculaneum, the faster her pace became until she slipped behind a door that had a sign indicating an apothecary shop.

Just who was this woman?

CHAPTER 3

TIBERIUS

STARING AT THE DOOR of the apothecary shop, I hoped to get another glimpse of her. After thirty minutes and seeing nothing, I went to the balneae, got cleaned up, and headed toward my father's home. I stood in front of the door for a long time, wondering if I should have sent word ahead that I was coming home. Would it be a burden to them that I was back?

Gazing down the street, I took a deep breath before reaching for the door when a seven-year-old brown-haired girl peered through the window and her eyes grew big.

"Tiberius!" she shouted, and when she flung open the door, it bounced against the wall.

"Nepia," I said as she threw her arms around my shoulders and I wrapped her up in a giant hug.

"Tiberius?" a soft voice asked from beyond the threshold.

"Mother," I said, losing my breath in relief. It felt so good to see her. I put Nepia down and went to my mother, who wrapped her arms around my waist and wept.

My heart sank, then it sped up as I wondered what was causing her to cry. "Mother, what is wrong?"

"You are home?" she asked.

"I am."

"For how long?" she asked, barely above a whisper.

"As long as I need to be."

"Your father will be so happy to have you home," she said, stepping aside just as my other sister came through and nearly knocked me over.

"Hi, Septimia."

"Hi, Tiberius. Are you going to tell us all the stories from your travels? How was Macedonia? What was the farthest place you went? Did you see any pretty girls? How many people did you kill for the Emperor?"

"My goodness, you are full of questions." I chuckled. "Yes, good, Armenia, a few, and finally, I didn't keep count."

"Tiberius!" Mother chastised me.

"What? It wasn't like I had enough time to think, *How many is that today because Septimia is going to want to know how many died by my hand?*" I beamed at my sister. "Mia, I didn't keep count because I didn't like it, didn't enjoy it, and I don't want to do it anymore, okay? No more questions. You should be studying your letters."

"She is." Mother was smiling proudly at her. "Both of them are doing very well in their studies."

"Good. I won't have imbecile sisters."

"I won't have imbecile daughters!" Mother laughed. "They will hold their own with any man they are arranged with."

"Yes, Mother," they said in unison.

Just then, my father walked in, saying, "Avita, make a large dinner. I need to conf—" After stopping midsentence, he stared at me.

"Hello, Father."

"It's true," he said, taking a shaky step toward me. "Someone told me they thought they saw you walking out of the balneae, but I didn't believe it."

"It is me, Father." I took two long strides to him and held him close. He looked so much older than he was when I last saw him. The lines in his face had deepened drastically, but he still felt strong in my arms. I felt my father shudder against me and hold me tighter.

"The Emperor has returned you to us for how long?" he asked when he pulled away a moment later.

"I no longer work for the Empire, Father. I am here to help you with the business, if you will allow it, of course."

His eyes widened. "You may."

"Now, please tell me what I have missed here at home," I requested as we made our way to sit.

Days later, Father and I were walking down the street to meet with a business associate at one of the supply rooms when I saw her. She was walking with a man who resembled her but was much older. Her father maybe?

"What is it, Tiberius?" my father asked quietly.

"Who is that woman, Father?" I nodded my head in her direction.

"Which one? The one with hair of wheat or cinnamon?"

"Cinnamon," I said, my heart hammering. She was just as captivating as she had been the first time I saw her. There was a sensual sway of her hips that left me raking my eyes over every inch of her body. As if she could feel me looking at her, she turned and gazed in our direction, but I was partially hidden behind the barrels and my father.

Her eyes were bright, and the remnants of a smile on her face made my insides swim. Turning back to her father, she returned her attention to the person they had been speaking with. She tipped her head slightly, but it wasn't the usual greeting a woman in the Empire would give a man of higher status. She carried herself as if she were a queen. Damn, if that confidence wasn't sexy as hell.

My father was silent for a long moment, and when I looked at him, he was studying me carefully. "That is Sidonia Regillia. She is Alus Galerius Regillia's only daughter."

"Sidonia." Her name was almost a whispered prayer on my lips.

"She is unarranged," my father said, a small smile on his lips. "Are you looking for a wife, Tiberius? I could arrange it with her father. We work well with him. He controls the marketplace."

"No, Father. No arrangements yet. I wish to select my bride." *She wasn't married? Wasn't spoken for? How was that spectacular being not spoken for?*

I could not take my eyes off her as my heart spun in circles in my chest. She was a siren, controlling every ounce of my attention. I vaguely registered that my father was saying something, but I couldn't hear a word of it. This woman commanded respect from the people around her in a way that wasn't demeaning. She crouched down to talk to a child as if they were an equal, but when done, she immediately turned to another of her father's business associates and spoke to him in the same manner. It was fascinating.

"Tiberius," my father said, demanding my attention. I slowly took my gaze off her and looked at him to find him smiling. "You are enthralled by her, aren't you?"

I could do nothing but nod.

"Is this love at first sight?"

"I do not believe in such a thing. I just think she is beautiful, and I would like to get to know her. Love is not something that happens instantly. It is fostered. I know Mother says she fell for you instantly, but I just don't think of love as being something that happens that quickly."

"Your mother and I didn't know each other before the arrangement was finalized between our families. I came home from working with my brothers and was told that I would be wed in ten days to your mother. I knew I loved her the second she opened her mouth and demanded that if she was going to be arranged to me, she would be treated as an equal. She would not be a possession of mine," he said, smiling. "Your mother commanded respect, and that was the best endearment she could give me."

"I will give my wife no less." I flicked my eyes to her as she and her father strode down the road in the opposite direction we were heading. Her laugh flitted across the space, and it was a jolt to my senses, making me hard within seconds and yet softening my heart in a way no other woman had ever done.

"Father, do you think you could arrange an introduction?" I was practically begging him at this point. I couldn't let him know how desperate I was. If I did, he would make that introduction, but it would be an introduction and announcement all in one.

"I can, but it might take time. She and her father are rarely in the same place, and we do not have time now to happen upon them. Our associate will not wait long," he said, taking me by the bicep and pulling me along.

"I just want to get to know her. How long do you think it will be before we can arrange a meeting?"

"A few days, a couple of weeks. I will talk to her father and see what we can do. I have been thinking about meeting with him soon anyway, so we can talk then." He smiled, and I knew he could tell just how much I needed to know her.

I nodded and decided I would do what I did best: I would find out whatever I could about Sidonia Regillia.

Chapter 4

Sidonia

I TRIED TO RELAX as my bath attendant, Attia, washed my long brown hair by looking at the view out of the window. Mount Vesuvius was a beautiful being, and I reveled in it. I had to look through some of the crumbled buildings that were being repaired from the tremors, but Mount Vesuvius was standing tall and proud over the colony, proving that the Earth was still as stable as ever. Even this late into the summer months, with the dried-up grass littering the mountain, it was still beautiful.

I tried to think about anything other than the conversation with my father from that morning. It was *the* discussion, the one about me entering into a marriage arrangement. When he had stopped listening, I had turned on my heels and stormed out. I had my weekly appointment at the balneae, anyway.

Sighing heavily, my focus centered on the grasslands of the mountain, and I felt content and relaxed. Every seventh day, I came to the private balneae where Attia attended to me with the best of care. It was the busiest establishment in all of Herculaneum, and the wealthy came from all over the Empire to relax in our colony. My family had been here for generations, and we'd done well for ourselves. It'd allowed me to enjoy some privileges others couldn't afford.

"Sidonia. You've been up on the mountain again, haven't you?" Attia asked with a knowing smile as she rinsed my hair and got to work cleaning my arms and back.

"Gathering herbs for Mother and Grandmother," I answered carefully.

"Herbs," she said, sighing but with a smile on her face.

"Yes. Herbs." I sat up straighter to allow her better access to the small of my back. "We are lucky we can find what we need on the mountain without having to go all the way to the larger Pompeii markets."

"I understand, my lady. However, you must be careful. You don't want the Empire to ask questions. What if they found you up there?"

"We would merely be on a walk enjoying *what the Gods gave us*," I bit back.

"But Sidonia," she stammered, but I interrupted her.

"Surely Emperor Titus hasn't deemed it illegal to wander the countryside," I said pointedly. She nodded in understanding, saying nothing further.

"Thank you for your concern, Attia," I said, my voice lower now. "It is appreciated, but we have been careful for generations. The Roman Empire isn't going to scare us into stopping our practices and helping those who need our help."

"It's just . . . I heard from the guards that came through here a couple days ago that Emperor Titus didn't care much for . . . special apothecary shops. I would hate for something to happen to your family. You have business enemies, and we wouldn't want them to catch you unaware."

"Is that a threat, Attia?" I asked, eyeing her carefully.

Shock crossed her face. "Oh no, my lady! Never. It's just . . . your family has much status here. With that status comes power and influence, and there are others that want it. Your workshop is very well known here in the colony, and word is getting out even to Pompeii of your family's work."

We sat in silence as she finished her duties, and I looked back out over the mountain. She was right. There were many who knew of our practices, possibly too many. In fact, my grandmother, mother, and I had carved out quite a business. While my father looked over the markets of Herculaneum, the women in my family were not ones who just sat at home and catered to family life. My father enjoyed the extra coinage it brought, as it allowed us luxuries that other families didn't have, such as having meat on the table often, our morning fresh bread, finer cloth for our clothing, and stronger leather for our sandals. While his status in the colony would normally allow all of that, prices in the Empire were rising, and the coinage that came in through the workshop allowed us to keep things we would have had to give up, as Father refused to raise prices too much in the market.

My brothers, Lars and Severius, helped my father at the marketplace with whatever he needed them to do. Lars was eight years older than I and was married with two girls, while Severius was only five years older. Severius lost his wife last year while birthing their son, who the Mother didn't believe was ready for this world. It had taken years for her to get pregnant, and when Severius lost both of them, I wasn't sure what still held him to this world.

Father had expressed his want for him to remarry, but I believed Severius was too heartbroken over their deaths. Their marriage was a rare situation where love came before the arrangement for the marriage, not out of family agreements and status gain. I craved the same thing but knew that I probably wouldn't have that luxury. Grandmother and I wanted to repair Severius's broken heart, but there are some things that just couldn't be fixed with potions and herbs.

As Attia combed the knots out of my hair and a girl I wasn't familiar with applied colors to my face, I stewed over the fight between my father and me. He was absolutely insistent I get married and bear children. Granted, I was eighteen years of age and should have already married, especially with my family's high status. My father had set up a powerful arrangement last year, but Marcus had decided that he would rather go off to war with the Empire than marry me. I smirked as I remembered how I may have had something to do with that.

"Miss Sidonia, please keep your face still," the girl I didn't know said with a scowl.

"I'm sorry." I tried to keep still for her, letting my mind wander for a moment.

"Sidonia," Attia finally said after a few minutes. "Do you want the high braids like they do in Rome, or just pulled back?"

"Pulled back with the silver, please," I said. When she hesitated, I continued, "Attia, you know I'll pay you for it."

"Of course, my lady."

Attia pulled a section of my hair from the front on each side halfway back, clipping a piece of silver to each section, then pulled that section back to meet in the middle of the back of my head and clipped three more pieces of silver to secure it. She then placed a fine wreath with small gems on the sections of hair that had been pulled back, and it reminded me of the little folks' crown I had seen in one of my grandmother's books.

When she was done, she and the other girl helped me get dressed in my palla and sandals.

"Thank you," I said, paying Attia and headed out to meet Father in the market.

CHAPTER 5

SIDONIA

I WALKED DOWN THE streets of Herculaneum toward the forum, to the marketplace where my father worked. Father was the main proprietor. If you wanted to sell anything, you had to go through him. He had very strict rules and required only the finest and freshest of items to be sold there. He also made sure that all vendors kept their prices low enough that even the most modest of slaves could purchase most of what was offered. Father believed in equality and worked very hard to maintain that balance here in Herculaneum. While he agreed that higher rate items should be sold at a higher price, he wanted to ensure that every citizen of the colony could afford to provide for their basic needs.

The streets were still littered with crumbling rock as many slaves repaired walls to homes and shops. Some masters were nicer than others, regarding their help as part of the family, while others regarded them as nothing more than the dirt they brushed off their togas. My family had long since decided against hiring help.

Mother didn't even take our clothing to the local shop to get washed. She took them down to where the earth met the oceans and washed them there. She said the salt in the water helped clean them better than the shop did anyway, and without the need of degrading slaves to stomp around in urine. The urine did a fine job getting some of the harsher oils out of the cloth, but . . . I mentally shuddered. We just didn't see the need for it. We had also found that our clothes smelled cleaner and fresher than most.

When I arrived at the marketplace, it was full of vendors and citizens alike. Father had just received a fresh shipment of supplies from Pompeii, but there were a lot of hired workers repairing the cracks in the walls all around the marketplace, which had them fighting for room on the narrow walkways. Just because we didn't employ slaves full time didn't mean we wouldn't hire them for specific jobs we didn't have time to complete ourselves. Father paid his workers exceptionally well, so there was never any problem finding someone who wished to take a temporary job from him.

I wandered the market, taking notice of some of the new fabrics that had come in, as well as the new jewelry. I eyed one particularly beautiful piece that was made of silver that wrapped around the wrist and connected with a lotus blossom, complete with a sapphire in the center that shone brightly in the sun. After a few moments of admiring the piece, I paid the man the four aureus coins. It would upset my father that I paid so much for it, but I was paying for it with the money I had earned from our workshop, not with the family's portion of the funds. I slid it on immediately. The sunlight caught the sapphire, making it sparkle.

I passed by the meats and fish, wrinkling my nose at the smell. Some of that fish smelled like they brought it all the way from Pompeii . . . or maybe Rome. I made a mental note to speak to father about it and continued on to the herbs and oils stall.

"Madam Marulla," I said to the older lady behind the baskets of herbs. "How was your trip to Pompeii?"

"It was wonderful, as always. I spent time with my daughter and her family. Their home had some damage from the tremors, but it's being repaired quickly. How is yours?"

"Fine. We only had minor damage. In fact, they finished repairing it only yesterday. What else did you discover in Pompeii?"

"The farmers along the mountain have been having a hard time keeping the sheep alive on that side of Vesuvius," she said in a tone only I would have been able to pick up on.

"So, the rumors are true?" I asked, keeping my voice low but light.

"They are. Saw them with my own eyes. Sheep littered the landscape, looking healthy as can be but dead as stone," she said in a rush of whispers. After looking quickly to either side to make sure that no one else was listening, she added, "They think the Dark Witches of Moesia put a curse on them."

"The Dark Witches of Moesia? They haven't been seen in the area, have they?" I asked, leaning toward her. There had been rumors of them moving west and into some of those territories, but nothing this far south.

"There are rumors in Pompeii about three witches performing a ritual on men in the north, close to the Germania borders, and in the forests between here and Rome over the last few years." Her eyes were full of meaning that I didn't fully understand.

"Which ritual?" I had heard so much about the Dark Witches of Moesia, but when I asked Grandmother and Mother, I was always told they practiced a very dark evil magic that was handed down from generations almost as long as our practices had been. It didn't stop me from reading about some of those rituals in Grandmother's older books, though.

Madam Marulla hung her head with sadness. "I don't know, but they say that men and women are dying. Occasionally, they find people scattered around the countryside bound to poles with their necks sliced open. One of my associates said they found his eldest son like that just south of Rome."

I shook my head and sent a silent prayer to Mother Earth. The Mother would torment us for the rest of our lives if we ever took a life. I wondered what their deity did in retribution. They were practicing dark magic, so I supposed death came with the territory.

"Oh, Sidonia! I have the spell oils your grandmother wanted. Would you like to take them with you now, or would you like to have me drop them off later?"

"I can take them now," I said. "Also, if you have any turmeric, wormwood, and garlic, I'll take those, too."

"Turmeric," she said. "That's rare, but yes, I have some."

"I will pay, of course." I was confused that it was the second time today I'd said such a thing.

"Of course. I wasn't complaining, my dear. Only commenting on the rarity of it," she was quick to say.

I smiled at her as she ducked behind the sheet. The man with the smelly stall was eyeing me strangely as I heard him grossly overcharge for some fish. I would definitely talk to Father.

"What is it, girl?" he asked, snarling the words when the customer left.

"I was just wondering when your fish was fresh. Two, maybe three days ago?" My voice was sickly sweet.

He moved around to stand and tower over me. It was an attempt at intimidation, and I was not having it.

"Caught yesterday evening, three down from here," he said, his rancid breath flowing over my face. I reached up to cover my nose, and he caught my hand.

"Do I offend you?" he said, moving closer, and my stomach rolled. "Maybe I should take you around that corner and teach you just what kind of respect a woman is supposed to give a man."

I lifted an eyebrow at him. "Please let go of my wrist."

He pulled me forward two steps before his groin painfully met my knee just as I had intended. The string of inappropriate language that came from him had women covering her children's ears.

"You whore," he seethed and grabbed my wrist again. "You're going to make this feel all better right here and now."

I twisted my wrist around, grabbing his fingers and hearing the satisfying crunch as I broke two of them with the movement. When I brought my elbow to his nose, I smiled as I felt a crunch and witnessed how the blood sprayed onto the cobblestones. I sighed as I realized a few specks also landed on my palla.

His eyes burned in hatred as he held his nose and reached for something to stanch the bleeding. "Women are not property, and you don't get to do with them what you wish just because they have a pretty face. Now if you'll excuse me, I have some shopping to finish before I meet with my father, Master Regillia."

Eyes widening, he stomped back behind his stall and told his workers to pack things up for the day. I chuckled because I would now have to explain to my father how blood was on the cobblestones, but I took satisfaction in the knowledge that he would make sure that the man could never sell merchandise here again.

A moment later, Madam Marulla came back with a bag and handed it to me. "I added a few others that your mother is always looking for. No charge, of course."

"Thank you, madam," I said, smiling and handing her ten aureus.

"Oh! Sidonia, that is too much."

"Keep it. You deserve it. You've always done well by us and kept our lives safe," I said, meeting her eyes meaningfully.

"As you have with mine. Thank you." There was a mutual respect between us. She knew exactly what we were. She was also one of the few shopkeepers we could get some of the rarer herbs from. There was a high risk in even transporting them through the Empire, as they were used for not much else than for our healing potions.

CHAPTER 6

SIDONIA

WHEN I FOUND MY father, he was standing with a man and another who looked so much like him, only younger. It had to be his son. When my father saw me, he reached out toward me and smiled. "Ahhh, Sidonia. My sweet, sweet garden flower."

"Father," I greeted, giving him a welcoming hug. When he pulled away, his eyes narrowed at me as they focused on a spot on my left shoulder.

"Why is there fresh blood on your palla? Were you not just at the balneae?" he asked, almost hesitant to know the answer.

"I was. I stopped by and picked up the items needed for the workshop, and there was a vendor who did not appreciate that I wasn't receptive to his advances," I said carefully, noting the men standing with him.

His eyes narrowed again, but there was a small lift to the corner of his mouth. "Is that what the commotion was about?" I just nodded once, and then he let a smile cross his face as he turned back to the two men and said, "Sidonia, I believe you know Decimus Avidius Vispania."

"Yes. How are you today, Mr. Vispania?" I tipped my head in respect.

"Doing well," he said as the ground started shaking under our feet. Fruit fell from their baskets in the nearby stall, tents shook as if someone was trying to shake the dust off them after a windstorm, and bottles fell over in the various stalls around us. I grabbed a canister of water to keep it from tipping over and then . . . just as quickly as it started, it stopped.

"Well, doing well, considering all these tremors. Herculaneum is a great, prosperous colony. I'm not sure why the Gods feel it necessary to shake fear into the people around here." Mr. Vispania looked to the sky as if it held the answer.

"I agree, Decimus," my father said, eyeing me. We didn't view the Gods the way most did around here. We worshiped the Earth and the sanctity of what she could give us. By respecting her and taking only what we needed for our spells and potions, she blessed us with a small amount of healing power to help others. We were never to harm. That was the first and most important rule.

Behind Mr. Vispania was a man who, when his eyes met mine, smiled and stood up straight. He was a few inches taller than I and strong enough to show the outline of his muscles in his arms. His brown, slightly curly hair hung halfway down his ears, and his eyes sparkled like the sapphire in my new bracelet. I felt my heart skip a few beats when our eyes locked.

"Father, won't you introduce us?" he asked in a voice that had a smooth cadence to it I couldn't place.

"Yes, of course. Sidonia Regillia, daughter of Alus Galerius Regillia, I'd like to introduce you to my eldest living son, Tiberius Maximus Vispania," he said.

Tiberius took a step forward, took my hand, and kissed it gently. "Sidonia. Beautiful name for such a beautiful woman."

Now, it wasn't that I wasn't used to men getting flustered over me. Only with Tiberius, when his lips touched my hand, it felt as if a fire had been lit within me. My stomach tightened in a way that it had for no man before. He looked up at me again, and there seemed to be a heat in his gaze that made me wonder if he felt that fire as well.

Not only was he handsome, but he didn't seem arrogant or have an air of being entitled like so many other men who had clamored at my feet. We stood there looking at each other, his hand still in mine, a moment too long because out of the corner of my eye, I saw my father look between us, and the corner of his lip twitched up.

"Thank you," I muttered, attempting to get control. I took a small step back, forcing him to let go of my hand. When I met his gaze again, I gave him a look to tell him to leave it alone, but sometimes I could swear he could read my mind. I had to be careful because at the slightest hint of finding him interesting, my father would jump at the chance to arrange for a marriage, regardless of our agreement. Memories of my last arrangement burst across my mind, and I shoved them back into the recesses of my memory.

"Tiberius, how is your wife?" he asked like it wasn't obvious he was asking if he was married. I inwardly groaned at the subtlety of my father, trying not to roll my eyes and fixing my face to be as neutral as possible. By the smirk on Tiberius' face, I suspected I had done a horrible job of hiding it.

"I'm not married, sir. I've been away for many years as an advisor for the Empire." Tiberius answered my father without missing a heartbeat. His focus hadn't left me, and I did what I could to not look at him again.

Those two sentences made my stomach fill with butter-flies and then fall through to the floor. He wasn't married, which meant he was available, but an advisor for the Empire? My family couldn't afford to be too close to anyone associated with them. While they had been very accepting of just about any religion, which was how they could cross and conquer such vastly different cultures, but Earth worship, no. No one was that accepting. We had run into too much trouble in the past. We operated our workshop as a private apothecary, but those who took our shop seriously knew that we helped with more than just mixing herbs and oils together.

"And are you still with the Empire?" my father asked. "Or are you here to help your father?"

"The Empire and I . . . well, shall we say, had a difference in opinion. I'm no longer associated with the Empire. So, I came home to help my father and build a home for myself." Tiberius was looking at me with a hint of questioning in his eyes.

"A home," his father said with hope written across his entire face. "I'm so glad to hear that, son."

"We haven't talked about anything other than business, Father. Though if you don't mind, I would like to take the opportunity to ask Mr. Regillia and Ms. Sidonia"—he paused and looked at me like my opinion actually mattered—"if I may take Ms. Sidonia for a walk around town." The words were said to my father before he turned to me. "If that is okay with you, Ms. Sidonia."

Mother, he was bold. I couldn't hide the blushing now. Yes, I wanted to spend time with him, but it wasn't a good thing to show such interest. This was not good at all. Instead, my mouth betrayed my head and I said cheerfully, "Yes, I would like that very much."

"Though it is not usual protocol . . ." My father looked Tiberius over, then his father, and finally glanced at me. "Very well. Have her home before the ships arrive from their day fishing."

My father gave me a hug and a kiss on the cheek.

"Father, can you give these to Grandmother and Mother?" I said, handing him the bag of herbs and oils I had gotten from Madam. "There are extra items in there, including some . . . rare varieties," I said, trying to impress their importance.

"Of course. Excuse me, Decimus, I need to deliver this to my wife."

"Yes. Yes. We shall discuss other matters later." He turned to Tiberius and sternly told him, "Obey her father's rule. Have Ms. Sidonia home before the boats come in. I will meet you back at home where we can discuss our matters."

"Yes, Father." Then Tiberius turned to me. "Shall we?"

I smiled softly and nodded, trying very hard not to let the blood rush to my cheeks.

CHAPTER 7

TIBERIUS

GODS, SHE WAS BEAUTIFUL. When I first saw her up on the mountain, I knew I had to make her mine, but when that heat burst through me the second I kissed her hand, I was very glad that my clothing hid my hardness.

I didn't just want her in a physical sense. There was intelligence behind those brown eyes that screamed to be let out. When she mentioned she was the cause of the commotion a few minutes ago, every protective instinct I had came to the surface.

She had defended herself against someone nearly *twice* her size. Who was this goddess?

Then I noticed the expression she gave her father. I saw every muscle twitch in her face, telling him that while she may have an inquiry of me, that he was not to rush us into an arrangement. What worried me, though, was that shadow that had crossed her face as she stared at him. Just what had happened that she was still unwed?

"Shall we, Ms. Sidonia?" I asked, extending a hand. She looked at me for a moment then slowly placed hers in mine. That heat burst through me again, and every nerve in my body became hyperaware of her. I could almost feel each breath that she took to calm her nerves. "Nervous?"

"No," she said too quickly. I gave her a small smile, and she blushed. "A little."

"Why?" I asked without thinking.

"I don't think we know each other well enough for me to answer that yet, Mr. Vispania," she replied, standing up too tall.

"I mean no disrespect, Ms. Sidonia," I said, meaning every word. "Please, call me Tiberius. Mr. Vispania is my father."

She simply gave me a small nod as we reached a rug merchant. She stopped, studied it for a moment, and ran her hands down the mesmerizing design. I studied her, not in a way that a man usually studied a woman, but her stance. Solid. Pure. Confident. The way she moved through the crowd. The way she spoke to the vendors.

Yes, there was a lot of intelligence in that mind of hers. I had the very real impression that should her father be unable to run the marketplace, she would be able to do so from the shadows and make it flourish.

"What of your family, Mr. Tiberius?" she asked, pulling me out of my thoughts.

I was so taken with her already. The Gods must be messing with me. No woman had ever captivated me so wholly.

"Tiberius?" she uttered, turning to me.

"I'm sorry." I shook my head. "My older brother died in one of the occupational wars in the north, and I had a younger brother who died from a sickness that raged through the Empire a couple years ago."

Her eyes narrowed slightly. "No girls?"

My shoulders relaxed, and I smiled brightly at her. "I have two younger sisters at home. They are bright and adventurous girls. I'm almost sorry for their future husbands. They will have their hands full with them."

"You love and cherish your sisters," she said with admiration in her voice.

"I do." They were bright suns in my life. "I haven't really been around the last few years to see them grow up. I kept in contact by messenger as much as possible, but I have enjoyed being home recently to see the wonderful young women they are becoming."

"So, what led you to become an advisor to the Empire?" There was an edge to the question. I knew the tone—probing, assessing.

"I was about your age when, of course, I was being pushed to marry. At the time, there was no one I was interested in, though many were available. I refused to marry just because it was socially required. Instead, I left home and headed to Rome."

Her face questioned me. "Really. I had no intention of becoming involved with the Empire. Along the way, I made contacts and a name for myself. I learned the ins and outs of a lot of the underground societies, including the assassin and slave trades, the pagans, witches, and Earth Worshipers—"

She stopped dead in the middle of the road, grabbed my hand, and that intelligence flashed bright in her eyes. "Earth Worshipers? What did you learn about them? Who they are? Did you find out who the oldest families are?"

"Those are interesting questions," I said carefully. Earth Worshipers were one of the few groups the Empire wouldn't tolerate. She tried to hide it, but there was an earnestness in the way she looked at me that was only confirmed by the tight grip she had on my hand.

I stared at her for a little longer, until her eyes met mine again. Damn, I wanted to get lost in them. My eyes flicked to her lips, which were tight, waiting for my response. Right. Earth Worshipers.

"We found quite a few witches along the way. Most of them are harmless, others, like the Dark Witches of Moesia, not so much. Luckily, I only ran into one and was able to convince her just to leave me be. We didn't learn anything about who the oldest pagans or Earth worshiping families are, though. Most of what we heard was hearsay or legend. We found no solid evidence they actually exist."

Her voice became very tight, even if she tried to hide it. "And what would you have done if you had found them?"

"I would have let them be. Interesting cultures, I've heard, especially the Earth worshipers. It's my understanding that only the women show the gift, and there have been lines that completely died out because only men were born. I don't understand why the Empire opposes them so." I forced myself to look off into the distance. There was something intriguing about them. Then I continued, "A whole culture based on just helping people. What a world it would be if we could just have everyone do that, regardless of faith. Just everyone helping others because it's the right thing to do."

There was a distinct *thump thump thump* in my ears, and I turned to her. She was taking short deep breaths but was fighting hard to keep herself breathing calm. Her voice was calmer than the tense shoulders and her fisted left hand when she asked, "How did you learn all of that? Who told you that information?"

"Whispers. I never reported anything to my commander that I couldn't prove. Why risk people's lives unnecessarily? Without proof of the whispers, there was nothing to report." I stopped and glanced down the road. There were very few people here, and we were keeping our voices down, but it still wasn't safe to talk about the subject too much out in the open. How many times had I obtained information, just from people talking just like this, all because I knew how to stay hidden?

She was facing me, so I took a step toward her. She backed up, but I followed her until her back was against the wall. Placing one hand on the wall next to her, I bent down close. To anyone else, it would look like two lovers having a moment in the street, but I didn't dare touch her. As desperate as I was to know what those lips tasted like and what her body felt like against mine, I didn't dare get any closer. I knew, just *knew*, that if I touched her, I wouldn't be able to restrain myself. Besides, if she hurt whomever it was in the marketplace to the point of drawing blood, I both wanted and didn't want her to test those skills on me.

Her breathing hitched, and her eyes flicked to my lips, then up to my eyes. I looked down the street again, listening for anyone who could be eavesdropping. When I turned back to her, she was looking down my body, and her cheeks had turned a beautiful shade of pink.

"Ms. Sidonia," I said in almost a purr. Her focus flicked back to mine as I asked very, very slowly, looking deep into her eyes for emphasis, "Why are you so interested?"

She took a quick breath through her nose, and I saw her gulp before saying anything. The corner of my lip twitched upward at her trying to compose herself. It was adorable, and I clenched my hands into fists to keep from threading my fingers through her hair and kissing her right there.

I cocked an eyebrow at her. She smiled coyly, finding some inner strength, and batted her eyelashes. "Maybe I just find it interesting. Besides, we have only just met. I'm not letting you in on why I'm curious about such things." Then she straightened a pleat on my toga, and when her fingers grazed my chest, an involuntary, deep moan resonated from me. She smirked at the sound of it and said, "I have to leave something for you to come back to."

"Ms. Sidonia, I'll be back, that is for sure. Your beauty is one that is unmatched, and I find your candor and brass enticing."

"Enticing!" she exclaimed with a laugh, releasing any tightness in her body. I stepped back from her and she continued, "That's a new one. Usually, I'm told to watch my tongue or I'll end up causing trouble for myself or family."

"I can see where it could be trouble," I expressed, and without hiding the heat and want for her, I continued, "I like a woman who isn't afraid to speak her mind, though. What fun is it to just have her always obey?"

She smiled brightly at that. "Indeed. What is the fun?"

CHAPTER 8

SIDONIA

WE WALKED IN SILENCE for a few blocks before we ended up down by the boathouses on the water. I needed that silence to calm myself. That look he had given me made my stomach tighten and caused a very real heat to bloom between my legs. Never before had anyone affected me so much as he did. I'd known him for what, an hour?

I couldn't help it, though. When he had me against the wall, I could picture nothing else but wrapping my legs around him and letting him pound into me for all to see. It wasn't like sex in public was uncommon. It was just Tiberius wasn't even mine yet. We were already breaking so many rules being unaccompanied.

As we walked, his fingers had grazed mine a few times, and each time his hand touched my elbow to help lead me through some of the crowded areas, there was a spark of something in each of those accidental touches.

"Feel like sitting for a bit?" Tiberius asked, bringing me out of my thoughts.

"Sure, how about putting our feet in the water?" My toes were already itching to be in the sand at the mere thought of being near the bay.

"Sidonia, are you saying we get undressed on the first meet?" A sly smile lit up his face, and damn if that smile didn't make my insides swim.

"I, ahh . . . umm . . . just our sandals," I stammered. I could feel the heat in my cheeks.

He smiled, took my hand, led me down to where the earth met the water, and tossed his sandals off to the side and by a rock. I slipped mine off, closed my eyes to get my wits about me, and reveled in the feel of the sand between my toes. Oh, how I loved being down here. I took a deep breath and tried to relax, which was difficult to do with Tiberius standing only a few feet away from me. He was heart-skipping handsome, strong, came from a good family, and was saying all the right things.

I could feel Tiberius' eyes watching me, but he let me just stand there. I heard him take a deep breath, and when I opened my eyes, he was leaning beside me against the wall with his head up toward the sun and the wind in his face. My eyes studied him, and I may have taken a bit more of a critical assessment of him. Yes, I knew how vain that sounded, but if I was going to lust after this man, then what was the harm in enjoying the view?

And what a view it was. When I said heart-skipping handsome, I meant it. His arms were lean, but with just enough mass on them that they were solid. His chest was, well, for lack of a better word, gorgeous. And while I couldn't get a perfect view of his body through his robes, when he had me against the wall, I could tell that Tiberius was a very healthy, strong man. While his feet were callused, they were well taken care of, a sign that he still carried status with him even though he had left the Roman Empire's care.

He was still a good five feet from me, but I turned and let the wind and mist hit my face. I let the feel of the air and smell of the water fill my senses and sighed when the ocean tickled my toes. When the ground moved, my feet sank into the sand, and I started to fall backward.

Before I could grab the wall, Tiberius grabbed my hand and waist to steady me. When I opened my eyes, not realizing I had even closed them, our faces were mere inches from each other.

Was the ground still shaking? No. It had stopped as soon as it had started, but neither of us moved. I felt each of his hard muscles against my body. My free hand instinctively grabbed hold of his shoulder, and I felt it tighten under my touch. His hand wrapped tighter around mine, and I felt him pull me closer to him, enough that I could feel him hard against my hip.

I bit my lower lip as I looked into his sapphire eyes, just as butterflies burst into flight in the pit of my stomach. I tried to ignore the fact that when his hand pressed on my back, it felt as though hot rocks had been placed in their spot. His fingers tightened and pulled me closer, if that was even possible.

"Sidonia," he said, barely above a whisper.

"Yes, Tiberius?" I finally managed to say, but it was so lightly that even I barely heard it.

"I– No. Never mind." He blinked and stood me up straight.

I smoothed my palla and pushed the strands of hair from my face. When I turned to glance back at Tiberius, he was just looking at me with a small smile on his face.

"What?"

"Nothing," he replied, smiling bigger this time. His eyes caught on the bracelet I bought earlier. Then he shook his head.

"No. What were you thinking?" When he opened his mouth to answer me, I quickly added, "And don't say *nothing*. I can see that your mind is racing faster than the chariots in Rome."

He sighed for a moment and then asked me to sit down next to him. The tone in his voice instantly made me put my guard up. There was so much right about him, and I was preparing myself for the blow. I mean, no one can be this perfect, right?

I needed to remind myself that I was letting an instant crush blind me. We may have met earlier today, but there was something about him that made me feel at ease and comfortable. It was almost as if I'd known him for years. I sat down in the sand and said, "Sit."

He let out a heavy sigh as he sat down next to me. "Sidonia, I have to be honest. Today wasn't the first time I've seen you."

"What do you mean? We live in the same colony. Herculaneum isn't huge, so it would make sense that you have seen me before." Though, didn't he say that he had spent the last few years away from Herculaneum? We must have met sometime while growing up, right? I knew his name from when I was young, but no specific memory would surface.

"When I came back from Rome, before I returned into the colony, I spent a few days up on the mountain, on Vesuvius. I saw you picking herbs and grasses. Your beauty stunned me." He looked at me and smiled. "I have seen beautiful women from Rome to Stabiae and beyond, but not one could compare to you."

I thought back a few weeks ago and chuckled at the memory. "That was you? I thought an animal was following me down the hill. That or the . . . never mind." I shook my head. I had the fleeting thought that the Dark Witches of Moesia may have been up there. The rumors had been going for a while, but we didn't know where they were. "You had my heart racing. I cut the trip short and had to go back last week to get what I hadn't because of it."

"I am sorry about that," he mumbled. There was another pause before he sighed and continued, "Since returning, I have been watching you and even spoken to my father about you. I begged him to introduce me to you."

"Ok. That sounds a little . . ."

"I know." He looked at me for a long time, like he expected me to run home, and I probably should have, but when I didn't, he observed, "You aren't scared by what I just said?"

I shrugged. If I was being honest with myself, I wasn't scared. I didn't know what I felt, but fear wasn't it. Maybe it was the crush, maybe it was his honesty, or maybe it was . . . I looked out over the water. Maybe I was finally willing to marry and have a family of my own, and maybe, just *maybe*, that was because of him.

I shook my head.

Listen to me. Meet a good-looking man and a couple hours later, I'm already imagining my life with him? What was wrong with me? I was a complete idiot. I looked at him, and his face was covered in confusion.

"So, what have you learned about me in the last weeks?" I asked, not sure what to think or what else to say.

Tiberius shook his head and laughed. "That is what you have to say about what I just told you?"

I smiled. "Yes. I want to know what you found out about me in the weeks of skulking about in the shadows."

"Okay. First off, I wasn't *skulking about* in the shadows. I have been working with my father."

"I believe you, but didn't you just say that you have been watching me?"

"Yes, but I think I've learned more about you in the last five minutes than I have in the last weeks," he said carefully. "I know you gather herbs and work with your mother and grandmother in the best apothecary in the colony." A huge smile crossed his face.

"Now you're just trying to flatter me," I said, bumping his shoulder.

"I would never." He laughed but corrected himself when I looked at him sternly. "Okay, so maybe a little."

"What else did you learn?" I pressed.

"That you're caring, gentle, and respectful, and every morning on your way back from the bread maker, you always share a piece with Lucius Caldus' dog." His voice had a hint of reverence and a smile. "You can learn a lot about someone by how they treat others and animals."

"If you saw me every morning going to the bread maker and Lucius' dog, how did I not see you?"

"There is a reason I was an advisor to the Empire." He sat up straighter. "I'm very good at seeing and hearing things without being seen."

I shook my head. "So today? Was today your grand entrance?"

"No." He laughed, running his hand through his hair, and said nervously, "I . . . I really was working with my father today. Yes, I had asked my father to introduce me to you, but running into you today was just Venus doing what she does best."

"Oh? And what would that be?" I laughed lightly, playing with the hem of my palla awkwardly.

"Giving me a push . . . and leading me to love," he said, flicking his eyes to mine. I looked away quickly.

"Love," I whispered and looked out over the Bay of Naples. I glanced back at him and he was just staring at me. Not in a creepy way or anything, just looking like he was trying to figure me out.

We sat there, our gazes locked, for a long time when, out in the distance, I saw the fishing boats coming in.

"Oops." I giggled and pointed to the boats.

"I guess we better get you home then," he said, letting go of my hand. I hadn't even realized he had taken it. His thumb ran a small circle on it before he said, "I would like to see you again tomorrow."

"I suppose that would be up to my father, wouldn't it?" I teased as we grabbed our sandals and rushed down the street to my house.

The entire afternoon was a blur. I couldn't remember much of what we talked about. Did we talk at all after his confessions of sulking around watching me? There was something so comforting and easy with Tiberius Vispania.

When we got to my door, my father was standing just outside, looking for me.

"Sorry, Father. We were at the beach and we lost track of time," I said apologetically and gave him a kiss on the cheek.

"Yes. Yes. Well, get inside. Your grandmother needs your help," he said, leading me into the house. "Tiberius. Wait, please. I wish to speak to you."

"Yes, sir," I heard him say as I smiled at him and slowly shut the door. Tiberius smiled back with a sparkle in his eye.

I closed the door and sighed as I leaned up against it. What a wonderful day it was. *Thank you, Mother Earth, for giving it to me.*

CHAPTER 9

TIBERIUS

SIDONIA SMILED SOFTLY AS she closed the door behind her. I couldn't help but feel elated by that smile. Even after telling her I had been watching her, she still didn't run away. No, she continued to sit on that beach and just be with me. *Gods.*

"Tiberius," her father said, bringing my attention back to him.

I stood up straighter and faced him. It was ingrained in me from the time with the Empire. Anytime someone of authority spoke, you stood straight and listened. Most of all, you kept your mouth shut.

Her father took a deep breath, pinched his nose, and let the breath out in a long release. "Gods and the Mother, help me."

"I'm sorry, sir?"

"She is going to resent me for this, but . . ." He looked up at me and continued, "Your father mentioned you had asked to meet her."

"Yes, sir. I saw her on my way back into the colony and thought her the most beautiful woman I have ever seen." I glanced back to the door before looking at him.

"What if she had already been married?"

"Nothing would have come of it. She would still have been the most beautiful woman I had seen, but I would have no intention of moving forward toward her," I said carefully.

"Do you wish to move forward with her?" His words were just as careful and reserved.

I studied him for a moment. "If she agrees to it, I do."

"Would you offer her an arrangement if your father agreed to it?" Her father was bold, and I couldn't help but stiffen slightly.

"I have just spent the last few hours with your daughter, Mr. Regillia, and one thing I already know is that not only is she beautiful, but she is also fiercely intelligent and has the conviction to go with it. She isn't a soft, pliable woman. I don't think she would allow herself to be arranged with any man who could not meet that fierceness. No arrangement should be made without her agreeing to it as well."

A woman with long brown hair came from the street behind us, kissed Mr. Regillia on the cheek, and slid in behind the door. She must be Sidonia's mother. She looked so much like her. It made me do a double-take.

He studied me for a long time, and I knew not to say anything. What I had said was the truth. There was something in her history I didn't know, and I was hoping she would share it with me, but today was only our first gathering. I could only hope for more.

"Nothing further to say?" he asked, raising a single eyebrow and just one side of his lip.

"There is a lot to say, but we have only just met," I explained.

"You know of our family status. You know we can give your family not only higher status but also a very large dowry." He squared his shoulders. "She is past initial marriage age, and you are the first *she* has shown any interest in."

I studied him for a moment. "Is she a burden to your family?"

"No." Mr. Regillia shifted his weight just enough to let me know he was very uncomfortable with the direction of this conversation. "Not in the least. We will miss her in this house when she does marry. She is a benefit to our household."

Nodding, I thought carefully before saying my next words. I didn't want him to deny my time with her. "Sir, I'm sure my family would appreciate both the status and the dowry. However, one reason I left Herculaneum when I was initially of marriage age was that I wanted to have an arrangement with someone who I cared for and who cared for me. At the time, there was no one I was interested in, so I left. I came back to have a home and to help my father with his business. I did not misspeak when we met earlier, sir. That is still my plan."

"I will speak to your father then about the arrangement," he said, sighing.

"Sir, I mean no disrespect. I am vastly curious about your daughter. I wish to spend more time with her to get to know her. She lights something within me that has been cold and unfeeling for years. I cannot deny that." He nodded his head, but I knew he didn't fully understand. How could he?

I hadn't felt the warmth of someone's touch until her for a few years now. "However, I cannot agree to an arrangement at this time. Moreover, I must stress that Sidonia must agree to it as well."

"That may prove difficult," he said under his breath. There was a long pause, and I realized I needed to know one thing. I wasn't sure if it would make a difference, but I needed to know. "Sir, if I may be bold myself—" I started to say, but he cut me off.

"You want to know why she isn't already in an arrangement?" His voice was guarded, but there was a bit of anger in it as well.

"I don't say this to flatter or impress, but she is the most interesting creature I have ever met. I mean that in the intellectual sense. I want to understand why she hasn't become a cherished wife." Something settled fast and sure within me at the words.

I wanted her. No, I *needed* her. Needed to have her as *my* cherished wife. I silently vowed right then as I stared her father in the eyes that I would fight for her. There was no way I would not allow another man to step in and take her from me. She took my confession today with a solidness that made me realize she could handle me. All of me.

"She was in an arrangement years ago." Mr. Regillia sighed as he leaned against the wall of his home. A flash of anger and jealousy ran through me which I struggled to keep in check.

"Sidonia was arranged to Marcus Dulcitius."

My eyebrows knitted together. "Marcus Dulcitius? Vibius' son?"

He nodded. "The very same."

"What happened?" I asked in a tone that I had used before while questioning people for information. I had heard tragedy had fallen the family a couple years ago but knew nothing more.

"A couple of days before the wedding, he left. He didn't say where he was going and didn't say anything about the arrangement. Just left. Randomly, a couple of months later, he returned. Marcus had been with the Empire's army and training with them. All we know is that there were screams from his house, ones that hadn't been heard before. His mother ran out into the street, calling for the guards." Mr. Regillia took a shuddering breath and continued. "They found Marcus kneeling before his father's body. His head was several feet from where his body lay before Marcus. Marcus had decapitated him. He hadn't moved after he swung his sword but to kneel there in his father's blood as it pooled under him. His sword was still in his hands when the guards arrived."

"Gods," I whispered. "What made him do it?"

"No one knows. Marcus wouldn't speak, not even to Sidonia." His words were barely above a whisper. "She asked me to take her to Marcus so that she could speak to him. When we got to where he was held, he just looked at her. She told him she was sorry, and he just nodded to her like he understood what she meant. She would not elaborate on it. I do not know what happened. Neither does her mother."

We stood in silence as a few other families walked by. When we were alone again, I told him, "If Sidonia chooses me? I will never leave her like that."

"I don't think she liked Marcus. Not even as a person. That is what is so strange about the whole thing," he said with a small smile, pushing off the wall. "It did not upset her when she found out he left. In fact, she was relieved. I'm not sure what happened between them, but something did, and it infuriates me to the ends of the world to not be able to answer what it is."

I didn't say anything. I wasn't sure there was anything to say.

"A few months later, she made me promise her she could choose who she had an arrangement with. That she had to come to me to ask for it."

"Yet, you asked me for one tonight." I didn't ask a question. It was more of a statement of fact. I pondered the man that clearly loved his daughter so fiercely, claimed her as an asset to the household, yet broke his word on this matter alone.

He nodded. "You are the first and only person she has ever shown an interest in the slightest bit since she was ten years of age. At that age, I couldn't secure a successful arrangement to be executed later, so I waited. When she was of age, Marcus stated he wanted one, so I set it up. Told her, and she just nodded. After what happened, I've tried to keep to my promise."

"Yet, you asked me for one tonight," I repeated, trying not to grit my teeth. Anger filled me so fiercely, I balled my hands up at my sides to keep from punching him for the disrespect. "Why disrespect her like that? Is Sidonia that much of a burden on your family?"

"Gods no. I already told you she is a blessing, and carries her own weight through the apothecary," her father was quick to say. "It's just, I wish for her to be happy, and I think she is infatuated with you."

"Infatuation is not caring for someone," I said, trying to calm my heart. "I want a wife to cherish. One who I love and who loves me. It will be Sidonia's decision whether or not to have an arrangement with me." Even if it would kill me to have her reject it. I looked to the door she had disappeared behind, and I saw her father do the same.

"Then continue forward with her, Tiberius Vispania. Let me know when you two are ready and I will discuss terms with your father," he said, turning toward the door.

I stared at that door. There were so many layers to Sidonia. Would she let me peel them back to see her fully underneath? Would she like who I was enough to agree to an arrangement? Even if she didn't love me and agreed to one, I would spend the rest of my days trying to earn that love from her. I was just about to tell her father that when the door was thrown open, and Sidonia strode right into me.

# CHAPTER 10

SIDONIA

I SMILED AS I lightly skipped across the room to the workshop and opened the door slowly. "Grandmother?"

"Sidonia," Grandmother said quietly in her raspy voice. "Come on in and close the door behind you, please."

"Where is Mother?" I asked as I sat down to help her fill the bottles on the table.

"Finishing up the deliveries that could not wait until tomorrow." I knew she was making a point. The tone of her voice was enough to know I was about to sit down, work, and keep my mouth shut.

We sat in silence as I filled bottle after bottle with the bright blue elixir that Grandmother had been working on for the last week. This particular one was to help some of the older members of the colony with the stiffness in their joints, even though there were few in number. There was a sickness that ran through a few seasons ago, and while it improved our business, many of the older members and some of the very young were not able to fight it off and joined the Mother. We did our best to help them, but there was only so much our potions and herbs could do.

Mother returned just as we had finished filling the last bottle and sat down across from me. "Is there something you wish to tell us, Sidonia?" she asked with a soft smile in her voice.

"What do you mean, Mother?" I replied as I put marks on the tops of the corks of the bottles to indicate who I needed to deliver them to tomorrow.

"Would you like to explain why I saw you alone with Tiberius this afternoon down by the beach?" She was smiling with her hands on her hips and facing toward me.

"Tiberius Vispania?" Grandmother asked.

"Yes, Grandmother," I said with a sigh. How was I going to explain why I was alone with a man in the plain sight of the colony and unmarried.

"And you were unescorted today?"

"Yes," I answered, not turning around to look at them. I continued to go through the vials and sort the mixtures into the appropriate sections. There was total silence behind me. I knew they were waiting for more, but I would not break. I mean, what was I really to say? There wasn't really much to say at all.

"How long have you been speaking with him?" Mother asked, breaking the silence first. Score one for Sidonia, but I cringed. She and Grandmother were about to give me one strong tongue lashing.

"I . . . We only just met today," I mumbled weakly.

"Sidonia!" she said in shock. "You are not married to him, you are out unescorted, and, worse, you had only just met him?"

"It was with Father's permission. Didn't Father tell you I was with him?" I whirled around to plead my case. When no one spoke, I continued, "We met in the marketplace while Father was doing business with his father. We spoke, and then Tiberius asked if he and I could walk around the city. Father agreed but said I had to be home before the fishing boats arrived. We got home just in time."

"I shall speak to your father. I do not agree with this. However, if he gave permission . . ." She was half in thought, while I thought I heard Grandmother spew words under her breath.

I turned and started straightening the bottles and baskets on the shelves to pass the time, making note of which herbs we were missing and which oils we were getting low on along the way. Some of them I had given Father just this afternoon before I went with Tiberius.

"Mother?" I asked, staring at one of the supply baskets.

"Yes," she said. I was relieved to hear the tension had released from her voice. "Did Father give you the bag I got from Madam Marulla earlier today?"

"No. I was going to ask you if you had stopped by her stall or not," she said with her mind somewhere else.

"I did. She also had picked up the oils for us you had requested. Madam was even gracious enough to add some other various items. Yes, I paid her for them, even though she asked me not to," I added quickly when I saw her open her mouth to ask. She didn't want special treatment from the other workshops in the marketplace just because of who her husband was. Plus, Mother was of the mind that we should share our status and the benefits that come with it.

"Ask your father where it is," Grandmother said. "Then you can come back and put them away before we eat."

I nodded as I closed the door. Mother and Grandmother immediately broke out into hushed whispers as soon as the door was shut. I was sure they were having quite the discussion about me being unescorted today.

Technically, I wasn't supposed to be alone with a man who wasn't within my family. Some rules and customs must be followed, even without our unique family. Besides, there are those, such as the Empire's guards, that would think I was available for purchase for the night if I was alone and unmarried. That obviously wasn't true, so I could see where Mother and Grandmother would be concerned.

Father wasn't in the main room, and I didn't see the bag from Madam Marulla anywhere. Father had probably headed back to the marketplace. I opened the front door to head down there to get the bag from him and walked straight into a wall. Not a wall, but a man.

"Tiberius!" I put my hands up in front of me to brace myself.

He turned around quickly and smiled. "I'm sorry, Sidonia. I didn't think anyone would come out of the house."

His smile . . . I could feel the rush of blood to my cheeks and a smile grow on my face.

"No, my apologies. I was looking for Father." I turned my gaze to my father. "Father, where is the bag I had given you earlier today? Mother said she never received it."

"Now it is my turn to apologize," Father said, reaching inside his robes. "Here. I had not been home long when you returned. I was simply making sure Tiberius had kept his end of the agreement and had you home by the time the boats arrived."

I eyed him carefully, knowing that couldn't be why they were still talking, but he kept his face neutral, not giving anything away.

"I know we were a little later, but don't blame him, Father. I am just as much to blame as he would be. You've taught me well to gauge the time by the sun." I smiled and tried to lighten the situation.

"And why didn't you use it?" he said with a sly smile on his face.

"I . . ." I looked at Tiberius, blushed even redder, and turned back to Father. "We were talking by the water, and I wasn't paying attention to the sun's position."

How was I supposed to tell him I was having real feelings for a man I had only met a few hours earlier, with that very man standing right there? Father would have an arrangement done before I could snap my fingers if he knew that. I made a point to not look at Tiberius.

I let out a quick sigh. It didn't matter, I suspected. Most likely, they were already discussing it. I had to be honest with myself about that.

"I will leave you to your discussions," I said, keeping my head low, and went back inside the house before I said something that would either embarrass me in front of Tiberius or anger my father.

I swept across the main room quickly and back into the workshop. I didn't want to listen to the conversation. It would only infuriate and remind me I wasn't in total control of my life.

When I walked into the workshop, Mother and Grandmother were silent and busy grinding herbs for the next elixir they were working on.

"Father had the bag still," I told them quietly and went to the workbench.

"Did Madam Marulla find any anise seed?" Mother asked hopefully.

I carefully emptied the bag and set out the various items madam had given us. When I found the anise seed, I handed it to Mother and went back to filling and organizing the supplies. When I was done, I took inventory, again, of what we were still missing.

"Mother, we are still out of cistus, ginger, and tolermine."

"You can find them all on the mountain if you look carefully. Why don't you ask Lars if he can take you the day after next?"

"Why not tomorrow?"

"Because you need to catch up on the deliveries that you didn't make today," she chastised, putting down her mortar and pestle with a loud clank.

"Yes, Mother."

She got up, sighed, and put her arm around me, leading me out of the workshop. "Let's go get food prepared before your father returns."

"What about the—" I started to ask about the mix sitting on the counter.

"It needs to rest. I will finish it after we eat."

"Father is just—"

"Outside. Yes, I saw him speaking to a man when I came home," she said, looking at me and smiling. "And I'm guessing by the red in your cheeks that man is Tiberius?"

I nodded again and tried to hide a smile.

"Is he available?" she asked.

"Mother!"

"Well, you obviously have an interest. If he is available, I'm sure your father could make the arrangement."

"No!" I said too fast and loud. At the smug look on her face, I continued, "Mother. I only just met him, and I may have interest in him, but I don't know anything about him. Father is already discussing it right this moment with him, anyway." A feeling of defeat grew inside of me. "Please. You and Father both agreed to let me make the decision this time."

"Okay. Okay. I will ask your father to slow down, but keep in mind when your father decides on something, it happens," She stared as if she were looking through the wall and sighed. "You've not shown any interest in anyone since Marcus left."

"Mother, it isn't like I had feelings for Marcus. He was my betrothed and had been since I was thirteen. There was acceptance for him. That is all." I turned to prepare the fire.

After a few minutes of stoking the flames, I wondered if I was a burden to them. Yes, it is one more mouth to feed, but would it be any different if Lars' wife had another child? I finally sighed and asked, "Am I really such a burden to the family that you are in a rush to marry me off?"

"No, Sidonia. You are not a burden. It's just you are of age and already had one arrangement fall through," she said, making me look at her.

"Am I damaged goods?" I kept my head low. It wasn't like I hadn't thought of it before. There were already rumors that the arrangement fell through because I wasn't pure anymore.

"No, you are not damaged goods, Sidonia," she said with a soft, kind voice.

"The rumors claim otherwise."

She scoffed at the words. "Rumors. They are just from those who don't know what else to talk about. Anyone with whom your father makes an arrangement with will know better."

"Ok, Mother, but please, Father promised me he would let me decide as to whom I marry," I pleaded with her.

"And he is doing his best, dear." She kissed the top of my head.

I focused my attention back at the fire and boiling the water. I was also trying very hard not to think about what it would be like to marry Tiberius. The thought alone made my insides swim.

To change my line of thinking, I asked, "Mother, Grandmother, Madam Marulla said that the Dark Witches of Moesia may be to blame for the death of the livestock on Vesuvius."

There was silence, and when I looked up, they both were staring at me with strange expressions. They shared a look before Grandmother's focus moved back to me and she asked, "Any proof?"

I shook my head. "I didn't think they were this far south, though."

"Aren't they the ones responsible for all the deaths up north, near the Germania border?" Mother asked.

"They are," I said sadly.

Mother and Grandmother looked at each other as if they were having a silent conversation, but then Grandmother said, "Please, just be careful on the mountain, Sidonia. If you meet up with a Dark Witch . . ."

"It has long been ingrained in me to know better, Grandmother. I will run. I will not use the gift the Mother has given me to cause harm," I vowed.

"Good. Now get to cutting the vegetables or it will be halfway through the night before we eat dinner," Grandmother said, smiling.

"Yes, Grandmother," I replied, giving her a small smile.

CHAPTER 11

SIDONIA

THE FOLLOWING MORNING, I made my way to the bakery and picked up our usual order of biscuits and a loaf of bread. On the way back, I kept an eye out for Tiberius but didn't see him. He said he had been watching me for weeks, but surely if he had been watching me that long, I would have seen him, right? Did I even believe him? If he was following me, was he watching me now that we had officially met?

When I got to Lucius Caldus' dog, I figured he either wasn't watching or he really was that good at seeing without being seen. Where had he learned to be so stealthy? He said that he had become an advisor because of his abilities, not that he learned them from the Empire. Was that maybe why I didn't have any memories of him as a child? He did say he grew up here in Herculaneum.

He did, didn't he? I sighed as I crouched down, sat back on my heels, and gave the dog a piece of the biscuit. He nuzzled my leg and let out a heavy breath. I smiled and petted his back.

"See? Every morning," a voice said behind me, making my heart leap for joy and fright in the same second.

"So, you are following me." I forced myself to stay with the dog and not react and reached over to scratch behind the dog's ear. Slowly, the dog rolled over onto its back, and I gave him some belly rubs. A smile grew on my face, and my stomach swirled in excitement. How could he affect me this way? Why did I let him affect me like this? I was so giddy and smitten. It was not like me to act like any other young girl with a boy. It was so maddening.

I, Sidonia Regillia, didn't act like a blubbering buffoon around boys.

Well, you do if that person is a demigod dressed up as Tiberius Vispania, my inner voice said in a sultry, bedroom voice. Sighing inwardly at that inner me that couldn't get her hormones under control, I patted the dog on his belly. Looking over my shoulder, I immediately bit my lower lip when I saw him. No one should look that damn good first thing in the morning. Mother, help me.

"Sidonia, I am merely on the way to see my father," he said, rolling his eyes, trying to deflect me. Only, I saw the way his eyes heated, too, when our gazes met.

I stood up, crossed my arms the best I could without dropping the bread, and looked back at him. He looked so much more relaxed this morning, leaning against the building, smiling. It took everything I had not to lose the stern expression on my face.

"Is that so? I'm pretty sure your family and your father's workshop are on the other side of the colony," I said when he didn't say anything.

I met his gaze and just stared him down. His eyes narrowed slightly, like he wanted to continue to push me, but then something crossed his face and his whole body shifted. It looked like he had to move to keep from twitching.

"Ok. You got me," he said with a light blush on his cheeks. "I was following you again."

"I guess you are that good at not being seen." I was not intending to give him a compliment for being a stalker, but . . .

"So, you were looking for me?" There was a mischievous glint in his eye.

I shrugged noncommittally and turned to head toward home. I couldn't afford to be late this morning. There were already a lot of deliveries today to make up for my time with Tiberius yesterday. I might have to come home around the midday meal to pick up another round.

"I figured since we met yesterday, the least I could do is say good morning." He slowed his pace to match my stride. "Instead of just admiring you from afar."

"You haven't said good morning yet," I teased.

He laughed. It was light, airy, and one that could make anyone's day. "That is true. Good morning, Ms. Sidonia. I hope the Gods have blessed you this day."

"Good morning, Tiberius," I said, rolling my eyes and trying to keep the laughter from my voice.

We walked in silence for a bit, but it wasn't awkward. However, the silence allowed for my mind to wander. For instance, why was he following me this morning? There were a couple of times when I thought he was going to say something, but he clamped his mouth shut and just smiled.

I, however, thought about the conversation I had with Mother last night. Was Father already trying to make arrangements for me to be wed to Tiberius so quickly? Of course he was, but why had they spoken for so long outside the house? Why not come inside and have the full conversation? We were inside the workshop for plenty of time.

"What did Father talk to you about last night?" I asked as we approached the house.

Tiberius's face was full of shock. "That was direct and to the point." He avoided eye contact and ran his hand through his hair before continuing, "He . . . He wanted to know my intentions."

I stopped and just stood there looking at him, waiting for him to continue. This wasn't a shock at all. I was more surprised that Tiberius admitted to it actually. I thought he would have avoided answering the question and tried to change the subject instead.

"Judging by your reaction, you are not surprised."

"No. I'm not." Now I wanted to know his intentions, so I waited for him to go on.

He didn't say another word, and neither did I for a very long time. We just stared at each other, neither willing to cave. If we did end up marrying, would it always be like this? A battle of wills? I mentally rolled my eyes at myself.

"Are you available today?" he finally asked, not breaking my gaze.

"I am not." I stood up straighter. "I have deliveries to make today. Yesterday put us behind schedule. Mother made deliveries to those who couldn't wait, but there are still many who are waiting."

"Very well. We shall make arrangements for another time. I do not wish to keep you from your duties." He took my hand and then kissed it gently. The feel of his lips was soft and luscious, but that shock of heat hit me hard. I had to work very hard to keep standing because my knees had just about lost all ability to hold my weight on their own.

"Until I see you again, Sidonia Regillia," he said with a sly smile and in a voice that sounded like a perfectly sung melody. "Oh, and wear the bracelet you wore yesterday. With the sapphire and lotus. It becomes you."

One of my neighbors looked at me curiously as I stood there flushed, watching where Tiberius had disappeared. I smiled and dipped my head down as I retreated inside, grabbing the partial biscuit and putting the rest away before turning toward the workroom.

I stood there and nibbled on the biscuit for a few minutes while staring at the floor as my mind raced. What were Tiberius' intentions? Why didn't he answer me? He seemed to be interested in me romantically, but he was holding something back. *What was he hiding? Maybe I'd ask Father if I saw him in the marketplace this afternoon.*

I poured myself some water from the pitcher and gulped it to wash the biscuit down just as Mother stuck her head out into the main room, asking if I was ready to head out for the deliveries.

"Yes, Mother. Are they separated and ready?" I asked, walking back into the room.

"Nearly. Get your bag. I washed it the day before last." She pointed to the corner of the room where the towels were stored.

I found it easily and headed into the workshop. "Mother. Did Father say anything about what he and Tiberius talked about?"

"He did." She smiled. "He asked what his intentions were."

"And?" I asked. Mother always answered me directly. She didn't beat around the bush or tell me half-truths. If Tiberius wouldn't answer me, I'd get it from Mother.

"Tiberius is very much interested in you, and when your father asked to meet with his father regarding an arrangement, Tiberius begged to get to know you more before any arrangement was made."

"Really?" I was shocked. Someone else who actually wanted to make sure they liked the person before venturing into a lifelong agreement?

"Yes, Sidonia. Your father was very impressed with him last night. He wants to have a wife that agrees to the arrangement because she wants it, not because it is agreed upon between the families," she said then looked at me, raising an eyebrow. "Sound familiar?"

"It does, but I have not made that a secret. He worked as an advisor to the Empire, Mother. Surely, he knows how to get information about whomever he chooses without too much work. Maybe he is just saying that to get on Father's good side to make an arrangement. Plus, he's a man. All he has to do is say okay or point and say I want that one. How do I know if that is what he actually wants?" My voice sounded very childish.

"Such the skeptic, my daughter," Mother said.

"Am I wrong, Mother? Wouldn't it be easy for a man of his history and influence to get the information he desires?"

"True, but even if that is so, that means that he would want you happy about the arrangement instead of going into it because of family responsibilities," she said sweetly.

I didn't say anything else. What was I going to say that hadn't been said a hundred times? It wasn't a surprise that an arrangement was discussed. Of course, I wanted Tiberius. I knew I had a serious crush on him. That was obvious already. Painfully so. It was just strange for me. I had friends who would have crushes on four or five men before they had an arrangement. I just wasn't like that.

Besides Tiberius, there was only one other man I sort of had feelings for. Maybe it was because I had more than just being a housewife to think of. Not that the thought of being a wife was something I didn't want, I just didn't like the discussion being had without me.

Stupid society. Stupid laws. Why couldn't women have a say in their own lives before we had three kids and were declared independent? It was such a ridiculous law. I sighed, finished loading the bag, kissed mother on the cheek, and waved to Grandmother as I walked out the door.

CHAPTER 12

SIDONIA

DELIVERIES WERE GOING WELL today, and I was halfway through them when I arrived at Magistrate Octavianus Potius' home. I hoped to see his wife, who always had freshly baked muffins when I arrived. I'd made this delivery a bunch of times in the last season. It was always the same potions and oils to help with the magistrate's ailment in the knees without which, would render him bed bound. Madam Potius also ordered an oil mixture on a regular basis, for which she claimed relieved the pain in her back. Her story was that her back was severely injured during the birth of their youngest son, and she swore the mixture helped with the pain. At least, that was what she told the public. However, my family and I knew better.

The mixture wasn't for pain, but for stimulating arousal in men. Our family knew she was just protecting the magistrate's impotence, but we decided that as long as it wasn't hurting anyone, we would just look the other way.

She answered the door when I knocked, looking quite disheveled, and hurried me inside. "Oh, Sidonia. I'm so glad you have come. My back is in desperate need of your oil. I don't know how I have managed without it the last few days," she said as people passed her front door in the street.

"Madam Potius. The last batch we gave you was a two-week supply if used every day." I was astonished as she avoided making eye contact.

Magistrate Potius walked through the bedroom door and pulled his chiton over his waist haphazardly, just barely covering himself. He nodded to me and headed for the wine cabinet.

"Luculla. You may collect yourself and tell Flora she may leave but to return after dinner. I see Sidonia has arrived with a new batch. You two shall be busy this evening."

I quickly glanced at Madam Potius and noticed a look that was mixed with fear and concern, then she quickly shuffled off to the bedroom.

"Sidonia. I trust you will keep what you hear in this house to yourself," he said, sauntering toward me, wine goblet filled to the brim.

"Of course, magistrate," I said, curtsying slightly. "There are many secrets we keep in this town. I am here only to deliver our wares and move on to my next stop."

I could feel his eyes move up and down on me as he swallowed a mouthful of wine from his goblet. It made my skin crawl and shiver in a way that had nothing to do with the weather. Grandmother had told me many times not to appear weak, so I stood up straight but kept my eyes down.

He was still the magistrate, and just because my family ha
status, didn't mean he couldn't lower it.

"You have our supply?" he said in a voice that I was sure
he thought was sultry, but it only made me feel like I was in
a pit of spiders.

"Yes, magistrate. I brought another two-week supply."

"Only a two-week supply? I . . . I mean Luculla needs more
than just a two-week supply," he said, walking close enough
to me I could smell the wine on his breath.

"A few of the herbs that are used to make it are getting
increasingly rare," I tried to explain, raising my head slightly and keeping my voice strong. Reaching into my bag, I
placed them on the table just as he grabbed my arm and
pulled me close to him. I met his stare this time and said
almost through my teeth, "It takes more than a month to
make each batch and there are quite a few who order it."

"Maybe you should join Luculla, Flora, and I right now." He
breathed into my face while his eyes traveled downward to
my chest. My breasts were not small by any imagination,
and I usually did what I could to keep them from being too
much on display. His hand slid down and squeezed my ass
as he clenched my arm tightly in front of him, pulling my
hand against his flaccid manhood.

"Excuse me?" I jerked my arm back and looked up at him.

"There is always room for one more," he said seductively.

Out of the corner of my eye, I saw his wife, Luculla, and
Flora standing in the doorway to the bedroom.

"You can use those beautiful lips so that you don't become
unpure for whomever your father arranges you with. They
would look so *good* wrapped around my cock." He licked his
lips, then added with too much sweetness, "If that doesn't
sound enticing enough, you could play with Luculla or
Flora, if you prefer. I'd love to see your head between their

legs." The last part, he said with a bit of a growl, and my stomach lurched. I thought I saw Luculla give a quick shake of her head, as Flora's eyes were big as saucers. I was so stunned that I couldn't say anything.

I had made numerous deliveries to the local harem house, so I was not ignorant in the ways of sex or the wants of men. Just because I hadn't had sex myself, didn't mean I hadn't seen it or how the powerful men and women in our community used others for it, or knew how to pleasure both men and women. It also wasn't any secret some of the more privileged enjoyed the company of either sex and multiple at once in public. Many times, they had used the public balneae for just that purpose. However, to be propositioned so directly from someone in this manner brought back memories of the night at Marcus', and I instantly felt dirty and cheap.

"I'm sorry, magistrate, but I must decline," I said, pulling farther away from him, forcing myself to stand up straight and tall. I refused to let myself be seen as weak. I met his gaze and let every ounce of my defiance show through in my stance and stare.

"You must decline." A cruel smile crossed his lips before he continued, "I would watch who you deny, Sidonia. I am a powerful man and know things in this community that could hurt a lot of people."

"Don't forget, magistrate, that I, too, know things that could damage the reputation of a great number of people." I was filled with frustration but ensured my voice fed through the promise of a very specific threat as I eyed the oils I had put down next to us. This wasn't the only potion we delivered to this house, and he stared at me as he contemplated whether to push me on the matter.

"Indeed you do, Ms. Sidonia," he said, taking another mouthful of wine. Then he turned back toward the bedroom, taking the oils with him. "Well, you don't know what you're missing. Flora, I've changed my mind. Don't bother dressing. Luculla, pay Sidonia and return to me."

I looked at Flora, and there in that moment, I saw a girl not much older than myself, broken and shattered. What my future would have been had I not taken those drastic measures. Even though it was paid with a heavy price, I have no doubt I was looking at what I would have become.

Flora's body moved with seductiveness and the appearance of longing and lust for the magistrate as he entered the bedroom. No one would have known the difference if her eyes hadn't met mine and I saw just how dead of all emotion they were. Where was her family? Did she have any left? Was there anyone who cared for her? Why had her family allowed this? Why hadn't they come for her?

"2 aureus, 20 denarii, and 66 sestertii?" Luculla said, bringing me out of my thoughts and my focus back to her.

"Yes, madam." I pitied her. She had given the magistrate so much, and to be treated like this was heartbreaking.

As she handed me the coins, she held onto my hand. "Sidonia, from now on, I will come to the shop. You were lucky he let you off so easily. I'm not sure how you did it. No one has refused him like that before and not been . . . either forced into it or beaten."

Her hands were shaking, but her eyes were steady on mine, and I heard the magistrate tell Flora to get on her knees. There was a smack and then a choking sound. I moved to go help her, but Luculla gripped my hand tighter, holding me back, shaking her head.

"Flora . . . He likes to have Flora give him pleasure with her mouth."

"It doesn't give him the right to beat her or to abuse either of you. Why do you allow this, Madam Potius? Why not divorce him for his adultery?" I whispered. "You've given him three sons and two daughters. You would be independent. You have the basis."

"He's magistrate. I would be ruined." She pushed me toward the door. "Now quickly, you need to leave before he reconsiders."

"Luculla!" the magistrate said through panted grunts from the next room.

"Coming, master," she shouted over her shoulder as she pushed me out the door.

I turned back to say something to her but snapped my mouth closed when I turned and saw her mouth that she was sorry before shutting the door behind me.

CHAPTER 13

SIDONIA

I STOOD THERE IN the middle of the street, staring at the door, trying to classify what I had just experienced in the magistrate's house. His own wife had called him master. Only the slaves called their owners that. How could she allow herself to be treated so horribly?

It wasn't that they had started to have sex in the house. I had many times made deliveries while sexual acts were occurring. That wasn't what bothered me. It was the *abusive* domination that I didn't appreciate or understand: the forcefulness of the events, the fear and emptiness in their eyes, the way his own wife's hands trembled with that fear, and his ability to control them so completely.

Thankfully, a voice from around the corner grabbed my attention, shifting my thoughts. *Tiberius*. My heart skipped a beat, and I felt my cheeks warm. Without realizing what I was doing, I turned and headed for the corner. When I then realized that he was talking to someone else, I crouched down and hid behind a basket in the corner.

His back was to me, and he was talking to a guard. *What am I doing? Am I really eavesdropping?* I laughed at myself because apparently, that was exactly what I was doing.

"Tiberius. You have to admit, our stories are so similar," the guard said with a hushed sternness.

"Velarde, I was drunk. It was only a drunken dream. Nothing more," Tiberius said, voice light and humorous.

"Not drunk, *drugged*," the man named Velarde said quieter.

"Drugged?" Tiberius's voice trailed off, as though he were contemplating what the guard had just said.

"Drugged. Drunk. Regardless, the scar on your neck matches mine exactly!" Velarde pulled the cloth down, and I stretched to look, but saw nothing there.

"You can see mine?" Tiberius asked hesitantly.

I had spent enough time staring at Tiberius to know that there was no scar on his neck. This guard must be the drunk one.

"And it appeared mysteriously by the next morning?" Tiberius asked. There was a seriousness in his voice that made something stir deep inside me.

"I've covered it so I won't be asked questions I can't answer," Velarde said.

"No one else can see it. I've had mine for years, and no one has ever questioned me about it. A scar like that would get noticed. You didn't even notice it over the last couple years.

Since no one inquired, I stopped covering it," Tiberius said. "Don't believe me? Watch."

"Tiberius?" the guard hissed. "I may not have noticed yours in the past, but I did yesterday when you met me at camp. You don't have to prove it."

"I'm going to, though."

He moved farther down the street and walked up to a middle-aged man who was trying to pull a goat into a pen. "Mr. Tiladore, I'm sorry to bother you, but do I have anything on my neck?"

"No, Mr. Vispania. Nothing," Mr. Tiladore said, inspecting his neck as Tiberius craned it upwards and moved the fabric away to allow him to see it clearer.

"No marks, bruises, or scars?"

"No, sir," Mr. Tiladore answered, eyeing Velarde. "Is there a problem?"

"No, Mr. Tiladore. Not at all. Just settling a bet with an old friend is all." Tiberius laughed it off and headed back down the street toward where I was hiding just behind Velarde.

"That is strange. What do you think the Dark Witches of Moesia did to us?" Velarde asked Tiberius.

"I don't know." Tiberius ran his hand through his hair in thought. "And why do you think it was the Dark Witches of Moesia? Do you truly believe the rumors?"

"Tiberius, you have to admit, the stories are too similar to what we experienced."

"How long ago did you get yours?"

"Three weeks and two days ago. I won't forget the smell or the blood the next morning for as long as I live," the guard said in a shaky voice. "I still have nightmares of those three woman saying, *Fire from the Earth shall renew thee life,*" then the feeling of them slitting my throat. If that all happened, then how am I standing here?"

Tiberius stared at the guard for a long moment before saying, "I don't know, but those are the same words that play in my nightmares as well. I dream of them slitting my throat too."

Velarde sighed.

"How long are you here, Velarde?" Tiberius asked, his mind deep in thought.

"A week. Then our battalion moves to the north," Velarde said.

"Ok. I'll meet up with you later. Maybe you can join my family for dinner. I have a girl to find," Tiberius said.

"A girl?" Velarde laughed. "You realize that the harem is on the other side of the colony, right?"

"Nah. Not that kind of girl. This one is special," Tiberius said in a way that made my heart swoon.

"Are you seriously considering settling down? A family?" Velarde teased.

"If she will have me, absolutely," he said with a deadly serious look on his face.

"If she will have you? Just go to her father and demand an arrangement."

"Oh, her father has already started that conversation, but I'm not demanding anything. Not with this one. She's special enough to wait for," Tiberius said, with a gleam in his eye.

I smiled and backed around the corner before standing up, straightened my clothing, and walking out from behind the basket, acting like I didn't know he was there. Plus, I wanted to get a closer look to see if I could see any of these scars on their necks.

"Tiberius! What a pleasant surprise. You weren't following me again, were you?" I smiled innocently. I half-hoped he hadn't seen or heard what had happened in the magistrate's house.

"Speak of the goddess," Tiberius purred, taking my hand and kissing it gently. His arm slid around my back and I sidled up closer to him. He looked down at me and kissed the top of my head, sending warmth shooting down my body. I was sure I was shaking from the nerves, but then the guard broke through my thoughts.

"Tiberius, you have Venus on your side. She is quite beautiful," Velarde said, looking at me up and down appreciatively.

"Why, thank you, sir," I said. "Tiberius, are you going to introduce me?"

"Not sure I should. He may try to steal you for himself." Tiberius laughed, but I felt his fingers contract on my back, as if to hold on to me. "Sidonia, this is Velarde. We have known each other for years, and don't you even get any ideas about asking him anything about me."

"Ahh. Where is the fun in that, Tiberius? After all, we have only just met. I want to hear all the stories I can about your times with the Empire." I smiled seductively. Red crept up his cheeks before I turned to Velarde, first casually looking at his neck and then meeting his eyes. "Any drunken stories you two share that I should know about?"

I thought I saw a flash of fright in his eyes and knew I had hit the subject. I saw no mark on his neck and no immediate trace of a spell. All magic left a trace, and I couldn't see anything here. "There are many stories I can tell you about Tiberius drunk. However, I will heed his warning and leave it to him to share what he wishes you to know."

I fixed my best pout face on and asked again. "What? Not even one?"

"Sorry, my lady, but because I do know those drunken stories, I also know not to cross your Tiberius here."

The sound of him calling him *my* Tiberius interrupted any thoughts of scars or magic. However, it brought other things to mind, and that thought made the blood rush to my cheeks. If nothing else, it helped burn through the chill I had from that delivery.

"Sidonia, may I accompany you on the rest of your deliveries this afternoon?" Tiberius asked, dismissing Velarde.

"But Velarde?"

"Velarde needs to return to his station. I shall catch up with him later."

I looked to Velarde, who only nodded, bowed, and took his leave.

"Are you really that insistent upon spending time with me that you want to make deliveries with me?" I asked, a little surprised.

"Well, aren't you full of yourself? This gives me the opportunity to meet the citizens of the colony. After all, if I am to take over my father's position. I need to have at least met and mingled with them." He jabbed his elbow into my arm playfully.

"You really are planning on staying and making Herculaneum your home, then?"

He took my elbow and turned me to face him. "Yes. I hope to be a successful businessman, have a home and a family, but most of all, have a wife who will love me and be my equal."

There was something in his sapphire eyes I couldn't read, but I felt like I was falling into their depths. Damn those eyes. I mentally shook myself to clear my thoughts and studied them a moment longer. Was it hope? Was I just reading something in them that was a reflection of my own crush, or was there really hope flashing in them when he said that?

I'm not sure how long we stood like that. Seconds? Minutes? Hours? I shook my head and cleared my mind again.

"You want to make deliveries with me?" I repeated.

"Is there a problem?" he asked, taking a loose hair and tucking it behind my ear.

I looked back toward the house I just left, bit my lip, and shook my head.

"You okay?" he asked, putting a finger on my chin and making me look at him. "You look a little pale."

"No," I uttered before I realized what I said.

"What is wrong?" he pressed. There was so much concern in his voice that I thought about how best to answer him.

"I was just making a delivery that brought back some bad memories." I kept my head down and thought through any problems with him going with me today. "If you go with me today, you may not like what you see. You also can't tell anyone what you see or what you hear."

"What's wrong? Tell me?"

"I don't know," I said, refusing to look at him and playing with my fingers.

"Sidonia. I want to get to know you. You should get to know me. I want us to trust each other," he said gently.

"Did you agree to an arrangement with my father last night?" I asked.

He paused for a moment and tilted his head to the side. He knew I was deflecting.

"Did you agree to an arrangement with my father last night? You want us to trust each other? Answer me truthfully."

"I told him I would like one, but that I would not agree unless you did as well." He took a deep breath and then said,

"I also told him I want us to get to know each other first, and that I want a wife who will love me as I love her. We don't know each other. Love takes time to grow, but I would like to hope that it can with you."

I looked at him. His face was determined and his eyes were bright.

"Is that what was bothering you? A possible arrangement with me?" he asked.

Who was this man? He was so open with his statements and thoughts. How had he ever worked for the Empire? "No," I said honestly. "Don't you wonder why I'm not already married?"

"Your father mentioned a part of the story. He said he doesn't know what specifically happened, just that your last arrangement fell through because he left. When he came back, he killed his father."

His hands had slid down my arms and were holding mine now. I was not even sure when I put the bag down.

"You are serious? About wanting to know me and my history before entering an arrangement with me?" I asked, trying to keep the hope and dread from my words.

"Yes." Not one ounce of hesitation.

"Okay. I'll tell you if you promise not to think ill of me for it."

He looked me deep in my eyes and, after a moment, said, "Tell me, Sidonia."

I turned my back to him and saw my bag sitting a few feet away. Chewing on my thumb for a moment, I wondered how I was going to tell him what happened without telling everything. I couldn't chance that yet. He was an advisor to the Empire, okay ex-advisor, but he still had connections that could get me and my family killed. Mother, he could still be working for the Empire and just hiding it. There was no way I could take the chance yet.

My eyes flicked to his quickly and there was worry in the lines of his face, but something vulnerable as well. Could I trust him, regardless of what might become of us? Granted, if we did move forward with an arrangement, that would have to be disclosed, but I wasn't going to do that until we had to.

"Okay," I said through a heavy sigh. "But we need somewhere private to talk."

"Let's go down to the beach. The wind will cover our discussions in case anyone tries to overhear."

CHAPTER 14

SIDONIA

I INSTANTLY RELAXED WHEN we got to the beach and had our sandals off, toes in the sand. The soft grains rubbed against my soles, helping to soothe the tension away. He let me stand there a moment, and then I sighed, turned, and sat up on the wall. He hopped up to sit next to me and took my hand.

"Tell me."

"How do you do this?" I asked.

"Do what?"

"Get people to tell you their secrets," I said. "I haven't told anyone other than my grandmother the truth of this. Yet here I sit, about to tell a man I have not known a week."

He half-turned toward me. "I'm very good at what *was* my job. I'm not using those techniques on you, though, Ms. Sidonia. I'm simply asking you to talk to me so that we can learn about and trust each other."

I studied him, looking for any signs of malintent, but his face was open and clear, with no indication of lying. Lifting my hand to his face, I ran my finger along his brow. He sagged under the feel of it, and I did it again, this time letting what little power was in me search for deceit. A long, relieved sigh escaped me when I felt nothing but warmth from him.

"Okay, Tiberius. I'll tell you, but I swear, if this gets out, I will know exactly who told. I don't wish to create more problems for a family that has had enough." Gritting my teeth through the words, I forced myself to relax as he smiled. "Swear it."

Slowly, I let my fingers slide down the side of his face and along his jaw. He grabbed my hand and kissed the tips of my fingers. "I swear that if I betray you, you can carve my heart out and eat it."

Heat flashed through me at the sincerity and fierceness of his words. My fingers tingled, and as my eyes dropped to where his lips were still pressed to them, I swore I saw a soft glow at the tips. His eyes were still on mine, but that glow seemed to pulse.

"Father told you he left and killed his father upon his return," I said more as a statement, desperately trying not to think too much about what my fingers glowing against his skin could mean.

"He did," Tiberius said. He was trying to be patient. I could see that.

Taking a deep breath, I told him my deepest secret. "I had gone over to Marcus Dulcitius' family's house for full introductions and finalization of the arrangement. When I arrived at the house, the cloth over the windows was closed tight and the rooms were dark, even with the sun still high in the sky outside. There were a few candles burning throughout the room, but only a few, and not enough to light it up properly.

"I thought it odd, and I should have known something wasn't right about the household then. In my home, and in most of the other homes I had visited of my friends, the women held equal status among the family. Only in Marcus' home, all the women kept their heads low and never made eye contact with anyone at all. Not even with each other. It was worse than any servant I had seen treated. I suspect the Emperor treats his servants better and with more respect." I took a deep breath and looked at Tiberius quickly. He was studying me but was patiently waiting for me to continue. "When we went to eat our meal, I went to sit next to Marcus, as an equal." I gritted my teeth.

"As it would be in any house," Tiberius said, more in confirmation that I had done nothing wrong. It was like he knew something horrible was coming. He squeezed my hand, and I looked out over the bay.

"His father, Vibius, glared at me and pulled me away from the table by my hair. He told me the table was where the men eat, and that *the women* were to eat in the corner on the floor. I hadn't even noticed that was where they had gone to sit. Vibius had his hand raised to smack me when one of Marcus' brothers reminded him that it might be a good idea for him not to mark me until after the wedding. Instead, Vibius took me and that brother's wife into the back room."

I wiped an angry tear from my face. Slowly, I let out a shuddered and rough breath before saying, "I looked back at Marcus for help, but his eyes were on the bowl of porridge before him. When I looked at the brother, all I could see was a flash of rage in his eyes before he went back to eating his meal. Neither of them moved from their chairs or even so much as twitched to come help.

"When we got to the back room, Vibius tied my hands to the headboard, stripped me naked and literally threw the woman onto the bed. He tied her hands with mine, put a sack over her head, and tightened it around her neck. I could see the skin bunching around the cord and wondered if she could even breathe. She never looked up from the ground. She never even looked at me. Never made a sound." My mind had fully gone back to that room, and when the breeze blew over me, I could feel the pebbling of my skin, just as it had that day when I stood there naked.

"Release us," I had said to Vibius.

"I don't think so, Sidonia," Vibius said, eyes full of anger, lust, and pure evil. He strode closer to me, and I could almost taste the wine on his breath. Pressing me against the wall, he grabbed my breast, putting his knee between my legs. He pressed harder, grinding his knee against me, and tweaked my nipple.

"You will learn, Sidonia, that I run this house. I get and do as I wish within these walls. No one, not even Marcus, will raise a finger to save you." He ran his tongue down my neck, and I pressed against the wall to get away from him. When he reached my left breast, he looked up at me and bit down hard. I screamed in pain, and when he stepped back, there was blood on his lips.

"You will behave in my house." He licked his lips clean before turning his attention to the woman on the bed.

I moved my hands into the woman's and tried to give her as much comfort as I could as he threw her clothing above her waist and spread her legs wide. I tried to kick him, but he was just out of my reach. He knew exactly how to position us so that he was unhindered.

He looked me in the eye then let his gaze slide up and down my body as he pumped himself. "By law, I have to allow Marcus the first fuck, but I think I will enjoy breaking you into this family." Then, as Vibius' eyes locked on mine, he plunged into her with no warning.

Her scream rang through the air. I heard the screech of a chair moving quickly in the next room, but no one came through the door. Not a single one of them. Vibius' eyes never left mine as he defiled her, as he went about his so-called punishment. A smile crossed his lips as he pulled his eyes from mine and lowered them to between my legs.

"That tight pussy will be mine, Sidonia, and I will enjoy every minute of it." He growled with each thrust into her.

I squeezed the woman's hand, and she held mine tight. It was the only comfort I could give her. Hate and fear filled me, the likes I had never known. I couldn't do anything. I felt so helpless.

When he finished with her, he strode over to me and rubbed his wetness over my stomach. I remember doing everything I could not to throw up all over him.

"So pretty. You will be so much fun," he said along my neck, then he untied the other woman and told her to leave.

Once she left the room, he turned me toward the wall and pulled my hips back. He pressed against me and when he was hard again, he slipped between my legs. He didn't enter me but proceeded to pump himself against me between my thighs. I didn't remember much until after he released himself and ran his hand along my core, spreading himself everywhere.

After turning me to face him, he said, "I will fill you nightly, and you will allow it without complaint."

"He moved just far enough away that I lifted my leg and kneed him in the groin. He pushed me against the wall again, cussing into my ear. I felt him smile against my cheek before my hips were pulled back and my ass was spanked to the point it hurt to sit and I had to sleep on my stomach. He left me tied there against the wall afterward as he left to finish his dinner. A while later, he came back, spanked me some more, and then rubbed himself against my ass cheeks until he finished on my back. I remember going to the ocean later and trying to scrub him off me. There are bits I don't remember, and I'm not sure how long I was even in that house." Tears were running down my face when I turned to Tiberius.

His face was tight and I could almost hear his teeth grinding. "Were you hurt?" he asked softly.

I shook my head. "Not physically. Other than my ass being tender and the bite. It was discolored and sore for a few days. The bite marks eventually cleared up, but otherwise no. I'll never forget that night, Tiberius, even if I don't remember everything that happened."

We sat there for a long time, Tiberius studying me and waiting for me to finish. He knew there was more to this story. My eyes flickered to his again, and there was nothing but patience and fury for what had been done to me.

"When I was allowed to leave, Vibius grabbed my hand and pulled me to him. He was close enough that I could smell his rancid breath and feel him hard against my hip as he spat the last words he would ever speak to me. 'Speak out of turn again, and you will see just how restrained I was tonight.' Then I ran out the door.

"I knew I couldn't live there. I knew I would rather die than live in that house. When I got home after trying to scrub him off of me in the ocean, I went directly to bed, and I refused to speak of the visit with my family."

"Why didn't you report what was happening to the guards?" Tiberius asked.

I looked at him evenly. "He's a high-status man running his house. No guard is going to put a stop to it. They would have just told me to learn my place and not to provoke him."

"What happened after that night, though? Marcus didn't intervene, but he left shortly after."

I didn't say anything as I remembered the next morning—getting up and going directly to the back room to find something to put an end to it. I wasn't looking for a way to kill myself. I was looking for a way that I could end the wedding, and I found it. It was an older spell that required ancient herbs that were very rare. We had them of course, but I knew Grandmother and Mother would notice any amount of them missing. It took me a week, but I had perfected it.

"Tiberius, I can't tell you everything. Not yet. What I can tell you is that a couple days before the wedding was to occur, Marcus and I, with Lars as my chaperone, sat for a midday meal at the base of the mountain. Marcus had brought bread and fruits for us to eat and I prepared a special brew of tea and handed it to him." I remembered how he drank the entire thing as I mumbled the spell under my breath and waited for it to take hold. Once it had, Marcus' eyes glazed over and he looked at me with questioning.

"In that moment, I saw a broken man. I saw a man who had been belittled, beaten, and abused his whole life. I felt sorry for him." Tiberius squeezed my hand then ran his thumb across the surface of it as I smiled at him.

"I tried to think of a way that I could save him from this life." Guilt covered my face as I told Tiberius, "I batted my eyelashes like a love-stricken girl and lovingly suggested that maybe he should join the Roman Empire as a warrior. He was strong and already such a good fighter. His eyes lit up and the next day, he had packed his things for Rome, disappearing without a word to me or my family."

What I hadn't counted on was him returning after two months and killing his father. I had learned later that it was nature's balance for what I had done. My grandmother recognized the effects when she saw Marcus as the guards took him from the home and directly came to me with questions. It took her a good long time, but I finally opened up and told her what had happened that night at Marcus' house. She didn't damn me or tell my father and mother what had happened, but she did remind me that with every spell that is cast, nature must have balance. We are healers, and while my intention at the point of my suggestion was to free him from the pain of his father, nature had to find its balance.

"I've continued to have nightmares about that night, though they have diminished." I took a deep breath. "But sometimes there are days when things happen that take me back to that night at Marcus'. I never want to feel that helpless and worthless again. I have learned and made myself become an advocate for those who are in that situation. If I see it, I won't tolerate it."

There was a long silence. "But with what happened at the magistrate's today, it . . . brings it all back—everything that happened at Marcus' and what happened afterwards."

CHAPTER 15

TIBERIUS

THIS WOMAN. SHE WAS a fighter. A survivor. My heart ached for her. Even though she knew she was powerless to stop all that happened, she knew she couldn't stop fighting.

"You saved him from his own family," I said after a few minutes. She still had tears flowing down her cheeks and didn't turn to face me. I had moved my body tight against hers: the only comfort I could give her. I had never felt such a burning need to be with someone in my life. Not just sexually, but physically and emotionally. To be her defender. To be hers and to make her mine. Every part of my being told me to protect her.

I grabbed her chin and forced her to look at me. "Sidonia, if you chose me, I will ensure that any memory of those horrors are erased from you with love and dedication."

I leaned forward, bringing her forehead to mine where my lips were a whisper from hers. My hand tightened on her chin as I struggled against the need to kiss her. I forced myself to look into her eyes, and she raised her hand to sit on my cheek. My head leaned into it just the slightest bit, craving her in the deepest of ways.

"Why me?" she whispered against my lips. It was so quiet, I almost missed it.

I studied her for a long moment before saying, "There is a fiery intelligence and fight in you. I have been through and led war. I've lived and done some deplorable things because of it, yet today you told me how you lived *through* it. That is a strength that can't be matched."

"I've survived," she said, but it was laced with a meaning that I couldn't understand. It was more than just that night. There was just an inherent strength about her.

Where her hand held my cheek, a fire burned. "Sidonia." Her name whispered out of me. I couldn't resist one moment longer. I leaned in, bringing my lips to hers, and pressed in, soft and gentle. When she returned it, it was as if Helios himself had pushed the heat of all his suns into me, burning me and searing her essence into me. That fire etched her name on my soul, and I knew, in that moment, she would be the only one I would ever burn for.

My grip on her hip tightened, and she opened for me, and I deepened the kiss. Not daring to break the connection, I moved off the wall to stand in front of her and pressed my chest against hers. She met me every step of the way.

I felt myself harden, but I was careful not to press my erection against her, for fear of bringing back those memories she had just divulged to me. I would not jeopardize this. I would let her lead. I may have initiated this kiss, but I was going to let her tell me how we would proceed.

She pulled back and whispered softly, "By the Mother." Her head snapped back, and her eyes were wide as her hand covered her mouth.

I ran my thumb across her cheek and just stared at her.

Her eyes became wary. "Tiberius, I'm so sorry."

My eyebrows scrunched together. "What? What for?"

She stared back at me in confusion. Her mouth opened and closed. Opened again, but closed. After another long moment, she kissed me again quickly, breathing a sigh of what sounded like relief, and said, "I need to get my deliveries finished, and you need to meet the people of Herculaneum."

CHAPTER 16

SIDONIA

"WHAT TIME DO YOU usually finish with all of your duties?" Tiberius asked as we were nearing the house after making all the deliveries I had with me.

"Depends. Today was an . . . interesting day." I only hesitated a moment to keep what occurred at the magistrate's house, the memories that had been drudged back up, and all I had told him at the beach at bay.

"What do you mean, interesting?"

"There were the usual deliveries to some of the more privileged in the colony, including the . . . magistrate's home, which is where I had just left when I ran into you and . . . What was his name again?" I said, trying to lead the conversation.

"Velarde." He offered nothing more.

"How do you know him?" I asked as we got to the door of my family's home.

"We met in Vendelicia along the Germania border. He actually helped clean me up after one heck of a tavern . . ." A smile crossed his face. "I see what you're doing."

"What are you talking about?" I asked, but he just gave me a knowing look. When I didn't say anything, his left eyebrow raised, and it was such a strange look that I broke. "Ok, fine. Tell me something. Anything I can hold over your head for years to come," I said, relaxing and smiling.

"For years to come. I like the sound of that." He smiled brightly, and I blushed, rolled my eyes, and headed inside with Tiberius on my heels. Placing my delivery bag on the table, I headed to the side door of the workshop. I heard Tiberius sit down at the table behind me as I checked in with my grandmother and mother. I liked the fact he didn't wait outside for me, but also respected my business enough to wait in the living area instead of invading the workshop.

"Grandmother? Mother?"

"Finished so soon, Sidonia?" Grandmother said.

"Yes, Grandmother. All deliveries are made. Can you . . . No. I'll do it. Forgive me," I said, thinking better of it. I wouldn't want to put Grandmother or Mother in the position of having to go to the magistrate's home. Then I remembered Luculla's request. "Actually, Luculla Potius wanted me to let you know she will pick up all orders personally from now on."

"Did she mention why?" Mother asked. "It is really no problem to deliver it to them. You go right by the magistrate's home."

"She did not mention why, Mother. She need not." I kept my eyes low and hoped that Mother wouldn't ask for more information. I really didn't want to go into what had happened.

"Did he hurt you?" Grandmother asked without looking up. Her voice was tight. Grandmother missed nothing. Nothing.

"No," I said quickly as my mother's face quickly turned to me, and I could see her ready to check me over at the littlest of insinuations.

"He did not. H-how—" I stammered.

"I do not know why Luculla does not just leave him. She would be independent, and certainly has enough of her own fortune to make herself comfortable," Grandmother interrupted, still without ever looking up.

"She's scared," I said, pausing for just a moment before continuing. "She's afraid she would be ruined because he is the magistrate. I feel bad for Flora, too. He's controlling her even more so. He is using all his power to manipulate them both. They feel . . . trapped."

"Flora?" Grandmother and Mother both said, stopping immediately and looking at me. I froze. I assumed they knew about her.

"Flora?" Mother asked again.

"Yes. Flora is their slave. Sex slave was more like it, but I didn't tell you that. I don't know if he has purchased her or not. Anyway, the magistrate uses the oil for both Flora and Luculla," I said as my mother's blue eyes pierced mine with hints of worry, confusion, and then flashed with anger. I couldn't bring myself to explain any further. It made my stomach flip with disgust and made me want to cry for them. I was already feeling very raw from telling Tiberius about my similar experience. Those emotions were sitting much higher than I had allowed myself to have them for a very long time.

She turned and looked back at Grandmother, who gave her a curt nod. Mother then mumbled a few words under her breath, grabbed a couple of vials from the shelf, and stormed out of the workshop.

"What is she doing, Grandmother?" I asked as she stormed out the front door, not even acknowledging.

"It is probably best not to ask, Sidonia." She gave me a look, but I pressed.

"Grandmother. Do no harm. It's our number one rule," I said, my eyes flicking to the front door of the shop.

"She's going to shrivel his balls off." Then she put a finger to her chin and shrugged. "Or just leave him without his manhood. Now we need anise, ginger, tolermine, valerian, parsley and some dandelion from Vesuvius. Tomorrow, you can go to the market, get Lars, and then the three of you can head up."

I looked at her, shocked. "The three of us?"

"Isn't the young man Tiberius sitting in the very next room?" She set the vial she was filling down on the table and looked up at me with what can only be described as a grandmother who knows way too much smile.

"He is," I said, blushing. "Do you miss anything, Grandmother?"

"Oh Mother, I hope not. Now, take the rest of the deliveries there on the counter and deliver them. Tomorrow, you three can take the day to get what we need . . . Oh, don't look at me like that," she said.

"Like what, Grandmother?" I said, not fully understanding.

"I may be the oldest in this family, my dear, but I'm not stupid. You are beyond smitten with that boy, and I'm giving you an excuse to spend time with him. This time, however, you will be escorted by Lars. I don't want the guards getting the wrong idea." She pointed her finger at me to drive home the point.

"Grandmother?" I said carefully. She looked up at me with a loving smile. "I told him about Marcus."

She studied me for a moment. "Did you tell him about how you did it?"

"No, I'm not sure I will tell him exactly what I did," I breathed. "I told him about what happened at the house, though. I didn't keep any of that from him. I . . . I can't . . ."

"You really like this one, don't you?" she commented with no judgment in her voice. I just nodded. She looked out past the curtain that separated the house from the workshop to where he sat. Her head twisted to the side, and then her mouth fell open in surprise. "I can see you around him, Sidonia."

"What?"

Her face was slightly vacant as she said in a voice too distant, "The Mother may have chosen him for you. Your souls are entwined. It's so rare, but you two have been touched." She shook her head to clear it and pointed to the deliveries that needed to be made today. "Now, go. Market and deliveries. Move!"

I loaded the rest of the deliveries into my bag, and before I walked out the door, I leaned down and gave her a hug. "You're the best, Grandmother."

"Where are we off to now?" Tiberius asked, standing when I returned to the main room.

"All day? You want to just go from house to house all day with me?" I asked, smirking.

He came to stand so close to me, if I took a deep breath, our chests would touch. I could feel Grandmother looking out the workshop door, watching us. He bent down close to my ear, and where Grandmother couldn't see, he ran his fingertips up and down my arm as he said in a voice that was smooth, "Yes. Any excuse to be near you, Ms. Sidonia. Now, where are we off to?"

My arm felt as if it had been dipped in lava. My heart was racing, and it took every ounce of concentration to say, "The marketplace for some purchases, then more deliveries. Apparently, tomorrow we are to retrieve my brother and the three of us are going to the mountain. That is, if you are available?" I asked, grabbing my bag and trying not to let him see me blush, which I didn't believe was all that successful.

"That would be wonderful. I shall meet you here mid-morning after a meeting I have with a few of the magistrates."

CHAPTER 17

SIDONIA

THE NEXT MORNING, TIBERIUS met me at the house, and we walked in silence to the marketplace where we found Lars, who was ready to go. I had made the trip alone numerous times, but Grandmother gave me this opportunity to spend time with Tiberius, and Tiberius was apparently happy to be at my side since we met.

It was strange. Marcus never wanted to spend time with me. He never flirted with me, or really even tried to get to know me. He had said we would just spend the rest of our lives together, and I was a family tool, anyway. It wasn't like that with Tiberius. He wanted to spend every moment he could with me. I asked whether he was avoiding his duties to his father, and he had just said, "My father is thrilled that

I'm spending time with you. He said he's been doing it for so long by himself, that should we enter into an arrangement, he will look forward to the help after we are wed." Then he kissed me quickly on the cheek, and we headed toward the marketplace.

The three of us made our way through town quickly, and when we reached the trails, Lars turned to me and smiled. "Okay, little sister. Bet I can beat you to the rock up the third bend."

I laughed. Years ago, before I made these trips on my own, he would take me, and we would race to the best picking spots. He would always win, but that was just because he was bigger. Now, I had the advantage. I knew the path so much better and ran it often. I laughed and said, "Oh, you're going to lose and lose badly, brother."

"Will I?" he said, bumping me with his shoulder.

"Yup."

"Loser does the dishes?"

"Done," I said as I handed my bag to Tiberius, and when I was ready, we nodded and took off up the mountain.

I could hear Tiberius' laughter behind me, and I almost stopped to look back at him. It was a joyful, angelic sound that made me smile, but I really didn't want to do the dishes tonight. More importantly, I hated to lose.

I pressed my feet into the ground and pushed up the hill. Lars was just ahead of me, and when I reached him, he tried to block my path to keep me from passing him. Only, he did not realize that just up the path, it widened. When it did, I pushed past him.

I also knew the steepest part of the path was coming up and when I reached it, I had the footholds memorized and danced my way up. I continued to run the rest of the way up the hill, and when I reached the designated spot, I climbed on top of a rock and waited for Lars to arrive.

It took a minute, but I finally saw Lars and Tiberius walk up. "You've gotten quicker, my sister."

"And you've gotten slower in your age, my brother. Maybe Father needs to work you more."

Tiberius handed me my bag, and I opened the canister of wine that Lars had brought from the market and took a big, long drink. My throat was dry from the run, but my muscles felt alive. It was always a rush when I ran on the mountain. I felt as if Mother Earth was rejuvenating me. I tossed Lars the canister when I had my fill.

"Ha ha. Funny," Lars said, catching it with ease.

Tiberius and Lars both took a drink before Lars suggested that we continue up the mountain to find the dandelion first. We did, but when we reached the higher site, the smell of eggs that had stayed too long on the shelf filled my senses. I stopped dead in my tracks as I looked over the sight. Lars came to stand beside me. "Oh, Mother Earth, what has happened to you?"

There were lush green areas, just as they were last week when I was up here, and then dark brown patches, and patches where the grass had completely given way to the dirt. Around a small boulder was a small rodent that looked just as if it were sleeping, only it wasn't and had its tail sitting a few inches away from its body. I covered my mouth when the smell hit me again. Death, rot, and the rotten smell that filled my head had me reaching for the wine again, to rinse the taste from my mouth.

"What is that smell?" Tiberius asked.

We shook our heads.

"Vesuvius is . . . Why?" Lars asked disbelievingly, then he nodded to me, silently telling me he would distract Tiberius so I could examine the ground for anything that could have caused this.

"Tiberius, tell me about your time with the Empire while Sidonia gets to work." Lars led Tiberius gently in the opposite direction. "It will get us away from the smell, too."

I knelt on the ground, and it was warm from the sun, but it felt off. I pressed my palm to the ground, willing that healing power within me to come forth, and mumbled a silent prayer to Mother Earth for her healing.

Nothing happened. I felt nothing. There should have been a warm breeze, and the ground should have attempted to heal itself. I tried again, concentrating harder.

I felt nothing, but then . . . turmoil rocketed through my hands, hitting me hard in the chest, causing me to fall backwards onto my butt. Rubbing the spot, I felt as if someone had kicked me right between my breasts. I tried to take a deep breath but could only take in a few quick, short ones, and nothing deeper or soothing. No matter how hard I tried, it felt as if I had someone sitting on my chest.

Lars was doing a good job of keeping Tiberius distracted, but I needed to cast a full blessing to help heal the Earth. I didn't have any of the candles or the ingredients needed to do that with me, though.

I sat there for a moment, letting the dirt filter through my fingers. Something was wrong. Vesuvius was full of so much chaos and confusion. But why? The mountain has been so well taken care of. The citizens of the colony had made their offerings to their Gods, and hadn't my family respected the Mother? Why was the mountain destroying itself like this? There was no rhyme or reason to the damage, either. No fire had burned through. That was clear from the marks, and fire would have left a healing, renewal feeling, not discourse.

I sighed again and stood just as the earth under our feet shook violently. Lars and Tiberius both rushed to my side to steady me. "I'm fine," I spat. Both looked at each other with shock and confusion on their faces that they didn't voice.

When the shaking stopped, I stomped back down the hill, leaving them to follow me. I knew this mountain better than anyone and that included Lars. I didn't need them to show me the way down.

"Sidonia," Tiberius said, catching up to me and taking me by the elbow. It felt like flame had wrapped around my arm and I froze. Lars stood a healthy distance away, giving us some privacy.

I looked up at him.

"I . . . Are you okay?" he asked, bringing his hands to my face. My head was swimming. *Was the Mother ill? Was Vesuvius?*

I tried to look away, but Tiberius cradled my head in his hands, forcing me to look at him, bringing his face close to mine. "Are you okay?" he whispered.

"I'm fine. Vesuvius isn't, though, and I don't know why," I said, my voice cracking.

His eyes narrowed at me in confusion. "Why would you know what is wrong?"

I took a deep breath and kept my eyes low. "It's my job to make sure that Mother Earth stays healthy. That Vesuvius stays healthy."

When I tried to heal the earth, I felt the remnants of a curse that had been placed, but there have been rumors of the Dark Witches of Moesia cursing the lands. Since I hadn't run up against their magic before, I didn't know if I could even feel anything they did. I should, but their magic was dark, twisted, and so different from any other, that I suppose it's possible that I couldn't detect it. Had they cursed Vesuvius? I kept an eye out for any other clues to the sickness as I headed down and noted how, as the smell dissipated, the damage to Vesuvius did as well.

"I don't understand," Tiberius whispered against my lips.

"I know," I said, kissing him quickly and backing away from him to continue down the mountain. "You will soon."

I stopped at a clearing and started gathering the herbs Grandmother had requested. Lars and Tiberius stood nearby, talking and laughing, and when I was finished, I found Tiberius showing Lars some of the sword skills that he had learned while with the Empire.

When I had everything on the list, I sat down on a rock and watched them for a while, and I couldn't help but smile. Lars was soaking up the knowledge, and Tiberius looked to be really enjoying himself.

He was a natural teacher. He knew how to break the moves down into bits and pieces, and he explained the reasoning for each move and why your body had to be positioned in a certain way to get the right effect. Even I learned a few things by just watching them.

They were in a mock battle when Lars swung his "sword," which was nothing more than a stick, and landed a solid hit right on Tiberius' jaw. Tiberius fell back and crashed to the ground.

"That was unexpected," Lars said, more surprised than worried.

When Tiberius didn't get up, I panicked. "What do you mean, unexpected, Lars?" I got up and ran over to Tiberius.

"I didn't expect to make actual contact, so I swung hard," Lars said.

I knelt beside Tiberius and blood gushed down the side of his face from just below the eyeline. Tearing a piece of cloth from my palla, I worked on cleaning it up. It was only a minor cut, but the ones from the head always bled more.

I had learned that when I was nine and found Severius bleeding in the kitchen. My powers had come in much earlier than they were supposed to, and I had been able to seal the wound for him. Mother and Grandmother, who were shocked to see I had healed him without help, immediately started teaching me the basics of care and how to mix herbs and oils. It gave them additional time to prepare what would be needed when the battalions came through. Roman battalions stopped here for rest and aid on a near constant basis, so they were glad for the extra hands to help.

I wiped up the blood that had run down Tiberius' neck and took more time than was needed to clean it, looking for any hint of the scar he and his friend had discussed. Nothing. I ran my hand and pushed my power into him to see if I felt anything. A faint shadow filtered back within him, but I couldn't find what it was tied to. It sat deep within him, and while I could sense it, I couldn't touch it. I pushed to reach it, and it seemed to shy away from what The Mother gave me. I sighed heavily and pulled my power back.

I finished cleaning him up and once the bleeding stopped, I sat there looking at him for a moment longer when he smiled. "Should I enlist a painter to paint a portrait for you?"

I threw the cloth at him and got up. He took my hand before I could fully stand and pulled me back down to my knees.

"You were just lying there letting me take care of you?"

"I like the feeling of your skin on mine. It's warm, and I could feel that warmth spread through me." One side of his lips lifted, and there was a sparkle in his eye, and I didn't know what to make of it.

I looked down at his thumb where it was making small circles on the top of my hand. I didn't answer him, just watched his thumb. His touch was searing my skin and sending pulses of pleasure through my body. They stopped at the most intimate of places, and I could even feel my nipples harden for him.

"You are more beautiful than all the stars in the sky," he whispered. "How has no man made you his wife yet?"

I sighed and looked at Lars, who gave me a questioning look. "I already told him about Marcus, but . . ."

"I'll give you two some alone time to talk," Lars said, giving me a small, sad smile. He went off behind a boulder far enough away to give us privacy, but not far enough that he couldn't overhear if he wanted to.

Chapter 18

Sidonia

"I told you yesterday," I said, looking away from him.

"I'm sorry. I didn't mean to bring up that situation. Did the Empire put Marcus to death?"

"Yes. No. He was sent off not long after to be executed in Pompeii. There was no doubt he had done it. However, they ran into some trouble in the forest, and everyone died." How was I going to explain this? I looked down the mountain and onto Herculaneum, running my fingers through the grass.

"Sidonia?"

"I didn't want the arrangement to go through. I would have been better off a slave." I shuttered. "You know what happened."

"I do, and frankly, I'm glad it didn't." Tiberius waited a few moments before he asked, "However, that does not explain why another man hasn't made you his wife. You're sweet, gentle, caring, intelligent, and beautiful. Why didn't your family enter into another arrangement?"

"No one in my family has ever said it, but I'm damaged goods. I hear the rumors that go around about me. Most think . . ." I inwardly groaned, not really wanting to explain this to him. "Most think I'm not pure because of Marcus' arrangement. I think more people knew what was happening in that house than they let on. No one wants an arrangement with someone who isn't pure for their new husband."

"I would have killed him myself if I had known what had happened then," he said softly. "I won't let any harm come to you, Sidonia. Pure or not, that doesn't change who you are."

"I am, though." If he wanted us to continue, he had to know I was. It was important to me he knew I was still pure. I blinked, not sure why that was so important to me, but it was. "Like I said, he knew Marcus, by law, had to have me first. He didn't want to risk invalidating that marriage."

"Again, it wouldn't matter to me, even if you weren't. Sidonia, it doesn't change who you are," he said in a determined tone. "I don't care if you have been with other men or women. It doesn't change that I want to pursue us."

Ignoring him, I told him the other rumor. "I also hear that I'm cursed, which is why Marcus killed his father. Many blame me. I hear that in the streets, too. Father and Mother deny what is said, but I overhear the gossip when I'm making deliveries. I hear the whispers, but as you said, you can't prove whispers."

Tiberius took my chin and forced me to look at him and meet his gaze. His eyes were soft, radiant, but had a flickering of pain in them. "Sidonia. You are not cursed." Then he took his thumb and wiped the tear from my cheek. "Any man would be lucky to call you his wife."

Tiberius pulled me down and snuggled up behind me. He just held me as we lay there in the grass for a long while. He would on occasion just repeat that pure or not, it didn't matter, and there was no way I could be cursed, but Tiberius didn't know everything. I could be cursed. What if I was for what I did to Marcus?

But I didn't feel cursed in his arms. I felt like there could be happiness and warmth in life. His words had settled within me. I wanted him and realized I very well would be happy with an arrangement with Tiberius. My heart skipped a beat as he pulled me closer to him and kissed the back of my head. If this wasn't real, then he was one good actor.

When I rolled over to face him, he rolled onto his back, and I cradled myself up to him, resting my head on his chest. I could very much get used to this. The sound of his heart jumping at the small movements I made with my fingers brought a small smile to my lips.

I ran my hand down his stomach and back up. The sound that came from his chest had me aching for him. Yes, I very much wanted Tiberius. I wanted him in every way I could. Not just that, I needed him in my heart, *and* I wanted him physically.

I lay there daydreaming how if Lars wasn't nearby, maybe I would throw all caution to the wind and give into my need for Tiberius. It took all my self-control not to allow my hands to roam under his cloth and stroke him. I could have easily done so and kept my movements hidden. Glancing up, Lars was so immersed in drawing, I didn't think he would even notice. His back was to us, and short of us being extraordinarily vocal, nothing would pull him from his sketch.

Tiberius had taken to running his hand up my arm and down my back. The trail left my nipples erect, and I shifted my legs to adjust for the ache that was forming there.

I found my hand slipping lower and beneath the first layer of his clothing and could feel his hardness against my leg that laid over his. There was a content moan in his chest, and we both knew exactly what I was doing with my fingers.

The books in the workshop library were filled with ways a woman could please a man or a woman. There had been many days spent reading them with the hope that one day, I would be able to satisfy my future husband. Not to mention, all the public displays that gave me the visual of exactly how all of that worked. I knew many ways to please a partner, even if I hadn't physically had sex myself.

My mind was filled with visions of sitting above Tiberius and impaling myself with him, rocking my hips to bring him pleasure. I even thought I heard him moan as I thought of that.

Lifting my gaze to him, where his sapphire blue eyes met mine, I bit my lower lip, frozen in that moment. His free hand, the one that wasn't tight on my waist, reached over to touch my cheek. When his thumb ran across my exposed bottom lip, I moved my hand lower. He let out a hiss and his eyes closed in concentration when my hand brushed him. I simply ran one finger over the length of him, and his eyes rolled back.

"Sidonia," he whispered, lighter than the breeze. I smiled and moved my hand back below another layer of fabric, and he froze.

"Do you want me to stop?" I whispered softly.

"Gods, no, but Lars." He hissed that last part as I had made contact with his bare balls under the last layer and cupped them fully in my hand. "Gods, woman."

His hand hadn't moved from my face, and we just stared at each other as I took him in my hand. My fingers barely fit around his girth as I stroked him slowly. Running my fingertip around the head of him and through his slit had him holding onto my chin tighter as he tried not to move his hips while I pumped him.

"Tiberius," I whispered as his gaze stayed on mine, full of heat and lust.

"Sidonia," he whispered back and moaned as quietly as possible as I gripped him harder and fingered his balls. As I stroked him and pumped the bulbous head of him, his stomach tightened, and I felt his thigh muscles tense up in restraint as he tried not to move his hips.

Long moments passed between us, his eyes staying fixed on mine, as we tried to stay quiet and not draw Lars' attention. Every time his hand would tighten on my cheek, I would smirk and smile at him. When his breathing started to come in quick succession, his head dipped toward mine and he kissed me hard, and I swallowed his moan as he released in my hand.

Grabbing the cloth I had used to clean the blood from his face, I slipped it under to clean us both up.

"Are you sure you are not Aphrodite?" he asked, kissing my forehead. I smiled at him as he whispered, still half-drunk on his bliss, "I chose you, Sidonia."

Heart racing, I moved my hand back to his chest and curled back up next to him.

He said he chose me.

Was it because of who I was or just post-release bliss? Would he still choose me if he knew my biggest secret? His whole family would have to agree to keep that secret. Any daughters I would bear him would follow the same line.

Over the next hour, Tiberius just held me close. I tried to not think about what he said, and just enjoy our time here, because the more I thought about it, the more I feared Tiberius would run.

"We should get back into town," Lars said when the sun was getting low in the sky.

Tiberius got up, dusted himself off, and asked, "Did you get the herbs for your grandmother?"

"I did," I said as I looked back up at Vesuvius before we headed into town. There was something in his eyes that said he almost understood as I looked back up at the brown patches higher on the mountain and sighed.

When Tiberius took my hand, I studied him, but he smiled at me. Squeezing my hand, he led me down the mountain. What had just happened between Tiberius and me? Things changed, but in a good way or bad?

CHAPTER 19

TIBERIUS

Spending the day with Sidonia had to be one of the best days of my life. Gods, I wanted that woman. Anyone else, anywhere else, and I would have taken her right there on the mountain and worshiped her like the goddess she was. I was so hard at just the thought of her.

The way she moved on the mountain was enticing. It was like she was one with it. She cared for its well-being, but she had also said she was responsible for Vesuvius. What did that even mean? It was just a mountain, part of the Earth. As long as Herculaneum continued its offerings to the Gods, it would stand proud and protect the colony.

I sighed at the memory of how she just let me hold her up there. She had curled up next to me and put her head on my chest, and when she draped her leg over mine, my muscles had twitched with the restraint not to pull her on top of me and move our clothing aside. Just when I thought I was going to burn in Tartarus for all of eternity for the thoughts going through my head, she moved her hand.

That beautiful vixen turned those brown eyes on me and . . . Where and how did she learn how to do that with such precision? I knew what I said and thought afterwards, and I also noted she did not say it back. I could only hope she would find me worthy someday.

I walked back into the house, intent on heading straight to bed and relieving myself because damn, that woman. I just left her, and I was already hard for her again. I walked through the front door and stopped. My father was sitting at our table talking to Sidonia's father.

"Mr. Regillia," I greeted, trying to keep the panic from my voice. "I hope that this isn't about what I think it is. I believe Sidonia and I have *both* made our positions quite clear to our fathers."

"Tiberius, sit down," my father demanded, leaving no room for questions.

Sighing, I did as I was asked but said, "Father."

"You said you wanted a home," he said, looking at Sidonia's father.

"I did, but I didn't mean I would be setting one up with the first girl who showed any interest."

"There are few girls without arrangement around your age. Most of whom have already been married and with children. Consider this a blessing from Venus," he said again with no room for negotiation.

"I consider Sidonia a blessing from Venus, but that just means I do not want to push her into something that she isn't ready for. I do not want to push her into a lifetime commitment with me if she doesn't love me," I growled.

"That right there is why I came to your father, Tiberius," Mr. Regillia said. "The fact you don't want her just because she is beautiful, but you actually want to care for your wife and for her to care for you. I told you already that I had promised her she could choose. She still can choose. We are finalizing the terms here tonight, and then tomorrow she can decide if she wishes to continue with the arrangement."

"Tomorrow," I said incredulously. "We haven't known each other for more than two weeks, and you want her to make a lifetime determination tomorrow?"

"Yes," both of our fathers said in unison.

I stared at them and after a moment said, "I want Sidonia. I choose Sidonia, but only if she chooses me. I do not agree to . . . this."

"There are many arrangements that happen without the two ever meeting, Tiberius. It is your family obligation to follow through on this agreement," my father said.

"Father," I gritted out through my teeth. "Give us two weeks."

"Four days," he said. "If Mr. Regillia is agreeable."

Mr. Regillia nodded his head and said, "If terms are confirmed today, I will agree to four days."

I looked at them and said, "Please. Please give us more time. I do not understand the need to rush this. If terms are confirmed, what does it matter if it is in two weeks or a month?" I had to try. I knew it would not matter, but I could not go into this marriage without trying to give Sidonia more time. My mind had been made up and only confirmed every day since I saw her on that mountain. She was mine in my heart.

"You have made your objections about the speediness of this clear," my father said with total finality. "Now, you can either go to bed and brood or you can sit here quietly while we work out terms, and maybe even have some say. Mr.

Regillia has agreed that you are worthy of his daughter, which is more than most fathers consider in these arrangements."

CHAPTER 20

SIDONIA

EVERY NIGHT, FOR THE last three nights, I dreamed of Tiberius. He spent every moment he wasn't required to help in his father's business with me. The inappropriateness of how much of our time was spent together was intoxicating. My cheeks flushed as I recalled giving him another hand job in the alley alcove on two different occasions over the last few days. Every time Tiberius touched me, I felt like I was going to explode. Every night, I had to come home and put my hand between my legs in order to sleep. Last night, we had been just walking down one of the smaller, less traveled streets when he took a deep breath to steady himself.

"Sidonia. I need to talk to you about something."

"What's wrong?" Resting my head on his shoulder, he ran his thumb across my cheekbone and kissed me quickly. I looked at him carefully and repeated, "Again, what is wrong, Tiberius?"

Taking a deep breath, he said, "Our fathers have been making arrangements for our marriage."

He wouldn't look at me.

"Tiberius," I said softly, and when he still didn't look at me, I brought my hand to his cheek, forcing him to meet my eyes. "You think that is a surprise to me?"

His eyebrows knitted together. "You aren't mad? You have told your father repeatedly that you want to decide on who to marry."

"I have, but I also know my father. He knows I care for you. He will not chance me changing my mind. I can only hope that he allows us to determine the time frame."

He blinked. Then blinked again.

"Did you just say that you hope they allow . . ." His throat bobbed as he gulped. ". . . *us* to determine the time frame?"

I lowered my head, heat filling my cheeks. I hadn't told him I thought I was in love with him. I didn't want to ruin what we had if he didn't feel the same way.

He made me face him, and I had hardly registered the look on his face before he had me up against the wall and his lips crashed into mine. I didn't know whose air belonged to whom as our tongues fought for dominance. When he pulled back, his gaze met mine, and with a ferocity that had my insides swimming, he said against my lips, "You are mine."

I simply smiled back at him.

Chapter 21

Tiberius

When I knocked on Sidonia's door, it was late. Too late for a man to be knocking on a single woman's door to have a few stolen moments with her. However, when her father answered with a knowing smile that said he knew just how much I wanted to marry his daughter, I shook my head. I would ask for more time. I wanted more time for Sidonia. I had hoped I could ask immediately, but when he opened the door, she was standing right behind him. Later. I would ask for more time later.

"Mr. Regillia, I'm going to take Sidonia down to the ocean for a few hours."

Sidonia looked at me in shock, but her father smiled and said, "Keep her safe from the guards."

She looked at both of us, confusion and shock on that beautiful face of hers. I smiled at her and said in fierce determination, "I will keep her safe from the Emperor him-self."

I took her hand and hurriedly led her down to the water. It was one of our favorite places to go. We could be away from prying eyes, and no one could overhear any of our discussions.

Tonight was different. I needed to reassure myself that this was real. I had been in meetings all day with magistrates who belittled each other and then talked about swapping around their slaves like they were trash.

I needed to have something real and assuring in my arms tonight, and the only thing I was sure of was Sidonia. She was mine, and I was going to make sure she knew it tonight.

We had been down there for about twenty minutes, just standing with her in my arms, before my tense shoulders finally loosened. Taking a long breath, I turned her face toward me and kissed her tenderly. She twisted in my arms to face me and wrapped her arms around my shoulders.

"Sidonia," I whispered, feeling everything inside me warm with her touch.

I felt her smile against my lips. "I like when you say my name like that."

I smiled back and kissed her again. She deepened the kiss and more than heard my chest growl against her. Lifting her from the ground, I carried her down to the water's edge.

When her toes felt the water, she pulled back, smiling, and asked, "What are you doing?"

"I have a very special favor to return to you for what you did on the mountain . . . and in the alley . . . and the other alley," I whispered against her jawbone.

She tried to speak as I slowly set her down, letting her slide down my body, but there were no coherent words. I knew she felt my hardness against her stomach when she pressed herself closer against me and moaned.

"One day soon, Sidonia," I promised. It was the heat in her gaze that extracted that promise from me. I would love nothing more than to have her now. To lay her down on this beach and lose myself deep within her.

I wouldn't do that to her, though. She deserved to have her first time done properly. Not in a frenzy on the beach, but somewhere where I could take my time and show her everything.

No. Tonight I was going to show her appreciation for all the times over the last few days she had satisfied me and never asked for anything in return. Gods, I wanted to, but time was never on our side for me to repay that pleasure properly.

"Tiberius," she said as she threw her head back, and I kissed my way down her neck. "I . . ."

I threaded my hands through the hair at the nape of her neck and, shakily, I whispered in her ear, "I know. Soon."

My hand snaked down her back and to her hips. "Do you trust me?" I ask with a little grin.

"Yes. Why?"

"Mind getting wet?" I smiled at her, and she smiled at the double meaning.

"I can swim if that's what you mean," she said, tipping her head toward the ocean. She tried to back away from me, but I tightened my grip on her nape. She froze, giving me a mischievous smile and raising her eyebrows at me.

"Where do you think you are going?" I demanded.

"Swimming," she said, tearing off layers of clothing. When she was down to nothing, I wished for more light from the moon to see her properly.

I released her to strip myself, and the moment she was loose, she took off for the water. I couldn't strip fast enough, and but a minute later, I was wrapping my arms around her bare waist and lifting her back to me.

She giggled and squealed. It was the purest sound I had heard in my life. With the force of the waves, she wiggled herself free, and I barely caught her hand and swung her back against me before another wave crashed into us.

I moved to where we were barely waist deep and I could hold us against the waves. Turning her to face me, the moonlight sparkled in her eyes. She used the force of the next wave to propel herself up and wrap her arms around my shoulders. I held her there and leaned in to kiss her. Her legs wrapped around my waist, and when she locked her ankles behind me, she rolled her hips, causing me to almost lose all sense of reason. I moaned into her.

"Tiberius, my love," she said with a need that I wanted to pull from her again and again. My heart latched onto those words.

"Hold on to me," I ordered, bringing one hand to cup her ass and the other between us.

I ran one finger from one end of her to the other, stopping just short of that nub that I knew would beg for attention. Her head fell back, and I kissed her neck as I did it again, circling her opening. Her hips rocked against my hand involuntarily, and it was everything I could do not to remove it and plunge myself into her.

One finger slid in, just the slightest bit, causing a moan to come from her. When I used another to circle that spot closest to me, the sound from her was non-human. I smiled when she jerked against the added pressure of her nub.

Her head was back in unadulterated bliss as she stared into the starry sky. She was a siren, and I couldn't resist her call. "Sidonia. Look at me."

She slowly lifted her head, and when her gaze met mine, I pressed down firmer on that numb and circled it. Her mouth opened and then closed. As I pressed my finger against her opening again, she ground into my hand enough that I entered her and with a smirk, I thrust my finger in and out of her as much as I would allow myself.

She rolled her hips against me, and I felt myself hit her internal barrier. I pulled my hand back, and the sound that came out of her was adorable. Something between a moan and a growl of frustration left her. Her eyes narrowed at me as I lifted her up against me.

"Not here. Not now, love," I said with all the self-control I had. She huffed in frustration, and I chuckled. She moved her hips against me and slid herself along my cock. My eyes rolled back into my head as she did it again, giggling and kissing my neck. I knew that if we kept that up, we would cross the line, and I had promised myself better for her.

"You temptress," I said through gritted teeth.

I turned her around, so she was facing out toward the bay, wrapping one arm tightly around her waist and sliding the other between her legs. I rubbed up and down her slit and paid special attention to that nub of hers. She ground against me faster and faster, and it was only moments later that I felt her tightening. I pulled my hand away before she reached her climax. Her head fell back against my shoulder, and she hissed my name through her teeth.

Running my thumb against her stomach, I pulled her from that edge before teasing her to the edge again, and stopping.

"You do not play fair."

Giggling, I slowed and teased her one more time before kissing her, working her hard and fast. She rocked against me, whispered my name, and threw her head back as she orgasmed. The look of pure bliss and the way her ass had moved against me had me releasing against her.

Her head collapsed on my shoulder and her legs went limp. I wrapped my arms around her waist so she wouldn't slip away from me, and I chuckled in her ear.

Turning her back toward me, I held her there in the waves for a good five minutes before she tried to stand on her own. Her legs were still weak, so she wrapped her arms around me and rested her head on my chest.

"Thank you," she said, kissing my chest.

"After all the pleasure you've given me this week, you are thanking me?" I chuckled. "Sidonia, I just wanted to give something back."

Just then, a wave surprised us both, sending us under the water. I held her tight, and when we surfaced, laughter burst out of us. Setting her down, we made our way out of the ocean to find that whether we had stripped or not, even our clothes were now soaking wet.

We helped each other get dressed and laughed as we headed back to her house. I smiled and when we got back to her door, I pulled her close and said, "You are what I want for the rest of my life, Sidonia."

Her hand came to rest on my cheek as she rose on her tiptoes and kissed me. Against my lips, I barely heard her say, "My Tiberius."

CHAPTER 22

SIDONIA

WHEN I HAD GOTTEN back from the beach with Tiberius last night, soaking wet, I lied to my mother and said that I had fallen in when a wave surprised us. I thought she saw through it, but she just said to get some rest because we had a few last-minute deliveries to make early the next day. Within minutes of crawling under the blanket, I easily fell into a deep sleep.

I woke up the next morning feeling happy and relaxed. I dressed quickly, securing my palla with one of the ruby pins that was my grandmother's. My hair this morning was a completely different matter. I brushed it and remembered how it felt when Tiberius moved it to the side so he could kiss my neck. His touch lit me on fire. Blessed be the Mother, I had wanted to have all of him last night. The restraint he showed as I begged him for it was unrivaled. I took a calming breath as an ache was quickly settling there again, and I shook my head to clear it.

I quickly finished combing through my hair, pulled it back, and reset the jeweled wreath from last week on my head. Since I would be making deliveries again today, I decided to wear a few of the rings my father had bought me as a birthday present earlier this year, as well as the sapphire lotus bracelet that reminded me of Tiberius every time I would look at it.

My mind was wondering just where I might run into him today as I walked out from my sleeping chamber and into the main area, where I saw my father speaking to two other men, whose backs were to me in the shadows of the room. It wasn't uncommon for my father to have early-morning meetings in our home for the marketplace, so I tried to be quiet.

When he noticed me, I said, "Excuse me, Father. I did not realize you had associates over."

"No, Sidonia. Please. You do not need to leave," my father said encouragingly.

"I will be on my way in just moments, Father. There are deliveries to make," I said as I noticed there would be no need to go to the bread maker as there was already some on the table. The younger of the two men turned and stepped out from the shadows, and my heart leapt.

"Tiberius. What are you doing here this morning?" I asked, trying to hide the butterflies in my stomach. By the look on his face, I knew what he fland his father were doing here, and I groaned internally.

He looked at his father and then at me. "You may tell her, Tiberius," my father said, smiling.

"Sidonia, I know it is fast, and I would prefer more time—well, to give you more time. I want you to have a decision in the matter." He almost growled the words while looking at his father as if trying to make a point. By the look on his face, this was a discussion they'd had repeatedly.

"We are to be wed," I said strongly with a lift of my chin. The arrangement had been or was being finalized. Our fathers had decided they didn't want to wait for us to make a decision. I looked at my father, and my heart broke a little. I felt tears spring to my eyes, and I fought to keep them from falling. He had promised me I could decide. He wasn't waiting for my approval. His eyes went pleading for a moment but then shifted away from me.

"Yes. Our fathers have . . . They have arranged our marriage," he said, trying to look serious but yet unable to keep a hint of a smile from his face.

"Tiberius, we have discussed this," I said, looking only at him. He nodded, and I saw the glimmer in his eye. "While we have spent much time together over the last couple of weeks, we haven't known each other long. Is this arrangement agreeable to you?" I tried to sound strong, all the while attempting to keep the butterflies from flying out of my mouth.

He had said a few times he chose me, and I knew I was choosing him, but there was that little girl inside of me that wondered if all of our escapades were just for fun or if he was serious about this. Regardless, I tried very hard to keep a smile off my face as I asked him.

We had hoped our physical escapades had remained hidden, but there were some places that had been risky. Anyone could have seen us at the beach or near the balneae. Even Lars could have just been ignoring us while we were on the mountain a few days ago.

He reached down and took a hold of my hands and studied me a moment before answering, "Yes. I choose you, Sidonia."

His face was all business, but his sapphire eyes sparkled, letting me know just how much he agreed with it.

"Father also said that I would have a say in whom I marry. It was a promise made after the arrangement with Marcus had fallen through," I said, even though my heart broke at him breaking his promise to me. I looked pointedly at Father.

"Have you not enjoyed his company?" my father asked.

"I have." I met my father's gaze. I could not look at Tiberius.

"Do you not care for him?" he asked.

My face turned bright red. My voice would not come. Of course, I did. I was obsessed with Tiberius, but I didn't really know him, the *real* him. We had spent hours asking questions about each other, but that gave you an overview of someone. You didn't know the authentic person until you'd been with them for a very long time.

"Well?" Decumus, Tiberius' father, demanded. I could feel Tiberius' gaze on me.

"I do," I said, finally turning to Tiberius, whose face lit up like a thousand suns. "Though, there are things to know before we wed."

"Of course. Custom and tradition must be met for our families to be joined," Decimus said. "There is much my wife and I would like to know about you as well."

"May I ask a question?" I said, removing my hands from Tiberius so I could get through this conversation.

When my father nodded, I continued and tried very hard to keep a business tone. After all, this was a business arrangement, regardless of how Tiberius and I felt for each other. Right now, I really needed not to be touching Tiberius to get through this. He had to know, and I couldn't think straight while in Tiberius' arms.

"I do not wish to present disrespect, but for how long had this plan been in the works before we met?" I took a step back from Tiberius, letting our hands drop.

"It had not, Sidonia," my father said, coming around and taking my hands. "My daughter, I have respected your wishes to marry for love and to someone who will respect you, even more so after Marcus. I have known the Vispania family for generations, and I know they will take great care of you. If you had been eligible before Tiberius had left, then I would have arranged it years ago. It must be . . . Venus' will that you have come together now."

"Venus' will, Father?" I dropped my hands from his and eyed him carefully. He nodded slowly. Something raged inside of me. How could he use Venus like that? She played no part in my life. None. He should know better.

"If I am to marry him . . ." I looked at Tiberius and smiled weakly before continuing and trying to control my anger. ". . . shouldn't they know the truth? I mean, our children, my daughters, will and must be raised as I have. They will have my blood, will they not?"

My father's face fell slightly, as he knew he had crossed the line. "They will."

I saw Tiberius and his father exchange a questioning look behind my father.

"Yes. I care for Tiberius," I said, regaining my composure and the anger lessening when I saw Tiberius' smile widen and his sapphire eyes light up. Mother, those eyes, would they ever lose their effect on me?

I walked over to Tiberius. I took his hand and looked up at him, about to tell him my biggest secret, when the ground started convulsing. Tiberius grabbed me around the waist and stabilized me.

I looked up at him and then at my father. My mother and grandmother came out of the workshop just as Serveruis, my two nieces, Lars, and Juventia came out of the other room, when the shaking stopped.

"They are coming more frequently," Juventia said. "What is the Mother upset over?"

"The Mother?" Decimus asked.

Juventia's eyes widened. She hadn't realized that there were guests over and had made a slip—one that we were extremely careful not to make in public.

I sighed and turned to my family. Tiberius had not removed his hold on my waist, but held it tighter. "This is Decimus Avidius Vispania. He has arranged with Father that I will marry his son, Tiberius Maximus Vispania." I made it sound as formal as possible since we'd never even had him over for a meal.

My sister-in-law's eyebrows sprang almost to her hairline, and with her eyes sparkling and in a teasing voice, she said, "And he already has his hands about you? Sidonia, I didn't realize you were so accepting of an arrangement."

"The arrangement was made a few nights ago and finalized early this morning. Sidonia and Tiberius have been spending much time together over the last week," my father said.

Tiberius had warned me that our fathers were talking, but to hear it confirmed by my father hurt.

There was a long awkward silence in the room, and Decimus Vispania had not taken his eyes off of Juventia the entire time we spoke. I knew I needed to address it. We shouldn't have to hide in our own homes. We wouldn't. This was the one place we didn't need to watch what we said.

I would not hide in my new home, either. How could it be a home if I had to? However, there were Tiberius' two younger sisters to think of.

"Decimus Vispania, I think you need to know something about the family I will be coming from, as I *will* bring them with me into yours." Taking a deep breath, I stepped away from Tiberius. I couldn't touch him and feel the rejection as I said the words. My eyes flicked to Mother and Grandmother as they walked into the room, and when Grandmother gave a quick, curt nod of her head, she said, "You may tell them, Granddaughter."

I nodded to her and looked to Tiberius' father, because I couldn't look at Tiberius. "Tiberius, you need to know as well. If, after I tell you, you wish to cancel out of the arrangement, I understand. My father will not hold any ill will and will not hold you responsible for breaking such a commitment."

"Sidonia!" my father snapped with authority. My mother and grandmother both snapped their heads toward him. I could see the frustration in them. "It is not your place to make such promises. You do not know the full arrangement, and you cannot make such a demand on me."

"I will not join a family under false pretenses, Father. I realize you may not agree. I realize it puts the family in danger, but you cannot make such a demand on me. This is our way. You have no say," I snapped back, matching his tone. Out of the corner of my eye, I could see Grandmother glare at my father in a way that dared him to push the issue.

When my father's eyes met hers, he immediately backed down. I had rarely used my authority through our line to overrule him. He knew that if I was taking this step, that it was nonnegotiable for me.

"Tiberius, she is such a fighter. Are you sure you wish to marry someone so outspoken?" Decimus asked his son.

"Yes, I do, Father. I have witnessed it occasionally the last few weeks, and I love her all the more for it," he said, smiling with satisfaction.

My heart stopped, and I looked at him. *Love.* He said love.

His eyes shone brightly as his eyes met mine. "I do not want someone who will just be agreeable to everything just because I say so. I want someone who will be a partner in every decision and tell me when I'm being an idiot. There is no doubt that Sidonia will do that."

Did he just say that he loves me all the more for my defiance? Was there anything I could say or do to throw him off? I huffed a laugh. I guessed we were about to find out.

Juventia gave me a warning look, though. I could understand why she was concerned. Her family was part of ours, and she had two young girls to consider. They had the same blood that my mother and grandmother did and the older of the two had already shown signs of having the touch. However, it was Grandmother's nod of encouragement that gave me the strength. She was head of the Earthly family here. One day, I would be head of the Earthly family over Lars' girls, and I would be responsible for protecting them as if they were my own in this.

I turned back to Decimus and Tiberius and took a deep breath to calm myself. "The women in my family are Earth Worshipers, which is why we are the best herb and medicine purveyors in the colony."

I held my breath and let them process that. I held my gaze on Decimus, for fear of seeing disappointment, hatred, or anything else in Tiberius' eyes. I didn't know what exactly he had learned of Earth Worshippers in his travels, and many times when people heard of us, they thought of us as being against the Gods, which wasn't wholly true.

Decimus just blinked and looked at me, to my father, and then back at me. I crossed my arms and cocked an eyebrow at him.

"Pagans," Decimus said with a shocked calm.

"No, we are not Pagans. We are more closely allied to druids, though that is not a clear representation of our belief or practice either. No matter how you want to classify us, we do not conduct animal or human sacrifices, and only the women in the family hold the touch to practice." I held my gaze upon Decimus. If I was going to be part of his family, he must understand that I would not be a submissive woman in the house.

Decimus blinked and looked at me, to my father, and back to me again. I wished I could figure out what he was thinking. It did not surprise me he would jump to the conclusion of paganism. Pagans were not well liked in the Empire.

"And that explains why you are the best healing purveyors in the colony," Decimus said quietly.

"One more thing you need to know, which my father would not have told you. The woman in the Earthen house run the household. While in the colony, my father may be the head of the house, it is actually Grandmother that is. That means in any home that I live in, I would need to be respected as head of the house as well. One day, I will be head of the Earthen home for our family and oversee Lars' girls and any I may bear for Tiberius. I will be head of my house. While living in your home, I will, of course, respect you and your wife, as well as Tiberius as my husband, but I will not be a housewife or at your or my husband's call. I must continue my work here in the apothecary."

I still did not dare look at Tiberius, though I felt him come stand closer to me and brush his hand down my forearm. My stomach flipped, squirmed, heated, and flopped at the simple caress. Because that was what it was. A simple caress. I knew that, but I still couldn't look at him.

It was quite a while before Decimus or anyone else said a word. "Your father had mentioned that you would need to continue your work in the workshop. I thought it odd that he would make such an absolute demand, but . . ." He looked at me and then to Mother and Grandmother before he said, "Now I understand."

Then he looked at Tiberius and gave him a quick nod that I could easily have missed had I not been paying such close attention. It was his way of telling Tiberius that the decision was up to him now.

Tiberius had been way too quiet. What was he thinking? I allowed myself to admit it terrified me that he might reject me, but it was better he did now than after we were married, even if he had touched me like he did while I was talking to his father.

I still could not look at him. Decimus was looking at his son, trying to gauge his reaction. Tiberius took my hands, placed them in his left, then settled them over his heart. It thudded to a steady beat under my hand, but there was the occasional quick one. He took my chin in his right hand and gently forced me to face him. I averted my eyes from his, which only focused my attention on his lips. Heat instantly flooded me.

Wrong move Sidonia! Wrong move.

Even with all the fear, my body went feral for him. His hand suddenly felt too hot, like someone was pressing a hot ember to my chin. However, it was easier than looking into his eyes and seeing the betrayal in them. I would endure the burning to keep from having my heart shattered.

"Sidonia, please look at me." His voice was so gentle, it shocked me. My traitorous heart swelled with hope. Surely, this was a ruse? A way to get me to look at him? My eyes stayed set on his lips.

"Please," he said again in a soft, pleading voice. I studied the lines of his mouth and jaw. There was no hardness, and his jaw was relaxed and soft. I could practically hear my family behind me holding their breath. Slowly, I raised my gaze and met his eyes, ready for the disappointment I knew I would see there.

Only, when I gazed into those sapphire orbs, there wasn't any. All I saw was understanding and something else I could not place. I blinked, not sure what to think.

"I don't care."

My head cocked to the side. I didn't understand. What did he mean he didn't care? I just told him, someone who worked for the Empire, that I was a traitor to the Empire by their standards. Just by being associated with me, he was putting his whole family at risk. If the Empire found out, they would all be sentenced to death with no question.

"I don't care," he said again as he released his hold on my chin and smiled. "In fact, it does not surprise me. It makes perfect sense. You never speak of the Gods, and you hesitated when I mentioned I thought Venus had given her push. Considering what I know of Earth Worshipers from my travels, everything you do, the way you move, the way you situated yourself when we were on the mountain, not to mention the way Lars attempted to distract me when we saw all the damage done on Vesuvius, confirms this. Even that day on the beach when you told me about Marcus, you talked of the Mother and not the Gods."

He had noticed. I had slipped up and praised the Mother and not his Gods. He had noticed but hadn't called me out on it. Hadn't . . . cared. "But my beliefs and practices will not join yours. I will not go to the temple and worship Hercules, Venus, and Apollo. They are great beings, but not worthy of worship in my practices," I said, searching his face for something, anything, to tell me this whole wedding was a bad idea. Standing here, though, with his hands in mine, it all felt right.

"This is something you must keep a secret if you wish this wedding to occur, Decimus," my mother said behind me. I stood there, still waiting for Tiberius to call it all off. "It is for all of our safety that you do. It is something we normally . . . would not disclose until after the wedding, but as you can see, Sidonia is very strong-willed."

"Tiberius. Are you sure of this? This is what you want? Remember, there are your sisters to consider as well," Decimus said.

"Yes. I am sure," Tiberius said without hesitation. His eyes sparkled, and I saw nothing but happiness in them. I couldn't see anything at all that would speak to the contrary.

I turned to look at Decimus. "If you wish to allow this arrangement to proceed, I promise to do everything within my power to keep your family safe, just as we have done here. If you wish, I will keep my practices hidden from your daughters as best I can. We do not need to endanger them unnecessarily, as they will be of age and marry into other families in a short time. Most of my time and work would still need to occur here, as I have responsibilities. However, once I bear my own daughters, I will teach them openly in my home. If this is not satisfactory to you and your wife, we will relocate. Any sons I may bear will know of our life but will not have the same power that I do. It manifests only in the female line."

"I would appreciate that very much. You are a very bright woman, Sidonia, smarter than most men I have dealt with in the past. I can see why Tiberius is captivated by you. Maybe you can help me with some of my business arrangements," he said, smiling.

I turned to Tiberius. "You understand that should this proceed, that I will be head of the house. I require the house to be run as an Earthen home. I will discuss issues with you, and we can work together, but it will be an Earthen home."

His lips twitched, and his eyes burned with a heat I felt in my core. I could see how much he was restraining himself from kissing me right now. "Yes, my love. As I told you before, I choose you, Sidonia Regillia."

I rested a shaking, tentative hand on his cheek. "And I choose you, Tiberius Vispania."

Tiberius' father turned to Father then looked to my grandmother. Mr. Vispania then said, "Then, I agree with the arrangement and will get the connubium this afternoon."

After more discussion, they decided we would be wed the following morning. I tried to object as I really wanted to have more time, but I was told that there was no need to wait, as we had already stated that we had feelings for each other and the dowry was easily exchanged.

I turned to Tiberius, sighing in defeat and anticipation. "We are getting married. Tomorrow."

"We are," he said, smiling brightly. Then, surprising everyone in the room, he leaned down and kissed me. I was so shocked that it was over before my brain registered what had happened. "And I can't wait."

CHAPTER 23

SIDONIA

THE NEXT MORNING, MY mother was shaking me awake. "Mama. The sun isn't even through the windows yet." I rolled over, away from her.

"Sidonia, today is your wedding day. You must run to Vesuvius before sunrise. You have to do the blessing. Come, I have our things." She threw my blanket back and pulled me out of bed.

"Aye! Okay, Mama." I slipped my sandals on, and we ran out the door.

"I'm sorry it is so late. Grandmother reminded me of it less than an hour ago. She wondered why you had not left yet," she said as we passed the last building in the colony and made our way through the grass and trees. I could run this in my sleep; I was running it in my sleep. It was the same path I took every couple of weeks to gather the herbs we needed.

When we got to where I did most of my picking, she explained the ritual I needed to conduct to allow for a successful transition into my new life. We quickly laid out the items needed, which had to be done before the morning light, but the sun was already lighting the sky.

I took a deep breath and centered myself, lit the sage, and purified each of the elements: wind, fire, water, and, finally, earth. I could feel the warmth of the earth at my feet and knew that the Mother was listening. Facing the mountain, I asked Mother Earth and Vesuvius to bless the life Tiberius and I were starting together and for a painless transition into womanhood. I quickly doused the sage, smearing the ashes on my wrists and chin, before resting my forehead on the ground. Then, I hoped the rushed ritual would appease them as the sun crested over the horizon, lighting my circle. As it did, the circle glowed bright purple and then faded into the earth.

Mother let out a relieved sigh and just said, "The purple is an acceptance of the ritual."

On the way back to the house, I tried to calm my nerves as I thought how two hours after dawn, Tiberius and his family would come to retrieve me, we'd declare our intentions, eat, drink, and my family would follow me to our new home.

When we arrived back at the house, I bathed quickly, and Mother and Grandmother went to arrange my hair into an intricate mixture of braids and flowing strands. They dressed me in a tunica recta, belted it tight with an elaborate knot, and added the orange wedding palla overtop. It was the same garment my mother wore on her wedding day to my father. Grandmother then placed a sapphire-jeweled necklace around my neck that perfectly matched Tiberius' eyes and a few of my mother's rings on my fingers. A few minutes later, my father walked in with a couple of arm bands he bought for this day and slid them up my arms. They were gold with three sapphire gems on the outer side of the bands that matched the necklace Grandmother had put around my neck. Slowly, he added the bracelet I had bought in the marketplace that Tiberius loved so much. I could see the pride and happiness in his eyes when he saw me standing there.

"You are beautiful," he said. "A mirror image of your mother on the day I arrived at her home to marry her."

"Thank you, Father," I whispered as he headed back into the main room.

Playing with my fingers, I hoped my nerves didn't show. I was leaving the only home I'd ever known to live with Tiberius. A smile spread across my face at the thought of that. When Tiberius touched me, my body came alive, and that had never happened with Marcus. Marcus was a duty to my father to marry and bear children, to continue the line. However, this, with Tiberius? This was more than just a duty to my father. This was me allowing myself to be happy.

My eyes roamed around the room and it looked so empty. Being the only unwed woman in the family meant that all the items in this room would go with me. We packed all of my belongings into a couple of chests that my brother Severius built for me when I was betrothed to Marcus. In the last day, he had made extensive modifications to it to symbolize and honor my new arrangement.

My mother raised the back part of the palla over my head, and she and Grandmother left the room. Tradition said that I was to stay in there until Tiberius and his family came for me. Some of the old traditions were really stupid and degraded women, in my opinion. Though, I was a bit more of a free-thinker than most in this world.

I laughed lightly. That was saying something, considering in other places, your status was based on the color of your skin and nobility. Our region differed from those of the desert or the forest. You could go from slave to nobility with hard work and a little luck.

I sat there at the edge of the bed, playing with my fingers. It was so quiet and left my mind to think of all the things that were about to change. Yes, I would still work with Grandmother and Mother in the workshop, but I wouldn't be living where I was. I had already made one very strong demand on my new family, and I would have to bend and cater to their lifestyle now. I was going to be a wife to Tiberius and give him all of my priorities. Everything was about to change.

The thought of being Tiberius' wife left a smile on my face and butterflies in my stomach, but I also admitted to myself that it wasn't all butterflies. I was scared.

I was getting what I wanted: a new family that was willing to allow the arrangement to go through even after finding out about my practices and marriage to a man that I cared for. I was very lucky in that aspect. However, normally arrangements took time to cultivate and grow, which allowed the two betrotheds to get to know each other more, but this . . . This arrangement had happened so fast.

I kept thinking that. Why? Was it going to change anything? Was it going to suddenly make things slow down? No, it wouldn't.

I also did not know the details of the dowry, and it made me wonder what I was worth to my father. If they had indeed only spoken of the arrangement over one night and finalized it in a morning conversation, who had more leverage over the other to allow such a quick agreement? Had that shift of power changed since my demands and revelations yesterday? Both families were equal in status, at least publicly. Both had successful workshops and women in the family who were able to bear children.

My hand flew to my stomach. How soon would I be expected to give birth? Would I be able to bear children? What if I were barren and unable to give Tiberius heirs? Would he still want me? Would he require separation? A mistress to give him children?

What if I couldn't satisfy him? Sure, over the last few days, he seemed happy enough. At least he had found his release, multiple times, but that wasn't the point. I had never physically been with a man before, but he surely had been with his share of women while with the Empire. He had made that abundantly clear with his skills. What if I were a disappointment to him?

My stomach and head were swimming, and I suddenly felt very overwhelmed by the whole situation. These were not thoughts I thought I would have this morning. I even started to get mad at my father for rushing the arrangement, but then I took a deep breath and let it out really fast to ease any of that ill will. There was no justification for it.

Yes, everything would change, but he only moved quickly because there was an eligible man who was part of a family who had plenty of status in their own right, and that eligible man was someone I actually cared for. It was a blessing, from whichever Gods you worshipped, that he happened to also care for me.

A knock on the door interrupted my thoughts. That sound made my heart race, and my breathing came in short, quick breaths. Was it Tiberius to come and make me his wife, or had things indeed changed overnight and now my father was coming to tell me it all was for naught.

"Sidonia?" My heart instantly calmed at the sound of my name.

Tiberius had come for me.

CHAPTER 24

TIBERIUS

I WOKE UP BEFORE Helios had the suns in the sky, regardless of how little sleep there was to be had. Finally, I just gave up. Last night, I had rearranged this room to accommodate the belongings that would come from Sidonia's home.

When I got up this morning, I moved things around again. I was just finishing up when Septimia snuck in and told me she was very excited to have a new sister and looked forward to having her in the house.

Sighing, I knew I had to lay out some rules for my room. My sister and I had always had an open policy, and the few things I wanted to keep from her were stowed away in a small chest in the corner. She knew and respected that some things were just off limits. Sidonia's books, though, how were we going to keep her from going through those?

"You know that there will be rules about coming into this room from now on?" I said to her gently.

"Mother said I have to knock first, and then I have to wait for your permission before coming in. She made that second part very clear," she said, scrunching her little nose and rolling her eyes. "What if you aren't home and neither is Sidonia? Can I come in and get a book to read?"

Books. I rubbed my jaw and thought about how to answer that. Sidonia would bring several books to our room that we didn't want either of my sisters getting a hold of.

"Septimia. There are going to be some books that you will not be allowed to read. I will talk to Sidonia about which ones of hers you can read, though, okay?" I said carefully.

She nodded but asked, "I thought you said I should read any book I can get a hold of. You said smart girls get smart men."

"And they do, my sister. However, please respect Sidonia's rules. If I know you like I think I do, you will not like them, let alone understand them," I said, smirking at her. I remembered way too many times she told Mother and Father that certain rules around the house were stupid.

"So even if they are stupid rules, I have to listen to Sidonia?" she asked, crossing her arms and smirking at me.

"Yes, Septimia. Your sister, too. Neither of you are to break any rules Sidonia makes okay? She won't impose a rule for stupid reasons. She is fiercely smart and wants to teach you lots of things. Listen to her. Ask questions, but respect her." I stared her down to impress the importance of this. Father, Mother, and I would keep her family secrets, but we were going to keep the girls out of it.

"Yes, Tiberius," she grumbled finally.

"Thank you."

"Are you happy with Father's arrangement for you? Do you like Sidonia?" she asked me as I stared at the floor.

"Yes. I like her very much. She is smart, determined, and fierce," I said, smiling. "Just like someone else I know."

She laughed, and then there was a knock on the door. "Come in."

Father walked in and smiled. "I was wondering where you were, Septimia."

"I heard Tiberius moving furniture, again, so came in to talk to him," she said sweetly. "I think he's nervous, Father."

"Are you nervous, Tiberius?" Father said.

"I am," I said through a long breath. "What if we don't find a balance in our lives and we end up hating each other?"

"I saw the way you two looked at each other. She loves you already, even if she just hasn't put it into those words," Father said. "Septimia, please go help your sister. We need to leave soon to retrieve Sidonia and bring her home."

"Yes, Father." Septimia came and kissed me on the cheek and then ran off to find Nepia.

"I spoke to your mother last night after you finally went to sleep. She agrees to keep things away from the girls. I didn't tell her everything. Only that there were some trade secrets she would need to bring here with her, but that she would try to keep the girls uninvolved," he said quietly.

"What about after they leave? Will she allow Sidonia to be open at home? I won't let her hide herself."

"She will, as long as it stays within the home and we don't have trouble with the guards or magistrate."

"Her family has been doing this for generations. I don't think there will be any issues," I said, a little surprised he thought there would be.

"I know." He clamped his hand down on my shoulder. "Finish getting dressed and let's go get your wife."

"My wife," I repeated in amazement.

Sidonia was going to be my wife.

CHAPTER 25

SIDONIA

"SIDONIA?" TIBERIUS SAID. I stood as the door opened, and I held my breath. Decimus and my father stood with their backs to us at either side of the door as Tiberius walked in. I couldn't tell you what he was wearing. I was only focused on his face. He was smiling as bright as the sun, and when his eyes met mine, those sapphire orbs sparkled, but there was something else in the look on his face.

"Sidonia," he said, barely above a whisper, in such a way that made me blush. "You, you look like a goddess. I'm not sure who to compare you to, for I have lots to learn from you and . . . the Mother, but I can assure you that your beauty surpasses them all."

He used the name of the Mother. He was accepting me and my life. There was much I needed to learn about him, but I had told him my darkest secrets. I had told him of the abuse at Marcus'. I had told him about my way of life. He was accepting all those things.

He came to stand in front of me, took my hand, and kissed it gently. It was like a bonfire had ignited in my hand and ran up my arm. He kept his hand in mine as he lowered his and then took my other hand, but sighed.

"Tiberius. What is wrong?" I asked hesitantly, a million and one thoughts running through my head. *Did he change his mind? Was he backing out of our arrangement? Was I too much of a risk? Was my dowry not enough? Had what I said yesterday put his family in so much danger that he couldn't chance allowing me into his home? Were his parents telling him it was too much to burden the family?*

Tiberius stood before me, squeezed both of my hands, and dropped to kneel before me. The look in his eyes was searching, "Sidonia, I want to marry you. I'm not sure I have wanted anything more in my entire life. I have traveled all over the Empire and not found a woman who matches me more perfectly. You are a woman of whom any goddess would be jealous." Then he stopped and smiled. "You are also stubborn, independent, passionate, strong-willed, and defiant. There isn't anyone else in the world I would rather bind myself to for life."

"But?" I said hesitantly.

"But I want to make sure that you are willing to marry me for me. Not for the arrangement made between our families," he said, looking at my hands. "There is much you don't know about me. I have ravaged, pillaged, tortured, and done horrible things in the name of the Empire. Through my work, I caused decisions to be made that led to both the saving and destroying of entire civilizations. I'm not a good man, Sidonia."

I studied him for a minute. I had once asked him about his time in the Empire, and he wouldn't talk much about it. *Now, at the moment we are to be married, he'd decided to tell me?*

I looked back to where our fathers were standing in the doorway, and they were trying to look like they were not listening in, but I could tell they were both holding their breath for my response.

"Tiberius," I finally said. "Please look at me."

He slowly raised his eyes to mine, and I could tell he was guarding himself for the painful words he thought would come. I could only speak them because of what I saw in his eyes: his total commitment to me as his wife. He loved me.

"I will honor any arrangement that my father makes for my marriage," I said, and as I saw the hurt in his eyes, I quickly added, "However, this arrangement is more than just a legal binding of families for me. Yes, there is much I still have to learn about you. What is your favorite wine? How do you like your meat seasoned? What are some of your favorite activities? How many books have you read? Where have you traveled while working with the Empire? And where would you go back to if given the chance?"

"Anything red, medium with simple seasonings, reading, Gods only knows, there are too many to count, so many places, and Britannia. Britannia is beautifully green and lush. I think you would love it there," he said, answering each of those questions. How he could even remember them all was beyond me. I smiled and shook my head, squeezing his hands tight in mine.

"You said you watched me for weeks before we met, right?"

"Yes." His voice was small, and he sounded ashamed.

"You think that after we met, I didn't listen for word of you? I didn't watch how you interacted with the people of Herculaneum? I didn't ask about you?"

His head popped up, and he cocked his head to the side. "What?"

"You once said that you could tell much about a person by how they treat animals. I've watched you, Tiberius. I've heard how others speak of you. You are good. You may be ashamed of what you did while in the Empire, but you also left because you couldn't live with that. You couldn't be responsible for what occurred. That says much of your character, Tiberius."

His eyes lined with tears, and I squeezed his hands so that my next words would be made perfectly clear.

"All of that aside, you must understand that for me, I am marrying the man I very much care for and cannot see myself living without. You said that I match you, but you forget that works both ways. You match me. You are caring, independent, strong-willed, and passionate. I love you, Tiberius, and *that* is the reason I am marrying you today."

"You . . . You love me?" he said, as if he couldn't believe the words. Standing up, he pulled me close, kissed me quickly so he wouldn't mess with the paint on my lips, and whispered in my ear, "And I love you, Sidonia."

Wrapping my arms around him, I could feel every curve, ripple, and muscle in his body against mine. Our bodies and souls fit into each other perfectly. There was a fire building in the pit of my stomach, and I could not wait to take this man to bed. I wanted to feel every inch of him inside me. Then, a thought from earlier snuck back into my head. *What if I couldn't satisfy him?*

He pulled away from me and released a jagged sigh. Was he thinking the same thing? He met my eyes, and I could see love and lust mixed there.

Then, in a voice loud enough for everyone in the main room to hear, he announced, "I have come to collect my bride, Sidonia Regillia."

I smiled brightly as he offered his hand to me. Having memorized the script many years ago, I placed my hand in his as I responded, "I am here, ready to be collected by my agreed-upon husband, Tiberius Maximius Vispania."

We stood there looking into each other's eyes and smiling for, well, I was not sure how long, when we were reminded that we needed to leave the room by Decimus and my father clearing their throats. Tiberius led me into the main room, where three tables had been joined end to end in order to accommodate the numerous people who were standing around, waiting for us to arrive. When I saw Magistrate Potius standing at the head of a table with a quill and ink next to a piece of paper, I hesitated a half-step before continuing on. He looked at me like nothing had ever happened. I didn't know whether to feel relieved or sick. I looked at my mother, who gave me a knowing smile and mouthed, "It's been taken care of." She then made a motion with her hands that clearly conveyed she had shriveled his balls. I nodded and then looked at Tiberius again.

Tiberius led me to the magistrate, where we bowed in respect before Tiberius said, "Magistrate, I wish to make Sidonia Regillia my wife."

"Have the families agreed to this arrangement?" He looked to our fathers for confirmation.

"We have," they said in unison.

"Tiberius Maximius Vispania, please make your mark here, and Sidonia Regillia, here," he said, pointing to the two lines below the text for us to sign on, which we did. As I finished my signature, Magistrate Potius said, "It is with honor that I join these families. I declare you husband and wife under the Roman Empire, and with the blessing of . . ." He hesitated just a moment as he looked at me and then at my mother and grandmother before he continued. ". . . the Gods. Tiberius, you can seal it."

Tiberius swung me into him and placed one hand on the small of my back and the other on my cheek, bringing my face just millimeters from his, our eyes locked onto each other, and then he whispered my name against my lips before kissing me.

It started soft and gentle, just as before, but something was rising inside of me that felt real and wild. I threw my arms around his neck, pulling him closer, and I kissed him back with every ounce of emotion I had within me. He lifted me off the ground and held me close. He was mine, and with that thought, all of my worries from this morning evaporated away.

CHAPTER 26

TIBERIUS

"TIBERIUS MAXIMIUS VISPANIA, PLEASE make your mark here, and Sidonia Regillia, here," he said, indicating the two lines below the text for us to sign on. I took the quill, signed my name, and handed it to Sidonia. She signed hers in a beautiful, elegant script I couldn't help but marvel at, and as she finished, Magistrate Potius said, "It is with honor that I join these families. I declare you husband and wife under the Roman Empire, and with the blessing of . . ." He hesitated just a moment. There was a look of fear in his eyes as he looked at Sidonia, her mother, and grandmother. I could have sworn her mother gave him a little smirk. He swallowed hard and said, "The Gods. Tiberius, you can seal it."

"It's about time," I muttered. I'd wanted to fully kiss her since the moment I opened that bedroom door. I twirled her into me, placing one hand on the small of her back and the other on her cheek, and brought her to meet me.

"Sidonia," I whispered in a needy breath, and our mouths met in a scorching kiss that had me wishing we could head right to the bedchamber. It started softly, as we had an audience, but that did not seem to matter to her, as she threw her arms around my neck and kissed me back with a fierceness I knew was a raging fire within her. I could feel all that heat spread within me, branding her forever to my soul. I would not have been surprised if flames had burst from our skin.

This was the woman my soul needed. This was the woman that the Gods and Mother named for me. No matter how long I lived, there would be no other. It was Sidonia or no one.

I picked her up, needing her closer. I hardened for her, and when her lips separated from mine, there was a smile that meant everything to me. My erection pressed against her, and her eyes instantly filled with lust. I could not wait to get her to my bed.

When I put her down, there was a roar that filled the house and spilled out into the streets.

"We feast!" our fathers shouted together, and they led us to a space at the end of the very long table and served an enormous goblet of wine with plates full of fish, bread, and root vegetables grown in our garden in the back.

Lars and Severius toasted our union and drank through a cask of wine all on their own. Each time they offered me a fresh glass, I declined. I did not want to be drunk when I could finally have Sidonia in my bed. I wanted to remember each and every moment of it.

CHAPTER 27

SIDONIA

THE MORNING WAS FILLED with food, wine, bread, and laughter. Lots of laughter. When the sun was high in the sky, my brothers gave us one last toast and drained their glasses.

As I left my childhood home, I felt a pang of sadness but dismissed it. I was going to be back the next day for work. Some potions needed to be made and oils and herbs had to be delivered. It was just that it was no longer my home.

The entire way to the Vispania residence, our families laughed and banged pots and skillets together, making as much noise as possible. Of course, my brothers were knocking everything down that would have been standing in the street. Mother had to help keep Severius standing up, and Juventia was attempting to keep Lars upright. Decimus and my father were leaning against each other, all the while refilling each other's goblets. There were a couple of times, I heard my mother swearing she was going to need a cart to bring the boys home in. Tiberius' mother said she had one she could borrow. I laughed loudly at that.

As for Tiberius, he said he didn't want to have much of the wine because he wanted to remember this day. That didn't stop his father from trying to refill his goblet each time he would reach over to kiss me.

I laughed when Juventia almost dropped Lars on his butt a couple of streets from my new home.

"Serves you right, Lars. You shouldn't have drunk so much," I shouted over my shoulder.

"It's naa . . . not every day your baby sisterrrrr getssssss married! Issssss it?" he slurred as Juventia straightened him up again and this time didn't even bother hiding the eye roll. "You . . . You better taaake care of her, Tiberius!"

"Oh, trust me, I will take excellent care of her," he said with a growl, pulling me into him and kissing me deeply, which fueled the fire burning within me once again. When he let me down, he growled into my ear, "I'm never going to get enough of kissing you."

"You have our lifetimes now," I whispered.

When we rounded the corner to my new home, there was every government official, work associate, and friend we had in the colony in attendance, including Velarde, dressed in his Roman Guard uniform, at the door, as if watching over my new home. It shocked me to see so many there to celebrate the joining of our houses.

There was a flash of someone just at the corner behind everyone that filled me with dread. I blinked and looked again but saw nothing. It wasn't possible. When I blinked again, Tiberius put his hand on the small of my back, leaned down, and whispered in my ear, "What's wrong?"

"Nothing. Just thought I saw someone from my past," I said, then I looked up at him. "Really, it's fine."

I walked up to the door and turned to my mother, who handed me the oils and herbs to bless the home to the Earth. A similar ritual would occur in the "traditional" home, but with pig fat and a blend of oils instead. Our words of blessing were different, but whether you believed in the traditional ways or in mine, the point was the same. The only difference was, I didn't decorate the door with wool, which would brand me as a domestic wife. Everyone knew I would continue my duties at the family workshop.

Once I completed the ritual, as was custom, Magistrate Potius opened the door, and Tiberius lifted me into his arms and carried me inside.

"Welcome home, my wife," he said, hesitation in his voice as he set me down.

I looked around and found the home was nicer than what I had grown up in. I hadn't expected that. It was open with plenty of light. The tables and chairs were more intricately designed, and the kitchen had nicer furnishings than what I was used to. The wall to the left, where the dining table was situated, was adorned with a beautiful mural of the Gods Hercules and Venus, standing and looking down upon a mountain with a city below. It was a beautiful representation of Vesuvius and Herculaneum.

There were three doorways along the back wall, one for his mother and father, one for his sisters, and one that was decorated with garland and flowers, which signified our wedding chamber.

Our sleeping chamber. The thought left me nervous and scared, but it also filled me with a raging fire that made me smile brightly. I was now Sidonia Vispania, and I would be one with my husband. I would be his wife, partner, mother to his children, and lover. I turned back toward him and said the words everyone was waiting for me to say, "I am honored to be part of it, my husband."

With that, our wedding was complete, and there was a loud thunderous cheer and the clanging of pots and skillets—everyone who was outside poured into the Vispania home, our home.

For hours and hours, people drank, danced, and celebrated. There was only one instance where Tiberius left my side. It was as if he didn't dare let go of me for fear that I would disappear into thin air. One of his father's business associates demanded some of his time, and it was then that Velarde came to talk to me.

"I am happy for your marriage, Sidonia," he said with his fist over his heart as he gave a quick bow.

"Thank you, Velarde," I said, smiling.

We stood in silence for a moment before he said, "I have traveled all over the lands with your Tiberius." He paused as I looked over at Tiberius, who, at that very moment, looked over at me and smiled before turning his attention to the man he was talking to.

"Tiberius has been a good friend to me, Sidonia," Velarde said, but there was a note of sadness and longing in his voice.

I looked at him carefully, and when his eyes met mine, he said, "A few years ago, we were on the border of one of the forests of Germania, and I remember getting into a fight in a tavern. I got separated from Tiberius and a few of the other soldiers we had gone with."

His eyes flickered to where Tiberius was quickly before he said, "I woke up with a split lip. I was missing my sword and a personal item." My eyebrows pinched together, and I wondered what the point was to the story but let him continue.

"I made my way back into the colony that we were stationed just outside of and back to the tavern. I found the guy I had fought with the night before, retrieved my sword and that item from him. By force." He rubbed at his side, just below his heart, then looked back at me. "He was so mad, he broke one of the bottles on the table, stabbed my side, and took off. It was deep. Tiberius walked in just then, and if he hadn't, I likely would have died. He carried me back to the camp, cleaned and stitched me up himself."

I looked back at Tiberius. "You are his friend. He cares for you deeply. Anyone can see that."

Velarde nodded. "I would give my life to protect him. Tiberius saved mine on more than that occasion, but I have saved his as well. We became inseparable in battle. No matter where we were sent, no matter what was happening on the battlefield, Tiberius and I would always fight side by side."

"Were you two lovers? Do you love him?" I asked, and his eyes widened in shock. "It wouldn't bother me if you were. I know lots of soldiers find comfort both emotionally and sexually in the field."

"I do love him, but not as a lover. He is my brother. He always will be, and I would go to Tartarus and back for your husband, Sidonia. Tiberius loves you, even if he won't say it or even knows it yet. I can see it. He's been fascinated before. He's been with other women, but the way Tiberius looks at you . . ." He paused and sighed. "I believe that you and Tiberius are connected by the Fates. I don't think that even the Fates would be so cruel as to unweave the two of you. Not so sure they could. Because of what you mean to

Tiberius, I will also go to Tartarus and back for you as well. No matter where you are, if you need help, you can send a message through the Empire, and I will find you."

I studied this man who laid his love, dedication, and loyalty at my feet. His eyes burned with a determination that I had only seen a few times in my life. I reached up to touch his face, and he flinched.

"May I? It won't hurt. I promise," I said, just above a whisper.

Slowly, he bent down toward me, and I ran my finger over his brow and let my power run through my fingertips. His eyes shuttered, and his shoulders relaxed. I felt nothing but warmth and certainty from him. I pulled my hand back, and he stood up, taking a shuddering breath.

"Wow. I don't know what you just did, but I've been fighting a headache for days and it's gone," he whispered.

Suddenly, arms were around my waist, and I was being swung around in a circle.

"Not trying to steal my wife already, are you, Velarde?" Tiberius' chuckling laugh sang near my ear.

"Gods, no," Velarde said with a bright smile. "Not that she isn't worth the attempt, but I wouldn't dishonor my brother in that manner."

"Brother," Tiberius said wistfully. "You haven't called me brother in over a year."

"Well, that's because you keep doing stupid shit, like running into battle with only your sword. Or leaving the Empire. Or moving back to Herculaneum and finding yourself a worthy wife," he said, laughing. "Okay, so finding a worthy wife isn't stupid. I'm happy for you, brother."

"Thank you, Velarde. You know where to find me if you ever need my assistance," Tiberius said, putting his fisted hand over his heart.

With a nod, Velarde turned and walked out the door. When I looked at Tiberius, love and respect were shining in his eyes as he watched him. Velarde turned back just before disappearing around the corner. It may have been the light, but I could swear that Velarde was crying.

It was late afternoon by the time people slowly left our home. I was grateful for it but felt anxious all at the same time. It had been a long and exhausting day. Over the last hour, Tiberius had made it his mission to tease me and ensure that once everyone was gone, that the bedroom was going to be our first stop.

On more than one occasion, his hand had slipped under the multiple layers of cloth and grabbed my ass. I may be anxious, but since I kissed him, sealing our marriage, I had thought of nothing else but about how I wanted to pleasure him tonight.

When it was just his parents and sisters left, his father said, "We will stay at my sister's this evening."

"You will?" I asked, a little surprised.

"We thought you might want to spend the first night alone instead of having to worry about what we might overhear," his father said.

His mother, a little more red in the cheeks, said, "We will be back in the morning."

"But," I tried to say, but his father put his hand up, gathered his wife and two daughters, and left the home.

I stared at the closed door for a moment before turning toward Tiberius. He was still staring at the door in complete shock.

I waited for him to turn toward me and when he didn't, I put a finger on his chin, turning him to face me, as he had done so many times to me this week, and said, "Tiberius, I don't plan on wasting our time alone. Will you please stop staring at the door and take me to bed?"

CHAPTER 28

TIBERIUS

"HOLY GODS, WOMAN. YOU don't have to ask me twice." I picked her up as she wrapped her legs around me and pressed her lips to mine. Every time she did, Helios' suns burst through us. I would take the heat and burning every time she kissed me to have her.

I carried her to our room and kicked the door shut. I didn't care if no one else was here. In case someone came barging in, I wanted it made clear to leave us alone. I planned on taking my time with her. She was going to have every inch of her body worshiped.

Her hips rolled against me and I moaned, loud and deep. When we reached the bed, she unwrapped her legs reluctantly from my waist to kneel on the bed. I removed my toga without breaking our kiss and kicked off my sandals. She reached behind her, slipped hers off, and threw them

168

over my shoulder. When her hands were free, they slowly ran down my bare chest.

"Sidonia," I whispered when we pulled back for a breath. She looked up at me through her lashes, running two soft fingers along the length of my cock, and I swore it took all the concentration in the world not to cum right there.

I reached to unpin her palla, but she stopped me with a firm squeeze on my cock, pumping it just once to get my attention. She kissed the hollow point of my throat and said in a throating purr, "I have been looking forward to doing this since our time on the mountain, so stand here and let me attend to you."

She kissed her way down and positioned herself at my hips. When her tongue licked along the base of me, my cock twitched. I watched her as she looked up again through those lashes and tongued the head of me, causing a wave of pleasure to rush through my body.

When she took me into her mouth, I growled in ecstasy. I hit the back of her throat, and she slid to the head, letting her tongue trail along the underside of me. This time, when she took me fully into her mouth, she adjusted her head and sucked harder on the way back up.

"Jupiter is going to be jealous of what you can do with that mouth, woman," I said, grabbing a hold of the footboard of the bed. She chuckled, and the hum that went through my body made me quake.

Sidonia repeated the motion and found a rhythm that had me quickly reaching the precipice. Soon, my hips were moving of their own accord, and she took each thrust. Even the women in the brothels in Rome could not please me like this. I moved her hair out of the way as I groaned again at the feel of her sucking me off.

"Sidonia, I'm . . ." She grabbed the base of me, squeezing and kneading my balls just as I thrust into her mouth and spilled myself down her throat, a deep moan erupting from my chest.

She licked me clean before I fell to my knees before her. The look of satisfaction on her face as she licked her lips was pure, but the heat and lust in her eyes made me pull her close and kiss her. I faintly tasted myself on her tongue, and it was such a damn turn-on.

I reached over and undid the pin on her palla and slid the fabric to the floor. Her family had tied her tunic tight with an elaborate knot, one that I wished I could have just cut off. Instead, I worked through it with one hand while reaching under and running a single knuckle down the center of her. The shudder that went through her was so satisfying.

I nibbled on her ear as I got the last of the knot undone and flicked her. She gasped, and I fingered her opening, spreading her wetness.

"Tiberius," she breathed. I moved both of my hands under her tunic and lightly ran my hands up her thighs, across her hips, raising the tunic with me. When I reached her breasts, I kneaded them softly before pulling the tunic over her head.

Bending down, I ran my teeth along her neck. She arched toward me as I ran a thumb across her two pink peaks. Each one commanded my undivided attention.

Wrapping my arm around her waist, I kissed her while laying her down on the bed. Her hips met mine in a cry for attention. While fucking her until she was screaming my name was on my list tonight, I also knew how it could be for someone their first time, and I was determined to make sure she enjoyed every moment.

Kissing my way down to her breasts, I swirled my tongue around her nipple as she ran her nails down my back. After a quick nip that had her moaning, I left a trail of kisses down her stomach.

Holding her legs and spreading them wide in front of me, I still couldn't believe this woman was all mine to devour. I doubted she had ever been so open to a person, and all that thought did was make me hard again.

As I ran one single finger through the mass of curls between her legs, her back arched as she moaned. I kissed down her knee, creeping closer to her, taking my finger and circling her entrance. I repositioned myself so that I was kneeling just off the bed and grabbed a hold of her hips, pulling her to me.

Without warning, I ran my tongue slowly from one end of her to the most sensitive spot that drove any woman wild. I flicked that little nub once, and her gasping moan filled the air around us. That was all the encouragement I needed.

I clamped down, licking and sucking every inch of her. Gods, she tasted divine, like candied fruit in the heat of summer. I slid my tongue inside, and her hips rocked against me. I gripped them tight and took just one finger and slowly slid it inside her as I continued to lick and suck her.

"Tiberius," she moaned, and when I looked up, she had both of her breasts in her hands, kneading and pinching her own nipples. Dear Gods, it was beautiful.

Slowly pushing my finger deeper inside her and moving around to help stretch and prepare her for me, I inserted a second finger into her just as I clamped down on that nub. She rubbed against my face, begging for more friction and moaning loudly. I could feel her getting close to her first orgasm of the night. I was a knuckle deep when she clamped down around my fingers and screamed my name in ecstasy.

Taking one last nibble at her, making her whole-body spasm, I pushed her up farther onto the bed. The glazed look of satisfaction in her eyes just about undid me right then.

She took my face in her hands and kissed me. I moaned at the need and desire in that kiss. I reached down and rubbed her again, and there was a gasp of air and a rocking of the hips that had me rubbing my cock up and down her slit.

I forced myself to open my eyes and look at her. "Sidonia?" I asked.

"Tiberius, please. I am yours," she begged.

Those words. *I am yours.* I was trying so hard not to completely unleash myself on her. There would be time. She was mine.

I smiled and teased her again by rubbing my cock up and down her center. Her hips rocked against me, and I kissed her as I positioned myself just at her opening. Her hips lifted just enough that the head of me was in her. I groaned and shook at the restraint it took not to plunge myself wholly into her warmth.

CHAPTER 29

SIDONIA

I WAS STILL REELING from the first burst of pleasure he had given me. I had heard and read that kind of satisfaction could be given orally, but Mother, I did not know it could be that intense.

He rubbed himself up and down my center as I rocked my hips, begging him to take me. I wanted nothing more than to have him fill me. I was not sure I wanted anything more in my life other than him, just like this.

"Sidonia?"

When I met his eyes, there was a question there. *Did he really think I didn't want this? Did he think I wouldn't want him to take me in every way a man could take a woman?*

"Tiberius, please. I am yours," I begged him.

He just rubbed himself up and down on me again and kissed me. I couldn't take it anymore. I rocked my hips and just the head of him entered me, and I knew that this was going to hurt, but I wanted more of him. It burned slightly, but I quickly adjusted to him.

Tiberius froze, and I could feel the restraint in his muscles to not take me in one stroke. Instead, he reached down and played with that damn spot as I rocked against him, forcing more of him into me. I wanted all of him. Now. He pulled out just a little more, and when he moved to enter slowly, I raised my hips, forcing him deeper than anyone or anything had ever been.

There was a quick sharp pain that was quickly replaced by a burning sensation. Tiberius chuckled as he nibbled my ear. "So impatient."

He didn't move, he just lay there and let me adjust to the size of him. I'd seen other men before, and Tiberius was by no means small. Just when the burning started to subside, he rubbed me, delivering more pleasure to distract me from any pain as he pressed himself fully inside me. The feel of his hips solidly against mine gave me a satisfaction that made me feel purely evil.

"Sidonia?" When I opened my glazed eyes at him, he asked, "You okay?"

"Yes," I hissed, and then to make my point, I rolled my hips so that he would move inside me. A deep moan emanated from each of us at that. He pulled out and then slowly, with a wicked grin on his face, filled me again.

"Mother be!" I groaned as he did it slowly, over and over again. My back arched, and I felt like I was burning in a raging wildfire. Every nerve in my body sparked for him. I raked my nails hard down his back, and he moaned in response.

I raised my hips to meet him at each stroke. I could feel my pleasure mounting again, and when he gave me one particularly powerful stroke, I clenched around him and moaned loudly.

Tiberius took a deep breath of control and before I had fully come back down. He was taking long, powerful strokes, one after the other. Each time, he filled me to the hilt.

"More," I whispered. I wanted more. He slammed into me again and then froze at that command, giving me a wicked smirk as he did so. Instead, he rolled his hips, hitting a spot inside me that made my toes curl.

"More," I moaned as he nibbled on my ear and kissed down my neck.

Over and over again, he repeated that sequence of movements: a slow withdrawal, powerful thrust, and then rolling his hips to make me moan loudly each time he hit it.

"Sidonia." He was panting now. "I . . ."

"Harder. Take me harder, Tiberius. Give me everything you have."

"I don't want to hurt you," he said, moving the hair that was stuck on my face from the sweat that covered us both. "There will be a day, one soon, when I give you all the enjoyable pain that you can handle." There was a lustful need in him that promised years of sexual fulfillment.

He slowly retreated from me and filled me again. Before he had a chance to play with me, I pushed on his chest and forced him onto his back.

Straddling him, I let myself slide across him a few times as he moaned and writhed under me.

"Sidonia," he said in a warning need as he held my hips.

"Tiberius?" I teased him and slid along his length once again.

"If you take me like this . . ." He tried to say, but I slid him into me and rolled my hips as I fully sat upon him. "Gods," he moaned, his head thrown back in pleasure.

The feeling of being on top of him, taking control, was exhilarating. When he raised his hips to meet mine, though, he filled me farther than he had before, and the pleasure was instantaneous. I clamped down on him, but, refusing to stop, I rocked my hips.

With his cock filling me and that damn spot rubbing against him like this, I was already so close to shattering completely. There wasn't anything at that point that could have stopped the collision course I was on.

I rocked against him fast and furiously and he met me for every movement. His hands moved to grab ahold of my breasts, and he gripped them tighter the faster I moved.

With each faster and harder stroke, he brought me closer to that raging bliss. Just when I was on that edge, he pinched both of my nipples, sending a wave of pleasure through me so fiercely that I screamed out his name, climaxing on a level I had never felt before. It so wholly consumed me that I could have sworn a pulse was let out into the world to let it know we belonged to each other.

I fell forward on top of him, legs shaking as my orgasm rocked through me. He grasped my waist, forcing me onto him as he pounded into me and then bit down on my shoulder hard enough I knew there would be blood, but it didn't hurt. Instead, it sent another wave of pleasure through me, extending my climax as he released himself within me.

CHAPTER 30

SIDONIA

I WOKE WITH THE sun shining brightly upon my face and a newfound contentment. I lay there, taking in the smells of my new life. There was the clean, crisp air, with just a hint of muskiness that was all Tiberius. There was the smell of flowers blooming outside the window, the faint smell of eggs being cooked in the breeze. It was the smell of a home. If I woke every morning of the rest of my life like that, then I knew I would die a happy woman. I closed my eyes tight and took in the feel of the soft bed and Tiberius' bare body against mine. His arm was draped around my waist, and the slow rise and fall of his chest against my back was a feeling I would not soon forget.

As I lay there, I thought back to our first night as husband and wife. For all the worrying and apprehension I had of becoming a woman, Tiberius made it feel easy and effortless. Our bodies responded to each other with the lightest of touches, and it had only taken us a few minutes after that first time to look at each other and want more. Tiberius was a very generous lover, to say the least.

I remembered running my fingers over his chest, seeing the bumps rise where my fingers left. There was the way his stomach muscles rippled under my touch and the way his back muscles contracted as I ran my nails against them in pleasure. Our bodies fit into each other with total perfection, even as we were curled around each other this morning.

I took a deep breath and released it. It was jagged and full of nervousness. The wedding happened so quickly that there were so many things that still had to be worked out. What would be my schedule at the workshop? Would I still work there every day? Or would my duties in my new family restrict that? What would my new family require of me? I had made it clear that I would not be a domestic wife. Hopefully, that expectation hadn't changed since that discussion. I wouldn't budge on that.

"Mmm, good morning, my wife," Tiberius said as he pulled me closer and kissed my bare shoulder. Then, he ran his finger up and down my bare stomach, which left a trail of embers in its wake. As I turned to face him, he continued the motion up and down my back, sending lightning down to my toes.

"Good morning, husband," I whispered as he pulled me close enough that I could feel him hard against me. I instantly felt heat fill my body, and I could have sworn there was a fierce *thump thump* between my legs. *Could I ever get enough of Tiberius?*

"What do you want to do today?" he whispered in my ear and then kissed my neck.

"I know I have to work out a schedule between what my new family will need me to help with along and my workshop duties," I said, trying not to think about the way his hand lightly ran down the side of my body and up my back with the lightest of touches. His lips had moved to my shoulder, and it was making it very hard to concentrate. "There is also organizing our space to accommodate what I brought over."

"And there are several boxes." His voice was rough, gravelly, and made me want him all over again as he nibbled on my ear and drew slow circles on my back.

"Where do you think is a good spot for . . ." My voice hitched as his fingers ran down the back inside of my thigh, sending a fire raging in the pit of my stomach and a bolt to my core. The image of him between my legs the night before, and the pleasure he gave me, made my eyes roll back.

He murmured something, but it didn't register. I only felt my breasts tighten, and when the air hit them, I felt my nipples harden as well.

I rolled him onto his back and straddled him. He was fully hard against me now, and I ground against him as he held my hips. I let a small smile spread across my face as I leaned down and kissed him. I may be sore from last night, but my body responded to his so intensely, there was no way that a full-fledged conversation was going to be had right now.

There was something feral rising inside me that screamed for him. When I pulled back just that little bit, I saw a gleam in his eyes that was full of a hunger, and I was more than willing to feed him.

I rolled my hips again and in one swift motion, I impaled myself on him.

CHAPTER 31

TIBERIUS

THE SMELL AND FEEL of her next to me this morning was intoxicating, but when she slammed herself onto my cock, an inhuman sound came from my chest. The sight of her now rolling her hips, demanding pleasure from me, was more than any man should have to withstand.

Sidonia was a natural at sex. I looked at this woman riding me in awe and appreciated every inch of her. Aphrodite would take offense to the creature in front of me. She would smite Sidonia where she stood for daring to be more beautiful and vibrant than her.

My hands ran up her sides and back down as she rose and fell upon me. When she was fully seated, I smacked her ass, and she froze for half a second and looked at me, a shadow crossing her face.

Every muscle in my body stopped moving at that look. It took me just a moment to remember back to that day on the beach when she told me of what happened at Marcus' house. His father had assaulted her. He had spanked her to the point where she couldn't sit or lie down. Gods, how could I have been so careless?

When her eyes met mine, there was intrigue, confusion, and lust flitting around them. She rose and slammed down on me again and again then said, "Do it again."

"Are you sure?" I said carefully.

"Yes," she said, grinding against me. So, when she thrust back down upon me, I spanked her again, and her back arched, nipples hardened, and she moaned.

"Again, and harder," she moaned, and so I did.

"Mother. The pain, pleasure, and the feeling of you filling me." She reached back, bracing her hands on my knees, and rolled against me. I smacked her ass again, and she moaned. I could feel the exact moment that pain turned to pleasure. Her inner walls gripped me tighter each time.

I ran a single finger down between her breasts and along her stomach before I said, "I will teach you all the ways I know of mixing the two, Sidonia, but we have time." Gripping her hips, I thrust into her in long, powerful strokes.

Slowing, she bent over to kiss me, and I wrapped my arms around her waist, holding her close to me as I slowed and rolled my hips against hers.

She moaned again, and I asked, "Do you trust me?"

Freezing, she looked at me and gave me a sly smile. "I do."

Rolling so she was under me, I flipped her on her stomach and pulled her hips up to reach mine. Her ass was divine.

"Tiberius," she begged, wiggling that ass at me. I ran my hands over her and then, just as she was about to beg again, I slapped it hard. There was a half-second of dead silence before she wiggled again. I slapped the other cheek and there was an instant moan from her.

With another slap, I buried myself deep within her, and she screamed in pleasure and said in a needing groan, "Again."

Over and over, I buried myself in her and slapped that ass. It was red, and when I rubbed my hands over them, she pushed back into me. I grabbed her, brought her back to my chest, and reached around, rubbing that sensitive spot.

"Mother," Sidonia said through panting breaths. "Don't stop. Harder."

I felt my balls tighten at her need. I slammed into her, and before I allowed myself release, I slapped her ass and flicked that spot again. When Sidonia clamped on me, she screamed in pleasure, back bowing into me. I pulled her head around to face me, and I kissed her as I thrust into her deeply twice more before releasing myself within her.

We fell forward, and I rolled just to the side, pulling her close. When she found her breath again, she rolled over to face me. I searched her eyes, looking for any of the darkness that I suspected had crept in from what we had done.

"You okay?" I asked, running my thumb along her cheek.

She blinked and studied me for a moment. "Yes. Better than okay." Then it was like her head cleared enough to understand what I was really asking. "When . . . When you first did it, I was brought back to that moment, but then I felt you."

I cocked my eyebrow at her, but then she smiled. "Yes, I felt you inside me, but more than that, I felt you in my soul. I knew I was safe. A second later, it turned to pleasure, and . . ."

"I'm sorry. I didn't think about it. I just did it. I should have talked to you first," I apologized, and she laughed.

"I liked it. More than liked it," she said, then there was a blush that crossed her lips. "I'm sure there is a lot you can teach me about sex. I know I'm not experienced."

"Yet, you pleasured me up on the mountain so expertly, the alleys, and then, when your lips were wrapped around me last night . . ." I wasn't making coherent sentences. This woman may not have been physically experienced, but . . . "How did you learn to do any of that?"

"There are books that have been handed down for generations. Grandmother found me reading them one day before, well, that day with the picnic. She understood why I wanted to learn. So, she let me read when Mother wasn't around." Her voice was so vulnerable and sweet. "I may have a book knowledge of sex and seen many performed acts around the colony, but that doesn't mean I know how and what to do. I need you to teach me how to pleasure you."

I looked at her, amazed. I'd never had a lover satisfy me how she had in our time together. "Teach you?"

"Yes. You need to teach me what you want and what you like. I want to perform my wifely duties to the best of my abilities for you." She looked up at me through her eyelashes, and I was instantly hard for her again.

I took her hand and placed it on me. "That. That right there proves that you can do no wrong."

She wrapped her hand around me, and I rolled on top of her. "Oh no, Sidonia, hands will not be an option for you. You want me to teach you all the things I like? Here is your second lesson," I said, taking one of the clothes next to the bed and securing her hands above her head. "I want to stay in bed with you all day until you are so weak from finding your pleasure, you can't walk."

Then I kissed her and plunged myself into her in one deep thrust. Her back arched and there was a silent, ecstasy-induced scream on her face.

"Mother, help me," she said before I went to work, finding all the ways to make her scream my name.

CHAPTER 32

SIDONIA

AFTER WE GOT DRESSED, we discussed everything I tried to talk about earlier but were effectively distracted. We had spent the last few hours enjoying and teaching each other what really turned us on. I was sore from my head to my hips, but the mere thought of why I was so sore just left me hungry for Tiberius all over again. Would this want and love for him ever ease?

I forced my gaze to the items that my brothers had brought over. I needed to distract myself. Bending down and opening the crate, I felt exhaustion and a soreness that had me half-swallowing a moan at the thoughts racing through my head. Eyeing what was before me, I focused on my workbooks and the problem at hand.

"Could I ask my brothers to build me a bookcase to store these?" I asked him as he finished securing the fabric at his waist.

"I would like to see them locked up so my sisters don't get into them. Once they are married, we can have them open in the bedroom, but for now, I'd appreciate having them secured," he said as he looked down at how many of them I had.

"There are more than I realized." I sighed. "I thought most of what was on my shelves at home were standard books. Much like yours, actually."

"Your regular books we can make room for there, but these—"

"You're right. I am not trying to fight you on this. It's just going to be a pain to dig out which book I need from the bottom of the crate." I was frustrated. I never had to hide this at home. I did not want to hide here, but I knew we had to just for the sakes of his sisters. That was part of the arrangement.

"Septimia, the oldest," he clarified at my frustrated look, "is going to have a hard time with having rules about our room. We've talked about it, but she's always been welcome to any book she can get ahold of in this house. I've tried to teach them that the more they read, the more they know, and I would not have stupid sisters. Father, Mother, and I want them to have an arrangement with someone who will want them for their intelligence and to be a beneficial part of a household, not just a woman to bear children."

I was on him and kissing him instantly.

"What was that for?" he said with his eyebrows high.

"I got lucky. Not only are you, well, you, but your family has values that not every Roman family has. You value things other than beauty and money." I was in awe of him.

His finger guided my chin to him, and he gave me another quick kiss. "So, your books. What if we get a locking cabinet? Septimia may still try to get it open, but you would have easier access to them. It might at least deter her for a little longer, until we find a permanent solution."

I nodded.

"Hungry?" When I smirked and held him closer, he continued, "For food. You need to keep your strength. I can't have you passing out halfway through sex. Smells like Mother is home and cooking."

I faked a disappointed look, and he chuckled. "Aww, don't you look cute. Big lip and all," he said, nipping at it.

I looked at him through my eyelashes again and splayed my hands across his back and stuck my bottom lip out farther.

"Gods. How did I end up with a woman with a sexual appetite such as yours?" With a forced sigh, to keep himself under control, he muttered, "Like I said earlier, there is nothing I would like to do more than to stay in this room and fuck you all day long."

I smiled. "All day?"

"The bed. The floor. The desk." He nibbled on my ear as he growled. "Against the wall."

My toes curled, but then there was a soft knock on the door.

"Yes?" Tiberius said, a bit painfully.

A small voice on the other side said, "Breakfast is ready."

"Thank you, Nepia. We will be right there." He tried to release the want in his voice. His forehead met mine, and I saw him fighting for some inner control. I recognized it for what it was because I wanted nothing more than to push him back on that bed and swallow him whole.

"Come on. Mother is an amazing cook," he said, leading us out to the main room.

I stopped short as I came into the family room, suddenly not knowing what to do. His arm pulled taut, and he nudged me along. Usually, I got up and headed to the baker for fresh bread, then into the workshop for deliveries, lessons, or crafting. *What did I do now?*

"Sidonia. Come and sit down. I've already made breakfast," Mrs. Vispania said.

Tiberius, sensing my uneasiness, pulled me to the table. As I sat down, Mrs. Vispania smiled and said in a simple voice, "Sidonia. We are family now. I know we haven't had a chance to talk, but I want to know you better."

"And I want to get to know you more too. It's just—"

"You're feeling a little out of place," she said, smiling. "Don't worry. My husband explained to me you will need to spend most of your days helping with your family's workshop. Is that correct?"

"Yes. There will be deliveries to make, wares to craft, and much more, but I don't want that to sound like an excuse not to help you here at home."

"It will be nice to have some additional help, but I fully understand. I've been doing it all by myself for so long that I don't mind."

"I've been helping with some of the cleaning, too," Septimia said enthusiastically.

Mrs. Vispania smiled at her daughter. "However, now that Tiberius is home and you are here, there will be additional laundry that will need to be done, and more food, and so on."

"I can do the laundry and help with food and cleaning. Whatever you need," I said after swallowing a very delicious bite of eggs. "Your eggs are delicious. How do you get them so fluffy and light?"

"Goat's milk," she said, laughing lightly. "And how does your family get your laundry so clean and fresh smelling?"

"Mother has always washed them in the sea. I can show you one day if you will teach me to cook like this." I looked at Tiberius, who was smiling. "I'm not saying I can't cook, but your mother can cook lots better than I can. My food will be very boring in comparison."

"As long as it isn't like what we ate when I was on the road with the Empire, you will be fine," he said, chuckling.

"They had cooks, though, didn't they?" I asked, taking another bite.

"I didn't say they didn't have cooks. Just implied they were not very good." He smiled and his eyes lit up again. "Though Mother's cooking is one of the best I've ever had. I just learned to appreciate it that much more while gone."

"You are just trying to butter me up," Mrs. Vispania said. "Now don't forget you have a meeting with your father this afternoon after lunch."

"Mother. I thought I could spend the day with Sidonia. After all, we just got married," he said sweetly. It was so adorable to see him practically pouting with his mother. It made me smile.

"That is what I tried to tell your father. However, he said he could handle the rest of the meetings today, but that one you had to be there for. Apparently, it's with the Roman general who is in town."

"That explains it," he muttered, looking down at his plate, his smile fading from his face.

"Know him, I take it?" I said as I squeezed his knee under the table, and he brushed it against mine in thanks.

"Yes," he almost hissed as an answer. "He and I have been involved in more than just a few fights over the years. I always wanted to take a more strategic approach to things as not to . . . well, lose lives unnecessarily. He just wanted to go in, rush line tactics, and pick up the pieces later."

"And your friend Velarde is under his command," I said with a hint of sadness in my voice.

He nodded. I was studying his face when there was a knock on the door. I made to stand when Mrs. Vispania stood and said sternly, "Sit down. You're a guest until tomorrow. Your Grandmother said you have the day off. We will do laundry tomorrow morning, and then you can head to the workshop."

CHAPTER 33

TIBERIUS

MOTHER OPENED THE DOOR and took a document from the messenger. "I'm sorry to bother you, Mrs. Vispania, but this came for you, and Mr. Vispania asked me to deliver it to you immediately."

"Thank you," she said, looking at who it was from before turning ghost white.

"Mother?" I asked, getting up and rushing to her side

"It's . . . It's from my sister," she said, then she looked to Sidonia. "She lives on Capri."

She turned the letter over a few times before opening it. Sidonia looked at me, and I lowered my voice as I told her, "Her entire family is on Capri, and when she married her husband, they fought and essentially disowned her. Her sister has only sent messages to her three times, to my knowledge."

"Four since you were born," Mother said, staring at the paper in her hand. "Once to say that she had married, once to say that she had three children and was now independent since her husband had passed a few months before, once to say our mother had died from the illness that spread through here, and finally about her and father fighting, and that she, too, was disowned."

"So, not usually good news then," Sidonia whispered, looking at her sadly.

"No, not usually," Mother said, sighing and breaking the seal on the back. I saw tears in her eyes, though they didn't fall, as she read the letter, and then confusion crossed her face.

"Mother, what is it?" I asked.

"My father is dead, but he left everything to my sister and me. I don't know why. He disowned us, didn't want anything to do with us. The last words he said to me were that I would never see a coin of his money and that he never wanted me and wished I had been a son. He would at least have seen a redeeming quality in me then." She chuckled and shook her head. "Not that it was much of a surprise or anything. She says the money, which is quite a sizable amount, has already been placed in my name and is available at the treasury."

"Mother, I'm so sorry," I said, even though I knew she had little respect for her father.

"Sorry?" she said, looking at me incredulously. "Why are you sorry?"

It was Sidonia who spoke. "Your father is dead. You said that you did not get along and hadn't spoken, but—"

"I made my peace with it a long time ago." She smiled then turned back to me. "I know just what to do with that money.

Your father and I don't need it. I will have it transferred into the names of Tiberius and Sidonia Vispania immediately."

"No!" I shouted at the same time as Sidonia.

Mrs. Vispania threw her head back in laughter. "You two are perfect for each other, aren't you?"

I couldn't help but blush. "Mother, keep the money. We will make our own way."

"No, my son. We have more money than we could spend in multiple lifetimes. Consider this *my* wedding gift to you. The fact you both declined it immediately means my decision is the right one."

"Mrs. Vispania—"

"Atia," she interrupted. "Please, call me Atia."

"Atia. Really, we can't. Tiberius is right. We will make our own way."

"And like I said, we have enough to last many lifetimes." She studied us for a moment before she said, "Do you know we declined any dowry? I know your family could have paid for it, dear. We just don't need it. The only thing we needed to have was the satisfaction and assurance that Tiberius would be happy. Don't tell your fathers I told you, though. I expect they would be embarrassed. They may even demand the Gods smite us."

I looked at Sidonia, whose eyes were as wide as mine. When I looked back at my mother, I whispered, "I am happy, but Mother—"

"Don't *but Mother* me," she said with a smile. "The matter is settled. No more discussions."

Then the house shook and a roar sounded so loud, I had to cover my ears. I looked at Sidonia and grabbed her hand as we ran outside to see what had happened.

As we rounded the corner to the marketplace and looked up, I saw a sight that frightened me to the core.

The top of Mount Vesuvius was blowing massive amounts of smoke into the air.

Chapter 34

Sidonia

Around me, people fell to the ground, praying to their Gods, grabbing their families, telling them to take what they could so they could leave, and then there was Tiberius and me. We stood there, our hands clasped tightly, and when I turned to look at him, he was just staring at me. Then he pulled me close.

"It will be alright," he chanted. "I will keep you safe."

When I regained some of my composure, the only thing I could think of was getting to my family so that we could go to the base of Vesuvius and offer a blessing to stop this. "Tiberius. We need to get to the workshop."

"Mother, wait here for Father with the girls," he said, pushing her into the house.

She nodded, and Tiberius, still grasping my hand, led me to my family's home. When we got there, Severius was trying to calm the girls down as Juventia lay on the ground covered in rubble from where the roof fell in just on the other side of the doorway. Her head was caved in, and there was so much blood. Too much blood.

"I know, girls, but I need you just to look at me, okay?" Severius said. His voice was thick and hitched at the end. His eyes met mine, and when I looked from her to him, he simply shook his head. I fought back the tears as I looked at Tiberius. "Help Lars and Severius. My Father should be here soon," I said as he nodded.

Lars was standing in the doorway just staring at Juventia. "Lars, let me help you." Slowly, Lars turned to face Tiberius, and there was a bob of his throat, tears streaming down his face, but he gave a quick nod.

As I entered the workshop, Grandmother was opening the secret compartment behind one of the shelves with my mother standing there, bug-eyed.

"What? You thought nothing was kept in there?" she said with a smile.

"Sidonia. Juventia—" Mother started to say.

"I know. Tiberius is helping Lars. Severius is trying to keep the girls calm. Are we going to bless Vesuvius? What do you need help with?" I asked calmly. I knew it would do no good to freak out. The best way to help was to keep my composure. Granted, I was taking more deep breaths than usual to keep the hysteria away, but as long as it worked, then I was functional.

"Once we get to the base of the mountain. Maybe we can slow this down enough for everyone to escape," Grandmother said.

"What?" I asked. "What do you mean, slow this down? Can't we stop it?"

"This isn't the first time a mountain has gotten angry, spitting fire and smoke among its people. It can't be stopped, Sidonia. I remember my grandmother telling me stories her grandmother would tell her about them. Once the mountain is angered, it will spit fire, smoke, and devastation upon the people. The only question is in which direction," she said with an easy calm.

"What did she say about the colonies around it?" I asked hesitantly.

Grandmother looked at Mother, sadness in every line of her face, before Mother said, "Total devastation."

"What do we have to do?" I asked after a quick moment to absorb what she said.

There was no way that I was going to let Vesuvius stop my happiness. I just got married. I was going to have kids, teach them the ways of Mother Earth, and, most of all, spend all my years loving Tiberius.

I would have my forever with Tiberius. That thought settled deep within me, and my focus went to the storage area that Grandmother had just pulled the books out of, then it shifted to one of the older tomes in her hands.

Shifting my gaze to the shelves, I strode to them and grabbed the purple shamrocks. Rubbing them between both of my hands, I chanted the words for the spell I had seen years ago. There was something about it that made me memorize it.

Mother, I give you this,
Mother, I give you love,
Mother, I give you Tiberius,
Mother, I give you us,
Mother, I ask only for forever.

Repeating it thrice, I smeared the purple on my forehead, walked out into the other room, and did the same to Tiberius, who just looked at me confused as I took his hands in mine after smearing it on his forehead, rubbed the shamrocks between his hands, and said the verse thrice again. When I ran his hand over my brow and then his again, there was a fiery heat that burst through me, letting me know it had taken root.

Then, I turned on my heels and walked into the back room where my mother and grandmother stood there slack-jawed. "I don't want to hear it," I said.

"When did you learn that?" Mother asked.

"She's been in those books for years. What I'm more surprised about is the fact her hands glowed white as she did it, and then her and Tiberius' brows glowed to match. It took root," Grandmother said, cocking her head to the side in contemplation. "It will fade before we leave this room, but . . . it will stay. By the Mother, it took root!"

"What took root?" I heard Mother ask.

"Are we going to go and slow down Vesuvius or not?" I turned to them, hands on my hips, daring them to push me. I refused for this to be the end of us. There was going to be a happy ending.

My grandmother was still looking at me with awe, but it was my mother's confusion that had me asking, "Mother?"

She blinked and gave a quick shake of her head. "Vesuvius."

After gathering what we needed, we walked into the main room.

"We will be back soon. We are going to bless the mountain to help stave this off," I said, kissing Tiberius and full of all the fear I was trying not to show. He held me tight and gave it back to me.

"You're what?" Tiberius asked when we broke the kiss. Worry and fear were tight on his face.

"Giving an offering to Mother Earth and casting a blessing in hopes to slow it down. Maybe it won't be Herculaneum that the mountain is mad at. Go get the family. Tell them to meet us back here in an hour. I promise that is all I will be," I said firmly.

He nodded and then pulled me close, my head in his hands. "Sidonia, I only just found you. I won't lose you. If you aren't back in this room in one hour, I'm coming after you." Then he kissed me hard. It was full of love and tenderness, but there was tension that assured me he wasn't lying about coming after me.

"One hour," I said, kissing him quickly once more. Grandmother, Mother, and I ran out the door, thankful we didn't have to slow much at all for Grandmother to keep up with us.

Twenty minutes later, we were standing at the same clearing on the mountain that I had been in just yesterday morning before marrying Tiberius. We set up quickly. Grandmother drew a perfect circle around us while Mother set up four candles in the position of the stars. I dusted salt around the outer perimeter of the circle and grabbed three additional candles from the bag Mother had brought and handed them out.

We each knelt facing Vesuvius, lit our candle, and started the blessing.

Through the smoke and darkness
Grant us thy protection

In thy protection, give us strength and understanding
Mother, Daughter, Spirit, Earth
Forgive the ill that we have done
Forgive the pride that we have shown
Forgive the words that have spread like vermin
Protect our homes and our families
And in the love of all those existences
Forgive our wrongful doings and
Mother, Daughter, Spirit, Earth
Surround and protect us through these hours of night.

We repeated the blessing four times as each candle was lit in the element's place. When the final one sprang to life, a green light circled us where Grandmother had drawn the circle for us to sit in the middle of.

We each raised our candle to Mount Vesuvius, lowered it to the ground, and snuffed the light with our hands. As we did, the green faded out just as the ground shook again.

Grandmother looked at my mother and me. We all knew that was not a good sign.

"Do we try it again?" I asked, my voice shaking slightly.

"No," Grandmother said. "As I told you, we cannot stop this. We can only hope it will be enough to delay, allow us passage out of the destruction, or prevent destruction landing upon us."

Rock and debris were starting to fall from the sky, and I just looked up toward the peak of the mountain. I couldn't see it through the dust and smoke and my heart sank.

Still kneeling, I put my head to the ground and said, "I'm sorry, Vesuvius, for not protecting you enough. Please spare Herculaneum, and I will live the rest of my days proving to you we are worthy." I let the tears fall now.

Mother's hand was on my back. "Come on, let's get back to the house."

"No. It was my responsibility to take care of Vesuvius," I yelled at her. Tears were flowing hotly down my cheeks. "I failed."

They just looked at me with love on their faces as I whispered again, "I failed."

"It is not all on you, child," my grandmother said, kneeling in front of me. "That weight is also on your mother and me. We should not have left that to you."

"I will stay and allow Vesuvius to take me as payment," I said, swallowing any despair I felt.

"No," Grandmother said sternly.

I turned toward Vesuvius. "I offer myself as a sacrifice for the payment of all wrongdoings of Herculaneum. Take me and allow all to live."

"No," Grandmother and Mother said in unison.

I turned to them, pulling what the Mother gave me to the surface, and pushed them out of the salted circle. Kneeling in the center, I took the knife from the bag and sliced each of my palms. I vaguely heard Grandmother scream in horror as I slammed them onto the dirt. The ground trembled under us as my blood met with the earth. Then there was nothing but a deathly silence in the air.

Closing my eyes, I let my love for Tiberius come to the surface and the Mother's blessing pool in my hands. Warmth flowed through me as I chanted the words.

I give myself freely
I give myself to right the wrongs
For the failure of my blood
For the failure of my duty
I offer myself freely
I give you all.

Lifting my hands again and slamming them down, the ground trembled, and I repeated it.

I give myself freely
I give myself to right the wrongs
For the failure of my blood
For the failure of my duty
I offer myself freely
I give you all.

Again, I raised my hands and slammed them down, the ground trembling once more, as I repeated it a final time.

I give myself freely
I give myself to right the wrongs
For the failure of my blood
For the failure of my duty
I offer myself freely
I give you all.

I lifted my head to the top of Vesuvius and saw my mother and grandmother banging on an invisible wall that rose from the salted circle.

There was a melodic song flitting through the air that I recognized as the Mother. How I knew, I was not sure, but I did with every fiber of my being it was her.

You bind yourself to your true soul-bonded love, and now offer yourself as a sacrifice?

"Yes," I said, without hesitation and barely above a whisper. "If it means my soul-bonded love will live. Yes."

This is not your price to pay.

This is not a failure of your devotion to me. This is the work of other Gods. It is not your price to pay. I release you from your duties.

"Mother Earth," I begged.

You and Tiberius are soul-bonded. You will know him by his fiery touch. Much time shall pass until forever.

Be well, my child. For we will speak again.

There was a bright red-hot light that burst around me, the salt burned, and then Mother and Grandmother were in front of me. Tears ran down their faces, and they were looking me over to see if I was hurt. I raised my hands, and there was no trace of where I had run the blade through my palms.

"She rejected me," I said, crying.

"What?" Mother said.

"She rejected me. The Mother rejected me. I offered myself. She said it wasn't my price to pay. This was the work of other Gods." My voice trembled with the words.

"Come. Let us head back. Tiberius will be waiting," Grandmother said.

CHAPTER 35

TIBERIUS

SEVERIUS STILL HELD THE girls tightly. Sidonia's father and I had moved the table so that it blocked the view of Lars' wife in the other room. My mother and father were now sitting huddled with my sisters, and I could do nothing but pace the room.

"Tiberius, she will be here soon," Severius said, trying to calm me. Father looked over at me and just stared.

It was my mother who said, "Sidonia will be back soon. She is strong, Tiberius." While her voice was powerful, she held onto Septimia tightly in one arm and my father in another. Nepia was huddled between my father's legs and crying softly.

I had this nagging feeling that something was seriously wrong. Twenty minutes ago, I felt a fire burn through me, quick and painful. Worse than that, I felt it burn against my very essence.

The front door burst open, and Sidonia's grandmother and mother came through. My heart stopped when Sidonia didn't follow. "Where is she?" I growled.

"She was right behind us," her mother said, panting and out of breath.

I vaguely heard my father yell at me as I ran out the door and down the street. It had started to rain. Not rain. *Rock.*

And not just any rock. I caught one in my hand, and it was lightweight and full of holes. They were hard but eventually crumbled in the palm of my hand.

Bigger, harder, faster-falling rocks started raining down, and a pot smashed to pieces beside me. There were some stalls ahead of me, and my heart jump-started as I saw Sidonia jump into one. Rocks smashed and crashed on the roof, and I could hear nothing but clay and canisters breaking everywhere.

I ran to her, turning the corner, just narrowly missing a larger rock that landed beside me. I threw myself into the stall and pulled Sidonia into my arms.

She shrieked and pushed against my chest, but when her eyes met mine, she fell into me again. "Oh, Tiberius!"

Sidonia looked up at me, wrapped her arms tight around my neck, and kissed me.

I kissed her back. "Gods, I was terrified something had happened to you. You didn't return with your mother and grandmother." My voice was shaking, and I struggled to control the shivering of fear through my body. I had been in war, fought in battles, but the thought of losing Sidonia? It was too much. "Don't scare me like that."

"I love you, Tiberius," she said, whispering it against my lips as if it were her only prayer.

"And I love you, Sidonia," I whispered back against hers

She placed her hand over my heart, took my hand, and placed mine over hers. "I will always be yours," she said softly.

"And I will always be yours," I said, bringing my forehead to hers. When they touched, heat raged through me from our foreheads and hands. I could feel her. She was here, she was whole, and she was mine. I could feel her love and warmth.

Rocks crashed around us, and she looked at me wide-eyed. Then she started speaking so fast that I didn't have a chance to respond. "What did Herculaneum do to deserve this? We were prosperous, but not gluttons, at least most of the people. Sure, there were people like Magistrate Potius who flaunted his power, but most of this colony were good, whole, and spiritual people. We did our rituals, and the Mother said it wasn't her doing. It was the doing of other Gods. Certainly, Hercules and Venus wouldn't punish the entire colony for actions like his? Would they?"

"I don't even know what to think about the Gods anymore," I whispered to her. She was so sure in her faith, but I had not seen the Gods help us in anything we had done in the Empire. There was plenty that was done in their name, but there was no reward for any of that atrociousness.

"I offered to stay as a sacrifice to the Mother to make it stop," she said just loud enough I heard it, and my heart stopped.

"Why?" I sat back and put her head in my hands. "Why would you do that?"

"If I could save you and Herculaneum, it would mean a good death," she said, bringing her forehead back to mine.

"Sidonia, I just found you. You can't leave me. I won't be able to live without you by my side," I begged, my voice cracking. I surprised myself with those words. This woman had become such an integral part of me that the thought of losing her was inconceivable.

The ground shook violently again, and the stall we had taken shelter in creaked and groaned.

"Come on. Let's get back to the house before this one falls in on itself. The entire family is there," I said, taking her hand and leading her from the stall. Just behind me, I heard it crash to the ground. I glanced back and the roof of the stall fell in on itself, just where we had been kneeling.

In the little over an hour that had passed since the initial smoke vaulted from the mountain, most of the citizens had gathered what possessions they could carry from their homes and started to leave the colony. I wondered if our families would want to do the same, or would Father and Mr. Regillia want to stay here to protect their business ventures? While I knew that Sidonia's grandmother led their house, I believed they would follow our fathers' lead. They could rebuild the workshop in any city.

Out of the corner of my eye, I saw a huge rock flying directly toward us. Grabbing Sidonia's hand tighter, I pulled her into one of the buildings we were running past just in time for the rock to crash into the wall. The stone shook and as we ran out toward her family's home. I looked back to see it cracked with the force of the rock colliding with it.

Gods, it had just missed us.

CHAPTER 36

SIDONIA

WHEN WE FINALLY REACHED my family's home, everyone was there waiting for us to return. The look of relief on their faces was one I matched when I saw them, including Tiberius' two little sisters, sitting at the table. Juventia was the only one we had lost. My nieces were with Tiberius' sisters. Faenia, my youngest niece, played with some wooden toys, which made me feel better. Bella, the oldest, however, was looking off to the corner and smiling. I had to wonder what she thought that could make her smile. When my eyes met Lars', all I could see was pain. I couldn't help myself and ran to him and threw my arms around him.

"I'm so sorry, Lars. I'm so sorry," I murmured.

"It isn't your fault, Sidonia. The roof fell in, and I wasn't fast enough to push her out of the way," he said as he held me tight.

"It isn't your fault, either, Lars."

I felt warm, hot tears on my cheeks and when I pulled back, I did my best to hide them. There would be time later for grieving.

It was Mr. Vispania who broke the silence as we all stood there, staring at each other. "The general said that there is a fleet stationed just off the coast. They may come to our rescue. We can wait down in the boathouses."

"Shouldn't we go to the temple?" Mrs. Vispania said. "We should pray to the Gods. Hercules could save us."

I looked at Mr. Vispania, and he looked at me with a glint in his eye. He hadn't told her the whole of our secret. I had wondered just how much she knew after breakfast this morning. Well, I had my answer.

Mr. Vispania's lip turned into a small smile, and he said reassuringly, "No. Sidonia's family has done that already. That is where she, her mother, and grandmother were when we arrived."

"The boathouses are strong. They should be able to carry the weight of all the rock that is falling. Our homes were not made to withstand that kind of weight. The boathouses, however, are as strong as Hercules himself," Severius said. I gave him a thankful nod.

"Then we make for the boathouses and wait for the Roman fleet," Father said, nodding. "Do you have any extra lanterns? We packed ours, but we don't know how long the smoke will stay overhead. It could be a few days before it clears enough for the sun to shine through again."

"We packed them, along with extra oil and all the bread and water we could carry," Mr. Vispania added with a laugh in his voice. "Left a lot of items that if my grandfather were still alive . . . Well, let's just say he would skin me alive, but what good would they be if we die from hunger or thirst."

"Daddy?" Bella said, not necessarily sad, just quietly. "Are we going to die like Mommy?"

Lars rushed over to her. "No, baby. We are going to go somewhere safer, where the roof won't . . ." A lump caught in his throat, and his eyes were full of sadness. "Where we can be safe until the mountain stops."

I watched as Bella reached over and touched her father's face. "It's ok, Daddy. Mommy is ok. She is with the Mother now." As she wiped away the tear on Lars' face, I could have sworn that I saw a small glow under her hand and Lars' smile slightly, but then his eyes shot wide and he grabbed her hand. "What did you just say?"

"Mommy is with the Mother now. She is okay," she said in a whisper.

"Oh!" I said and turned to Grandmother, who was beaming brightly. However, when I looked at Mr. and Mrs. Vispania, their faces were covered in confusion. Tiberius' face was a little harder to read.

"Did she . . . speak to you?" he asked her hesitantly.

Bella's laugh was musical and light. "No, Daddy. You know that isn't how it works."

"How . . . what . . . works?" Mrs. Vispania asked.

I sighed, knelt before her, and took my mother-in-law's hands in mine. "The morning that the arrangement was finalized for me to wed Tiberius, we told them our deepest secret. We are Earth Worshipers, and before you jump to conclusions, no, we are not pagans, druids, or witches. We are different. Each woman in the line holds just an ounce of power, which we use for healing only. It is why our potions and oils are so successful. We hold a strong vow not to do harm."

"Are your kind causing the shortage of sheep near Pompeii?" she asked.

I had to stifle a laugh. That was what she wanted to know after what I just told her? "No. Supposedly, it's the Dark Witches of Moesia. We have no relation to them," I said lightly.

"What are these . . . powers you speak of then?"

"We only use them for healing and for imbuing our herbs and oils. However." I turned to Grandmother. "Bella is so young. She shouldn't come into hers for another five or six years."

Grandmother thought for a moment. "It may have to do with the mountain, but I do not know. Yours came in earlier than usual too, but—" The ground shook again, cutting her off.

"But we should get down to the boathouses before the rest of the roof caves in on us," Father said with an authority that ended the conversation.

CHAPTER 37

TIBERIUS

WHEN WE FINALLY REACHED the boathouses, there were already a lot of people down on the beach. One of my father's business associates, Magistrate Brillino, ushered us into inside where his family was and then closed the gate behind us.

After we settled in, Magistrate Brillino said he had stopped by Magistrate Potius's home and found the magistrate and his wife crushed under a pile of rubble. The boys and their families were gone. Flora was also nowhere to be found, and they assumed that she had left town with some others. It was a relief to me that his vileness was now gone from this Earth.

As I sat down next to Sidonia, she said, "I wonder how Attia from the balneae was fairing? Was she even still alive?" I wrapped my arms around her as she looked up at Lars and Severius. I felt a wave of pain flow through me. Juventia should be here with her girls, and Severius should be surrounded by his family as well. It was so wrong.

I'm not sure how much time had passed when there was a commotion outside. Someone yelled, "Ships!"

We got up and ran to the ledge, and out in the bay you could see the Roman fleet. We jumped, screamed until our throats hurt. We waved our arms, but it was all to no avail. They were headed for Pompeii, not Herculaneum. They left us to ride out the storm.

As more and more realized it on the beach, some took off into the water. Were they hoping to swim out to the ships? They would tire long before they ever reached them, if they even stayed there. Instead, the ships would be long gone by the time anyone would be far enough out to be rescued. They would drown or would fall prey to the creatures of the bay before they ever reached help.

Fights broke out along the beach as people panicked and tried to steal rations. I took Sidonia's hand and led us back into the boathouse. "Father, you should come inside."

"Is there anything we can use to secure the gate?" I asked, looking at Magistrate Brillino. Visions of so many colonies that we had trekked through where villagers fought over just one jar of wine in situations like this flashed through my mind. "That group is going to escalate much worse before it settles down. There's no help coming, and I've seen it before. Citizens will lose their minds when they realize they are on their own in a disaster."

"What do you mean, there is no help coming?" Mrs. Brillino asked.

I looked to the magistrate, who nodded and calmly, and said, "It just means that we will have to ride out the storm here or we leave, but I don't know which direction will be safe for us to run in."

I only thought of Sidonia. If I thought I could make it out of here with her and survive, I would have done it before even going back for my family or hers. She was all that mattered anymore. She was my present and future.

Sidonia curled up next to me and just kept whispering how sorry she was.

"Shh. I've already told you that you are not to blame for this. You have nothing to be sorry for. Just stay with me. Just stay with me, Sidonia," I said against her hair, kissing the top of her head.

After they secured the door the best they could with rope from the magistrate's cart, Severius passed out some more water.

"Grandma's coughing is getting worse," Sidonia said, looking over at her. The air was dry and growing hotter. I knew it was probably from all the smoke and dust, but there wasn't much we could do about a cough created by that.

CHAPTER 38

SIDONIA

MINUTES TURNED TO HOURS, and because the smoke had covered the sun, we did not know how late it was or even how long we had been in there. It was getting blisteringly hot, and my clothes were drenched with sweat. I looked around and everyone's hair was sticking to their skin, and you could see where their clothes were wet and sticky as well.

I had gotten up and handed out some water and bread to those in our chamber a while ago, but when I got up again to give out some water, I found that much of it was already gone.

"Did I fall asleep?" I asked Tiberius, who shook his head that I hadn't. "Did someone else give out more water?"

"No. Why?" Mrs. Vispania asked.

"The water is already half-gone from here. When I last handed some out, there was more than this left in this container." I checked the containers we hadn't opened yet and they, too, had lower water levels. "Severius, you filled these to the top, right?"

"Yes. Some even leaked out when I put the tops on to help keep them from spilling," he answered, getting up and checking the rest of the water containers. "Magistrate Brillino and Mr. Vispania, can you check yours as well?"

As they did, they noticed theirs had lowered even though no one had gotten into them. There were no leaks, no spills, the water was just . . . gone. There was a knowing look that spread through the group. No one said anything, but as if our bodies knew, we all became much more parched. I passed out another round of water to my family and then sat back down with Tiberius. Even though the girls had all settled down and were resting, I could not sleep. I knew I should. If anything happened, they would need me to help mend the injured.

The ground continued to shake occasionally, and there were the distant sounds of homes falling and crumbling. As they became more frequent, I couldn't help but cringe at the thought of who might be losing their lives in the falling debris. I tried to tell myself that there was no one in the building, that they had fled or were down here with us.

Hours went by, and my nerves were on a sharp edge that wouldn't dull, no matter how much I tried. Tiberius just held me and told me that everything would be ok. I knew he couldn't guarantee that, but it still made me feel better. I would be fine if I met my end as long as I was in Tiberius' arms. Until then, I would help my family and try very hard to stay calm.

When Bella woke up a little while later, Grandmother and Mother started talking to her about what it meant that she was getting her power, and how important it was that she hid it. Bella, of course, said she understood. She was so smart and really had been beyond her years, but she was still only seven years old. Was just a kid, but I remembered when I went through the transformation; I didn't feel like myself. However, there were things I loved, like connecting with the earth, the ability to help my mother and grand-mother with the workshop, learning what herbs went with each other to help with ailments, and all that had consumed my life. With all of that came the responsibility of having to hide a part of ourselves, knowing that others were not as accepting as some about our ways. That had become much more important since the Roman fleet had spent more time in our colony.

"How can they talk to Bella so openly about the Mother with the magistrate's family here?" Tiberius asked.

"A couple of years ago, the magistrate's wife was very ill. My family was able to cure her, but it took more than just the herbs and oils to do it. We had to call upon Mother Earth to help her, and when she woke back up, she knew. The magistrate said there was a gentle green glow around her as we chanted. Since then, the magistrate has worked hard to help our secret stay a secret and has assisted my father in anything that he ever needed," I said, smiling at the thought.

"More than just the herbs and oils?" he said, looking down at me.

"Yes. Like I said, her power is rising. It's not much. The Mother gives it to us so we can imbue those herbs and oils, and sometimes, on very rare occasions, we can ask the Mother to send it into a person to help heal them. It is said that only those descended from the original families can do it. There is a rumor in our family history that we were, but until that moment, we didn't know for sure. We just knew she was going to die if we didn't try."

"Which is why, when we first met, you asked if I knew who the original families were? You were just protecting your family."

I nodded my head, and he smiled. "Sidonia, you are full of surprises."

I looked up at him and kissed him. "You have no idea."

Our moment was cut short as we heard a thunderous roar and the shaking started again, but not like before. No. Before, it felt deep and achy. This was more on the surface. The roar was getting louder, and Tiberius pulled me closer.

I reached my hand up and, letting my power shine at my fingers, I ran it along his brow and took his hand to do the same as I said the prayer trice again.

Mother, I give you this,
Mother, I give you love,
Mother, I give you Tiberius,
Mother, I give you us,
Mother, I ask only for forever.

Lars held the girls and Severius sat with his knees to his chest, murmuring the name of his one love, the one that he never really recovered from. My mother and father were holding Grandmother and from the look in her eyes, I knew the Mother was coming for us.

I looked up at Tiberius and saw my fear mirrored in his eyes. "I love you, Sidonia Vispania."

"I love you, Tiberius Vispania. I will find you in another lifetime," I said, looking into those sapphire eyes that swallowed me whole.

"And I will find you," he vowed. "Even if it takes me two thousand years, I will find you again."

The fear vanished, and I was filled with nothing but love. If the Mother decided this was how I was to die, then at least I was surrounded by my family and in the arms of the man that I loved with all my heart.

Off in the distance, you could just barely hear screams and buildings crashing to the ground. Then it was hot, *so, so hot.*

It hurt to breathe. It reminded me of the time I had fallen in the fire when I was little. I had inhaled the heat and was unable to eat solid food for three days' time.

Tiberius' eyes bored into mine, and in the split second the dark, hot clouds engulfed the boathouse, I felt my skin boil, and I vaguely heard a scream before the darkness overtook me.

CHAPTER 39

A PHOENIX RISES

TIBERIUS

I TRIED TO OPEN my eyes, move my arms, legs, anything, but I couldn't. I'd been struggling and trying for a while now with no success. Then a burning pain washed over me again, and I blacked out.

It was the fourth time it had happened.

I was coming to again. That same damn poem repeated in my head.

By the powers
Of the moon and stars
Latch onto his soul and hold it tight

Hate and envy he will always know
Tainted, infected, a poisoned kiss
Strength of a thousand men he will have
Once burned by the fire of the Earth.

I shook my head to make it stop.

I can move! I thought as the poem continued.

Love he shall be find
Love he shall be lost
Their love shall bind
Once burned by the fire of the Earth.

I could still feel Sidonia in my arms, only she didn't feel like she should. Slowly, very slowly, I opened my eyes. It burned and felt like sand coated them.

When my eyes finally focused, what I saw before me couldn't be true.

Out of reflex, I dropped her and scooted away, only to back up into yet another charred skeleton. Ash flew up all around me, filling the air and making me cough.

Sidonia.

No. Everything crashed in on me at once, and I crunched my eyes shut again and covered my ears. There was a thunderous voice pounding in my head.

Fire burns the skin
Fire renews the soul
Fire from the Earth shall renew thee life.

No.

No, this was a bad dream. I opened my eyes again and saw the charred remains of what was Sidonia Regallia Vispania, my wife.

No. This really couldn't be. Sidonia was just in my arms. Sidonia was telling me how much she loved me.

Just moments ago, she . . .

I stared at her charred skeleton and then around the room. I saw Mr. and Mrs. Regillia, my parents . . . my sisters. My heart dropped like stone. They were nothing but charred bone.

I reached out to touch her, trying to convince myself it was an illusion or a dream, but when my fingers reached what should have been her cheeks, I touched nothing but bone.

Charred bone.

Cool. It was cool to the touch. If everyone burned, then shouldn't they still be warm?

I looked down at myself, naked, with skin that was red and tightly stretched. I touched it, and it hurt.

My touch was too hot.

"No," I said. Only, it didn't sound like me. The voice was too raspy, too hoarse. I went to where the water jars should have been, but they were busted wide open. I looked around and saw my whole life in a charred, ash-covered state. I knelt before Sidonia, staring at what was my future. All the emotions, heartbreak, and pain came crashing down on top of me.

"I'm so sorry I failed you. I swear on everything I am that all I wanted was to make you happy. Give you children and a happy home," I said to her. Tears streamed like a raging river down on my cheeks, and I didn't even try to hold them back. There was no reason to.

Everything I was, everything I was going to be, my whole being lay before me in the remnants of those charred bones.

I sat there and let the tears flow.

I wasn't sure how long I was there, but eventually, light broke through the clouds. My heart would never recover from this, but I knew somewhere deep, really deep, inside me that she would not want me to just sit here and cry over her. She would want me to get up and live. Live my life. To find her again.

I *would* find her again. Whether it be in this life or the next, I would find my Sidonia again.

I reached out and ran my fingers along her skeletal brow. Fire and light seared through me and I committed it to memory. Every touch of hers had set me on fire, and for as long as I lived, I would never forget it.

I would find her again.

I was not sure where I found the strength, but I stood, every muscle in my body screaming in protest. I was weak and parched. I needed something to drink. Wine. Water. Anything to wet my throat.

I made my way out of the boathouses and saw the beach littered with bodies, just as what lay behind me. I forced myself not to look too closely and stumbled up the stairs to the main portion of the colony.

As I climbed, I found myself getting stronger with every step. My skin tightened and was red, but at least it didn't burn anymore, and it was healing. Quickly. Too quickly.

Sidonia had mentioned that she could imbue healing if needed. Did she imbue me just before the heat and smoke engulfed us? Was that what she had done?

I looked back at the boathouse. "Why, Sidonia? Why save me? I'm nothing without you," I whispered through a parched throat.

When I reached the top of the stairs, I took a deep, ragged, painful breath. I wandered around the colony, looking in building upon building for anyone else who could be alive. There was no one in any home, no one in the marketplace, but when I arrived at the temple, I saw a man standing at what used to be the statue of Hercules.

He stood naked, just as I was, skin just as tight and red. I had to blink repeatedly.

"Velarde?" I asked, wondering if I was hallucinating.

"Tiberius!" he shouted back.

He grasped my arm, and I cringed at the icy touch. "Sorry, my skin is sensitive."

"Mine as well." Then, after a moment, he asked, "Tiberius, how are we alive?"

"I don't know." I looked back to where Sidonia was entombed, and my heart broke all over again, but I didn't cry. Maybe there weren't any more tears available. If Velarde was here, it wasn't Sidonia who saved me.

"Sidonia?" Velarde asked, as if he could read my mind, and I shook my head. His eyes filled with tears, and I saw his throat bob before he nodded, a lone tear dropping on to his cheek.

"It appears we are the only ones alive. The colony is ruined," I said.

My head started pounding, and both Velarde and I grabbed our heads in our hands. Fleeting images of the forest to the north flashed through my mind. A scene that I had dreamed of too many times played in vivid color.

I saw the tavern fight, the three women walking toward me from the fire. I could almost smell the substance being poured around my feet, and then I could feel the blade of the knife the witches held to my throat.

FIRE FROM THE EARTH SHALL RENEW THEE LIFE!

The voices of the three women rang through my head with thunderous purpose, and when it stopped, I jerked my head up and saw Velarde do the same.

"Did you?" Velarde asked.

"What?" I said hesitantly.

"Did you . . . just have images of the night . . . you got your scar?" he said as he brought his hand to his throat.

I couldn't say anything. I just looked at him. How could he have known? Unless . . .

"It really happened?" I mumbled.

"What did those women do to us?" he asked.

"Who were they?" I asked, then remembered what Sidonia had said about the people of Pompeii believing that their land had been cursed by . . . "The Dark Witches of Moesia."

"There has been rumor they have been killing the sheep off outside of Pompeii. Before I came back to Herculaneum, there was a rumor of them moving south. Do you have any other suggestions on why we lived through the Gods' torment and no one else did?" Velarde said as his eyes met mine and pleaded for me to understand. Then he just sighed and looked up at the statue of Hercules that was nothing more than a body. The head was somewhere in pieces behind us. "Do you think . . . if it was them outside of Pompeii, that they would still be near enough to find?"

"I don't think that anyone around this mountain is alive," I said sadly and turned to walk out of the temple.

He met my stride and followed me. "Then where do we even start?"

"Where it started for us. We have to travel back to the forest bordering Germania. Back to where our dreams occurred. We will find answers there. We have to."

I tried not to think about what I was leaving behind. All my hopes and dreams were now just piles of charred ash and debris.

And I tried not to think of the one thing I would need most of all. *Sidonia.*

Eternity's Flame

Part Two

CHAPTER 40

TIBERIUS

80 AD

"SHUT HER UP, VELARDE," I growled. Eight months of roaming across the Germainia countryside, and now we were staring at a blonde-haired, black-eyed Dark Witch of Moesia, who wanted nothing more than to emit a high-pitched tone that grated on every one of my nerves.

I tightened the bindings on her legs and wrists. I needed to know why I was here and Sidonia wasn't. We needed answers for why we lived through Mount Vesuvius blowing up and destroying the entire colony of Herculaneum. Everyone but us.

When Velarde came to stand by my side, he crossed his arms across his chest and planted his feet wide. She narrowed her eyes at us, the high-pitch sound growing, when a cruel smile crossed her lips. Black and yellow teeth spread across her face before she said, "You were made by the Clothea Sisters."

"What?" Velarde said, and the sound stopped.

"You were at Vesuvius eight months ago, weren't you?" she said, her head rolling from side to side as she studied us. "Three of you were made that day. Only two of you are here?"

"What do you mean, three of us?" Velarde growled.

"He's not with you?" She smiled as she hissed the words, and I swore I saw a bug crawl out of her mouth. "Oh, the Clothea Sisters will be so thrilled to see you two looking for them."

Her eyes went pitch black, her body twitched, and then she froze. Then, in a voice that was many, she said, "Three created that day, two stand here. Caleus Lars Velarde, your soul has yet to be born. She will rise in a century plus, when more shall be made. Tiberius Maximus Vispania. You left your soul in Herculaneum. She will rise again, but not until the time has passed that you've said you would wait for her. The two shall cross in time from now to your future. Know them by their fiery touch."

"What do you speak of, witch?" I growled. "What do you know of my Sidonia?"

"She will return to you, Vispania. She will return. You've stated the length of time you shall have to wait for her. You both will die many times before you find each other again. To unite forever, she must willingly drink from your neck or life from you must be created within her. She will be the only one able to carry the life you create."

The witch froze, twitched, jerked, and went rigid before saying in that voice that was many, "Death will not find you. Eternity is thy gift given to you. For if you are mortally wounded, rise you will again. All souls will reunite in time. All will be right in time."

The words hung in the air as she slumped forward and crumbled to ash.

I stood there staring at those ashes.

"Tiberius," Velarde said, taking a step toward me.

I continued to stare at that spot, and then I fell to my knees.

"What did that all mean?"

I couldn't breathe. My hand immediately covered where her lotus bracelet sat in my pocket.

Sidonia.

I would get her back, but it would take lifetimes.

CHAPTER 41

KELSEY

PRESENT DAY

"GRAB ME A BEER, bitch," Izzy called out to me as I stuck my head in the fridge.

"You're perfectly capable of getting off your sexy ass and getting one yourself," I shouted back to her.

"But you're already in the fridge," she whined back.

Grabbing Izzy a beer off the back shelf, and one for me just for good measure, I strode back into the living room where she had our textbook on Ancient Tibetan mythology in her lap.

I leaned against the doorjamb and smiled. Her appearance hadn't changed much since I met her during our sophomore year in high school, and I would be lying if I said I wasn't a little jealous. She had walked into that English class like she owned it, sat down next to me, and winked. She'd been my best friend ever since.

She reached behind her for the beer, but I just set it between her boobs, and she moaned. It was hotter than hell today, and her head leaned back against the leather couch in appreciation of the cold against her skin.

"I would normally yell at you for that, but I just can't right now," Izzy said.

"By the way, we're out of ice cream. Your turn to get more. I'm not going back outside. It's over a hundred out there, and while the AC may not work perfectly, at least it's in the 90s inside."

"I'll make Vel bring some when he comes over tonight."

"More beer, too," I said as she picked up her phone and sent him a text message.

Her phone buzzed back, and she frowned. After a few more texts back and forth, she sighed. "No beer tonight because I'm not going out in that weather either."

"Why can't Vel just bring it for us?"

"He has to do some work for Max tonight." She typed furiously on her phone for a minute, and then her lips disappeared, which could only mean one thing. She didn't agree with what they were doing.

Maximus "Max" Vispania was the local hotshot of the area. He was not only a billionaire, but he was also the one you went to when you needed something fixed but couldn't go through legal channels. Maximus Vispania and Caleus Velarde ran the entire town of Trenton, California. I had never met Max, but everyone knew enough about him to stay clear.

During our junior year in high school, when Izzy told me she was dating Max's right-hand man, Caleus Velarde, I nearly choked on my soda in the middle of the cafeteria. She sat right there and told me like we had been discussing Mr. Jones' math test last period. He was about five years older than her and often got his hands dirty for Maximus Vispania, who inherited his empire from his father.

Vel'd been immensely supportive of us, so I couldn't hate the guy. Other than treating Izzy like the rightful queen she is, he helped get us into the very competitive University of California, Trenton, history program. He knew some folks and pulled strings to get us on the list.

Three years after transferring, we were almost done with our bachelor's. I wanted to petition to get my master's at Sac State, but Izzy wasn't sure. Trenton's master's program wasn't as good as Sac State's, but she didn't want to leave Vel, so we stayed put. They had fought, as all couples did, but always made up over the years. They also had never "taken a break" from each other like most high school sweethearts, not even when we were at Foothill College in the Bay Area. In order to transfer as quickly as possible, we took as many classes as we could and finished our associate's in a year and a half.

I knew one day soon, I would watch her walk down the aisle wearing a black wedding dress, because there was no way in hell she would wear white to marry him. I had no doubts about that. The way they looked at each other, it was what made me believe in true love, unlike my parents, who had divorced when I was two.

There were years of bouncing between the two of them before my grandmother took me in, and I would forever be grateful for it. My parents made no attempts at contact since my freshman year of high school, and I had no plans to ever talk to them again.

Taking a sip of my beer, my heart sank at the thought of my grandmother. She passed away last year, and I was going to school on my inheritance. I had to get good grades and graduate. School was my only, and therefore, number one, priority.

I was going over my notes when Izzy sighed heavily and threw her head back against the couch again. "Idiots," she mumbled.

"Do I even want to know?"

"Probably not. Max is moody right now. History is coming back to throw him into a spiral of chaos, and he isn't happy about it."

"Obviously."

"Not that I really blame him. It's a long feud and sometimes it's been . . . bloody," she said, twisting the cap off the beer and downing half of it.

"Izzy!" I said, blinking at how fast she was chugging the bottle.

She just rolled her eyes, chugged the rest, got up, chucked her bottle in the recycle bin, and grabbed another from the fridge. Her phone went off again, and I heard a groan from her before there was a loud crunch. When I looked back through the door, her fist was against the freezer door. Looking at the impact as she pulled her fist back, I sighed at the bent metal.

"You break it, you buy it?" I said, trying to diffuse the tension, but she just glared at me. "Wanna talk about it?"

"No. Let's get back to studying. This test isn't going to ace itself."

CHAPTER 42

MAX

"WHO IS IT?" I called out without looking up while studying the world map spread out on my desk. There were marks of my past all over it, and I cringed at the memories.

"The only asshole willing to deal with you right now," Velarde grumbled, coming in. "Could you be any more of a dick on the phone?"

I glared at him. "Could you give me just a little bit of a break?"

"Tiberius, I haven't in two thousand years. Why would I start now?" he teased, but when I didn't respond and just kept looking at the map, he groaned. "Shit. Not again. Where has he shown up this time?" Vel headed to the sideboard and pulled down two glasses, pouring us each some whiskey. Downing one quickly and refilling it, he handed me one of the glasses, and I downed it in one shot.

237

"Sacramento." I slid my gaze to him without moving my head and waited for his response, which came instantly.

"What? He's never shown up this close. Last time, at least he was on the other side of Europe from us during the World Wars." He downed his drink quickly before saying, "What's in Sac?"

I shrugged. I had been trying to figure it out for over a week since I heard the rumor that Marcus was in California, then I got confirmation he was, indeed, in Sacramento earlier today. We had tried and tried to find out who he really was, but the only name we could ever find on him was "Marcus."

Roughly every hundred years, he would show up just to tear apart everything I'd worked for. Sometimes, it worked, other times, not so much. It'd been such a vicious cycle, but I did not know why he always targeted me.

The years that I let Velarde lead a town or territory, he left us alone. It was only when I was in charge. *Now he wanted Trenton? Fat chance, fucker.*

Trenton had felt like home the moment I arrived in the early 1800s. After running a few towns in the South, I moved west, set up in Texas for a while, and then landed up here in Trenton. Being at the foothills of the Sierra Nevada Mountains had its benefits. Mostly, it kept me from feeling caged in by modern society. With the mountains so close, I would escape often to get away from the "hustle and bustle." During those first years here in Trenton, Vel ran the local bar and brothel. I sat back and spent my time in the hills, looking for gold. Made a fortune doing it, too. We'd been here ever since.

Over 200 years, we'd been running this town. We'd rotate out every few decades, one of us hiding out here and there. Took it from a stop on the trail to a metropolis that major corporations who wanted to be out of the big city flocked to. Sacramento was a quick hour-and-a-half drive down the main highway, but there wasn't much need for it with technology nowadays.

To the public, I was a generational businessman, but most everyone knew I ran the underground as well. I had half the city's police department and lawyers on payroll. The mayor had always been handpicked by either Velarde or myself.

I looked up at Velarde, and he was texting furiously into his phone.

"Tell Bella I said hi and I'm sorry for ruining your booty call." I walked over to the bar and poured another drink.

"You know how much she hates that you call her *Bella*, right? Why can't you just call her Izzy, or Isabella even?" He gave me an even look, and when I smirked at him, he said, "You are such an ass. Anyway, I told her we had work to do. She's pissed, but she'll get over it. At the end of the day, she understands."

"Did you tell her what, or who, exactly, had come up?" I downed the drink and poured another. I really wished I could get drunk off this shit. That was one thing I missed from my life in the Empire: just drinking to get drunk and washing away all thought.

"Yeah. She wanted to come help, but I told her she needed to stay with Kelsey. Help her out. They have a huge test coming up."

"Not much she could do, anyway. She's a smart girl, but we've done years of research on Marcus. She's unlikely to find anything new. There just isn't anything."

"Even the others like us can't figure out why he has been so Underworld-bent on destroying us," Velarde said, running his hand through his long curly hair, which he finally pulled back into a ponytail. He'd cut it short during the

1300s during the Black Plague but had it long ever since. "Franco give you the heads-up?"

"Yeah." We had run into Franco during the 1500s while fighting in the Brittania and French wars during the time. I mentally chuckled at the memory of how many times we had killed each other on the battlefield, only to crawl up from under the mass of bodies two days later.

There was a knock on the door, and Velarde went to open it. I turned and stared at the bookcase, my eyes falling on the only thing that I had brought with me, no matter where I went. Every hundred years or so, I had a new case built for it so it didn't continue to degrade. A few years ago, I had hired one of the top restoration companies in the world to clean it and put it in a custom-built container. There was a biometric mechanism on it and automatic climate control now, but I didn't know if it would survive being cleaned again.

A cloud moved and let the sun shine through the large window behind my desk. When the light hit the sapphire stone in the lotus, it was like a punch in the gut. Almost two thousand years later, I still missed Sidonia. I could still hear her tell me she loved me before the pyroclastic flow had hit us in the boathouse, still feel the heat of her touch. No one had ever lit a fire within me like she did. Everyone's touch, including Velarde's, were always ice cold.

"I don't give a fuck! Find him or it will be your head I take and shove up the other's ass," Velarde screamed into the hallway.

Sighing, I turned and went to the door to see three men dressed in suits. When they saw me, all the color drained from their faces.

"What seems to be the issue here?" I asked, leaning against the door.

"Nothing, sir," they said in unison.

"Now, why don't I believe that? Because if that were true, then Velarde here wouldn't be threatening such a messy end to your existence." I looked down and brushed a speck of nonexistent dust off my blue suit before crossing my arms across my chest. "Though he could just be cranky because he ain't getting laid tonight."

Velarde gave me an even look, and I winked at him. He rolled his eyes and turned back to the men standing there. "Go find the rat. When you do, bring him to me in the basement."

They scurried out down the hall, and I couldn't help but huff a small laugh.

"What was that about?" I asked, smirking at him.

"Just one of the dealers. He ran off to L.A. with about 200K in cash that was supposed to go to us." He sighed. "Don't worry about it. I'll deal with it. I'll track him down and call you once I have something. You worry about finding Marcus."

CHAPTER 43

KELSEY

"FINE, VEL. JUST HURRY back," Izzy complained into the phone as we pulled into the mall. "Find the fucker and come home to me, okay . . . ?Yeah, yeah, yeah. Tell him to fuck off, too. Love you. See you soon."

"How long this time?" I asked, really wondering just how long I would have to deal with a cranky Izzy before he got back. He hadn't come over last night, and only just returned her phone call. She had stared at her phone all the way through classes today and only half-listened to me ramble on about the lecture from this morning.

"He says just a couple of days." Her knee was jumping so I wasn't sure what the story was there, but she knew more than what she was telling me.

"Well then, sounds like it's retail therapy time!" I said as I got out of the car. "Ice cream is on me."

"And this is why you are my best friend, Kels," she said, slapping my ass.

We walked into the mall and sighed as the air conditioning hit us. I heard Izzy moan at the feel. "Air conditioning. The only way to live in the valley."

I took her hand, led her down the hall, and stopped in front of Creswells, the adult shop. I turned to smile at her, and she just shook her head.

"You have to be the horniest girl I have ever met," she teased. Laughing, she strode in behind me without hesitation.

"Well, when I find a man that I burn for, maybe it will be different, but right now, this girl needs a new toy."

As we were wandering the rows of dildos, I noticed a man in his mid-twenties following us. I poked Izzy and flicked my eyes to him. She didn't look up but nodded. She had noticed too.

"So, do I go with the purple one or the pink one?" I said, holding each up in my hand.

"For you? The purple." She smirked. "While we're here, you need new rope, too. The last time Vel and I used it, I sort of broke what was left."

"What!" I said, a tad too loud for the store. About four people turned around and looked at me. "Hey, y'all would be mad too if you just found out your best friend and her boyfriend broke the last of your rope."

"Fine, I'll buy you a new bundle." Izzy chuckled and shook her head. "You have no shame."

"When it comes to sex, Izzy, not one damn bit." I smiled back at her.

As we walked by a couple, they chuckled and murmured something about having to find out just what Izzy and Vel could have been doing to break the rope.

Looking through the ones they had, I noticed the man again. He wasn't much taller than I was, had brown hair, and was decently built, but not too much to look at.

I was bent over, looking at the options lower to the ground, when he walked behind me and ran his hand across my ass. I whirled around, fist ready to punch him, when Izzy caught it mid-swing.

Looking beyond her, I tried to find the creep but didn't see him anywhere.

"What the fuck, Iz?"

"You were the one about to take a swing at me. I should ask you the same thing."

"That was not your hand that just touched my ass," I ground out through my clenched teeth.

"What? No. I didn't touch you." Her eyes narrowed in confusion.

"I know. I know what your hands feel like, Izzy, and that was a male hand on my ass." I was still looking for the asshole, but we didn't see him again while we finished our shopping at Creswells. Once we checked out, I dragged Izzy toward the shoe store. "I need some new boots."

Natural Leathers was the best place to get boots, whether you wanted cowboy boots, dress boots, thigh-highs, or booties. If it was a boot, they were the ones to go to. They just launched an online catalog, but the store was much nicer. As I turned to look back at Izzy, I froze. The man was leaning against the escalator and boldly staring at me. "Izzy."

"I see him," she said, taking her phone out. After a few texts, she said, "He won't be a problem much longer. Now, let's go get you a new set of boots."

We shopped for hours without seeing Mr. Creeper again. She bought me my new boots and got a matching pair for herself. They were brown with embroidery on them and were instantly comfortable on my feet. She then promised that we could wear them to the bar this weekend if we did well on the Tibetan mythology test Thursday.

We were sitting at the restaurant, which was extraordinarily busy, when the server came up. "Whatcha girls want?"

"Iced tea, please, and could I get some yellow packets of sugar, please?" I asked as I stared down the two things on the menu I was trying to decide between.

"Same here," Izzy said.

"I can take your food orders, too, if you know what you want," the perky girl said. Her boobs bounced slightly too freely, and her short shorts were ones I owned and wore often. I let my eyes wander a little too long down her legs because, well, I was a perv. I could appreciate a woman's body just as well as a man's, and this girl had *it*. The other servers were dressed much the same as she was, but she was the one rocking it.

"Bacon cheeseburger, avocado, and waffle fries," Izzy said without hesitation.

"Predictable much?" I laughed and turned to the server. "Grilled chicken club, extra crispy bacon, side salad, honey mustard dressing on the side, please."

"Would it kill you to get a cholesterol burger?" She laughed at me.

"Not all of us have a sexy body without having to eat right and work out," I said, gesturing to myself.

The server looked me up and down and winked. "I'll get it in the queue, babes."

"I think she may be interested," Izzy suggested, waggling her eyebrows at me after the server walked away.

"Interested, but not interested." I sighed. Izzy gave me a look. "I dunno, Izzy. It's hard when everyone feels just, meh. I want someone to light me up from the inside. Make me crave every inch of them."

She smiled at me sadly, and I knew she understood. When we were in high school, she told me it was the main reason she had started dating Vel. He lit her up. Made her feel hot, wanted, and sexy. Said he still did to this day.

When the server came back with our iced teas, she handed me another drink, one I hadn't ordered, and said, "From a man at the bar."

"I'm sorry. I don't accept drinks from unknown persons," I declined politely.

"I can guarantee he didn't touch it, if that helps," she said.

"I appreciate that." I twisted around, looked to see who it was that she had indicated, and my stomach flipped. *Mr. Creeper.* "But I will not be accepting the drink from that man."

"Is there a problem?" she asked carefully. Her eyes flicked to his, and I saw her discreetly hit a button on her screen.

"There isn't if he leaves," Izzy said, her eyes narrowing.

"Ms. Edelmann." A man with muscles big enough that he looked like a mountain moved to stand before us.

"Jayson," Izzy said.

"What seems to be the problem?" Jayson asked.

"The gentleman in the suit at the end of the bar looking our way," the server explained.

"He's been following us around the mall," Izzy said quietly.

"I'll have him removed." Jayson's voice was serious and held a note of death that made me cringe just a little inside.

"Just escort him off property so Kels and I can eat in peace, please," Izzy said, sighing. "And don't tell Vel or Max, please. No need for either of them to go all alpha on him."

"Yes, ma'am."

I refused to look behind me as the security moved in that direction. Izzy, however, watched to ensure that the man had actually left the building. She was studying him carefully.

"Do you know him, Iz?" I murmured.

"I'll comp your meal, ma'am," the server offered with wide eyes and trembling fingers.

Instinctively, I reached out and took her hand. "Please don't."

"But you . . ." She hesitated as she looked between Izzy and me. "If Mr. Vispania hears of this, he will be furious."

"None of this is your fault. That creep has been following us all afternoon," I tried to reassure her, even going so far as to run my thumb back and forth across the back of her hand. Her breathing eased slightly at the comfort before she nodded and hurried off toward the kitchen.

"Gods, I hope Max doesn't get overly protective. He was just a stupid creep." Izzy sighed. "But Max tends to get extra alpha-holey when Vel leaves town."

"Well, he *is* Maximus Vispania, all things alpha," I grumbled. "Fucking asshat."

Izzy just gave me a look and smirked before looking back to the door Jayson had led Mr. Creepy through. We sat in silence for about ten minutes before I saw Jayson give us a quick nod, letting us know he was gone.

"Any idea who he was?" she asked.

"Nope. You?" I asked. When she looked back at me, I said, "You had that look on your face that made me think you recognized him from somewhere."

"Yeah. I don't know. Maybe . . . ," she trailed off in thought, then she did a one-eighty on me. "Anyway, what are we going to do about getting you laid?"

"We aren't." I glared at her as I drank from my iced tea. "Like I said, I think I'm going to take a bit of a break from people for a while. Hence why I needed a new B.O.B."

She laughed as the server walked up and handed us our food.

"Seriously, Iz. I'm just tired of the one- to three-night stands and then moving on because there is no connection," I told her, and then I reached over and stole a waffle fry.

"Hey, bitch, that's mine. You're the one who said she needed to keep her figure."

"Yeah, I do, but that doesn't mean I ain't gonna steal a couple of your fries."

CHAPTER 44

KELSEY

"Vel disappears sometimes. He'll get back to you," I told Izzy as we drove up to the bar. We had indeed aced the Tibetan mythology exam, so we were going to party it up before we had to dive into the origins of Christian theology.

"It's been eight days. He disappears for a couple days at a time, but never over a week." Izzy chewed on her lip. She was tapping her phone against her knee, and I slid into the last parking spot in the lot. "Even if he takes off for this long, he at least answers me. There's been nothing."

"You have Max's number. Call the asshole. If Vel was doing a job for him, then he should be able to tell you where he is or at least tell you he's not dead in a ditch somewhere," I encouraged, getting out of the car. She bent down when she rounded the hood and put her wallet in the small pocket inside her boot. "By the way, did I mention how fuckable you look?"

She rolled her eyes. "Thanks, but the only one I want to get fucked by has disappeared on me."

I looked her up and down and didn't resist licking my lips. She had this naturally sexy and elegant look about her, and I couldn't help but be jealous. She just threw her curly dark-brown hair up into a messy bun, making her hazel almond-shaped eyes sparkle in the lights. Because her mother was Egyptian, she was naturally sun-kissed brown. Tonight, she wore a short jean skirt, red crop top, and the pair of stitched brown shit kickers she bought the other day that matched mine.

We were like night and day. My white skin paired perfectly with my red hair and freckles. Izzy would tan if we spent any time in the sun, and I would be a lobster. Yay, European heritage. Tonight, I wore just a plain white tee with some jean shorts that barely covered my ass. I knew I looked good, but everyone would go after Izzy if there was a decision to be made.

"Well, I would do ya, but Vel may kick my ass. Last time I tried, he promised I could only have you if he could watch or join in. Guess I'll just have to find someone else." I shrugged, and she just shook her head and smirked at me.

"You've been on a dry spell, girl. Haven't changed your mind after our mall trip?" she asked as we neared the entrance to the bar.

"I don't know. Just seems like something is coming. I'm just . . . I can't explain it." I really could use a good railing. I'd been with my fair share of both men and women, but it was hard to have any attachment when everyone just felt cold to the touch.

Grandma spent plenty of time with me at specialists trying to figure out why I couldn't feel anyone's heat. I felt the pressure of their touch, but I just couldn't feel any warmth from them—that included my grandma and Izzy. My nerves worked fine. There was no neurological damage. To make it worse, there had been no other case anywhere that reported someone unable to feel the heat of anyone else.

I handed my ID to the bouncer at the door, who scanned it, looked me up and down, and licked his lips when he saw me. "Hey, Kels, if you don't find a ride tonight, come see me when you leave."

"Fuck off, Brandon," I said, laughing. I'd known Brandon since we first moved to Trenton. He'd even helped me get my job at the coffee shop a few blocks over. "Ridden that ride and not interested tonight. Maybe another night, though, okay?"

"Anytime, Kels. Always here for ya," Brandon said with a wink.

"Now, if you wanna ride Izzy?" I half-suggested, smiling at him.

The expression on his face as his gaze shifted to Izzy was comical. "Izzy, no offense sweetheart, but fuck no. I ain't crossing Vel."

"No offense taken, hun, but he'd have to be around to get pissed. If you see him, tell him his girlfriend is gonna cut his balls off," she told him a bit too seriously.

Brandon then motioned over to the metal detector. "Gotta run you guys through. Big crowd tonight, so the boss man is taking extra precautions."

"You know I got a knife in my boot," I told him, hands on my hips. Heat flooded over me like my own private hot flash, and I blinked, taken by surprise.

"And there's one in mine, along with the switchblade in my pocket," Izzy said.

"You gonna call Vel to get you vetted?" Brandon asked, crossing his arms. He knew we were good, but he had a job to do, and we had to bust his balls for it.

"Do I have to?" Izzy fired back. Very rarely did she ever use Vel's authority to get what she wanted. She had apologized repeatedly for using her connections to Vel and Maximus Vispania to have the creep removed from the mall and restaurant. I had just told her it was one of those times it actually came in handy.

"Thought you said he up and disappeared." Brandon smirked at her, and his eyes lit up with laughter. She held his gaze, but his moved past us, and he nodded his head before saying, "Go ahead, ladies."

I turned to see who he had nodded to, and when I saw him, my eyes narrowed. Maximus Vispania was leaning against a stairwell door in a dark-blue suit that had to have been custom-made. It fit every curve of his trimmed body.

He was drop-dead gorgeous. Six-foot three, maybe taller, with brown hair that was short on the sides, but long and curly on the top. Strong jaw, with just the scruff of a beard, which was without a doubt the biggest turn-on in men for me. I actually felt myself pulse between my legs looking at him, which did nothing but piss me off.

But by the Gods, he was a fucking Adonis. I tried to hide the gasp as he turned his bright blue eyes to mine, and a flame lit somewhere so deep within me, that it had never seen the light.

"What the . . . ," I breathed, grabbing Izzy's hand.

"What's wrong?" she said, swinging around to look in the same direction I was then groaning. "What is *he* doing here?"

My heart raced, and the longer he looked at me, the hotter I felt. *Why did this man's gaze make me feel like this?*

It was like someone had lit a bonfire inside my soul and it was trying to burn every ounce of rock-hard ice on the way out. The ice fought back, and it was the strangest mixture of pleasure and pain as it cracked.

I started shaking and breathing fast. It was impossible. *How could someone's gaze turn me inside out like this?*

"Kels, what's wrong?" Izzy's voice was full of concern, but I couldn't turn my gaze from his.

"I . . ." I couldn't say the words, but then his face changed to confusion as well. My gaze was still focused on him as the man's eyes widened and his arms dropped to his sides. His features had turned to inquisitive shock, and it almost looked as he had the breath knocked out of him.

Forcing myself to close my eyes in an attempt to shake the feeling, I took a deep breath. When I reopened them, he was halfway up the stairs.

"Kels, you're scaring me. What's wrong?" she asked, taking my face in her hands and forcing me to look at her.

"Izzy," I said, coming back around and seeing her in front of me. The heat had disappeared, and I felt somewhat normal again. My gaze flicked to the stairwell and then back to Izzy. Blinking, I shook off the thought that his royal alphaholeness had just lit me ablaze with a look. *Nope. I was mistaken. That wasn't Maximus Vispania. It was someone else entirely.*

"What . . . ?" she half-asked, confused. She stared at me then back toward the stairwell. Her brows knitted together. "Come on, let's get you a drink."

<hr>

We drank and danced for hours. I didn't see him again, though every once in a while, I would feel a wave of heat hit me. Sometimes, it would stay on my face, and at other times, it would trail down my body.

I was dancing with a particularly pretty blonde when I felt that wave of heat against my back so fiercely, it burned. I turned around to see where he was, but the blonde had just grabbed my ass and started grinding against me. Her hand slid into my pocket, squeezing me, but I excused myself.

When I met back up with Izzy, her phone buzzed a few times. She checked it and just stuck her tongue out at the message. I asked her who it was, and she just said it was a friend of Vel's that was giving her a bunch of shit. When it went off nonstop, she finally sighed and excused herself, saying, "I'm going to call him. Be back in a few minutes."

"I'll be at the bar. I need a drink."

She nodded and stomped off, disappearing in the crowd. It was only midnight, so we still had a couple of hours before we had to be out of there. I had no plans on going home anytime soon and half-wondered if Izzy would do a skinny dip run-up to the lake. Gods, it seemed like forever since we'd done that.

"What am I getting you tonight, Kelsey babes?" Sasha said, sliding up in front of me.

"Do I really need to be telling you that, Sash? You're the one who got me addicted to them."

"Oh, you are on edge. Alright, extra bitters on the pisco sour for my girl." He pulled the egg whites and lime from the fridge under the bar as I reached into my boot to get my card for him and felt the prick of something against my stomach. When I stood up, there was a business card in my pocket. A picture of the blonde I had been dancing with stared back at me, along with her name and phone number. Only, my eyes didn't catch on that, but where it stated the Coven of Moesia. *No way.* First of all, they died out centuries ago. The Dark Witches of Moesia didn't exist anymore. They had long since been lost to myth. Hell, what was known of them was little and ugly. Secondly, even if she was one, she wouldn't be so stupid to announce it on a business card, would she? I closed my eyes and shook my head. She probably just sold trinkets, saw the name, and adopted it, not knowing any better.

I slid the card in with my license, and when Sasha came back with my drink, I took a small sip, savoring the light lime flavoring and sourness. He waved me off when I handed him my card, saying he would just keep a tab running for me.

I'd been at the bar sipping my drink for about five minutes when a man with short-cropped brown hair slid up next to me. That wave of heat hit me again from above this time. I looked up but saw nothing past the mirrored windows above me. Whoever that was, whatever was happening, I wanted it to stop.

"Kelsey Stillthorn," the guy next to me said. When I looked back at him, his deep brown eyes were playful.

"What's it to you?" I asked, looking him up and down. He was nothing too special, wearing clean cut, nice jeans, a pair of sneakers, and a tight-fitting band T-shirt that showed he was trim, but not ripped. So not a total gym junky. Might not be a bad fuck, but I wasn't feeling it. Too bad for him.

"Your eyes are as green as grass," he said.

"What?"

"Your eyes haven't been green since . . ." He tapped his lips and smirked. "Not since you were a servant in the House of Tudor."

"I don't know how much you've had to drink, but I think Sasha needs to cut you off."

"No, Kelsey. I know more about you than you do." The man looked me up and down, and I wanted to pop his eyeballs out of his head. He licked his lips and ran his thumb across his bottom one before shaking his head appreciatively.

I shifted, feeling the reassuring weight of the knife in my boot. There were too many people here tonight for me to get to it efficiently, and I realized I really should start carrying something in my pocket, like Izzy.

"Again, what do you want?" Just then, the lights from the dance floor shifted over his face and I recognized him—the creeper from the mall. I felt my facial features harden. "Actually, just leave. Now."

"Why don't we head outside, where we can talk more directly," he said, his face becoming more serious.

"No, thank you. I'm good."

"You sure about that?" He looked up to the two-way mirror above the bar and smirked before he said, "Your whole life is about to change, baby girl, and I'm about to show you just who will own it."

"I'm not your baby girl," I retorted.

"You will be."

"Pass," I said, giving him a bratty smirk.

"Oh, that is yet to be seen."

"Again, let me be clear. Hard pass," I said, stronger this time, and stood up straighter.

He looked at me again and smiled before downing his drink. "It's nice to see you again, pet. I think we will be having a lot more fun this go-around." His eyes once again shifted up to the two-way mirror, and heat like a match had been lit against my skin burned through me as he smirked at whoever he was looking at.

Just who was he looking for? Who was up there?

Looking me up and down again, his eyes rested on my ass as he stood. "Yes. I'll be having much more fun this time around. Will enjoy playing with that ass, too. I'll be seeing you again very soon, Ms. Stillthorn."

Just as I saw him disappear into the thinning crowd, Izzy showed up and asked Sasha for a double. I raised my eyebrows at her.

"Not now." When Sasha put it in front of her, she downed it like it was water. "Another one, please."

"Izzy. How many is that tonight?" Sasha said, putting his hands on his hips that jutted out drastically. He was the most eccentric man I have ever met. I loved him to pieces, but he was not to be messed with. If you were one of his people, he would throw hands immediately.

"Tell Vel and Max to pay for the fucking things," she bit back.

Sasha reached over and hit one button on the phone, calling the manager on duty. After a moment, he said, "Very well, sir." He hung up the phone and looked our way again. "Guess all your drinks are on the house tonight." Confusion lined his face when he turned those eyes on me. "Both of you."

Sasha put another drink in front of us both, and when Izzy downed that one, he kept them coming. I knew Izzy could hold her liquor. Hell, I had never seen the woman lose a drinking contest. She could drink the entire bar under the table.

"Who was that talking to you just before I got back?" Izzy demanded.

"Just some creeper," I deflected, taking a long drink.

"Kelsey. Who was that?" she asked more sternly, staring me down.

"The creeper from the mall. He didn't give me a name. He came over and started talking to me." I shrugged it off.

"Did he know your name?"

"Yeah, but one of the bouncers probably gave it to him. Everyone who works here knows who I am, Iz. How many white redheads are in this room right now?" I bit back.

She looked up at the mirrors and let out a long, deep breath.

"Who's up there?" I demanded.

"Where?"

"Who's behind the mirrors, Izzy?" I crossed my arms over my chest. It was only a moment before I gritted my teeth against the heat that hit me then.

"Max," she said, letting out a long breath. "That's where I was. I was talking to Max."

"Did you find out anything about Vel?" I asked, putting my hand on her arm. That immediately dissipated the anger, but the heat was still flowing through me. She looked upset, and she never drank like this unless there was something wrong.

"Vel's fine. Talked to him on the phone while I was up there. Max actually wanted to know about you," she stated, giving me a critical look. When I said nothing, she continued. "Why didn't you tell me you *felt* him?"

"I've never touched the man, Iz," I said, deflecting again. She was the only one alive who knew that everyone felt cold to me.

"No. Why didn't you tell *me* that you felt heat from him?"

I looked at her. "How . . . How did you know that I felt him like that?"

"Kelsey," she demanded. "You felt him. You don't feel anyone. So explain."

I didn't know what to say. I couldn't explain it.

"It makes sense it freaked you out, Kels."

"I don't know what you want me to say, Izzy. I don't know what happened, alright? Of course, feeling the heat of someone's gaze freaked me out. You know how it is for me." Picking up my drink, I downed the last of it and then half of the next one, shaking my head as the lime hit all at once. "I don't want to talk about it. I want to forget it." I turned to Sasha, "Since his royal assholeness, Max, is paying, Patrón shot, please. Two actually." Sasha, bless his heart, just poured and handed it to me. I tipped it back and looked at my best friend, holding her gaze as I shot the second one.

As the liquid flowed down my throat, I felt anger with a touch of fear fill me. Max Vispania really was the one that had made me feel that raging inferno? Well, fuck. That was a huge hell no. I would rather stay in the cold sea than explore that with the man who literally ran the darkest parts of this city.

Her eyes narrowed at me. "Well, that isn't likely to happen. You have his attention now."

"I don't want it. Next time you talk to Mr. Maximus Vispania, you can tell him to fucking leave me alone. I don't want anything of his. In fact, I can pay for my own drinks." I reached into my boot, grabbed my credit card, and practically tossed it to Sasha.

"No, ma'am," he said, flipping his hand in the air and then pointing his finger at me. "No way I'm taking your payment. Boss man says he's covering it, so he's covering it."

"Take me home, Izzy," I said, growling in frustration. I threw back a shot Sasha had sat down in front of Izzy and headed for the door. Just before I got there, though, a wave of heat filled me, and I turned.

I could just barely see the outline of a figure behind the mirrors above the bar. "Leave me the fuck alone, asshole," I muttered under my breath, and then I flipped him off for good measure.

CHAPTER 45

MAX

I WATCHED HER THROUGH the mirrors as Bella confronted her about what had happened. Fucking Gods, what had happened? How did I feel her gaze like a flame-tipped spear to my gut?

I reached over to the row of buttons on the edge of the mirror and pushed one to overhear their conversation. I had microphones installed every few feet at the bar for our bartender's protection. Too many times, they had been accused of illegal acts. Too many times, my microphones had saved us from having our ass handed to us in the courts. That was when the judge wasn't already paid off.

"No. Why didn't you tell *me* that that you felt heat from him?" Bella said, downing her drink. "It makes sense it freaked you out, Kels."

"I don't know what you want me to say, Izzy. I don't know what happened, alright? Of course, feeling the heat of someone's gaze freaked me out. You know how it is for me. I don't want to talk about it. I want to forget it."

What did that mean? What had happened to her? How *what* was for her?

Kelsey turned to Sasha. "Since his royal assholeness, Max, is paying, Patrón shot, please." I huffed a laugh. His royal assholeness. Been called worse, but that was a new one.

"Well, that isn't likely to happen. You have his attention now," Bella told her. She was right, but I didn't know why. I needed to know everything about Kelsey Stillthorn. I knew the basics, like how old she was, her major at UC Trenton, that she had no one left in her life except for Bella. Knew all of that because of her best friend.

"I don't want it. Next time you talk to Mr. Maximus Vispania, you can tell him to fucking leave me alone. I don't want anything of his. In fact, I can pay for my own drinks," Kelsey said. She reached down and grabbed her credit card. I chuckled when she tried to hand it to Sasha. There was no way that man was going to take it.

"No, ma'am," he said, flipping his hand in the air and then pointing his finger at me. "No way I'm taking your payment. Boss man says he's covering it, so he's covering it."

A moment later, she downed the rest of her drink and three shots before she stormed out of the club. Just before she reached the doors, I flipped the mirror off, allowing her to see me when she looked up. I smirked and my cock twitched. Out of nowhere, I felt heat spear me in the spot just below my heart. My hand moved to cover it as my head cocked to the side. *There was no way.*

"Mine." My voice was a distant growl and commanding. I stopped short at hearing myself. I stared at her. Only once before in my long now immortal, life had that feeling ever flowed over me: the need to have her, to claim.

Looking back up at her, I smirked when I saw her flipping me off as she strode through the door. She was a fiery one, that was for sure. I half-smiled at her for it.

My phone rang just then, and it was Velarde. When I answered, he said, "Bella just texted. Said Kelsey—"

"Don't," I cut him off, rubbing my face to clear my thoughts. Regardless of what just happened, I wouldn't go down that path. "I don't know what just happened, but that woman is not my Sidonia." I had long since given up hope I would ever find her again. Changing the subject completely, I said, "What did you find in L.A.?"

"The rat was dead. Still had about 120K on him, so I've confiscated it for traveling expenses. And before you ask, no, I didn't kill him. He was dead with a needle in his arm when I found him. Seems he liked some of the harder street quality down here," he said, sounding a bit perturbed.

In a city the size of Trenton, we wouldn't be able to keep the drugs out, but we damn well could control how much got onto the streets. By some miracle, we were also able to keep some of the more deadly varieties away. Opium was just a way of life and had been for centuries. The shit hitting the streets nowadays, though, was brutal. One hit and you were royally fucked. Nothing else would meet that high. The ecstasy, the marijuana, the prescription drugs, those were easy to keep control of. The new variants of narcotics were getting harder to keep out of our alleys and back rooms.

"I ran into one problem. It's being handled, but just so you know, it leads back to Marcus." Vel's voice was tentative on the line, and there was some muffled discourse on the other end. He waited a moment, as if collecting his thoughts or allowing me to gather mine.

"Spit it out, brother."

"Some guys showed up as I was staging Sanchez's apartment." There was a muffled humpf, and Velarde said, "Damn it, now there is blood on my boots. You're buying me new ones, brother."

I chuckled. "Like I care. Get to the point."

"These guys here say that a man who only goes by Marcus, who they claim is a white dude and I quote, '*not some cholo*,' is taking something called nightwhispers to Sac." There was a muffled scream, and then Velarde said, "Tell him what you told me."

"Hernandez. He works for Marcus. Hernandez is taking it to Sac but said that Marcus was looking for someone. Someone in . . . Trenton. A girl. Said he had a history with her and wanted what was promised to him long ago," the voice said.

Fuck. What in the hell was going on? "Velarde, get what information you can about who this girl is and get back here."

"Yes, sir."

"And Velarde," I said. "Find out what the fuck nightwhispers are. I don't want any new designer drugs in our town."

CHAPTER 46

KELSEY

"Where are we going?" I asked Izzy.

"We need to stop by Vispania Tower." She winced when she said it. She knew I had a long-standing dislike for Max, but she was tied to him whether I liked it or not. "Sorry, Kels. I promise it will be quick."

When we walked in, the receptionist barely looked at us as she hit the button and the glass doors opened. People moved out of our way to allow us through, and when we got to the elevators, guests and staff alike just moved aside to allow us on without waiting.

"Why does it always surprise me that people just get out of your way like the building has your name on it?" I asked her as the glass doors shut. The entire north side of the tower was made of glass, and I had to admit that as we rose to the 12th floor, being able to watch the mountains rise out the windows was cool.

Izzy just looked at me evenly. "Are we going to have this conversation again? If Vel and I broke up, no one would think twice about it. I would be just like everyone else out there on the street."

"Give yourself credit. Vel ain't stupid enough to fuck shit up with you. He knows what a catch you are." I looped my arm around hers. "He knows he could live a thousand lifetimes and not find someone better for him."

Izzy squeezed my arm and chuckled. "Damn straight. Remind him of that when he decides to grace us with his presence again, okay? Right now, I'm still considering cutting his balls off."

I pulled her to a stop and acted like a kid on Christmas morning. "Can I hold him down while you do it? Oh, come on, Izzy, please?"

"Of course! I need you to . . . ," she trailed off as we heard a commotion at the end of the hall, then Maximus Vispania walked out of the second door from the end, wiping his hands off on a towel. There was too much red on that towel to be all his, considering how he was holding himself, but without looking up, he froze. I swore I saw the muscles in his shoulders tense from where we were standing. There was no way he could have seen us yet. It was almost as if he felt us standing there. Did he feel my gaze?

His head swung toward me, and there was nothing but rage in those eyes. I took half a step back. That fire in my chest burned again, and I took a slow, deep breath.

"I asked you to stop by hours ago," Max said to Izzy.

"Well, she was busy," I said, not able to keep my smart ass in check.

"Kels," Izzy said under her breath.

His eyes narrowed as he finished cleaning his hands on the towel and chucked it into the room behind him. There was a dramatic sigh from him before he shut the door and came to stand before us.

"Where is Vel?" Izzy said.

"Working," Max answered, then he looked at me. "What is your name?"

"Like you don't know, asshole."

His eyebrows rose as he looked at Izzy, and she just smiled at him. "She's not wrong."

"About which part?" I asked. "The part where Maximus Vispania is an asshole or the part that he knows exactly who I am?"

He was looking at me now with humor and exasperation on his face.

"Both," Izzy said, laughing loudly.

"Formally, I am Kelsey Stillthorn, Izzy's lover." I sighed. When Izzy choked a laugh, I said, "Alright, fine. I'm second to your best friend, Caleus Velarde. You know all of that, though. So, I'm not sure why you're faking niceties with me. You are Maximus Vispania, not only a billionaire from very old money but also the crime boss of Trenton."

"Crime boss," he said, his eyes glinting with amusement. The fucker was enjoying this. "I don't think I've heard that one before."

"You won't deny it," I said as he shrugged. "You take care of things for people. Just like you were doing when we got here. Who did you just kill, Max?"

"You are a bold thing, aren't you?" Max said, looking me up and down. The heat trailed that gaze and made me squirm in all the right, or maybe wrong, places. Izzy groaned and murmured something about me shutting the fuck up.

"Max, why did you need me to come here if Vel isn't here?" Izzy asked.

His eyes narrowed at her, and there seemed to be a silent conversation being had between the two of them, but she sighed. "When is Vel gonna be home?"

"When he gets home," Max said, as if he were holding back his anger.

"Don't be a dick," I bit back. He looked at me again, and my entire face bloomed with heat. I rubbed my cheeks. "Stop looking at me, please."

"Why, Kelsey?" Max said in almost a seductive tone. Gods, if anyone else had said my name like that, I would be a puddle on the floor.

My eyes met his, and I said back through my teeth, "Because I don't like how it feels."

I could have sworn I heard him say, "That makes two of us."

Pulling on Izzy's arm, I begged, "Can we go now?"

"Yeah. I'll meet you back at the elevator," Izzy said. "Let me have a quick conversation with Max."

"Wait," Max said, "Before you go, you said there was a guy following you at the mall the other day, right?"

"Yeah, how did you . . . Jayson. The bouncer at the restaurant." I rolled my eyes, feeling stupid at the obvious way he would have known about Mr. Creeper.

"Your lover here . . . ," he said, his eyes sparkling and the corner of his lips rising. Shit. It made him look like the sexiest man alive. There was that *thump thump* between my legs at that look. I blinked carefully and tried very hard not to pinch my legs together. "She said it was the same one that gave you some trouble at my bar."

"It was, but that isn't really your concern." I tried not to let on just how much that look had turned me on like a faucet.

"My mall. My bar," Max said in a tone that left no room for me mouthing off. "My best friend's girl."

"The creep harassed me. Not Izzy."

He shrugged, and I noted a few specks of blood on the crisp white shirt. He noted where my eyes landed and sighed. He took the shirt off, and Izzy made a show of how disgusted she was at him stripping before us.

I, however, noted each curve, each ripple in the definition of his muscles. Goosebumps trailed as my gaze studied those muscles, but my eyes settled on a single tattoo just below his heart. It was beautifully done, and I couldn't help but stare at it. Max hissed and jerked back a bit. He tried to hide it, but I couldn't take my eyes off that tattoo. Something about it pulled me in. The lettering was Greek. Ancient Greek at that. A really old dialect that was rarely seen anymore.

I didn't realize I was reaching out to touch it until Izzy's hand was around my wrist. I looked at her, stunned. "Don't, Kelsey Ann." Her voice was thick with a heavy meaning that I didn't fully understand. Not to mention, she used my first and middle name. She *never* did that. Lowering my hand, I looked back at the tattoo.

"Sidonia," I whispered, translating it instantly.

"Drop it, Kels," Izzy said. Her eyes went back to Max as he took a step forward. She put a hand on his chest and, without looking at me, said, "I'll meet you back at the elevator."

I nodded and headed back to the glass windows to wait for her.

I could hear them arguing, but I was far enough away I couldn't understand exactly what they were saying. The trees swayed in the distance along the edge of town as I crossed my arms over my chest and watched them. Max sighed and when his gaze flicked to me again, there was almost longing in that look. When he looked back at Izzy, I shifted my focus to the trees outside.

Who was Sidonia? Maximus Vispania had never had a significant other as far as I knew. The news would have been all over anyone he had taken an interest in. Who was this woman that he had cared for so much that he tattooed her name under his heart? Why did I care? I was so lost in my thoughts that I didn't hear Max and Izzy walk up behind me.

"You will have a security detail with you 24/7," Max said.

"What?"

"Guards will be assigned to you for your protection. That creep has found you twice and harassed you."

"And that's *my* problem," I said defiantly.

"And as you said, I take care of problems." The corner of his lips rose again, and damn if it didn't heat me in all the wrong places.

"I don't want your help."

"Well, ain't that too fucking bad. I'm taking care of the problem," Max said, taking my hand and practically throwing me into the elevator. "Now, Izzy will have your schedule on my desk by morning. Have a nice day, Kelsey Stillthorn."

The doors closed just as Izzy entered the elevator. I was looking at my hand that still felt like I had dipped it in a fire pit. I blew on it and shook it out.

"I tried to talk him out of it. He won't budge."

"Did you flat out refuse?" I asked, still shaking my hand out.

"Kels," she said carefully.

"One doesn't refuse Maximus Vispania. I know. I know," I said, sighing and giving up. My fight wasn't with Izzy. "So, what's first? Ice cream or the grocery store?"

It had been a few days of Vispania detail, and they weren't very inconspicuous about it either. On more than one occasion, the media had followed us, or me, shall I say. Today was one of those days.

I just got to work, and about twenty minutes later, a news team came in and up to the counter asking, "So what's your relationship with Maximus Vispania?"

Kira, my boss, immediately noticing my discomfort, came over. "Excuse me, please do not harass my employees."

"What is your relationship with Maximus Vispania?" the reporter asked again.

"There is no relationship. Please leave or we will call the Trenton PD and they can escort you out of the shop," Kira said.

Izzy showed up then with Vel, who had apparently just returned, and my current overseer, James. "Leave," Vel said.

The reporter looked Vel up and down hungrily before saying, "And what is your relationship with Kelsey Stillthorn?"

"Look here, bitch," Izzy said, her finger waving away in the air. "Kelsey is my best friend. Vel is my boyfriend, so you can put those eyes away."

"Izzy," I said carefully. Vel just shook his head.

"James, if you are going to be guarding me, please remove the media," I commanded. "I have a paycheck to earn. They don't pay me to deal with personal shit on the clock. I get paid to make coffee. So, unless you're going to order a coffee and pay for it, get the fuck out." I said the last part with determination.

Kira laughed. "I will take it one step further. Your business isn't wanted here. Yours or your coworkers'. No one from KMTN is welcome here any longer. You are to leave."

James and Vel took the cameraman and the reporter by the elbows and all but tossed them out of the coffee shop.

Turning to Kira, I said, "I'm so sorry, Kira. I don't know why they're here following me or anything."

"Are you involved with Maximus Vispania, Kelsey?" she asked, her eyebrow cocking up.

"Not in any way that you think. My only connection is through Izzy and Vel," I said.

"Then why has he given you a special protection detail?"

"Because he's a controlling douchebag," I muttered.

"He's being safe," Izzy encouraged, taking Vel's hand and threading her fingers through his. "Kelsey and I ran into a creep who has been stalking her a bit. Max has extended the protection Vel would usually give to me in these instances to Kelsey as well. Much to her annoyance, as you can see."

I narrowed my eyes at her. We had agreed not to tell anyone about the creeper, but we also both knew that there was more to this than what Izzy was saying, not that I knew everything, but she obviously did.

"Okay. Back to work then, Kelsey," Kira said. "But please keep whatever is going on between you and Mr. Vispania out of the coffee shop?"

"There isn't . . ."

"Regardless, Kelsey," she said sternly.

"Yes, Kira." I said.

"Thanks, Iz," I said after Kira went back into the office. "Any chance we can go out for a drink tonight, or are you going to be busy in the playroom with Mr. Muscles here?"

Vel groaned, and I smiled. "Or do I get to hold him down while you cut his balls off for being gone for so long?"

Vel's eyes turned to Izzy and sparkled with amazement. "You threatened to cut my balls off? Ahhh, how sweet."

Rolling her eyes but still blushing a little, she said, "Yeah, I'll be at the apartment tonight. He just got back and has to go fill Max in on everything from L.A."

"Okay. I'll see you about six then. I'll stop by for more ice cream and waffle bowls. Chocolate sauce or caramel tonight?"

She tapped her chin for a moment. "Chocolate, but I want the stuff that gets hard and you can crack it to pieces." I saw Vel and James both stiffen at that one.

Laughing, James took up position next to the door with a book, Vel leaning back in a chair a few yards from him. Thirty minutes later, James escorted another cameraman out. An hour after that, there were two more of Max's goons sitting at the coffee shop.

I apologized to Kira repeatedly all day. She tried to assure me she understood, but how could she when even I didn't. When I left, Vel and James both went with me to the grocery store, where I was followed all the way to the door.

"What do you need, Ms. Kelsey? I'll go in and get it for you while you wait in the car with Velarde," James said. I gave him the list and as he went inside, and Vel practically carried me back to the car.

Vel had physically removed two reporters from hovering around the car just so I could get in. By the time he was finally in the back seat with me, I was fuming.

"Sorry, Kels."

"Call Max, now," I demanded.

"I'm not so sure that is a good idea."

"Not a good idea?" I said incredulously. "I told him from the beginning that I didn't want his security detail. He has no claim over me, and there is literally no reason I need to have someone with me at all times. I can't even go to the fucking grocery store, Vel. Call. Max. Now."

"Kelsey."

I reached over and pulled his phone out of his jacket pocket and held it up to his face to unlock it. He frowned at me, and I stuck my tongue out at him.

Just as I was about to hit the button to call him, his phone rang in my hand. Looking down, it said, *The Asshat Brother*. I smirked at Vel and he rolled his eyes, slapping his hand on his face.

I hit the accept button, putting it on speaker phone. "Just the fucking asshole I was going to call. Thanks for saving me the trouble."

"Good evening, Kelsey. Vel, what the fuck is going on?"

"Your fucking detail has brought a plague to my life. That is what is going on. Do you have any idea how many fucking reporters that James had to kick out of the coffee shop today, Maximus Vispania? I'm going to lose my fucking job over it."

"You don't have to worry about money."

"I *do* have to worry about money. Not all of us can just come from generations of printing money out of our asses," I growled at him.

"I'll handle it." His voice was all dominance that even had Vel's eyes knitting together.

"You won't. I need my job, and I'm going to lose it all be-cause you insist upon having me followed by your security detail. Now the whole town thinks we're in this super-se-cret relationship and wants to have the breaking news for the day," I said. Vel was smirking now.

"The detail isn't going anywhere, Kelsey," he said, his voice dropping to a deathly low tone.

"I told you once. I'll tell you again. I don't want it."

"Has Vel told you how many times the creep has attempted to contact you since the detail started?"

I went deathly still and my eyes narrowed at Vel, who had the sense to tighten his lips and look slightly ashamed. "No. He hasn't," I said, my voice hard.

"In the last week alone, Kelsey, he has been deterred by that detail sixteen times," Max said through the other end of the line.

"Do we know who he is?" I said, my voice getting smaller, my heart racing.

"We don't," Max said as James put my groceries in the car and got in the driver's seat. "We are working on it, Kelsey, but the detail stays."

"Can you make a statement or something that there is no connection between us?" I said, trying to change the subject.

"Feel free to tell them that yourself. It's smarter if they believe you have the detail for reasons that are personally related to me than for the actual reasons."

"I have told them that there is no connection, that the only connection is because of Izzy, but they don't believe me," I said, grinding my teeth.

His voice was softer and more understanding than I had ever expected to hear coming from him. "And they won't, Kelsey. It will burn off. They will go in search of another story."

"My bigger problem is that they're disturbing me at work and I can't even go to the grocery store without being mobbed." I groaned, leaning my head back on the seat as James headed down Chambers Blvd toward the apartment.

"They stay. James or someone else can get your groceries for you," Max told me, and I heard James sigh dramatically. "I heard that, James."

"Sorry, sir. Yes, sir. Whatever Ms. Kelsey needs." I made eye contact with him in the rearview mirror, and he smiled brightly.

"Vel, after you ensure Kelsey is safe at home, get back to the tower. We have work to do."

"Fuck off, brother. Can't I have one night?"

"You can, but not tonight," Max chortled. It was such a genuine sound from him, it took me off guard. "She will forgive you. She always does."

"Not the point, asshat." Vel snapped and just reached over and hung up the phone.

"Detail stays, Kelsey," Vel said, smiling sadly at me.

"Doesn't mean I have to like it," I muttered.

"No. No, it doesn't."

"At least James is good to look at. You, on the other hand?" I lifted my hand and moved it back and forth a bit, and James burst out laughing as he pulled into the apartment parking lot.

CHAPTER 47

KELSEY

I WAS DRESSED IN Viking war leathers and strapped my sword and shield on. "Get the rest of the shield-maidens. We leave to retrieve Bjorn, Lars, and the others immediately," I said, striding out of the temporary structure we had built.

A woman dressed much the same, and looking a lot like Izzy, strode forward. "The boats are ready, my lady."

"Are you ready to retrieve Lars, Lady Bella?" I asked.

"I am, my lady. I will fight by your side to the death," she answered, standing proud.

I wasn't sure how this Egyptian woman and Mediterranean man had so firmly established themselves in our community, but they both had fought with the clan on more than one occasion. Lars had a brother south of here, but he never came to visit. Sir Lars and Lady Bella had been with us for ten years now, and while they talked of his brother, Maximus, often, I'd never met him.

Time flashed forward, and I was standing in front of a man with long brown hair and brown eyes that flashed with need and hatred.

"Come to retrieve your husband, have you, Freydis?" he said, jerking his head toward where Bjorn was. The whole place smelled like piss and shit and it was hot, which only made it worse.

"I'm not sure why you make me do this over and over again," he said, sighing, as he twirled his sword in his hand.

I cocked my head to the side. "I don't know what you are talking about, but I suggest you release what is ours before you know the might of the Bloovollr shield-maidens."

"What is yours?" The man laughed. "What do you know of what is yours, maiden? Is he yours? Have you borne him sons and daughters? Has he made you burn with need and desire? What do you know of what is yours? For years, I have worked to reclaim what is mine. Just to prove a point, I shall show you." He turned and gestured for one of his men to lead someone out from the back of the pack.

His head was down, which caused his hair to cover his face, but I heard Lady Bella hiss beside me. They lifted his head, and it was so swollen, bloody, and busted open that I could hardly make out any features.

The man turned to face us, smirked, and then ran his sword through Lars' chest. The scream emitted from Lady Bella was shattering. Each of the maidens behind me drew their swords and thumped them against their shields, showing they were ready for my order.

I looked at Bjorn, whose eyes were wide and distraught, just as Lady Bella burst past me and swung her sword, embedding it in his right leg. She pulled it out with a wet sucking sound before whirling around and slicing it deep across his stom-ach.

He collapsed to the ground, holding his stomach, but Lady Bella was not done. She put her foot on his neck and then took the tip of her sword, plunged it into the wound in his stomach, pulling the ropey insides out and onto the ground with a slosh.

"May Odin's ravens feast upon you this evening," she said, ensuring it would not be a quick death for him. Chaos ensued as the man's soldiers swarmed us.

Sometime later, Lady Bella, Bjorn, and I were kneeling before Sir Lars, covered in blood. Blood still ran down my face, and I could taste the iron tang on my lips. The taste of an honorable battle. As I looked around, I felt pride in my clan. There was not a single soldier left.

"Lady Bella. Do you wish us to give him a pyre?" Bjorn asked.

She stared at Sir Lars on the ground, eyes staring to the heavens.

"No. I will take him to his brother. Leave me a horse and we will make our way," she said, easing his hair back from his face.

"Do you wish an escort?" I asked, putting my hand on her shoulder to lend her strength.

"No. I must do this on my own." She looked at me, and her eyes were filled with an emotion I could not describe.

"Very well," I said, rising, and everything faded to black.

I blinked and rolled over in my bed. I ran through the dream that felt so real. There had been so many of them since last weekend, but why did this feel so much more important than the others?

Slowly, I sat up and took a deep breath. The apartment was silent, which meant that Izzy was still in bed or hadn't left for work yet. Neither of us had class today, and when I looked at the clock, I still had a couple hours before I had to be at the coffee shop for work.

I tiptoed through the living room, in case she was asleep, and looked out the peephole to see the two guards that Max still required Izzy and I have with us. Sighing, I knew I needed coffee, minimum two, maybe three cups, to deal with all that bullshit. When I got to the kitchen, I saw Izzy sitting there, staring at her coffee mug.

"Didn't realize you were up," I whispered, giving her shoulder a quick squeeze as I passed. She didn't react, didn't twitch, didn't so much as register I was there, so I gently put my hand on hers. "You okay, girl?"

She blinked quickly at me, clearing her thoughts. "Just a lot on my mind."

"Well, hopefully you got a better night's sleep than I did." I reached for the coffee pot to pour my cup of happy bean juice and asked, "Can you give me the creamer?" She handed me the bottle from the table without even looking. "I just woke from the most vivid dream. You know those dreams where you can smell and taste what happens?"

"What was it about?" she said, still half-distracted.

"I was a viking. A shield-maiden actually. Head of a clan that went to rescue my and a friend's husbands." I smiled. The bond I had felt between them was so strong. I looked at Izzy. "She sort of looked like you."

Her eyes narrowed and she studied me as I took a sip of my coffee after putting a bit more creamer and a lump of sugar in it. There was a knock on the door.

"Hold that thought," she said as she went to get it.

"Hey, sexy," I heard Vel tell Izzy when she let him in.

"You need to hear this," Izzy told him.

"Hear what?" he said as they both came into the kitchen.

Izzy blinked and turned her head to the side. "Tell us about it."

"Why does he need to hear about my dream?" I asked, half-glaring at him. It wasn't that I didn't like him. He treated Izzy like she was a fucking goddess because she was, but I hated what he did for a living.

"What is this about?" Vel asked.

"I was just telling Iz about a dream I had last night."

Izzy gave him a meaningful look that conveyed way more information than I could have ever deciphered from it.

I sighed. "I was a shield-maiden, and this man had captured my husband, Bjorn, and my friend's husband, Lars." Vel blinked rapidly and instantly became more alert.

"My friend was a woman who reminded me of Izzy. Her name was Lady Bella." I scrunched my nose at the name and giggled. "I remember when people in high school used to call you Bella. You would get so pissed and tell them to call you Isabella or Izzy. How many times did they end up with your foot on their throat for emphasis?"

"Lady Bella?" She drawled out the words carefully, but it sounded so much like I had said it in the dream. She stared off into the distance, but then, in a voice that I couldn't really place, she continued, "You had a dream of a woman who looked like me named Lady Bella? Was she Norse? English? Shield-maiden or other?"

"Other, I think." I thought about it. "I want to say she was Egyptian, but since she looked so much like you, I'm probably just inserting a familiar person I know."

She continued to study me. "What else happened?"

Vel had gone completely still. He could have been a statue for how still that man was leaning against the doorjamb.

"What? It was just a dream, you two."

"Kels. What else happened in the dream?" she demanded slowly.

"The man killed Sir Lars, Lady Bella's husband, we slaughtered everyone, and then Lady Bella took him to his brother south of wherever we were," I said, and when Izzy's eyes widened, she tightened her mouth as if she were keeping from saying something. "Seriously, Izzy. It was just a dream."

She slowly took a seat at the table again and looked to Vel. His eyes moved to meet hers, but he still didn't budge.

"Have you had any others?" she asked, shaking her head. "Other dreams that felt real like that?"

"Not any that felt that real, but yeah." I looked at Vel, studying him. "In fact, there was one . . . No. I'm not remembering properly. I'm just inserting familiar faces into unknown ones." I shook my head, taking a long sip of my coffee, but I still didn't take my eyes off of him. "That's what our brain does. It puts faces into our dreams that we have already seen. It's basic science." I was rambling and I knew it.

"Why are you still staring at me that way?" Vel asked, narrowing his eyes.

"Because it was just a dream, but you fit his description exactly," I said and turned my back to him. "It was just a dream, fucker."

He moved, and after I blinked a couple of times, he was leaning over the kitchen table, hands flat on the surface, staring me down, still as stone. If this had been when we were in high school, I would have jumped at how fast he was, but he had always moved quicker than anyone else I knew. With a voice he rarely used on me, he said, "Kelsey Ann Stillthorn, tell me now."

"Don't you fucking use my full name. You know how much I hate it. I will kick you in the balls so hard, Izzy won't be able to chop them off for a week because she'll have to wait for them to descend." He, at least, had the brains to wince a bit at that. He'd been back for a couple of days, but she was still pissed as hell at him for disappearing with no communication like that.

Backing away just the littlest bit, he asked again. "Please tell me about this dream you swear I was in?"

I sighed. "I need another cup of coffee if you're going to demand I retell every historical dream I've had over the last week and a half."

"You've been having more of these dreams?" Izzy asked.

"For the last week and a half?" he asked, his eyes flicking to Izzy and back to me. "It's been about that long since you guys went to the bar, right?"

"Yeah, but what does that have to do with anything?"

"Nothing," he said in a way that I knew he wasn't telling me everything. He shifted his whole demeanor, though, and teased, "Dream with me in it? Was I rocking your world, Kelsey?"

"Gods, no," I said, almost spitting out the sip of coffee I had taken. "You're all Izzy's. Now, if you want to share her? Then let's talk." I waggled my eyebrows, and even Izzy laughed.

"It was fun last time. Maybe we'll even let you watch next time, babe," she said, kissing him on the cheek.

Rolling his eyes, he said seriously, "Dream, Kelsey?"

"It wasn't much, really. Just, I was peering around a corner, looking at someone I cared for a lot. No. I think I may have been in love with this man, but his back was to me. I could feel my heart racing at the sight of him in front of me. He was talking to someone who looked . . . exactly like you in a . . ." I had to think about it a bit. "Pre-Alexander the Great, Roman Empire garb."

Vel got stone still again. I swore some of the blood left his face. "Where?"

"There were stone buildings, casks of wine, grain, and there was a giant mountain in the background," I said, trying to picture it all. I smiled. It was a happy dream. Even just the memory of it left me feeling good. "Don't you dare ruin any of it either. It's the best dream I've had in the last week. It was filled with so much love and hope. I don't want to lose that."

"Anything else?" he asked thickly. "In regard to the two people talking, that is."

"They had known each other for a long time. The one I loved had walked down to talk to a merchant and was asking about a scar on his neck or something, and then you two talked some more before I approached them. Well, the me in the dream obviously."

Vel's legs gave out from under him, and he stumbled as he took a seat in the chair, putting his head in his hand. "Hun, get me something strong to drink." His eyes bored into mine. He was looking for something.

"What are you looking for? It was just a dream," I said, looking between the two of them. "Why is this such a big deal?"

Izzy put a glass of whiskey in front of him, and as he downed the first one, she rolled her eyes and plunked the bottle down. He poured himself a full cup and downed it before he spoke again. "Kelsey, have you ever thought of doing past life regression?"

"No."

"Do you believe in soul reincarnation?" he asked carefully.

"Yes. Very much so. I believe that we have lessons to learn, and each reincarnation is a lesson."

They looked at each other and did that whole silent conversation thing.

"I have to get to work," I said before slamming my cup of coffee down on the counter. "They're just dreams. I'm a mythology and occult major. I live in history. Why does it seem strange that I would have dreams about the past?"

"Because you so adamantly swear that it was us in those dreams, Kels," Izzy said, staring at me the same way that Vel was.

"Our brains fill in blank faces with familiar ones. Every face you've ever seen in a dream is one you've seen before. It's what our brain does," I said, thoroughly confused and weirded out as to why my friends were acting so strange this morning. "Now, I'm going to get ready for work."

If they wouldn't have a straight conversation about what they were really talking about, then I wasn't going to have the conversation either.

Chapter 48

Kelsey

For three days, Izzy spent her days and nights at Vel's house. It was only a matter of time before she just moved in permanently with him. I enjoyed a quiet house, but I missed having her around. When I woke this morning, though, I heard her messing around in the kitchen. She must have gotten home after I passed out.

I had gotten up for work this morning and dragged myself in the shop after having dreams of fighting in one of the World Wars. There was a recurring theme showing up in them, though. Three times, a woman who looked like Izzy had been one of my companions, and twice a man who looked a lot like Vel had shown up. What was worse, the man from the mall that had given me the creeps almost two weeks ago was appearing in every single dream. Not in a good way, either. Each time, he was killing those I cared about, or abused me, or even, in one instance, had been the one to light the fire that then burned me to death. I had pieced it together yesterday on my lunch but hadn't told Izzy about it. She would have freaked out, and with Max's unshakable security, I suspected it was only going to get worse if I told her.

Max had been calling me nonstop to find out if the creeper was still bothering me, and I sent him to voicemail each time. Today, when I sent him to voicemail, he called Izzy, and she put him on speakerphone in the middle of the courtyard for everyone to hear Max Vispania scream, "Kelsey, when I call, you answer the fucking phone."

"Controlling asshole," I said loud enough for a couple of students to raise their eyebrows at me. I didn't care. It was no secret how I felt about his royal heinie. If he was going to scream at me for everyone to hear, they could hear me tell him to fuck off.

"A controlling asshole, I might be, but I'm trying to keep you two safe, Kelsey. So, the least you can do is answer the fucking phone when I call you." More than one person had given me a pitiful look as they walked by.

"I didn't ask for your damn security, I didn't ask for your protection, and I certainly didn't ask for you to become entwined in my life," I said through my teeth, trying not to yell in public. "Don't you have some criminal to keep out of jail or something?"

When there was silence on the other end, I reached over and just hung up on him. Izzy had looked at me for a good thirty seconds like I had literally lost my mind.

"What?" I asked, taking a sip of my coffee.

"You just hung up on Max," she said, shock written all over her face. "You just hung up on Maximus Vispania."

"I did. Now, can we get back to the notes for the Mayan cultures test this afternoon?"

Izzy shook her head and pulled out her notebook, but then she said, "Have you had any more dreams of people that look like me and Vel?"

"I have, but not that many."

"This morning, you were thrashing in your sleep and crying." Her hand reached out for me, but I pulled mine back. "What was that one about?"

"It didn't have you two in it. Didn't have anyone I knew in it." I felt my heart race as the details came back to the forefront of my mind, but I said, "Please, Iz, can we talk about something else? I'm not trying to just change the subject here. I really do need help with studying for this test."

"Okay, but you know if you need to talk."

"You'll be the first I go to. Now. Mayan cultures?"

"Mayan cultures."

"Hey, Kelsey?" John, one of my coworkers, said, popping his head around the corner from the back storage area.

"Yo!"

"There's someone out here asking for you. Pretty good looking too, if you ask me. If you don't want him, can I?" he asked, smirking.

"Horndog." I smiled. "Sure. But if I want him, hands off. Deal?"

"Deal!"

When I turned the corner, I hesitated for just a moment and steeled my nerves. "Hi. You were asking for me?"

He grinned, his white teeth fully on display. "Do you remember me?"

My heart stopped, stuttered, and restarted again. I balled my hands into fists to keep from shaking and tried very hard to stay professional. I wouldn't give anything away until I knew more about what the hell was going on, so I just said, "Unfortunately, I do. I wasn't nearly drunk enough not to remember that encounter. Nor was I drunk when you were stalking me at the mall. What can I do for you?"

John stood just outside of sight and gestured to see if I needed him to call the police. I shook my finger for now, indicating no, but I did have questions.

"I would like to sit and have coffee with the beautiful Kelsey Stillthorn," he said. "Unfortunately, today is the first day I've been able to get past your very elaborate entourage to ask for a coffee date."

"I'm sorry, but you have me at a bit of a disadvantage. I still don't know your name because you've refused to be an adult and give it to me," I said, crossing my arms and staring him down.

"I've gone by many names over the years. Let's just go with Dom," he said. "You get off in, what, thirty minutes? Why don't I take an Americano, black, a glass of water, and wait for you in the corner? You can join me there, where your coworkers can watch to make sure you stay safe while talking with a not-so stranger."

"Dom. Like Dominic? No last name Dominic?" I looked out into the courtyard and saw Vel keeping watch over me, as he had been since he returned.

Dominic shrugged but just said, "I'll wait in the corner. Get my coffee for me, pet? I'll wait for you there."

"I have people already waiting for me. How about never, okay?" I said in my best customer-service voice.

"Now, now, Kelsey," he said with a glimmer in his eye. "Why don't you just give me a few minutes? They can wait for you while we talk."

I studied him a moment longer and sighed. *Just let him say what he needs to say, then you can go on and get back to your normal life.* Maybe Max would finally get the constant guard off my back.

"Fine. I'll see you in thirty." I turned my back on him and asked John to get him his coffee.

Over the next thirty minutes, I saw Vel paying much closer attention to the shop while eying Dominic carefully. His phone was in his hands constantly, and a worried look crossed his face. Dominic didn't help matters by never taking his eyes off me. This guy gave creepy a whole new meaning.

After I clocked out, I noticed that Izzy and another man had joined him on the bench. I couldn't be sure, but there was a part of me that knew it was Max.

My phone buzzed, and I looked down to see it was Izzy texting me from outside.

Smeexy Bitch:
I'm waiting outside with Vel.

Kelsey:
I'll be a few.

Smeexy Bitch:
Why?

Kelsey:
Mr. Creeper dude wants to talk.
He says his name is Dom. Short for Dominic, I think.

Smeexy Bitch:
Max wants to talk to you.

Kelsey:
That's nice. He can wait.

I don't really want to talk to him. I have no reason to.
In fact, tell him to fuck off.

Smeexy Bitch:
Nope.
You can tell him to fuck off yourself.
He's royally pissed at you still for hanging up on him.

Kelsey:
Sucks to be him then, doesn't it?
Creeper dude will be no more than a couple minutes.
I promise.
Just wait. Keep your G-string on.

Smeexy Bitch:
Fine. BTW.
Vel's been trying to get a look at his face but can't.
Says there is something familiar about him. We'll wait.

I looked up to meet her gaze, and she looked really worried. I smiled at her and shot her one more text: *I love you.*

She responded without even looking down. "Love you, too. Always have, always will."

Taking a deep breath, I went and sat in front of Dominic. Crossing my legs and then crossing my arms over my chest, I said, "So, Dominic, what do you want to talk about?"

Dominic smirked and ran his eyes up and down my body. It gave me the feeling of being encased in a tub of worms.

"Please don't do that," I bit out at him.

"What?" he said, trying to be innocent.

"Look at me like I'm a prize or a snack for your enjoyment."

He giggled. "But you *are* a snack for my enjoyment. You *are* my prize."

"Do I get to just tell you to fuck off and walk away now, or do you want to tell me what you are so desperate to tell me, *then* I can tell you to fuck off and leave me alone for the rest of your life?"

"You always have been defiant. My father tried to teach you a lesson, but that didn't work out so well."

"I have no idea what you're talking about." The statement made me think of the dream Izzy had woken me from yesterday, though, causing me to shiver. He noticed and smirked, but I ignored it and said, "I think you have me seriously confused with someone else."

"Oh, trust me, Kelsey Ann Stillthorn." His voice lowered like he could intimidate me. "Like I told you, I know more about you than you know." His eyes flicked to where Izzy, Vel, and Max were. "Had any strange dreams lately?"

I blinked.

He let out a short, amused laugh. Then, when he spoke, the corner of his lip curved up. "You are remembering. Happens occasionally. Wonder what the catalyst was. Caleus? Maximus? Isabella?"

"I . . . I don't know what you're talking about. Just tell me what you want to tell me, then you can leave me Gods damn alone."

"That won't be any fun though, Kelsey. See, half the fun is tormenting the three out there that are so protective of you."

My eyes flicked to them, and I thought I saw Iz pull her switchblade from her pocket. Vel already had a knife in his hand, the blade lying flush with his forearm, hand firmly around the handle.

"Who are you?"

"I told you. You can call me Dom."

I narrowed my eyes. "Not going to happen because you are not my dom. Why are they overprotective of me?"

"Now you are asking the right questions, my pet." He smirked, drinking his coffee. "Because they have finally figured out what I have known for many of your reincarnations."

"My . . . reincarnations?"

"Those dreams you are having, Kelsey. Those are your past lives."

I blinked but then dismissed it immediately. "No. I just dream. There's nothing to it."

"You may not be ready yet to understand," he said, draining the last of his coffee. "But I have one question for you. Just one I want the answer to. Then I will get up and let you join your friends."

I stared at him as his eyes flicked to them. I reached over and took a drink of the water that was sitting there. There was a hint of sweetness to it, but I said, "First and foremost, whatever this conversation is about, leave them out of it. They have nothing to do with it."

He burst out laughing. "That is where you are so, so wrong. This has everything to do with that man you call Maximus Vispania. More importantly, though, it has everything to do with you." He paused, leaned forward, all emotion leaving his face and, with dead eyes, said, "And me."

There was a door that creaked open in the recesses of my mind that had me recalling all the dreams I had with the man sitting before me destroying everyone I had cared about. I could feel my hands shake as my mouth dried out, and I reached for the glass of water again, taking a sip. "You said you had a question for me."

He looked at the glass of water, smirked, and said through clenched teeth, "Just how many of those dreams you've had, have me in them? Am I the villain or the hero?"

The world splintered like someone had punched a glass window; it was spider webbing, and I was trying to look through it. I took a drink of the water again, closed my eyes, and swallowed hard, regaining my composure before saying with as much bravado as I could muster, "Those are two very separate questions."

"Fine. How many of them have I been in?" He glared at me. I saw something shimmer in his hand, and I took a deep breath, making it appear like I was thinking about it, but I slid my leg higher and reached into my knee-high boots, gripping the handle of my knife. I had taken to carrying it with me all the time, and this man was why.

"I don't really know how to answer that," I said, trying to make my voice sound small, but it wasn't totally an act. I was suddenly feeling very groggy, like I had taken too much allergy medicine.

"Answer it."

I flicked my eyes up to him and said, "No."

Rage and fury flashed in his eyes, and he repeated, "You will answer me, woman, or . . ."

"Or what?" I bit back, fighting against the need to close my eyes. "We're in a very public place. I'm sure each of my coworkers have a phone in their hand to call the police, and *if* my friends are as protective of me as you say they are, then I don't think you'll leave here alive."

"Oh, my sweet Si . . . Kelsey. I have died more times than I can count. You can't do shit to me. Take that knife you have your pretty little hands on and slice it across my throat. Let me bleed out here on this table. It will not rid you of me."

"We're done. You can leave," I said with determination. I felt my chest shake in fear, and I only hoped that my voice sounded strong enough and he didn't know just how much he'd gotten to me.

He chuckled. "We will meet again, Kelsey. You won't die on me this time. You will be mine." He rose from the table, put the hoodie over his head, and strode out of the shop. Vel's eyes tracked Dominic as he walked out, but Dominic made sure to smirk as he walked by me in the window.

I rubbed my temples and eyes, trying to shake the fuzziness filling my head, and waited a good three minutes to calm my nerves. My heart was racing, and I could feel my hands shaking. Izzy texted me repeatedly to see if I was okay. I had to get my nerves under control. It didn't help that heat bloomed across my back and had taken to just burning on my right shoulder. It took almost all of my concentration to not turn toward that heat. Every ounce of me was drawn to it.

I shook my head and rubbed my eyes again. I couldn't think.

Texting Izzy, I asked her to tell Max to stop looking at me, and a moment later, my shoulder cooled. I took a few deep breaths, and I was able to get my heart to slow.

What the fuck just happened? What did he mean I wouldn't die on him this time? Could all those dreams be my past lives? Vel had asked if I had thought about past life regression, but . . . I chewed on my thumb for a moment before I slowly stood up and headed outside to meet up with Izzy, stumbling occasionally. My legs felt like lead weights.

I was five feet from the three of them when Izzy lunged for me, her arms around my shoulders, holding me tight. I held her tight and didn't let go when she tried to move back.

"You okay?"

"No." My voice was shaking, and I felt so damn cold inside. How could that man have known? Every instance of him destroying the people in those dreams flooded back. I shook off the last of the images and held Izzy tighter for a moment.

She leaned back and put her hands on either side of my face. "Honey, what is wrong?"

"I . . ." Then I saw Max and Vel talking behind her, and I froze. Time wavered, and I saw myself in that street, Vel in a Roman uniform, standing with the man I had loved so fiercely.

"Tiberius," I mouthed the word with next to no sound, but Vel and Max both turned to face me, wide-eyed.

I cocked my head to the side. "Aren't you going to introduce me?"

My eyes met Max's. He took three long strides toward me, anger, hurt, and . . . fear in his eyes. His hand reached for my bicep, but then he hesitated.

"Do it. You know it's her. Verify it again if you have to, you stubborn fucking ass," Izzy said fiercely. At least that was what I thought she said.

"It can't be her, Isabella." The male voice sounded like salvation.

"It is the only way to know, Tiberius," Vel said.

"Tiberius," I whispered, my head turning slightly to face him. His blue, no—his sapphire-blue eyes pierced into mine. My heart swam in those eyes. My voice was distant as I repeated, "Aren't you going to introduce me?"

"How does she know that name? It hasn't been used in five hundred years."

Nothing was making any sense. I was so disoriented. My vision was bouncing between past and present.

But when Max's hand gently stroked my forearm, a vision of standing in a room telling secrets and a soft comforting caress flashed before me. Heat flooded me so fiercely that

I felt like someone had put all the suns in every universe within me.

I looked back at Izzy.

"Who am I, and what is happening to me?" I whispered.

Izzy's eyes were wide as my vision tunneled toward Max. His sapphire eyes were the last thing I saw before everything went dark.

CHAPTER 49

MAX

VELARDE LAID KELSEY DOWN on the couch in my office and put a blanket over her as I just stared at her.

When we got to Isabella and Kelsey's apartment to have her lie down, the whole place had been trashed. Someone had gone through and completely ransacked the entire place. What were they looking for?

I had about three different street crews looking into it. I wasn't going to let someone invade Bella's sanctuary like that.

Bella went with some of Velarde's most-trusted guards to pick up their things from the apartment while I watched over Kelsey. Velarde and I decided on the way back to Vispania Tower with Kelsey that both of them would stay at the 14th floor apartment until we sorted all of this out. Whatever that guy had said or done to this girl had made her hallucinate. It made her know things she should not and could not possibly know.

Now, I was just staring at this woman lying on my leather couch. The pull to protect her was getting stronger, the need to make her mine, but none of it made sense. She was beautiful, yes, but also fierce. No one had ever talked to me the way she had and gotten away with it. This girl. She cussed me out on the regular. She wanted to be independent. She *was* independent, in every essence of the word. She took care of herself and didn't need a partner. No, she was a woman who would only take a partner who could not only deal with her attitude, but also give it back to her in equal parts. She would make a remarkable wife to any man, but that person was not me.

So why the absolute need to have her, to protect her, to possess her? My very soul craved her, and it was total and utter bullshit. My soul belonged to Sidonia, and I wasn't getting her back. This *girl* was not Sidonia.

"Brother," Velarde said carefully.

"No," I spat. "This pain in my ass is not Sidonia."

"Tiberius, it's been two thousand years."

I turned to him, anger and rage flowing through me. "No, Caleus."

His eyes turned sad. I only ever used his birth name when things hurt too much. When we talked of *her*. "You know how much I want Sidonia back. It has been two thousand years since I held her in my arms. Do not give me that hope I lost long ago." I felt my voice crack a little at the end and cleared my throat.

He lowered his voice, looked at her, then back at me. He didn't back down. "What did it feel like when you touched Kelsey?" I glared at him. His eyes flicked to the redhead on the couch then back at me. "I have seen you unhappy for too long, brother. I will never forget the pure joy and hope you had in your heart on the day you wed Sidonia."

"Caleus," I said in a warning tone.

"No. I've never told you this, Tiberius. When I left your home that day, Sidonia looked at me as I crossed into the street and looked back. She saw me hold back the tears. I walked around the corner into an alcove and cried for you. I cried for your happiness. Of all the people I have known, you deserved it. You still do. It is why I have stood by your side for two thousand years. I have only truly cried three times in all my life, Tiberius. Now, to reiterate, the day you married her"—he pointed to the woman sprawled out on my couch before finishing—"was the first day I had ever cried. You were there for the other two."

I was, and I had cried for him as well. It had renewed my hope of finding Sidonia, but that had long since faded away again.

"I just can't. I can't have that hope again, just to have it all taken away, Caleus."

"I know, brother, but you need to answer me. What did you feel when you touched Kelsey?" I didn't look at him, but he knew what I had felt. "That's right. You felt her. You know it is her. Or at least what was once her."

"You have known her for eight years, Caleus. You never suspected?" I said, looking at her.

"No, I didn't. She's not mine. Even if I touched her now, I would not know. I caution you, though, Tiberius. If Kelsey is the reincarnation of Sidonia, she is not *Sidonia*. Kelsey is all fire and brimstone. Where Sidonia played by the rules of the time, this girl? She will tell you exactly what is on her mind and whoop your ass while doing it."

We stood in silence for a long time. As much as I wanted to sit here and deny I felt her fire when I touched Kelsey earlier that day, I couldn't. It was just as it had been that day on the beach when I first kissed Sidonia. The suns of Helios had burned into me again just with that simple caress that I had given her before she passed out. Had she felt it?

"She hates me." My voice came out smaller than it had in a very long time. "She has every right to. I am the asshole she claims. I deal in depravity all day long. I control the drugs on the street. I take care of difficult problems for people."

"Then prove to her you are more than your reputation."

My head turned to the box on the shelf. The sapphire shone brightly in the sunlight that came through the window. I let out a sigh as I took in the beauty of the piece of jewelry that had once belonged to my love.

"Prove it to her."

"Is the apartment ready for her and Bella?"

"Yes," he said and then turned to me. "Want me to carry her up?"

An involuntary territorial snarl came from my throat.

"For fuck's sake, Tiberius," he said, his eyes wide.

I took a deep breath and strode over to her. Kneeling before the couch, I took a strand of her hair that lay across the smattering of freckles on her face and smiled. There was a natural beauty about Kelsey. I had noticed it before when she told me off that day in the hallway, and fuck if it hadn't turned me on. I could think of nothing until I got back to the apartment and rubbed one out.

"Maybe I've known since that first night I saw you at the bar, Kelsey," I whispered under my breath. The night she had flipped me off, my cock had twitched at her defiance of me.

Sliding that strand of hair behind her ear, my fingers burned where our skin touched, and her head turned as if to be cradled by my hand. She mumbled something under her breath, and I sighed at the warmth that spread through my whole body.

Putting the blanket between me and her, I wrapped her up and lifted her in my arms and made for the elevator.

"Tiberius." She turned toward me, and my heart skipped a beat.

"You shouldn't know that name," I said quietly as Velarde and I got into the elevator. He pushed the private code for access, and the doors shut.

She curled up closer to me and rested her hand over my heart, right where Sidonia's name was tattooed in ancient Greek. "It's all going to be alright. I'm right here, Tiberius. We are together again," she said, moving her fingers along the marks. Not loosely, but exactly as they were in my skin.

I nearly dropped her. I would have if Velarde hadn't half-caught her as well.

"What kind of game are the Gods playing?" I growled, my eyes wide as I looked at Velarde, who helped readjust her in my arms.

"I don't know, Tiberius." He looked from me to her and back to me before he said, "But this is more than just you and her finding each other again. Whoever he is, this Dominic is involved."

We said nothing more until we settled Kelsey into the bed. There was only the Alaskan King bed in the apartment, but Bella had already said there wouldn't be an issue with them sharing it. They had shared a bed before, and even if Vel and I came to lie in it, there would still be room for all of us.

My eyes traveled up and down Kelsey, studying her, as I heard Bella come back into the room.

"Who is this Dominic?" I said, pulling my eyes from Kelsey on the bed to look at Bella.

"He's the creep that's been following her. All of us have been looking into him and he's a ghost." Bella said, running her hands through her hair.

"How did he get by you today?"

"I don't know, Tiberius," Velarde said. He was pacing, and he only did that when shit was really fucked-up. "Fuck. I'm sorry, brother. I messed up."

"You did, but here we are. At least we have some sort of name to go off of."

CHAPTER 50

KELSEY

We had been down here for about twenty minutes when I turned toward him and he kissed me tenderly. I wrapped my arms around him, knowing that he was right. No matter what, he was right. He was what my soul needed, and I would give a part of me to prove it.

"Sidonia." He whispered my name as a sweet caress, and I smiled against his lips.

"I like when you say my name like that."

He kissed me again, and I deepened it. A need filled me, and I felt him rattle against my chest with that same need. He lifted me up and then my toes were wet.

"What are you doing?" I asked, smiling at him.

"I have a very special favor to return to you for what you did on the mountain . . . and in the alley . . . and the other alley," Tiberius softly said against my jawbone.

As I slid down his body, I felt every hard ridge of him. When I felt his cock against me, I pressed against him, needing him. I let every ounce of heat show in my gaze as I stared back at him.

"One day soon, Sidonia," he whispered as if it were a sacred promise.

"Tiberius," I said as I threw my head back, and he kissed his way down my neck. "I . . ."

His hands threaded through my hair, and the command in it made my insides swim with need. His voice was shaky when he breathed out the words, "I know. Soon."

"Do you trust me?" he asked after a moment.

"Yes. Why?"

"Mind getting wet?" He smiled a bit wickedly. The double meaning in that statement had me smiling back with a mischievous gleam in my eye.

"I can swim if that's what you mean," I said, tipping my head toward the ocean. I tried to move toward the water, but he tightened the grip on my hair, and I couldn't prevent the moan that escaped me. I wanted him to pull it tight as he filled me.

"Where do you think you are going?" he asked.

"Swimming."

Moments later, we were naked and in the water. When he grabbed a hold of me, I squealed in surprise and turned toward him. The heat in his eyes was too much.

"Tiberius, my love," I begged.

"Hold on to me, okay?"

He ran one finger from one end of me to the other, stopping just short of my clit. My head fell back as he kissed my neck and circled my opening. I rocked my hips against him, begging him. I whimpered when he slid his finger into me and then used another to circle my clit again. Slowly, he fingered *me and rubbed that bundle of nerves, and I jerked when he increased the pressure there.*

I threw my head back in pure bliss. "Sidonia, look at me."

Forcing myself to do as he bade, I saw those sapphire eyes full of love for me as he pressed and tweaked my clit. Mother, it felt good, and I ground against him, forcing his finger deeper within me.

When he pulled his hand back, I whimpered and then growled when he didn't replace it.

"Not here. Not now, love," he said with what I suspected was the last shreds of self-control that he had. Just to show him what he was missing, I smirked at him and moved my hips so that my pussy slid up and down his cock.

His eyes rolled back, and I continued the motion.

"You temptress," Tiberius said through gritted teeth.

I rolled over to find my hand between my legs in a bed that was too soft to be my own. There were also too many blankets on me. I sat up quickly and scanned the room before I was even fully awake.

"Kels," Izzy said, rushing to the side of the bed. "It's fine. We're in the . . . Well, we're in Vispania Tower. The 14th floor apartment, to be exact."

The pounding between my legs was still clearly at the forefront of my mind, but I looked around and saw floor-to-ceiling windows that showed the expansive landscape of the city.

"Izzy, why are we here and not at our apartment?"

"After what happened at the coffee shop, Max carried you home, but when we got there, we found that someone had broken in. The place was completely trashed. They were looking for something, but I don't know what," Izzy said. "So, Max said we could have this apartment for now."

"I don't want that asshole's charity," I said through gritted teeth, but it didn't come out as vicious as I would have liked because that dream was still very much at the forefront of my mind. Grasping for anything that seemed normal, I noticed the bed was massive. "I mean, what kind of person has an Alaskan King bed in an apartment? Who has an apartment like this anyways?"

"I'm going to go out on a limb and say that Max does." She smirked at me, and I rolled my eyes. "No one lives here. Vel's is just a floor up, and Max's is on the 16th floor."

I studied her for a long moment before she said, "What were you dreaming about just before you woke up?"

"I was having a dream about a woman named Sidonia and her lover Tiberius." I shrugged. "It was getting pretty hot before you woke me up. So, unless there's a vibrator in here that I can use finish myself off or you're gonna do it for me, I'm going to jump in the shower and clean up."

"Always trying to get in my pants, aren't you, hun? Bathroom is there to the right." Izzy was smiling as I crawled to sit on the edge of the bed. She kissed my cheek before saying, "Not that I'm complaining because you are a good fuck."

"But . . . Vel." I winked at her. While I wouldn't mind sharing her bed often, I thought it was sweet and enduring how she was trying to stay monogamous to him now. They had discussed it, and any future sex outside of their relationship would have to be expressly consented to beforehand. I loved her, but I didn't want that kind of relationship *with* her.

"What about me?" Vel said, coming into the oversized bedroom.

"Nothing. Private discussion." I sighed.

He leaned down and kissed Izzy, and my heart warmed for them. They were so madly in love with each other. I wanted that for myself, but I was too much of a slut, and my life wasn't a love story. Hell, if those dreams were my past lives, it was proof they weren't a romance novel.

I felt Max before I saw him standing just outside the bedroom door, and it almost killed my mood, but I just turned to Izzy and said, "Now, if you don't mind, I'm going to go shower and give myself a massive orgasm after that dream I had."

Behind me, I heard Vel choke a little before asking, "And did she tell you what dream she had?"

"Apparently, a real steamy one with Tiberius and Sidonia," she said, chuckling. It didn't escape my notice she had been looking at Max when she said it.

Just before I closed the bathroom door, I heard Vel's laughter and Max punch the wall. Well, it was his wall to repair.

Twenty minutes later, I came out in pjs and a towel around my head to find Vel cooking and Max, indeed, repairing the wall. I raised my eyebrows at Izzy, who smirked and handed me a beer.

Twisting the top, I took a long drink as I glared at Max standing there. I couldn't exactly tell him to get the fuck out when it was technically his apartment.

While taking another long drink, I couldn't help but let my gaze travel across his jawline, down his chest, and back up to the strong nose and sexy as sin lips, all so similar to the man in my dreams. I was mid-drink when my focus was back on those piercing sapphire-blue eyes. They had a dulled spark that I had a feeling would burn brightly again for the right person. It was then that I saw both men, the one standing before me and the one in my dreams, superimposed over each other, and realization hit me with the force of a hurricane. I sputtered and took two large steps to the sink to keep from spitting beer all over the kitchen floor. Everyone turned to look at me. I put the bottle in the sink and backed away as quickly as I could.

"No," I said, my heart racing. My breathing picked up, more and more dreams of him flooding my mind as I just kept whispering, "No. No. No."

"Kels, what is wrong?" Izzy asked.

"No. There is no way." My head was shaking back and forth as fast as I could. I pointed to Max, took a couple steps back, and said, "No. No. Way. There is no . . . That cannot possibly be."

Vel looked between us, and something clicked for him as Max hung his head and pinched the bridge of his nose.

"Kels." Izzy's voice was careful and tentative as she came up to me and turned me so my back was to both of the guys. "What can't possibly be?"

My eyes were wide as I turned to look at Max again. Then I looked at her with a murderous rage that had my hands balled into fists. There was way more going on than what was being told to me.

"Vel, honey, I'll finish up dinner. I think it might be best if you two leave," she said, not taking her eyes off mine.

"No. We aren't leaving you two unguarded," Max said evenly.

I turned toward him, took a knife out of the block on the counter, and chucked it. It missed him by inches and landed with a clear *thunk* in the wall.

His head turned to look at it, and Vel whistled. "Girl got good aim. That's hot."

Max growled in warning as Vel and Izzy chuckled.

"I'll fix that hard-on in your pants later, Vel, with Izzy's permission, of course. Maybe she'll just join us," I said, trying to bring down my temper. Humor. It was the best way to calm my ass down. As long as Max didn't say anything, as long as I kept my eyes off him, I would be okay. The heat from his stare was not helping, though.

Whatever it was on the stove started to burn, and Vel turned and said, "Well, grab your shit and get some clothes on, Kelsey. Guess I'm taking you out to eat."

I raised my eyebrows and waggled them a bit.

"Slut," Izzy said as I felt a raging heat wave barrel into me.

My eyes met Max's again, and I still couldn't believe it. I took another very deep breath to keep the panic at bay. "I have one question."

Max gulped but nodded.

"And don't you dare think of lying," I said, taking another knife from the block. Vel and Izzy stepped back, but Max stood his ground.

I flipped the knife a couple times in my hand. How was I going to ask the man staring back at me how he looked exactly like Tiberius in each of my dreams?

His eyes narrowed, as if he knew exactly what I was going to ask. "Ask me, Kelsey. Go ahead. Ask me."

Staring at him a moment longer, I felt my lips tighten as I tried to restrain myself. When there was a glint of humor in his eyes, I flipped the knife in my hand one more time before I said, "Why do you look exactly like Tiberius in each of my dreams?"

"Oh, fuck," Vel said slowly. While he had figured it out, I didn't think he expected me to ask it so directly. "Kelsey, you don't want that answer right now. You are not ready for that."

"I didn't fucking ask you, Vel. Stop running interference for him," I said through gritted teeth. "Now, Max, answer me. Why do you look *exactly* like Tiberius in my dreams of him and Sidonia?"

"Velarde is right. You are not ready for that answer," he said, but there was an emotion in his voice that I couldn't place. His throat bobbed, and I didn't know why it hit me in the chest so hard, but it did.

"I'm not ready for the answer, or you aren't ready to give it to me?" I held his stare. Fire raged within me. I could feel him, and that alone connected us in a way I needed to know answers to. There was so much more going on, and no one was telling me anything. Even Izzy knew and was saying nothing.

His Adam's apple made another distinct movement in his throat, and when he didn't answer me, I let the other knife fly. It landed on the other side of his head. He hadn't even twitched.

"Holy fucking Gods," Vel and Izzy said together.

"So many fucking secrets." I turned on my heels and headed back to the bedroom to change. "There are too many fucking secrets in this apartment, and *I'm* the ignorant one?"

While in there, I sat on the bed for a hot minute, trying to calm my racing heart. It was purely impossible. There was no way that he could look exactly like Tiberius. Even if there was an ancient bloodline, the dreams I had of Sidonia and Tiberius were from about two thousand years ago, give or take a hundred years, but there would be too much diluted blood for him to look . . . exactly . . .

"What the actual fuck is happening?" I said in frustration as Izzy came into the bedroom.

"Kelsey," she said, trying to placate me.

"You know, Iz, and you aren't telling me. Why?" I got up and headed for the closet to change. Why was my best friend keeping secrets from me? A huge fucking secret at that.

My stomach growled, and I stomped my foot in frustration. I was hungry, but I was also hungry for answers. Izzy chuckled behind me, and I glared at her over my shoulder.

I slipped on a pair of jean shorts and a black T-shirt and grabbed my brown stitched boots. Izzy, or maybe Max or Vel, brought over most of my clothes and shoes. Not that I had a ton, but it was nice not to have to worry about what I was going to wear while being caged here. I ran my fingers through my hair, so it didn't completely look like I just got out of the shower, and sat on the bed to put the boots on.

Izzy's tone changed. "I'm sorry."

"Why?" I asked. "What part of all of this are you sorry about? The part where Vel burned dinner? Or the part where Max won't tell me why the man I keep having sex dreams about looks exactly like him? Or, I know, how about how you have at least an idea of what this is all about, or know exactly what this is about, and won't Gods damn tell me."

She came over and knelt before me. I heard the guys in the other room having an angry discussion, and I felt the heat of Max's stare as I looked up to see him standing just behind Vel in the doorway a few feet away. I glared at him as he murmured something to Velarde. The look on his face, though, was worrisome and full of . . . grief and fear. I pinched my eyebrows for a second, trying to figure it out, before the anger filled me again when Izzy's hand rested on my knee.

"Kels Bells," she said, bringing my attention back to her. "I can't because it isn't my story to tell." She looked over her shoulder and narrowed her eyes at Max. "It's Max's, and he better fucking step up soon."

"How long have you known about whatever this is?" I asked, looking at my fingers.

"I suspected when you first told me of the shield-maiden dream, and when you told me others, Vel and I went to Max," she said. "I'm sorry I betrayed you by going to him. I know you hate him and most of what he stands for in the public eye."

"I realize he is an extraordinarily intelligent man who runs a very successful legit company. I understand that the company has dumped more money into the Trenton Children's Hospital than anyone else, and that they use most of that money to help the families. I know he does good things through his legit business, but it doesn't excuse the rest of the bullshit." I got up to pace the room. "He does little to help the public directly. He controls all the underground. Pays off people so they don't have to go to jail. He controls the drug runs in this town. Probably runs most of the elections to ensure the right people end up in office. The shit I've heard of him doing? He came out of the fucking room the other day covered in blood, and when I called him on it and asked who he killed, he just avoided the question. How many has he killed? Too many to count, I would guess. He's a half-step short of a crime boss, Iz."

She looked to where Max just stood there, staring at us.

"He is here, Kels," she breathed. "I can't tell you why, but he is here for you. Not for me or Vel. For you, Kelsey. He's trying to make sure you're safe because whatever that guy did to you yesterday, it was bad."

"Yesterday?" I said, stopping in the middle of the room. "I slept for almost an entire day?"

"Yeah. Since then, Max has had people looking into who that Dominic guy could be and what he might have given you to make you pass out like that."

Vel was standing at the bedroom door now and said, "We can't tell you everything, Kels, but in the face of truth, he's actually been looking into him since that night at the bar when he approached you."

"So, since the night there was some sort of strange connection between Max and me?" I stormed by Vel and went to stand toe to toe with Max. He took two steps back until his back was against the hallway wall across from the doorway. Gods, he was even more handsome up close. There was a deep woodsy smell that reminded me of a campfire, and it made my toes curl.

An unnatural impulse had me reaching up and running my hand along his brow and down to his cheekbone, where he grabbed it. There was a sad shadow that crossed his face then. I looked at my hand, his fingers gently wrapped around mine, and I could have sworn it burned with a raging fire in it. His gaze followed mine.

I shook my head to clear the thoughts. "Is he wrong?" I whispered but didn't move to pull my hand from his.

"What?" His voice was hoarse, like he had to bring himself back from wherever those shadows had taken him. He returned his focus to my face, and I watched as it danced across my features before he met my gaze.

"You started looking into the guy from the bar after that night?"

He nodded, not taking his gaze off of mine.

"That was the night that you felt . . . it too, didn't you?"

He didn't move.

"Answer me, please," I said as angry tears formed in my eyes. One fell, and his other hand reached up to catch it.

"Yes. I felt it that night," he said, wiping away the tear and pulling his hand back. I could swear it was trembling slightly.

"And you won't give me answers," I said, staring at his chest.

"Not yet," he breathed, but I could just barely see his lips as they wobbled with the words. I knew he was staring Vel and Izzy down as he said them.

I took a long, deep breath, stepping back.

I looked up at him and waited for him to look at me. There were silent conversations happening between him and Vel, and when he looked away from them and back to me, shame lined his face.

I was lost in his eyes and realized I wanted to kiss him to wipe that expression off his face. But when his hand raised to touch my face again, I stepped away from him. My cheek still burned from where he caught the one tear that had escaped.

"I don't like you, Max," I said, trying to build some sort of wall between us. I was drawn to him. There was a pull other than this heat between us, and I wanted it. Damn, I wanted it, but I didn't like him. I didn't understand what was happening here, but I couldn't allow him to get too close until I knew the truth.

His face fell slightly at my words.

"I heard what you told Bella in the bedroom," he breathed.

"Bella?" I blinked and turned to look at Izzy. "Can I throw him to the floor so you can put your boot to his neck, or do you want the pleasure?"

She winced.

She actually winced. Vel gave her shoulders a small squeeze.

"Max has been calling me Bella for longer than I've known you, hun," she said, her voice cracking with the pain of saying the words. Her eyes were lined with tears, and I saw a lifetime of pain in them.

A huff of air burst from my chest at the weight of what was happening before me. I backed up from everyone and looked around the room.

"There are a lot of secrets in this room. Too many fucking secrets." I was holding myself back from crying at this point. "Izzy, you're the one person I've kept nothing from. Gods! You even know how I can't feel anyone's heat. Not until . . ." My gaze flicked to Max and back to her. "Izzy, you were the one person who I thought wouldn't hide anything from me."

"Kelsey." She was crying now and looking to Vel and Max for help, but neither of them said a word. "You fucking assholes. What I keep from her is just to protect you two."

"Where are my keys? Is my car even downstairs?" I asked, starting to frantically look around the room. I needed to get out of here.

Izzy tossed them to me, and I headed for the door. Max stood there. "You aren't leaving without us."

"Over my dead body are you going to boss me around. I don't care who you fucking think you are."

"I am trying to keep you safe," he said, grabbing my arms to move me back.

"Watch your . . ." I heard Izzy say as my knee met his groin and he bent over in pain. "Dick," she finished, saying it through a chuckle.

Grabbing my keys from the ground, I walked out the door. Izzy reached me just as I got in the elevator and slid in just as the doors closed, Vel and a limping Max a few feet behind her.

"Izzy," I said, grinding my teeth, "I really don't want to hear it."

"I know. I grabbed Max's wallet. We're going to dinner on his dime. I'll answer whatever questions I can."

CHAPTER 51

MAX

DAMN, THAT GIRL HAS a leg on her. It's been a long time since someone was brave enough to knee me so fully. I was still bent over as Bella grabbed my wallet from my jacket and raised an eyebrow at me.

"Go," I croaked out. "Make amends. The Rose. I don't care what the fucking meal costs."

Izzy took off down the hall as Vel helped me to my feet.

"Man, it's been a hundred years since I've seen that." He laughed.

"Fuck off," I groaned.

"Come on," Vel said, but I grabbed his arm.

"No. Let Bella settle her down first. She trusts her the most out of the three of us," I said. "We will just make it look like we tried to catch up."

Vel pulled me into the hall, and we were almost to the elevator before it closed. Spotting us, Kelsey flipped me off as Bella stuck her tongue out at me.

I bent over and continued to breathe through the pain. I really had forgotten how much that fucking hurt. Vel stood there snickering, so I swung around and nailed him square in the balls.

"Fucking . . . piece . . . of . . . Tiberius . . . you . . . mother . . . fucker!" he spat out as he fell to the floor.

"Teaches you to laugh at my pain." I chuckled, sliding down and sitting on the floor with him.

When he stopped gasping for air, he asked, "Should we follow the girls?"

"Yeah, we will in a moment. I'll let you get your legs under you again." I laughed. "Bella is heading to The Rose. I kind of told her I didn't care what dinner cost."

"Gods, I'm glad we set up code phrases," he said, leaning his head back against the wall.

It was quarter to eight when we pulled up to The Rose. The girls had been gone for about an hour, and I was sure they had at least a few drinks in them by now.

When the hostess saw us, she nodded in the direction she had sat them, and when I pulled a chair around to sit next to Kelsey, Bella's eyes narrowed. Vel sat next to Bella and said, "So, what did you order us?"

"I'm sorry, Izzy. Do you hear some annoying buzzing?" Kelsey said as she took a long drink, pointedly ignoring me.

I smirked, and I saw Bella's eyes light up.

I sat down next to Kelsey, leaned back, and brazenly looked her up and down. I could see her body reacting to my gaze, and I would be lying if she didn't turn me on with the most innocent of her looks every time I saw her. I may not be willing to fully accept what this all could mean, but whatever this connection was, it was real. The thought both terrified and excited me. Kelsey was not Sidonia. I knew that. Hell, she proved that tonight with the knee to my balls.

"Are you done, asshole?" she said under her breath. She had never even glanced at me.

I leaned forward, closer to her, and, in a husky voice I hadn't used in two thousand years, said, "I'm not sure. Are you still pissed at me?"

Her eyes fluttered, and I swore I saw her cross her legs a little tighter. I smirked and sat back. The server came by, and I told him to get my usual and Velarde did the same. Minutes dragged by, and the tension between the two of us increased as she tried to ignore me and talk only to Bella. It wasn't too long, though, before our food came out with theirs.

There was more than the tension between Kelsey and I in the air, so while we ate, I kept an eye out for anything unusual. As we finished up, Kelsey's focus zeroed in across the room, and she sat up straighter, slowly lifting her leg. The movement had it sliding against mine, and the ache to grab ahold of it and lay it over my lap was so strong, I had to ball my hands into fists. Her knee ended up resting on my lap as she moved to grab the knife from her boot. I didn't resist this time and laid my hand on her knee and rubbed my thumb against it. Her breathing hitched, and her eyes flicked to mine before they refocused on something across the room. I followed her gaze and cursed.

Slowly, Velarde and Bella turned to see who it was, and Velarde flat out said, "Well, fuck."

We watched him as he made his way through the dining tables, shaking hands with the various politicians that were in the room. Once he had passed, each of them looked at me with pleading, terror-filled eyes.

"Well, isn't this a surprise? The entire family is finally together." His voice was full of all the maliciousness that his grin projected.

"What in the fuck do you want, Dominic?" Kelsey said. There was something about his voice that reminded me of someone from our past. My brain flew backwards in time.

"I said to call me Dom," he demanded of Kelsey then winked at me. And I *knew* when he said, "I'm just glad to see everyone back together."

"Marcus," I growled. There was something familiar about the face, but I couldn't quite place it.

"Dom, Marcus," he said, moving his head from side to side. "All the same person."

Clear recognition spread across Velarde's and Bella's faces. My attention slid to Kelsey, and she studied him for a long minute before her gaze shifted to Velarde and then to Bella.

"Are you fucking kidding me?" she said in horror, then she narrowed her eyes as she looked at Vel, who had the good graces to wince.

"Kelsey has been remembering, hasn't she? Let's see, which lifetime has she placed me with," he said, tapping his temple. There were two guards behind him, both packing. Sloppy. There was no attempt at hiding them.

Sitting this close to Kelsey made it easy and natural to wrap an arm around the back of her chair. I leaned forward to whisper in her ear. She tensed but then realized the appearance I was trying to portray and leaned into me. Forgetting what I was going to tell her, I gave her a chaste kiss on the cheek.

Slowly, under the table, I moved my hand from her knee to rest it on top of the hand that she had gripped tight around the handle of her knife. She gripped it tighter, and when I squeezed her hand, she released the knife to give it to me.

Marcus rested his hands on the back of the vacant chair and leaned against it, making eye contact with Kelsey and smirking. "Let's start off with the most current, shall we? The whole of this story, to be told later, with the grand reveal being so very glorious."

"Rachana Rajbanshi, commander of the Nepal forces." He listed off more and more names, and my veins ran cold at just how many lifetimes Marcus had been involved in with Kelsey, who had gone stone still. She was trying not to react, but her fingers twitched occasionally as she identified these names as being her own. When he smirked and looked to Vel and Bella, I flinched.

"I know which one you all will remember: Fenryis of the *Bloovollr shield-maidens*," he said with a gleeful remembrance that made me go back in time. *Velarde and Bella had gone to the north. When they had . . . I turned to Kelsey. They had gone and spent time with the fiercest shield-maiden of the time.* Kelsey had reincarnated into Fenryis of the Bloovollr? Holy fucking shit.

Kelsey had gone exceptionally still at that name, except for the death grip she had on my arm. I hadn't even realized she had grabbed it. I blinked and looked at her, then at Vel who gave me the smallest of nods.

Fenryis of the Bloovollr. The Shieldmaiden. Bella had told us Kelsey had dreamed about a shieldmaiden, but hadn't mentioned a name. Holy Gods, Kelsey remembered her life as Fenryis of the Bloovollr.

"How?" Kelsey asked. Her eyes flicked to me, then back to Marcus.

"I believe you remember how I slaughtered one, Sir Lars," he said, putting his hand on Vel's shoulder.

"Shut up, Marcus," I warned. He was going to itemize this out in detail, wanting to hurt Kelsey, and that was only going to happen over my dead body.

He smirked at me, but his gaze flicked to Bella before he said, "Now his wife. She was pretty pissed when I ran that sword through Sir Lars. Sliced my gut open and left me for . . . Odin's ravens? I believe it was?"

I took Kelsey's knife and chucked it at Marcus. In less than a blink, it now sat just between his breastbone to the hilt. Everything happened in the span of seconds. Wet gurgling laughter came from his throat as he fell against the two goons behind him. On the way down, he pulled a gun, pointing it at Kelsey.

"No!" I screamed, and as the gun went off, Bella jumped to move in front of Kelsey. I pulled Kelsey toward me and landed on the ground, covering her body.

I twisted my head around and saw Bella with a bullet hole to the center of her forehead, eyes staring out into nothingness. I twisted to Velarde, who was repeatedly stabbing Marcus in the chest.

Shit!

How had things gone so wrong tonight?

I looked back at Bella. *Fuck!*

Kelsey had seen Bella die.

Kelsey twisted under me, and when she froze, she was staring straight into Bella's dead stare. An ear-piercing scream blew through her throat, damaging her vocal cords.

Pulling her up with me, I picked her up and looked back at Vel, who gave me a nod. "Knockdale."

Marcus' guards were dead, and Vel was now kneeling over Bella. Kelsey was kicking and screaming as I carried her out of the restaurant. I had to get her out of here and somewhere safe. Marcus would have a contingency plan in place if he didn't walk out right away. Marcus always had a plan.

I threw her in the car, locked the doors, and started the engine.

"Put your seatbelt on. We have to get out of here," I demanded.

"Izzy!" she screamed at me, but it came out broken and raspy.

"I know, Kelsey. Now, seatbelt." She listened. She actually listened to me, so I threw the car into motion, peeling out of the parking lot.

Kelsey sobbed hysterically for the ten minutes it took to get to the hotel. When I took the turn down Rosedale, she just shut down. She stopped crying. She stopped doing anything other than breathing.

"Shit," I muttered.

I had to get her there and make sure she was safe. Velarde would meet us there, but shit.

Shit. Shit. Shit.

I slammed my hand on the steering wheel as I drifted into the back drive, and the garage gate lifted automatically.

Once parked, we sat there for a second, just so I could take a moment to breathe. We were in the garage of The Knockdale Hotel, nowhere near The Rose. No one had followed us.

Protect her, Tiberius.

Get her inside.

Get her cleaned up.
Get her in bed to rest.
Get her safe.
Protect Kelsey.
Protect. Kelsey.

It was the most solid thought I had going through my entire body. I had to protect her.

Slowly, I turned toward her. "Are you hurt?" I asked as I looked her over. It wasn't the way I had looked at her during dinner. No, I was looking for the smallest sign she had been injured. She was covered in Bella's blood, but I didn't think she noticed. It was drying in her hair, and I needed to get her to a room and into a shower to get clean.

She looked at me and her gaze was dead. I raised my hands to make her focus on me, and my hands shook. I hadn't . . . I gripped her face in my hands. "Kelsey."

Her gaze cleared in recognition of me. "Are you physically injured?"

She mouthed the word no but pointed to her throat a moment later.

"Yeah, when you screamed, you blew out your vocal cords. It's gonna take a few days for them to heal. I'll get you a chalkboard or something so you can tell me to fuck off whenever you want, love," I told her and turned to get out of the car. She grabbed my jacket, flipped me off, and smirked. "Yeah, okay. You don't need to have anything to tell me to fuck off. Message received."

She didn't move from the car, and when I got to the passenger side, I opened the door slowly. When she didn't outright attack me, I reached out my hand for her to take it.

Kelsey looked at it for a moment and then put her blood-covered hand in mine. Gods, how I burned for her. I gritted my teeth, took my jacket, and put it around her. She was shivering as the shock was setting in.

Safe room. I needed to get her into the safe room.

I entered through the secret entrance and used the intercom in the small room to call Candy, the owner of the hotel.

"Candy," I said, trying to keep my voice calm.

"What in the fuck, Max?" she said. "I was wondering if you were going to come here. The media has your face all over TV with a redhead over your shoulder."

Of course, they did. "Great. What are they saying?"

"That someone was shot and you threw your girlfriend over your shoulder because she wouldn't stop screaming and fled the scene."

I looked at Kelsey. "Speaking of that redhead, we need the room."

"Just press **6948 on the phone and you'll rise to the 10th floor. Give me a moment before you do, though, and I'll give you a key card."

"Thanks," I said. "I owe you."

"Yeah, you do. I've had ten calls already from reporters asking if you or several of your aliases are staying here. I'm sure I'll be able to retire on what you'll pay me." She giggled into the phone. "Meals as well?"

"Please. Caleus will be here in a few hours. He has to take care of a few things."

"Shit, Max. You run this town. Must be pretty bad if first names are coming out of your mouth," she mumbled.

"It is." I ran my hand across my face, dried blood flaking off from where it transferred while carrying Kelsey to the car. Noting how much I was shaking, I took a few deep breaths. I never reacted like this. I was always cool and collected, had fought on many battlefields, led those armies throughout time, and tonight, I was shaking.

I glanced at Kelsey and back at the slot, waiting for the card. It was all because of her. Because Sidonia had come back with all the fire and rage that was Kelsey Ann Stillthorn. I paced a couple steps back and forth, running my hands through my hair. I had to get myself together.

A moment later, a key card slid through the slot.

"All set. Be careful, Max." Then the line went dead.

As I turned to Kelsey, I saw she had crouched down low to the ground and wrapped my jacket tighter around her.

I pressed the code into the keypad and as the elevator rose, I crouched down next to Kelsey and held her gaze. When the door opened, I wrapped my arms under her legs and lifted her against my chest. She didn't fight me, and I carried her to the room at the end of the hall.

I turned on the light and noted that the safe room, which was more of a suite, already had a few essentials—changes of clothes, both male and female, soap, towels, toothbrush, toothpaste, and the curtains were blackout and shut.

I toed the bathroom door open and gently set Kelsey down on the dark-grey stone counters. Sighing, I pulled the jacket off of her and cringed. Her entire left side was covered in Bella's blood. I had seen it on her, but I didn't realize just how much was on her.

"Come on, let's get you in a hot shower." I turned the hot water on and let the room get super steamy so there wouldn't be much for either of us to see.

Slowly, I removed her clothes, and surprisingly, she let me. I kept my eyes on hers the entire time. Once she was undressed, I couldn't help but run my hands down her arms and sides before resting them on her hips. I shook with the restraint not to lean in and kiss her.

This was not the time or place. Besides, after tonight, she would rightfully and truly hate me for her best friend dying.

I took her hand and led her into the shower. Her gaze never left mine as she stood in the water and I got undressed and stepped in behind her. Leaning her head back slightly, I went to work getting the blood out of her hair and off her body.

"Turn around so I can get your back," I said as she slowly peeled her gaze from mine.

As I cleaned off her back, her shoulders shook. It was instinct to wrap my arms around her and hold her. "Shhh. It's going to be okay. I promise. I'll protect you."

She turned toward me, looked into my eyes, and the tears were streaming down her face. "Izzy," she tried to say, but it was nothing but a hiss of sound.

I leaned forward to rest my forehead on hers. "I know." My arms tightened around her waist as she leaned into me and sobbed.

I had no idea how long we stood like that, but the water had long since turned cold and she was shivering again.

"Come on, love. Let's get you into something clean and into the bed," I whispered to her.

Reaching behind her, I turned the water off, making sure never to let my eyes go lower than hers. She met my stare the entire time. It took a moment, but she went from shivering in the shower to a light sheen of sweat coating her skin. I briefly wondered if mine had done the same.

I reached over and grabbed her a towel and started drying her hair, then I wrapped it around her. The Gods knew I wanted to run my hands over every inch of her, memorize her curves, and then prove to her she belonged to me.

She turned at that very thought and stepped out of the shower. I blinked. *Did I really just think that? Gods, did I say it out loud?*

I blinked again.

A few minutes later, I had her dressed in one of the T-shirts and a pair of men's boxers. She curled up in the queen bed under the blankets, and there was a ghost of a contented sigh that came from her.

"Be right back," I whispered, and she gave me a quick nod but watched me as I went to get another blanket out of the closet to set up a makeshift bed in the chair. There was a single pillow and a fuzzy grey lap blanket on the top shelf. Grabbing it, I went to the chair and turned to face her. Our eyes locked, and there were a thousand things I wanted to tell her, but I said sadly, "Try to get some sleep, Kelsey."

She sat up a moment, looked around, and tried to ask something, but the words were so broken and in a hiss, I couldn't make them all out.

"I'm sorry, but I didn't understand that."

She pointed to me then put her head down as if she were sleeping, shrugged her shoulders, and pointed to me again.

"Where will I sleep?" I asked, and she nodded. "I'll be fine in the chair. Get comfortable in the bed. You need the sleep."

She shook her head and patted the area behind her.

"I'll be fine." She shook her head again, reached over, and pulled me to the bed. I very well may be the asshole she believes me to be, but I couldn't refuse her. She tried to lift the blankets, but I put my hand on hers.

"Love." I sighed. "You are going to be rightly pissed at me in the morning. Let me protect you. It will be easier to do so if I'm on top of the blankets."

She nodded, and I lay down behind her. A few minutes later, she reached over and pulled me so that I was cradled against her and pulled my arm across her side and against her chest. I fisted my hand, and I could have sworn I felt her chuckle.

Eventually, she fell asleep, and about an hour later, Velarde let himself in.

When he saw us, his eyebrows shot to the ceiling.

"Shut up," I said, rolling my eyes, but without thinking, I held her closer. I could swear there was a contented sigh that escaped her as she slept.

"I'm getting in the shower, then we have to talk," Velarde said before disappearing into the bathroom.

CHAPTER 52

KELSEY

IT HAD BEEN TWO days. Two days since my soul sister died. That first night, I let Maximus Vispania take care of me. Let him bathe me. Let him hold me in the shower while I cried. Let him hold me all night as I slept. He was still holding me the next morning when I woke up. Once he felt me stir the littlest bit, he said, "Stay there, love. I'll order you something to eat that will be easy on your throat."

When breakfast arrived, I had only sat up and watched him as he fussed around, making sure everything was secure and we were safe. That I was safe. I wasn't sure what exactly had happened other than Izzy died after Max had thrown my knife into Marcus' chest.

I couldn't bring myself to stop Max from taking care of me, though. Every moment of that had felt . . . right, and I hated myself for it. Max wasn't good. Yet, there was a gentleness and kindness to him that he had shown me over the last few days that I could not deny. Were there two versions of Max? The asshole and businessman that the world saw and this possessive caregiver? What was worse was that there was a part of me that hated when Vel took over and Max left. This soul burning need to have him with me at all times was unnerving, to say the very least.

Max and Vel had been staying with me in shifts. It usually worked that Max stayed overnight and Vel was with me during the day.

"What is wrong, Kelsey?" Max asked as I sat on the bed. I was playing with my fingers and thinking about the events of the night Bella died: the things said, the way they were said, and how everyone looked at each other.

"Love, talk to me. Does your throat hurt? I can get you some ice chips. More ice cream?"

"You making me fat!" I squeaked out in mock anger. I could get partial sentences out, but it hurt to say too much. He smirked at me, but there was a glint in his eye as he chewed on his bottom lip. Heat spread throughout me.

Rolling my eyes, I took the notebook he had given me and scribbled:

When will Vel get here? I need to talk to him.

Max came over, and when he read it, his eyes died a little. "He will be here shortly."

He faced the fridge, took out the ice cream, and scooped out some caramel swirl for me. I licked my lips. I wasn't sure how he knew what my favorite was, but damn, I really was going to get fat on the stuff. There wasn't going to be enough sex in the next year to burn off the number of calories I was eating the last couple of days. While he dished it up, I looked him over from head to toe.

I would be kidding myself if I didn't acknowledge how much I appreciated the view. He was standing there, back turned, loose black pj pants low on his hips, no shirt, and barefoot. I chewed on my bottom lip for a second and could feel myself mentally reaching out to trace my fingers along his back. He had let me last night, and damn if it didn't take every ounce of strength not to push my luck to see if he would make a move.

He looked over his shoulder, and there was a playful smirk on his lips and glint in his eye. "Love?" He drew out the word. Damn if it didn't make my toes curl. I had realized that he had taken to calling me *love* instead of Kelsey the day after Izzy died, and it left me swimming every time.

I knew I was attracted to him, but with these dreams, it left a lot of doubts in my head. Did I want him because of the dreams? Was he just taking care of me out of guilt? Was there even still a danger from Marcus? I thought I had seen Vel stab him to death. In fact, I was almost sure of it.

Max put the ice cream away and brought the bowl he had made for me. When I didn't take it, he scooped a small spoonful and brought it to my lips. "You need to keep the inflammation down. It will help."

I gave him a look and mimed how he was just trying to make me fat.

"I'm not, love. Doesn't matter either way. I don't care about your size."

My eyes questioned him, and I cocked my head to the side. There was a blush on his cheeks, but the words could have meant anything. He lifted the spoon again and this time, I opened, and he fed me a bite.

I let it melt in my mouth before it slid down. I almost moaned at the cold feeling against the heated sandpaper that was my throat. Then it felt like there was a flame on my lips. My eyes shot open, and Max was staring at my lips as he wiped some of the ice cream from the right corner of my mouth.

"Sorry." He smirked again then let out a quick sigh. "Why do you need to talk to Velarde?"

He gave me another bite of ice cream as I wrote out my answer:

Had a dream I need to talk to him about.

"And you can't talk to me?" There was a resigned sadness in it, so I scribbled quickly:

It was about him. So, I need to talk to him about it.

He nodded and gave me another spoonful. I wrote quickly:

When I can talk, you and I have lots *we need to talk about.*

Gods. There were so many answers I needed.

"There is a lot we need to talk about, but . . ." I watched as he struggled with what he wanted to say before looking back at me with an emotion in his eyes I couldn't place.

"Me figure out," I croaked, my throat starting to burn again. They had told me I had to figure out the connection between them and me before we could really talk. Only, how did I know what I didn't know?

His lips pursed together, and he nodded. He gave me another spoonful of ice cream, and I couldn't help but lift my hand to his cheek and run my thumb across it. He leaned into it, and I swore I felt him sigh.

There was a rhythmic knock at the door, letting us know it was Vel, and I smiled softly at Max. He handed me the rest of the bowl as Vel walked in.

"How did it go?" Max asked Vel.

"Still nothing. No casualties, though. Everyone is alive and well." Vel's voice was one of relief.

Scribbling on the paper, I asked: *What happened? No casualties?*

"We are trying to find out more about the nightwhispers. About the only thing we can figure out is it's being used as a date rape drug and sleeping agent. We found one guy who said he remembered shit that he had repressed from his childhood. I have a theory that Marcus somehow gave you some while at the coffee shop, hence why you slept for an entire day."

"Water," I whispered.

"You need water?" Max asked.

I shook my head and wrote out: *At the coffee shop. I drank some water at the table we were sitting at. He probably put it in that.*

There was a meaningful look that passed between them, but Vel said, "We don't know numbers or anything else yet. We also have a few other, um"—he paused, glancing at Max—"business items we are working on, Kelsey. Please don't ask anymore."

I pursed my lips but nodded. Of course, there was other business. It was that side of Max I loathed. One moment, I couldn't help but feel like I was falling down a very deep well for Max, and then there was this side. The side that was all shady shit and full of all the reasons not to get involved in any way with Maximus Vispania. I didn't know what to do with what was waging inside of me.

I looked at Max, and when his eyes met mine, I picked up a spoonful of ice cream, ate it, and turned my back to them. I brought my notebook with me because I needed to write things out for Vel and that was going to take a hot minute.

I ate the ice cream, though, instead of writing. When their whispers stopped, Max crouched before me. He put his hands on my knees and rubbed his thumbs back and forth. Each pass sent a spark between my legs and made my heart jump.

"You sure you can't talk to me about this?" he asked.

I nodded, mouthing, "Only Vel."

"But we will talk about things once your throat is better, right?" he asked, and there was hope in his voice. I smiled as I reached out and caressed his cheek. He leaned forward, and I thought he might kiss me. I hated to admit it but I wanted him to. But he just gave me a quick kiss on my forehead, and I closed my eyes.

Time warped through my mind, and I gripped his cheek tighter and grabbed his hand so that I had something steady to hold on to while it flickered through me.

"Kelsey? Love?" His voice was worried, and I just kept my eyes squeezed shut.

Tiberius and Sidonia walking down a street, stealing small caressing touches. Tiberius and Sidonia diving into an alcove for stolen kisses. Tiberius and Sidonia surrounded by friends and family. Then, without thinking about it, I squeaked out, "Serves you right, Lars. You shouldn't have drunk so much."

Everything stopped at those words. I could feel Max's hand on my cheek and my knee, but there wasn't a sound in that room. I slowly opened my eyes and shook my head. Everything was fuzzy, and I couldn't read the look on Max's face.

I blinked and removed my hand from his cheek. I forced myself to sit back against the headboard of the bed. When my eyes met Vel's, they were puzzled.

"Max," Vel said warily.

I refused to look at Max. It was only a piece of what I was getting, and I would not say anything more until I could talk. I didn't even know how I was going to broach that subject.

Shits bits! I wasn't even sure I understood everything I was dreaming, or seeing, or what I thought was happening. *Could I really be the Sidonia that was tattooed over his heart?*

That didn't work. There was no way that could be. Yes, I believed in reincarnation, but even if I was Sidonia's soul, that didn't answer why Max looked exactly like Tiberius.

I took a deep breath and put my head in my hands, tipping the ice cream all over the bed.

That was enough to break his concentration, and he said, "I'll clean it up."

"Max," Vel said harder.

"It doesn't mean anything, Velarde."

"But . . ." Vel was studying me, and my heart dropped at Max's words. Even if I was the same soul, I wasn't Sidonia. I was Kelsey. I would not be Sidonia's ghost. Max didn't want me. He wanted his Sidonia.

That thought hurt more than I realized it would, and tears sprung to my eyes. I jumped out of the bed, and as I tried to pass Max, he grabbed me by the waist. I pushed him off me, but he held tight as the tears fell harder. The heat of his touch seared me to my soul. I fucking wanted him, and he said it didn't mean anything.

What I was dreaming didn't mean anything, was starting to accept, what I thought I was feeling for him didn't mean anything.

"Kelsey," Max breathed as I pushed away from him again and locked myself in the bathroom.

"Kelsey," Max and Vel both said worriedly through the door. "Are you okay?"

A piece of paper slid through the bottom of the door and a pencil. "Are you okay?" Max asked again in a pleading voice.

No. I'm not. Just need a minute. Vel is here. Go do your thing, Max.

"Talk to me. Please," Max pleaded after I slid my reply through the door. Then, he pushed the paper back under for me to answer him as he asked, "Do you need anything?"

You. I need you, is what my traitorous heart wanted me to say. Instead, I scribbled:

Trust me, you and I will have a discussion at some point, motherfucker.

I heard him leave, and I wasn't sure if I was relieved or disappointed that he hadn't stayed to fight it out with me.

It was midafternoon when I started writing everything down. Velarde was pacing in front of the room-length window and studying me the entire time. When he sat, staring at the ceiling in the chair in the corner, I asked him for some ice cream, and he got up and made me a bowl with two large vanilla with caramel swirl scoops. Looking down at the page that I had written out, I sighed.

He handed me the ice cream, and I tilted the notebook toward him.

We need to talk.

"Okay."

Have you started planning Izzy's memorial? She doesn't want to be buried. She'd want to be cremated and scattered in the mountains.

Vel tensed a moment before letting out a long breath and pulling his long hair back. "Kelsey, I can't talk about that right now."

"Caleus Velarde. She is my best friend, my sister . . . ," I rasped out. Each word hurt, but he had to know that we needed to do something for her. We may have been locked up here, but we couldn't leave her just to rot in a morgue somewhere. "I know you love her, too. We have to . . ."

"No, Kelsey." His voice was hard, and he stared me down. "Not now."

I huffed and swallowed my emotions.

"What else did you need to talk to me about?" His voice was distant, and there was something there I couldn't place, but when I looked at him again, I dropped it for the time being.

Fine, for now. First, I need you to promise me something.

"What is that?"

Max knows I need to talk to you today. The promise I need from you is that this discussion doesn't go to Max. You can't tell him.

"Kelsey, that is asking a lot."

I nodded but raised an eyebrow. I knew I was asking a lot, but I needed to have this discussion with Vel before I could talk to Max about the most important stuff.

Sitting back down in the chair in the corner, he leaned forward, staring at the floor, out the window, and then up at me.

"Shit, Kels." He studied me a moment longer. "You are serious about this. You don't want me to say a word to Max about this conversation?"

I slowly nodded my head.

"Athena, save me," he said, rolling his head up and looking at the sky. I huffed a small laugh. Like Athena would do shit. She would likely lead the war against Max if I asked her to at that moment.

"Alright. I promise that this entire conversation does not get to Max unless it passes your lips," he said, letting out a long breath. "Hit me."

How did Marcus know all the names of people I've dreamed about? I hadn't told anyone those names. Not even Izzy.

I looked down at the bowl of ice cream and moved the contents around, making it more of a shake-like consistency instead of it being ice cream. I had a feeling that Izzy and Vel were way more involved in my life than what was on the surface. I had the dream of the shield-maiden almost every night. It was trying to tell me something. I knew it.

"You knew all those names, Kelsey?"

A couple of them I didn't know, but yes. I've dreamed of most of them.

"How many dreams have you had of your different lives?" he asked in astonishment.

A fair few.

I giggled, and his eyes raised to his hairline before he said, "A *fair few*? Kelsey, he listed fifteen names before he got to Fenryis of the Bloovollr."

I shrugged, took a small scoop of ice cream, and let the cold slowly slide down my throat, soothing it. I scribbled my first question and then slowly looked up at Vel, who was studying me.

When he got to the shield-maiden, even you and Izzy panicked. Please don't lie to me. I'm tired of the lies and half-truths.

He looked at me a moment longer, and there was understanding in his gaze. He opened his mouth a few times to say something but then took a deep breath and said, "You are putting things together, but I'm not really sure I'm the right person to answer it, Kelsey."

"Max," I said out loud, and he nodded. My voice was getting better, but it still hurt to talk too much.

Okay, fine. Second, as he listed those names, something clicked for me when he got to the shield-maiden. I've been dreaming of men and women, where a man ruins my life. There were dreams of ~~Dom~~ *Marcus killing me, lighting me up to burn at the stake, sword through the chest, slicing my throat. Name it, I've probably died one way or another by his hand. But why is Marcus after me?*

"What the fuck, Kelsey!" he shouted, looking at me in shock after he read what I wrote. I raised my eyebrows at him. "You've been dreaming of your past lives? Why didn't you say anything?"

I just gave him an even look.

"You are sure about this?"

I nodded.

"What is the most current one?" he asked, handing me back my notebook.

The most recent dream was from World War 2. He killed my entire family in France. He brought soldiers to the village we were living in and personally barricaded the only 2 exits and burned the house down. We all died from the smoke. I was 12, Vel. Why would Marcus want to kill me at 12 years old? Why has he killed me or disrupted my life for centuries?

"World War 2, huh? Damn." His lips tightened, and then he read the end again. "As for why Marcus is focused on you, I don't know."

My eyes narrowed at him because while he answered the question on the paper, he wasn't answering what I really wanted to know. Frustrated, I held out my hand for the notebook. He handed it back to me and I scribbled out, *Fine. I'll ask plainly. How is he always the same person? The same face. How is Marcus always Marcus?*

I tossed the notebook back to him. When he read it, he looked at it for a long time.

"Always the same face. Not just a different version of him? Like, you are seeing the same Marcus? Not just recognizing the same soul?" Vel asked.

I raised my eyebrows at him and nodded my head that I was indeed seeing the same Marcus.

He leaned back in his chair and rubbed his hands across his face. He stared at the popcorn ceiling for a good five minutes, his lips moving too fast for me to make out what he was saying, before I kicked him in the shin and crossed my arms at him.

When he didn't answer me, I threw my arms out, and, in a croaked voice that burned like the depths of hell, I hastily whispered, "Well?"

His eyes met mine, and I could tell he didn't want to, but he said, "I don't know."

CHAPTER 53

MAX

I WAS BACK IN *that room. Our first night together as husband and wife. I was there, between her legs, enjoying the taste of her, rubbing my cock against her wet slit, and then I was taking her for the first time. When the memory of our first joining release hit me . . .*

I sat straight up in bed. I wasn't in Herculaneum. I was in . . . Trenton. Two thousand years later. I placed my hand over the tattoo of Sidonia's name and gripped it tight.

My eyes narrowed as I took in the redhead next to me. Last night, she had finger traced each letter without even opening her eyes. Each feather-light touch had been a blaze to my skin.

I climbed out of bed and went into the bathroom. It had been two thousand years. That person out there could not be my Sidonia. I slammed my fist on the counter as I rejected everything my body was telling me.

"Max?" she croaked. It had been days, and her voice was still so hoarse. She was using it regularly now, but it still cracked.

"Go back to sleep, Kelsey. Vel will be here soon." There was a long pause, and then she was standing in the doorway.

"You okay?"

"Just a dream. Go back to bed," I practically begged her. When she touched my forearm, I jerked back and fisted my hands. I couldn't look at her, but I saw her reflection in the mirror.

Rejection. The rejection hurt. She covered it quickly and said, "Good. He'll be better company." Then she turned on her heels and went back into the other room.

Every ounce of me wanted to go back to her, but fuck her. *She. Wasn't. Sidonia.*

Then why was I so drawn to her? Why couldn't I leave her? There had been no sign of Marcus since that night. I could leave Vel with Kelsey and sleep in my apartment.

Every night, I thought about it. Yet every night, I drove back here. I needed to be with her.

I slid down to the floor, put my face in my hands, and cried.

If she was my Sidonia, then what was I waiting for?

Vel showed up a few minutes later, tried to talk to me, but I just grabbed my shoes and jacket, stomping out the door. I had to get away. I had to get some distance.

All morning, I did nothing but drive. I should have been checking in on our suppliers, business associates, and what else was happening with Marcus. I should have been checking in on things for Bella. I should be looking into what nightwhispers were. I should find out who Marcus' contact was down on California Street and when the shipment would come in. When I thought about doing any of that, all I saw was red hair and green eyes. So instead, I left that to Velarde to work on.

I stopped midday at Jackson Lake. It was a popular place for people to swim. The lake wasn't big enough to allow too much boating and water skiing, but there were a couple of boats out that day.

For hours, I sat there with my arms on my knees as I leaned against a tree. There was so much that had changed in the last few weeks, and it started with Marcus showing back up. *What in the hell was he really after? Why always me, never Velarde? Why?* I had only known one Marcus in my entire existence, and he died. Was put to death by the Empire. Leaning my head back against the tree, I muttered, "Gods, that was a long time ago."

But what was the connection? I couldn't see it. Marcus had first shown up around the 1100s, when I was just running a small winery and brothel colony near Zadat, in what is now Croatia. He came in with an army and destroyed the entire colony. It continued for centuries. He hadn't bothered me for 200 years here. Why now?

He seemed to have a special interest in Kelsey, but why? It seemed they had a long history in her previous lives, but again, why? There would be no reason for it. If he was interested in her, then why try to shoot her in the restaurant? I hadn't crossed paths with any of Kelsey's previous lives. I would have known by her touch. Hell, just her gaze lit me on fire that night, and every night since. I couldn't even remember what I had gone downstairs for, but when her eyes locked on mine. . .

I rubbed my face in frustration, and then huffed a laugh as I remembered the rest of that night. She didn't give two shits about the billionaire buying her drinks. No, she had flipped me off through those two-way mirrors.

In fact, she believed in the worst parts of me. She didn't know the millions that I gave to St. Jude under about eighteen different aliases, or that every student at Trenton High who went to CU Trenton miraculously got a full scholarship. Or the dozens of other things I did with the money that just sat in my bank account. I'd learned the hard way over hundreds of years how to be a successful businessman.

Unfortunately, that came with the bad as well. It was knowing which fights to fight and which ones to control. The underground of Trenton was one that I couldn't win, but I could control. Yes, it meant that dealers and crooked businessmen would then owe me in one way or another in order to go free.

Keeping drugs and stimulants out of a town this size was impossible. 250,000 people came with their own set of problems. People would come to Trenton with their own histories and troubles. Drugs came with that. I couldn't keep them out, but I could help control what was here. So, I became the person that I needed to be. To have a home that I could be proud of, I also had to be a man people hated and feared. Everyone needed a villain. I was their savior and their villain wrapped up in one glass and steel tower in the center of town.

Then there was Kelsey, who hated my guts. Who fought with every ounce of her being. I had once said that she needed to have someone who would take her mouth and give it right back, but I wasn't that man. The problem was, I wanted to be. I had been. We verbally sparred like it was an Olympic sport.

I was primal around her. Every cell in my body reached for her. Craved her.

Then Bella died.

I needed to take care of her that night. I needed to be the protector, and she had let me. She continued to let me. She had shown the softness within her, and I had shown her what little there was in me.

She wasn't my Sidonia. Gods, no. Kelsey was so much more.

I stared out over the lake and played with a leaf in my hand. I couldn't deny it anymore. Kelsey was mine. I was hers. The thought settled into me with a sureness that melded into my bones.

Staring off at the reflection of the sunset over the lake, the words came unbidden and fell into the wind.

"I choose you, Kelsey."

When I got back, it was late. Really late. And Velarde had already texted me a hundred times, asking where the fuck I was. I opened the door as quietly as I could, and when I cracked it open, there was a gun pointed at my head.

I froze. It wouldn't have been the first time that I'd been shot, but that shit hurt. Though, I may deserve it at that moment.

"Gods. You fuck!" Velarde said, lowering the gun and holstering it. "You don't fucking answer me all day, you come back late, and . . ."

"How's Kelsey?"

"Pissed as Hades is at Demeter. You deserve it, though." He looked at me. "Did you really blow her off this morning?"

I flinched.

"Tiberius, you are such a selfish asshole!" he spat, and I froze. "She's asleep. Has been for hours."

I sighed a relieved breath. "Sorry, Caleus. I needed to clear my head."

"*Caleus* . . . shit, man. Alright. Since first names are being used, this calls for whiskey," he said, heading over to the minibar.

"It isn't like we can get drunk, dumbass," I said, rubbing my face, but when I looked around the corner to check on Kelsey, her face was soft with sleep. I walked over and knelt before the bed.

Resting my head on my hands, I stared at her for a long moment. Without realizing what I was doing, I reached out and tucked some of her hair behind her ear and ran my thumb along her cheek.

"You are finally accepting it, aren't you?" he asked with admiration. Velarde had been so sure she was Sidonia. He figured it out almost right away. He had *never* given me false hope, had always said that I would know when it was really her. Then Kelsey started having dreams. It couldn't be a coincidence that after that night in the bar, she started remembering her previous lives.

Nodding, I looked at my dearest friend. "She isn't her, but there are glimpses of her in there." I just knelt like that for a good five minutes before I said, "I can't fight it anymore, Caleus. She . . . Kelsey is under my skin. I've tried thinking it's just because she could be Sidonia, but it's more than that."

Vel just listened as I spoke.

I stood and plopped down in the chair as I ran my hands through my hair. "Every ounce of my being is drawn to her.

I tried all day to walk away. I didn't answer you because I was trying not to come back. I can't not come back to her."

She was a damn angel in her own flames lying on the bed, hair splayed out around her. A sigh of longing released from me. "How do you walk away from someone your soul calls to? She hates me. Blames me for killing Bella."

"Has she said that?"

"No. She mumbles it in her sleep. It's kind of adorable." I smirked as I threw back the whiskey he gave me. "Gods, what is this shit? While you're out tonight, get something decent to drink. Whatever this shit is, it is worse than what we had to drink during the Somairle's Invasion."

"Alright. No piss water." He chuckled.

He stared at me for a long moment.

"Just say it."

"Why are you waiting to tell her everything, Tiberius? If she is talking in her sleep, you know she has it figured out, or at least enough of it."

"That's just it. I'm letting her figure it out. If I just tell her, she's going to throw it in my face and tell me I'm full of shit. That I'm pressuring her to be someone she isn't. That I'm just looking for the only person I've ever loved in my whole life—before her."

Velarde looked at me, shock in his eyes. He opened his mouth but immediately closed it. I knew what I said, and Vel was the only one who wouldn't call me on it.

I looked at her sleeping form and whispered, "She has to realize who she is. Kelsey has to realize who I am. She can't just ask me and I give her the answers. She has to come to that conclusion on her own. Even if she is Sidonia, that would only be a part of her now. Her soul has had two thousand years of life to grow and become something else. What if our souls aren't matched anymore?"

When I looked at him, he was staring at me like I was crazy. "Seriously. That is the line of bullshit you are going to give me? I see the way she looks at you, Tiberius. There is something there."

"Hate and disgust," I muttered.

"That is also bullshit and you know it. I see it in her eyes," he said. "But I'll ask again, what if she doesn't figure it out? What if she walks away from *all* of us?"

"I don't know, Caleus," I answered honestly. I looked at her again as her mouth was moving faster than I could make out the words. The mere thought of having to walk away hurt. "I don't know if I can survive her walking away."

CHAPTER 54

KELSEY

IT HAD BEEN EIGHT days since Izzy died because of Max. My throat was finally getting to the point that I didn't have to use the notepad anymore, and I was bound to have that conversation with Max. Every hour that passed, my confusion over Izzy's death and Vel's reaction when I asked about a memorial increased.

"Vel?" I croaked.

His head shot up, and he gave me a questioning look. "Want some ice cream?" he asked softly. I nodded, and he got up and made me a bowl.

I wasn't looking forward to getting on a scale when I got home. Home. Where was home anymore?

"I need answers," I muttered just above a whisper, but I made my tone strong. "Please tell me I'm not crazy. Need you to tell me what is going on."

I stared at him, and he was pleading with me not to push it, so with a sigh, I nodded.

"Once you know the biggest truth of all this, I will answer whatever you want to know."

"The biggest truth," I said, sighing heavily. It was coming together each time I slept. More and more dreams had surfaced, and more and more of them had been putting the pieces together for me—dreams of one specific lifetime. "The one that connects Max, Tiberius, Sidonia, and me."

"Yes." His answer was quick and fast. "Max isn't the bad guy you think he is. I've known him for a very long time, Kels. He can't fix the underground, but he tries to keep the worst of it at bay."

"But he doesn't have to bail out people who should rot in jail," I said without the harshness I was hoping for, and I looked off to the side, a little surprised at myself. There was that little voice in me saying that Vel was right. Max wasn't all bad.

"Max and I have both, and I do mean *both* of us, had to make decisions that neither of us have been proud of. Some have cost lives; some have saved them. Some have even kept bad people from jail, yes, but there are good reasons behind it."

"There is a justification for everything, Vel. Even the evilest of serial killers can give you a convincing argument for why the person they killed had to die." I stared into the bowl and moved the ice cream around again before scooping up another spoonful and letting it coat my throat.

"I guess you will just have to sort out if what you are feeling for Max is enough to put those things aside." He ran his hands through his long hair and cursed when his finger got stuck in one of the curls.

"What I feel for Max?"

"Yes," he said meaningfully.

"I don't have feelings for Max," I said with not enough bite to be completely truthful. He gave me a look that told me he knew just how much of a bullshit statement that was.

I really didn't know how I felt about him. If what I suspected was true, I didn't know if what I might feel for him was because of that or me. The lines were blurring, and I just didn't know.

"He . . ." Vel got up and looked out the window for a long moment before he continued, "He loved someone so fiercely that it destroyed him. I don't know if he can separate the two, but the way he looks at you, it reminds me of how he looked at her."

"I will not be Max's ex's ghost, Velarde. If, and that is a huge if, there were anything between Max and me, I'm not *her*. He would have to love me for me. I'm not sure he's capable of that."

His head snapped around to me, and he gave me a questioning look. He swallowed, and I could see he abandoned what he was going to say and shifted to, "I think the lines are blurred for him right now. Max cares for you. You, Kelsey, and not because of any ghosts." He looked me dead in the eyes. "I think he wants to explore that connection between you two, but he feels like it would be betraying her."

"And that's why I don't know if I can tell him what I suspect," I said, as there was a knock on the door.

Max was back.

"And what exactly do you suspect, Kelsey?" It wasn't Vel who spoke, but it was his face that was full of hope. After revealing more than I wanted to, I saw the confirmation in his eyes. Vel's eyes shifted farther into the other end of the room to where Max was standing.

CHAPTER 55

KELSEY

WHEN I LOOKED UP, Max was standing there, arms crossed, but staring at the floor. Slowly, he looked up to Vel, and when their eyes met, Max gave him a short, quick shake of his head.

Vel's eyebrows knitted together. "It's been eight days. There should be something by now."

"There are signs in Marcus' camp, but..." Max's eyes were sad and confused.

"Didn't Marcus die?" I asked. "You threw my knife and chucked it into his chest. I saw him fall back before he shot at..." I looked between the two of them.

"I'm going to head out. You two need to talk." Vel leaned down to give me a hug, and before pulling fully back, he whispered into my ear, "Don't kill him, please, Kels. You will only hurt yourself if you do. Trust your heart. I don't want to lose you again."

I gave him a confused look, and as he passed Max, Vel patted his chest.

I looked at Max, and he met my stare. The tension between us was somewhere between raging frustration and the need to walk over to him, strip him bare, and memorize each and every inch of his body with my tongue.

"Fuck, this sucks!" I said in frustration, getting up to pace the other side of the room. We needed to hash this out. I'd been thinking about how to go about this since I woke from that dream that afternoon.

He just leaned against the wall and let me pace.

"I have questions, and I need you to answer them for me," I demanded, chewing on my thumb.

"Kelsey, I don't know how much I can tell you yet. There are things you need to learn before I can tell you everything."

"Yeah, yeah, yeah. That's what Vel said, too. Except, I think I know what y'all are keeping from me. Rather, what you hope it is, but I need you to answer me."

I walked across the room a couple more times before I said, "So why don't you tell me what I need to know?"

"Because if I tell you, you won't believe me. When you get it, I will confirm it."

"Why do you both keep saying that?" I asked, grabbing my hair in frustration. "You'll figure it all out, love. You need to know the main part first, Kelsey. *You* need to sort it."

Max came over and put his hands on my face, and his touch burned. Those sapphire orbs sparkled as he said, "Kelsey, you are fierce and smart, and I . . ."

He stared at me a moment, his eyes flicked to my lips, and just when his head moved a little closer to mine, I blurted, "What went wrong a week ago?"

His eyebrow cocked up and he released me. As he moved away from me, curling his hands into tight fists, he growled, "A lot."

"No shit, fucker." My blood pressure was spiking quickly. "Why can't you just answer the question?"

"I—" he started to say, but I interrupted him.

"I hate you," I growled, and I could almost *feel* him flinching. "I hate you. I hate that Izzy died because of you. I hate that I'm stuck here with you."

He turned to me, his face lined with hurt, and I met his stare. It was a punch to the heart, to my very soul, because I didn't hate him. It was saying those words and his reaction that made me realize just how far down a rabbit hole I had fallen since meeting him. My stomach flopped as I forced myself to say the words that I had been keeping bottled up. A lone tear plopped down on my cheek.

"Most of all, I hate that you are the only man I have ever met that makes me feel like I'm on fire and burning from the inside out. I don't mean just by your touch. Right down to my soul, Max. No man has ever done that. No woman either. I've been with both. No one. Ever. Not until you, Maximus Vispania. And I hate how much I want you. I hate how much I want to take every inch of you and make you mine. I want to erase every shadow that crosses your face from the memory of her."

There were so many emotions that went through his expression that I couldn't read them fast enough to get a handle on them. One moment, he was across the room, and the next, his lips crashed onto mine with a ferocity that I had never felt before.

I opened for him and grabbed his shirt, balling it in my hands, pulling him closer. He had one hand on my cheek and the other threaded into my hair at the nape of my neck.

Gods, his kiss. I couldn't breathe in enough of him. Every inch of me came to light. Every man and woman I had ever kissed had felt cold, and there had never been that shuddering feeling that people in love said they had for their partner.

Kissing Max was lighting up parts of me that had been so dark, so ice cold, that the intense heat was almost painful as he touched it. The last of the ice around my soul dripped away. His kiss was so searing upon its very essence that I thought I could feel a pulse fly into the world.

When he reluctantly pulled back, his eyes were closed, as his forehead rested on mine. We heaved breaths as if the other had stolen all of the oxygen from the other. When his eyes met mine again, his lips were light as a feather as he whispered my name with a reverence that no one had ever given me.

"Kelsey," he repeated. I took a step back, and his eyes turned questioning.

Time wobbled in front of me again. I saw Max standing in front of me on a beach, water glistening behind him, but he was whispering a different name. I blinked, and there was a loud creaking in the recesses of my mind, a door fully opening, and the final pieces of my and Max's story fell together.

CHAPTER 56

MAX

WHEN SHE TOLD ME she hated me, it had almost killed me. I thought my heart was going to shatter and stop beating forever, standing in front of her. Then she said the words that undid me, and I hadn't been able to hold back.

I was kissing her before I knew what I was doing. It had been just like it had the first time I kissed Sidonia. The suns of Helios shone within me again, and then she stole every ounce of my breath. When I pulled back and breathed her name, there was so much I wanted to tell her. I needed her. I wanted to hold and cherish her forever.

Her. Not Sidonia. Sidonia was a figment of Kelsey. Sure, they both had the strength of the Gods within them, both had that spark of defiance and duty. Kelsey, though, had taken the spark Sidonia had and cultivated it over the centuries until it was a raging inferno. I wanted that fire. I needed her in that fire. I needed Kelsey Ann Stillthorn.

She stepped back from me, and there were a multitude of expressions that crossed her face before she blinked, stared at me, and said, "Sit down over there. I need to think."

"Kelsey," I said after a few minutes, feeling my heart drop. She looked at me, and before I could fear the rejection, I asked, "Do you regret me kissing you?"

"Hell no," she said instantly, but she didn't stop moving. "But I can't talk now. I need to figure out how . . . Just shut up and let me fucking think."

Hours passed as she paced that room, then she sat on the bed, chewing on her finger, then stood and stared out the window. I tried to get her to talk to me, and she said, "There are too many thoughts. Too much . . ." She pressed against the temples of her head, and when I took her hand, she looked at it and smiled as I ran my thumb across the back of hers.

"You need to sleep," I said around 1 am and tried to lead her to the bed, but she pulled her arm away.

"You've been thinking for hours, love. Lie down. We can talk more in the morning," I said, trying again. "You will think clearer on a good night's sleep."

I took both of her hands in mine again, and I gently tugged on them to lead her to the bed. She sucked on her bottom lip and her eyes sparkled. Gods, she was sexy. Then, she pulled her hand away and said, "I am thinking clearly. At least, I am when you aren't touching me. Gods, I can't *think* when you're touching me."

"Okay," I said slowly and went and sat on the bed.

Leaning up against the headboard, I watched her pace and stare out the windows until the sun rose. Every hour that passed, I noticed the little things about her that were both Sidonia and Kelsey, but I also saw the clear differences.

The way they stood in place thinking was the same, but the way they fought back was different. Sidonia was stern and would tell you exactly how shit was going to go down, but Kelsey . . . No, Kelsey would take that knife in her boot and stab you with it to make you do what she wanted. She would not hesitate to put that knife into your throat to make her point.

When the sun came through the blinds, she stopped and turned to me, arms crossed and determined.

"I had a dream the other night, and I'm going to tell you about it, okay?"

"Okay." That was one way to start a conversation.

"I was on a mountain. Sidonia was on the mountain, I mean." My heart stopped as she worked her bottom lip with her teeth again. Gods, if she only knew what that did to me. I shifted a little to adjust for what was growing in my pants. She didn't miss the movement, and I thought I saw her smirk and her eyes light up before she continued, "I'm just going to tell this the best way I can, okay?"

I nodded. I was not so sure I would have been able to speak if she asked me something directly.

"Sidonia and Tiberius were lying in the grass up on a mountain, and she was teasing him. Sexually."

Oh Gods, of all the memories she was going to relinquish to me, it had to be this one?

He whispered her name in a way that told her exactly how he wanted her, and she smiled. She moved her hand below his clothes, and when she held his cock in her hands, he froze.

"Do you want me to stop?" she whispered softly.

"Gods no, but Lars." Tiberius had hissed the last part as she held his bare balls under the last layer of his clothes. When she cupped them fully in her hand, he murmured, "Gods,

woman." Tiberius had said it as if Sidonia were going to be his undoing.

His hand hadn't moved from her face, and they just stared at each other as she stroked him. As she continued to tease and pleasure him, he held onto her chin tighter, and he moved his hips in time to her stroking.

"Tiberius," she said, her gaze full of heat and lust. She wanted him, too. She wanted so badly to straddle him and give Tiberius everything. If her brother hadn't been there as a chaperon, she may have.

Long moments passed between them as they tried to stay quiet and not draw her brother's attention. Tiberius' head dipped toward hers as he kissed her hard, and Sidonia swallowed his moan as he released in her hand. Then, she grabbed a cloth and cleaned them up.

Kelsey hadn't stopped looking me dead in the eye as she told the whole story. Heat flashed in her eyes, and there was a knowing, wicked smirk on her lips. I shook my head and blinked to clear mine.

That was the first time Sidonia had ever pleasured me. Kelsey told it without some of the minute details, but there was no way she could have known unless . . . I looked up at her and blinked. She really had figured it all out. She knew who I was. Who she was. I felt tears in my eyes, and I took a shuddering breath to keep from letting them fall. I swung my legs over the edge of the bed and went to stand before her.

"Tell me what Tiberius said next," she said in a seductive voice that if this were any other conversation, would have brought me to my knees before her.

I gulped and stared at her. "Are you sure you want me to do that? Everything changes if I do. There is no going back."

She stood before me, our chests just a breath away from each other. Then, emphasizing each word, she said, "Maximus Vispania. Tell me what Tiberius said next."

So, I did what I had done two thousand years ago. I pulled her close and said with emotion thick in my throat, "Are you sure you are not Aphrodite?" Then I kissed Kelsey's forehead. I pulled back, just enough to make eye contact, and swallowed the lump in my throat before I said the words that would tell her everything.

"Say it, Max." Those green eyes burned with a fire that I knew was all Kelsey. "Finish what Tiberius told her."

My eyes flicked to her lips, emotion fueling every cell in my body, and I said, "I chose you, Sidonia."

She stared at me for a long moment before she rested her hand on my cheek and wiped a tear away. There was so much going on in that gaze from her. I trembled with the restraint not to kiss her again.

"I know I just confirmed so much, but I need to know. Do you believe it? Do you believe you are Sidonia?" I asked.

"I strongly believe in soul reincarnation, Max. I always have. It is how I'm okay and confident knowing that my soul is the same as the woman you loved back then."

I let out a heavy breath. Yet, there was a meaning in those words. She had chosen and said them very carefully.

"Sidonia loved Tiberius. Kelsey doesn't know Max. It's been two thousand years, and I don't know you well enough to love you."

I understood what she meant, but I still said, "You married me after only a little over a week. You chose me, and I chose you."

"It was a different time, Tiberius," she said, and we both froze.

"You called me Tiberius," I said after a moment, warmth and contentment flowing through me at her words. She had said it while exhausted and while dreaming, but she had never called me Tiberius coherently.

"I did," she said, reaching up and kissing me, feather-light on the lips. "I've fallen down the rabbit hole, Max. I know I feel something for you, but I can't be the living incarnate of a ghost. Like I said, Sidonia loved Tiberius. Kelsey doesn't know Max," she said, barely loud enough for either of us to hear. My heart hammered in trepidation, sadness, and, worst of all, fear.

Fear she would indeed walk away. Fear she would be taken from me again. Fear I could lose her forever.

There was a heavy breath from her before she backed up and sat on the bed. She rubbed her temples with her fingertips.

A moment later, she said, "The last few days, time has been a bit wobbly. I know you are my Tiberius, and while I believe I am Tiberius' Sidonia reincarnated and that I have been dreaming of all my lives since that day, it leaves a huge question for you to answer."

Oh Gods. The way she said "my Tiberius" had me weak in every way possible. I would die a thousand deaths for this woman. Kelsey was something else. She was thoughtful, intelligent, and sexy as hell. I wanted to push her back on that bed and make love to her.

I clenched my hands into fists and took half a step back, just to give myself a little more distance.

Velarde came in at that point and looked between us. I hadn't even heard him knock. He said, "I can come back."

"No, Caleus Velarde, Roman soldier, best friend, and brother of this asshole standing across from me, you can't. Sit your fucking ass down. We are all going to have a chat," she commanded him, but there wasn't that usual bite of hatred when she called me an asshole. In fact, she almost smirked when she said it.

"She's sorted it out," he said, looking at me.

"She has," I said, taking a seat because I knew what she was going to ask next, and it was going to be the hardest one of them all to answer. "Go ahead, Kelsey."

"She figured it out, and you are still calling her Kelsey?" Velarde asked.

I didn't look at him, but Kelsey's eyes snapped to mine, an inferno lighting inside me.

"Yes, because while she may have been my Sidonia then, the impeccable Kelsey Ann Stillthorn stands before us," I said quietly before saying to Kelsey, who had the ghost of a smile on her lips, "Ask it, love. Ask the question you really want to know."

"How are you Tiberius Maximus Vispania in truth? Not a reincarnation. Not a descendant, but actually the man I loved in 79 AD before Mount Vesuvius blew up and killed us all. I told you I loved you, you told me you loved me, I gave our souls to the Mother, binding them forever, and then we died. My skin boiled off me and we *died*. My father, my mother, my grandmother, brother, nieces, your parents, and your sisters, we all died, Max. Everyone in that colony. Everyone in Herculaneum died. How did you and Velarde live?"

"Holy. Fucking. Gods. She really figured it all out. Every detail," Velarde said in utter shock. I was sure that my face showed the shock that I was feeling as well. She really remembered it all.

"How, love?"

"Since Izzy died, every time I close my eyes, I remember my time in Herculaneum. There are things from before

Tiberius, but most of the dreams are of my time with him. With you. I have been reliving the entire two weeks with him since Izzy's death." She said every word as she gazed into my eyes.

I stared at her. Velarde stared at her. "Every minute?"

"Every minute." She turned to look at him and smiled. "I even remember the conversation we had on my wedding day. Tiberius was talking to his father's business associate. You told me about how Tiberius saved your life. How you loved him. I even asked if you two were lovers."

My eyes flicked to Velarde, and he was chuckling.

"I've always loved you as a brother. Get that look off your face," Velarde said to me.

"He did say it was only as a brother, even when I told him I didn't care if you had found comfort in each other. Then, he told me he would come to either of us should we need his help. Now, two thousand years later, you and he sit here, talking to me, just as you did when we were all alive in 79 AD on our wedding day. Before one of the most notable and well-known volcano explosions in recorded history."

My eyes flicked to Velarde and back to her. When her eyes returned to mine, she said, fiercer this time, "So, I ask again, how are Tiberius Maximus Vispania, my husband, and Caleus Lars Velarde, my brother-in-law, sitting before me?"

CHAPTER 57

KELSEY

MAX AND VEL LOOKED at each other, and the shadows in their eyes made my heart hurt.

"Kelsey," Vel started, his throat bobbing a bit.

"Love, it's a story we don't even have all the answers to," Max said without taking his eyes off Vel.

"Look at me, Max," I said carefully. His eyes slowly moved toward me, and I couldn't tell what he was thinking. He had put on that hard mask when he was blocking the world out.

I rose and stood before him. He wrapped his arms around my waist, and mine instinctively went around his neck. After he leaned forward and rested his head on my abdomen for a moment, I said, "Max, Vel, I need to know. Please tell me. No more lies. No more half-truths. Please."

Max looked up at me from where he was seated before me, and there was pleading in his eyes that I didn't know how to decipher. *Did he not know? Was he trying not to tell me?*

"Short story, Kels," Vel said in a long breath. "We've pieced together things, but since . . . Well, short story, okay?"

I turned from Max and stood a few feet back. They looked at each other again, and Max said, "I was en route to an encampment on the Germania border. I was in a tavern, got into a fight, and woke up tied to a pole. There were three women who spread this awful smelling goop across my chest and feet, chanted some bullshit, then they took a knife and slit my neck. I woke up the next morning covered in that goop and blood. I still smell it when I wake from the nightmares."

"A few weeks before I met back up with you and Max in Herculaneum," Vel said, but when he noticed the look on my face, he amended, "Sorry, Sidonia and Tiberius, I mean. I had almost the exact same experience."

"You were trying to tell Tiberius that you two had the same encounter in that meeting in the street," I said as realization hit me. "Something about a scar on your necks that matched? You tried to have one of the merchants verify it."

"What meeting in the street?" Max asked, looking between Vel and me.

Vel smiled. "The day Tiberius introduced me to his soon-to-be bride Sidonia."

Max blinked, and then a slow smile crossed his lips. "You remember that?" he asked incredulously, shaking his head, almost smiling. "Wait, Sidonia was eavesdropping on that conversation?"

I blushed and sat down in the chair. "Yeah, apparently, she was."

"And you knew?" Max turned to Vel.

"Not until she told me how she dreamed it back at the apartment." He smirked. "But yeah, I knew."

"So, back to the issue here. How does that relate to you still being here? You being *you*, I mean." I sat on the edge of the bed and looked at my fingers.

Max came over and knelt before me, holding my hands in my lap with his lips pressed against my fingers. His voice was tight, but then looked up at me through his lashes before he said, "Fuck."

I looked at Vel, and he just said, "You need to tell this part."

"When Vesuvius blew"—he took a deep breath and gulped—"and we died, I woke up two days later, my skin still healing from the burns. I freaked out, cried like a fucking baby, and then strode out to find out if anyone else was alive. That's an oversimplification of what happened after I . . ."

"This fucker found me staring at a destroyed statue of Hercules at the temple," Vel said, half-laughing. "Both of us were naked as the day we were first born. We went to find some clothes and set out to find the Dark Witches of Moesia."

I froze. "You're shitting me. You didn't," I said in disbelief, my eyes flicking back and forth.

"About what part?" Vel said.

"The Dark Witches of Moesia?" I said, my memory bringing up everything I knew about them. "They are the most fucked-up dark magic clan in witch history."

"You know of them?" Max asked.

"Max, I'm an ancient mythology and occult Major. *Of course*, I know of them. Who the fuck doesn't?" I said like *he* was the crazy one in the room. "Anyway, did you find one? And how did you leave that encounter alive?"

"We did find one. She channeled some of the other witches and told us we were made. Apparently, three were made when Vesuvius blew. We still don't know who the third was, and for all we know, they are dead by now. Anyway, she said we would live for all of eternity and every time we die, we would rise two days later, not a scar or mark to show for it," Max said.

"She also said that we would meet our soulmates in the future, and how Max could be with his permanently again," Vel said, staring at Max.

"And yours, Vel?" I asked when Max wouldn't look at me. I suspected he wasn't thrilled about sharing that information with me just yet. Vel just narrowed his lips and turned his head, refusing to look at me.

"The heat that you two feel from each other is how you recognize your mate, your soul-bonded," Vel said.

"And what of your soulmate, Vel?" I pressed.

Neither of them would look at me. *What the fuck with these two? What was I going to do with them?* Okay, well, one of them I wanted to toss on the bed and fuck until I didn't remember any of my names, and the other I just wanted to strip and throw out in a snowstorm, see just how long it would take for him to come back from hypothermia.

"Caleus Lars Velarde," I said, putting my hands on my hips. Both of them sat up and looked at me in shock. "What in the fuck are you hiding from me? You told me once I figured it out, you would answer my questions. Now—"

There was a loud boom that shook the entire room. Max was in front of me, and I was reaching for the gun Vel had put on the table, but he had taken it and was opening the door, gun up and drawn.

Time slowed as I saw a huge plume of smoke billow through the opening and a sword impale through Vel's chest. I saw the black metal rise through the smoke a split second before I heard the gun go off again and saw Max fall to the floor.

Screaming, I ran to Max, who looked at me, rested his hand on my cheek and said, "I'll see you soon, my love. Now run." There was one more raspy breath, and then his chest stopped moving.

"Max?" I said, shaking him. "Come on. Don't die on me."

He just lay there, his face turned toward mine like he was the happiest man on earth.

"Max?" I breathed. I felt every ounce of me plead for him to stand. There was a tether to him, I could feel it, but I couldn't put my fingers on it to pull him back to me.

"Max," I pleaded, but then there was someone standing at his feet.

I looked up and glanced around the room. Smoke filled the space quicker than I thought possible, giving me just a moment to do exactly what Max had told me to do. *Run.*

I crawled up under the bed and lay there for a moment. I didn't know which direction to go. Where would I run to? My apartment was trashed. The apartment at Vispania Tower was likely compromised, if I could even get into it.

Crawling out from under the bed on the other side of Max, I saw Vel lying there, staring at the ceiling. I stifled a sob and saw the bathroom door open. I moved, but when I closed the door to the bathroom and locked it, a familiar blonde woman with eyes black as night appeared. "Night night, Sidonia," she said as she blew white powder in my face.

I coughed, trying to expel it from my lungs, but just as my eyes met the blonde's, everything went black.

CHAPTER 58

KELSEY

"AFTER ALL THESE YEARS. You've finally caught her," a male voice said.

"I had her once. In 1383, during the Ottoman wars, but she slit her own throat to escape me," another voice said. It was so familiar, but I couldn't place it. It was a voice that spanned time in my head.

"What are you going to do? What if she slits her throat again? Or finds some other way to off herself?"

"Then she'll never find her precious Tiberius again. The witches were clear that they would only cross once. I, however, would have her time and time again," the familiar voice said.

"So slit her throat and take her in the next life?"

"Then I can't torment him for all of eternity. And where is the fun in life if you don't get to torture the ones who destroyed yours?" the familiar voice said.

I willed myself to stay still. My hands were tied above my head, and I was slumped on the ground, feet bound. An icy hand wrapped around my jaw, and someone said, "Open your pretty eyes for me, Sidonia. You've been out for two days. It's time to gaze at the rest of your existence, my pet."

When I still didn't move, stayed limp and didn't react, he jerked me harder. "Don't play coy with me, bitch. I know you are awake."

I blinked my eyes open, and as my blurry vision cleared, it focused on the face of that familiar voice. Recognition hit and hit hard, but it was . . . It was impossible.

A sweet smile crossed his lips. "There you are, my beautiful Sidonia."

The fog finally cleared from my head. I tried to skitter away from him but found the back of the wall too close for comfort. I sat there and shook my head. *Marcus.* The man who creeped me out, threatened me at work, just before everything started going to complete shit. "No. Max killed you."

"Yeah, about that," he said, chuckling. He came in close to my ear and lowered his voice to a whisper. "I can't die, pet. I told you at the coffee shop. No matter how many times you kill me, trying to escape, I will still be here."

I shook my head. "I don't understand."

"Just what do you think your name is?"

I narrowed my eyes at him. He had given me a long list of names at the dinner that night Izzy died. I didn't want to play into his games. I had to be smart if I was going to get out of here.

My heart fell at the realization that no one would be coming for me. Izzy was dead. Vel was dead. My heart clenched for a moment before I made myself think the next three words. *Max was dead.* Every one of them died. I was on my own.

"You know my name, fucker. It's Kelsey Stillthorn."

He tsked and shook his head. "I think we all know better than that, don't we, my sweet Sidonia?"

"Don't call me that," I spat before I realized what I had done. *Shit. I had just told him I knew who she was.*

His hand came quick and fast. I didn't feel the sting of it at first, but I felt the blood rise in my mouth and the throbbing of my lip. "You will show me respect in my house, Sidonia." He sat back on his heels, looking at me. He must have given some silent command because my hands rose above me, forcing me to stand. I tried to move my feet, but they were secured to the floor.

"You are a bit overdressed for my liking," he muttered as his gaze raked down my body, and he pulled a knife out of his belt. With an efficiency that proved years of training, he cut my sleeping shorts and T-shirt off.

When I was left bare before him, he moaned. Taking one breast in his hand, he kneaded it and growled, "Oh, a woman indeed." I forced the bile rising in my throat and the shutter that threatened to come through down. I couldn't show a lick of emotion. He slowly stepped behind me and let his hand caress my side, which made my skin crawl. "And such a perfect ass. As I said, I look forward to playing with that." He kneaded each cheek in his hands and gave the left one a quick slap as he came to stand back in front of me.

Slowly, his eyes looked me up and down. Licking his lips, he ran the blade of the knife down my chest bone, between my breasts, and stopped just above my belly button. It stung but didn't really hurt. I looked down to see a small well of red rising where it trailed. Marcus bent down and ran his tongue along that line, licking it clean.

I writhed under him, trying my best to get away, to kick him in the balls, but I couldn't get my legs high enough to reach. My right ankle burned with the jolt of a restraint. A dark chuckle came from him as he reached my neck and kissed it.

"I've had centuries of practice to ensure that when I had you for good, you wouldn't be able to do to me what you did to my father," he said.

I froze and blinked. Time wobbled again, and I whispered, "Impossible." Tears of genuine fear were slowly filling my eyes. It couldn't be *him*. He had been killed on his way to Rome.

He smiled. "You remember?"

I did. It was the one dream I refused to tell anyone about. Izzy had woken me up just as it had finished only once. Max had woken me just before the end without realizing what he had done a couple of nights ago. I had turned over to face him, feigning sleep, just whispering his name repeatedly.

"Marcus Dulcitius," I whispered in horror, my eyes wide. He smiled widely and gave my ass a quick slap with the knife blade. I gritted my teeth. I would not show him any emotion.

"But . . . But I set you free," I stammered.

"Yet you condemned me as well. Although, you did release me from under my father's thumb. It just meant that I could have you to myself. Oh, he was so looking forward to enjoying you. He told me often how sweet you tasted and that he was looking forward to making you his."

"Why the grudge?"

"I don't know what, Sidonia, but you did something to me," he said through his teeth. "Yes, I left. Yes, I went and joined the Empire. The entire time I was there, all I could think about was killing my father. It was like a worm, a parasite eating at my brain," he said, taking a finger and pushing it into my temple, twisting it back and forth.

"I didn't know."

"Didn't know what, Sidonia?" He spat the words and spit landed on my cheek. "Once that sword went through his throat and his head rolled to the side, that was when I was free. It was such a sagging relief to have that needling in my head gone that I just dropped to my knees."

"Why didn't you say anything when I went to see you?" I didn't even know why I asked. Did it make any difference?

"Because I didn't know what was happening. I thought they would take my head before I got out of the colony, and none of it would matter, anyway. They sent me to Pompeii instead. I was technically still a soldier. I belonged to the Emperor."

"Your group was attacked, and you died." My mouth was not going as fast as my brain. "The witches."

He smiled as he realized just how much I remembered and knew. Then I realized what Max and Vel had said. "Three were made that day."

"Three were made that day indeed." He smirked, his eyes trailing down at the blood slowly sliding along the cut he made. "I came back to Herculaneum to claim you. No other woman had made me as hard as you did. I had tried, and no one could withstand my bedroom tactics. With your ability to heal, you could keep all the bruises from festering and heal us all. Every bit of me needs to have you."

"I would have rejected the arrangement," I spat.

"Your father would have been forced to honor it had I gotten back just two days earlier. Only, when I got there, I watched you enter the Vispania's home as Tiberius Vispania's new wife. I lay there outside your chamber window all night listening to him fuck you. Listening to the sounds you made as he made you cum over and over again." He rubbed himself against my leg, letting me know just how hard he was for me right now. The roughness of his jeans grated along my hip, and I tensed against him.

"Then Vesuvius blew. I left town immediately. Figured you would head toward Pompeii with that *husband* of yours. Only you didn't. You stayed there to die. I tried to escape but suffocated on the ash."

He ran a thumb over my lips and another along my hips toward my center. I tried to move away from him, but he gripped me tight.

"Two days later, I woke up alive. Everyone else around me was dead, and ash was still falling from the sky. I looked for you, but I found a merchant I knew safely in Pompeii. He said that your family stayed. Heard you had barricaded yourself in one of the boathouses with your *family*."

I glared at him. "So, I was gone. You should have just moved on with your life. You had all of eternity to find someone to light your flame."

He let out a wicked laugh. "Not a chance. About a year later, I ran into the Dark Witches of Moesia. They told me I would find you again. Our lives were twined."

"Twined, maybe, but my soul belongs to another. I don't burn for you," I said through my teeth. "I don't want you. I never wanted you."

"The witches told me I would spend nearly two thousand years before having you for the rest of my life. So see, I knew I would take back what was mine." He ran his tongue along my jawline, kneading my left breast before he said, "They told me Tiberius had lived. Three were indeed made that day."

My skin crawled with his cold touch as he nibbled on my ear, and I flinched away from him. He chuckled. "Tiberius

Vispania stole what was rightfully, by law, mine. So I have destroyed him every chance I could."

He took a step back and took a crop from the wall. I stared at it. My eyes flicked to the wall and for the first time, I noticed all the restraints and crops, floggers, and other supplies that hung there. My eyes met his again, where they glittered with excitement.

"You are my pet. You are mine. This will be the best sort of torture for him. For centuries, Tiberius has wanted you back in his bed. Now that he has, it will completely destroy him to know that you are mine and pleasuring me. You were promised to me, and by law and right, you are mine."

Marcus didn't know that Max and I hadn't had sex, but only assumed it. I was only just accepting that I didn't hate Max's existence. Okay, I was well past that. I wanted Max, body and soul.

Marcus walked behind me and tightened the slack on my bindings and when I was spread eagle, he ran his hands over my ass. There was a brief moment before the slap rang through the air, followed by stinging pain. I gritted my teeth. I had been with partners who enjoyed this type of play many times, had enjoyed it then because it was consensual.

This was going to be painful, but I could ride this for a long time if needed. I knew how to pace myself. Spanking was low on the list of things that I had done in the bedroom.

He swung again and came around to face me. He took my chin. "By law and right. You. Are. Mine. My. Pet." He punctuated each of the last five words with swings of the crop onto my thighs. Each contact of the crop on my skin stung, but I didn't get the pleasure that would usually come from this. No, instead, I shoved the pain down and concentrated on not reacting.

What he said, though. The phrasing was specific. I looked through Marcus, could almost see the brick wall just outside of my little cell here. Could almost hear an older brown-haired woman tell me that the Mother would always protect those who evoked the old laws. Marcus was laying claim to me by those laws. He had said, *By law and right.*

The old laws.

"If we are playing by the old laws, Marcus Dulcitius." I swung my gaze to his and smirked before I said with determination, "My name is Sidonia Regillia Vispania. Daughter of the Mother Gaea. Wife to Tiberius Maximus Vispania. As my soul is whole, and my husband still lives, you have no hold or claim on me."

There was a musky wind that blew through the room, and I heard various voices gasp.

"By the three-faced goddess, the bitch evoked the old laws," a blonde woman who was standing at the entrance to the cell said. Then she turned toward another woman with flowing brown hair, who stared at me with no color in her face, as she said, "Did she say daughter of Gaea?"

Marcus growled, and I barely saw his fist flying toward me before everything went black again.

Chapter 59

Kelsey

Cold water splashed on my face, and I jerked awake. The blonde-haired woman who had captured me was standing there, hand on her hip, leg jutted out like I was a personal annoyance. I studied her for a moment and realized she was also the pretty blonde that I had danced with the night I had met Mr. Creeper.

"Jannessa," I whispered hoarsely.

"Oh, you got my card. I was hoping you did." She smiled, running a hand down her body. "While I may have been there for Marcus, you are too tasty to resist this time."

"Fuck off," I hissed.

"Marcus wants you cleaned before he comes back," she said, inspecting her nails.

"Then untie me so I can wash," I suggested, gesturing to the hand and feet bindings.

She looked me up and down, licking her lips. "Oh no. I get the pleasure of cleaning you. I heard you like both sexes. Is that true?" she asked, coming over and running a nail across my left nipple. It was warmer in here than when Marcus was here last, but her touch still felt like ice.

"You aren't really my type." I rolled my eyes after giving her a good look over. "Skanky desperate hos aren't really my thing."

She raked her nails over my stomach, leaving a trail of blood on them as I screamed in pain. "Careful, whore. I'm the closest thing you have to a friend in here. Every male in this building wants a piece of that pussy and ass. A few of them have been begging Marcus to let them take you all at once."

She bent over and presented her ass to me. I rolled my eyes again. She got the rag wet and started cleaning the dirt and grime off slowly, taking every chance she could to rub her tits against me. It was so blatant that there was no real sensuality in it.

When she got to my center, though, she spent a lot more time trying to entice me. I forced myself not to move and just completely shut down. If there was no reaction, she would stop, right? Mentally, I huffed a laugh as memories from other lifetimes showed just how ignorant and naïve of a thought that was.

She became so desperate that she stuck two fingers into me and finger fucked me as she leaned in and licked my nipple.

The act, under any other circumstances, would have had me wrapping my legs around her, but it just hurt. Since feeling Max's skin against mine, the coldness of her touch and the feel of her tongue on me felt like a block of dry ice. My body rejected every touch.

After a few minutes, she stood up, and when I met her eyes, they were solid black. I blinked and cocked my head to the side. "You're one of them."

"What?"

"You are one of the Dark Witches of Moesia." My eyes narrowed as I thought through all I knew. "Probably about 120 to 160 years old? How long have you been with Marcus? How long have you wanted to fuck him? How many times did he fuck you, thinking it was me? How many times did you beg him to make you his lover and he blew you off?"

There was just enough slack in the arm restraints that I could rest my arms at my waist, so I crossed them. She took two steps back, realizing I had the slack in the line. Her eyes flashed with the truth. I had hit close. Too close.

"How long have you been wanting Marcus?" I asked again, letting a sly smirk cross my lips.

"A hundred years," she breathed like she wasn't able to keep her mouth shut. "But he keeps going after you. I have seen you in three lifetimes now. You fucking skank. Why can't you just accept him?"

I blinked. *Three lifetimes in 100 years?*

"I don't want him," I said through my teeth.

"Why not?"

"I've never felt an attraction to him. Not as Sidonia. Not as anyone else," I said plainly.

"You were arranged to marry him?" she asked, sounding so young.

"I was, and I found a way out of it." I had used a spell out of my . . . I thought hard and it took a long moment for the memory to come back. I could recall things from several lifetimes. I just had to be patient and think through the multitude of memories for the right one.

"How?" she asked with hatred lacing the word as she glared at me. "If you are a daughter of Gaea, then you are to only do good. To do no harm. Earth Worshipers of your time could not use any power you had. If you even had it, you couldn't do anything but heal. How did you do it?"

"My grandmother had a really old book of spells. A grimoire, I guess you would call it." I tilted my head to the side as I watched her reaction. "I found a spell to influence change. Used it on Marcus. I didn't mean to hurt him or anyone else. I only meant to get out of the arrangement and to help him escape his family. He, ironically, was the kindest of his male relatives."

"Marcus . . . ," she said but trailed off. Then her eyes burned again as they snapped up to meet mine. "You set this all in motion. You wanted him chasing you for all of time. That is what this is about, isn't it?"

I didn't know what had happened until it was over and my foot radiated pain all the way up my leg. She stood, hammer in hand, and said, "I will enjoy destroying you with Marcus. At least I can have him that way."

Then, she picked up the water bucket, dumped it over my head, and stormed out of the room, leaving me with who knows how many broken bones in my foot.

Chapter 60

Max

"Come on, you fuck. You couldn't have died more than a few seconds behind me," Velarde was saying, slapping my face.

I groaned, and then realization came forth. "Kelsey!"

"Marcus has her," he said, waving a note.

I grabbed it and growled.

"I've been looking for her since I found you two," Bella said, and I sat up, groaning. I looked down at my shirt and confirmed that I had been shot in the chest. Gods, I hated being shot. "Vel didn't meet me at the tower apartment, so I came back here to look for you. Found you idiots laid out and Kelsey gone. Not going to lie, I freaked out. Then I saw the note attached to your dick, Tiberius."

I grabbed myself, and she laughed. "I won't tell you exactly how mutilated it was, but personal experience makes me believe you are all pretty shiny and new down there again. He got creative, though."

I looked at the two of them, and there was clear worry on their faces. "Brother . . ." Velarde was waiting for me to give direction.

I looked back at him, determination imbuing each word as I said, "We have to find her. I will not be this close only to lose her."

They looked at each other, and it was Bella who asked. "Do you want Sidonia or Kelsey?"

"Kelsey," I said without hesitation. They looked at each other, a little surprised. "In 79 AD, I chose Sidonia. Now I choose Kelsey. Her soul is whole. I am still alive. By right and law, I am her husband and will marry her again, if she chooses me."

There was an old, musky wind that blew through the room, shattering the bulletproof glass windows. When it stopped, I looked at them. Velarde met my eyes, just as confused as I was. Only Bella's face was full of awe and disbelief.

"Bella, what the fuck was that?" I asked when I noted her smile and the tears that were now falling down her face.

"Old law," she said in amazement.

"I'm sorry, what?" Velarde mirrored my bewilderment.

"And a bit of Sidonia's Earth Worship soul binding spell, I suspect," she said then got up to pace the room. "She's . . ."

"Isabella Edelmann Velarde," I said through gritted teeth.

She raised eyebrows at me. "You haven't called me that since the first time I married this fucker. Gods, that was what? In 1250?"

"1251 actually." Velarde smirked. "You made me wait until after the snowstorms that year because you insisted upon a spring wedding for our first. Stubborn woman."

I laughed at the memory. She had been stubborn about it.

"I wanted to marry you when I first met you on that battlefield in 982. When I saw you climb out from under those *crols*, throw arms and legs off you, dried blood coating every inch of you, I knew I had to make you mine. You knew it too. You just wanted me to prove it like the warrior you are. Then you made me chase you all over the fucking planet for two centuries before agreeing to marry my ass. So yes, I remember the year. Now the date, that gets a little fuzzy," he said, kissing her cheek.

"I love you guys, but Kelsey!" The panic was rising in my chest.

"You spoke the ancient words. For the elements to react the way it did, it means she has spoken them and claimed you as her lawful husband as well . . ." Bella blinked, trying to remember something specific. Fear and panic crossed her face, and she turned to leave the room but said over her shoulder, "We have to get her away from Marcus."

"Bella, what is it?" I scrambled to my feet and lunged for her, taking her hand to make her look at me.

"Before I started running from Caleus, remember how you both told me stories of Sidonia? You let it slip she was an Earth Worshiper. I had lived with them before I died the first time, so I know their ways." She looked at me and asked, "Do you remember me begging for the details of the spell she cast before you two died?"

"Yeah. I also remember how you made me remember whether they were green or purple shamrocks that she used for the spell too."

"I knew then it was a spell to bind the soul so the both of you would go together to the Mother. Since you died and came back, your souls didn't. I figured it was because whatever this curse is that makes us live for eternity had already been set upon you, but it did bind your souls."

"Get to the point, Isabella," Velarde demanded, and Bella turned and stuck her tongue out at him.

"While running from your royal sexiness, I was in Tibet for a bit. There was a Dark Witch of Moesia whom I had worked with on and off. I may have mentioned you two. Told her how my soulmate was chasing me across the globe with his brother and how much of a pain in the ass they both were. You know, the usual girl gossip."

"Bitch," Velarde teased.

"Gods, you two are sickeningly cute together. How have I dealt with you two without killing you a few times myself?" I grumbled, pinching my nose. They really did drive me crazy sometimes. "Not to mention, I haven't killed you yet, but am seriously thinking about it right now because you won't get to the fucking point, Bella."

"Killjoy. She told me of the Clothea Sisters, who went through and created about forty beings, like myself, around the Roman Empire. There was a huge hunt among the Moesia Elders for those who had been creating us. The Clothea Sisters were brutal in their attempts. Only one in like fifty survived. So, there was a long blood trail. She said the witch that created me was one of the last found and executed for the practice."

We headed down to the car, and as we got in, she said, "She reiterated that her soul would have to drink from your neck, Tiberius. She was very specific about that. She mentioned her soul could get pregnant, but you wouldn't have a chance of that happening before her soul would have to drink from your vein."

I froze before hitting the ignition. Velarde was staring at her in horror.

"You know how Tiberius has always felt about that," Velarde said.

"I know." Bella looked at me with a sad, conflicted expression.

"Then why have you never given him the warning?"

"Because he never found her soul. Never found Sidonia. Now he has, so I'm giving it now." She turned to me with pleading eyes. "The thing is, she has to be near death. Which means that if Marcus has her, he might kill her before she can drink from your vein. If you do not convert her in this lifetime, Tiberius, she will be gone from you forever. You get one, just one of her lifetimes to do this. That is all."

I felt sick to my stomach. I thought back to that day in Germania with the witch when Velarde and I caught her. She had said Sidonia would have to either drink from my vein or become pregnant with my child, but she had said nothing about us never having the chance to get pregnant.

"Velarde, you drive," I said, getting out because there was no way I could right now. When I sat down in the back seat with Bella, I asked, "So why are you in such a hurry to find her now? Don't get me wrong, I want her, no, *need* her at my side. I'm not debating that we need to find her right away. Who knows what Marcus is doing to her?"

"It's just, you stated your claim on her through old laws. The original laws of your souls. Judging by the fact that the bulletproof glass windows burst and wind came from nowhere . . ." She put her head in her hands. "Tiberius. Did Sidonia ever tell you if she was a daughter of Gaea?"

I looked at her and knitted my eyebrows together. "No. She never mentioned Gaea."

"But she was an Earth Worshiper who worked through a deity called the Mother?"

I nodded. "She once asked me if I knew who the original families were."

Bella let out a long, deep breath as Velarde pulled out onto the main road to the tower.

"And what was that about the old laws?" Velarde asked as we drifted through an intersection toward the underground.

Bella's eyes filled with fear and her body went impossibly still, as her mind raced backward in time. "The witch I talked to said that should you both lay claim to each other by the old laws, that it will set the timer running. You have thirty days to find her and convert her or she turns to ash again. There will be no rebirth."

CHAPTER 61

KELSEY

FOOD CAME, AND I slept for what I guessed was a couple hours by the way the light had moved across a window. I was just stirring awake when a voice said, "I was wondering when you would wake up. We may have given you a little too much." I blinked and saw Marcus sitting in a chair in the corner with a book that he carefully placed on the seat as he stood and strode over to me.

My foot hurt like hell. I glanced down and winced at the toe that was bending in the wrong direction. The whole foot was swollen and discolored.

"Jannessa says you didn't play well." His eyes flickered down at my injury before his gaze flowed up my long legs, over my hips, and he ran his fingers over the marks on my stomach. "She apologized for marking your stomach, but it's healed well in two days."

"Two days?" I croaked.

"Yesterday, when it was clear you would not wake and drink on your own, we had to force some water down your throat. I can't have you die on me now, can I?"

Two days. That meant that Tiberius and Velarde should be awake, if what they said was true. Would they even be looking for me? Would they even care? If what they had said about rising from the dead were true. *Shit, I was married to a zombie!* I huffed a laugh at the thought.

Marcus narrowed his eyes at me. "Find something funny?"

"So, I've been here three days then?" I needed to find out the timing of things.

"Four actually," he softly answered, inspecting a few spots on my body. "You heal quickly, Sidonia, except for this foot."

I narrowed my eyes at him as he smirked before he straightened the toe and the pain lanced through me. Gritting my teeth together and hissing, I tried to keep the tears that were in my eyes from falling. I knew that I couldn't show any weakness here, but fuck, that hurt like a bitch.

"I punished her for it," he said with a twinkle in his eye. My focus landed on the BDSM supply wall, and he chuckled. "Don't worry, my pet. You and I will spend much time playing with those. Soon."

I rolled my eyes to make it appear as if I didn't give two shits what he did. It backfired horribly, though, because he hit a button on the wall and I was spread eagle and in the air for him, my foot screaming in pain. He said in my ear, "Remember the fun my father had with you?"

My entire body froze. I could feel my legs and stomach tremble at the memory from so long ago. It wasn't even this body. It was what had happened two thousand years ago, and the memory and shame of that made this body react in fear.

"When he let Dante's wife out of the bedroom, the door was still left open slightly. I sat in the chair in the main room, pretending I was reading, and watched every moment while my father taught you the first rule of our house."

I closed my eyes and willed myself to calm. Marcus ran a finger down my neck and said, "I remember every detail. It was one of the most erotic things I have ever seen in my life. The way he—" His voice cut off. A scream ripped through me as he bit down on my right breast. When I looked down, time wobbled, and Marcus was his father, then he was Marcus again.

"No. Please," I felt myself say.

"Please what, Sidonia?"

"Please don't. Please don't do this, Marcus."

He smiled, and just as it had been on that day in Herculaneum, blood covered the Dulcitius male's lips. Marcus Dulcitius stood there and stripped before me, and I tried so hard to shut down. I tried to remove myself from everything, but Marcus came over, pulled on a mechanism, and I was forced to lean forward.

He walked across the room and came back with a stand that had two horizontal pieces of wood connected by a longer piece in the middle. He put his hand on my throat, squeezed tightly, and pushed me backwards slightly, allowing him enough room to have my hips line up with one of the boards. "This should at least keep you in position."

With one hand still on my throat, he reached down with the other and pumped himself. I swallowed and closed my eyes. "Open your eyes and look at me," he growled, squeezing on my neck, and I couldn't help but open my eyes.

"Look at how hard you make me, Sidonia. I wish you could see how gorgeous you look right now." He continued to stroke himself as he walked behind me.

I stiffened and tried to move my legs to close them, but I was already in so much pain from trying to balance on one foot and the brace. It pinched and hurt against my hip bones.

Running his hand over my ass, he smacked it with a crop. It stung, but I bit my lip to keep from screaming, knowing that was what he wanted. Again and again, he swung that crop down onto my ass. It was just as it had been with his father. I wouldn't be able to sit for a long while after this.

"Scream for me, Sidonia," he growled through labored pants.

"Fuck you," I spat as another swing landed. That time, I felt the skin split.

He ran a finger along the cut and laughed. "Your blood is delicious."

Smack.

Smack.

Smack.

"I told you to scream for me," he demanded through gritted teeth.

Smack.

Another area of skin split.

"Fuck off," I said from the recesses of my mind where I had retreated.

I forced myself to remember to breathe.

I would pace myself.

Smack.

I would not give in. I would *not* give in.

Smack.

Smack.

Smack.

He tossed the crop to the side and ran his fingers down my slit as I wiggled to avoid him, but then he was rubbing the head of his cock against me, and I clenched myself as tight as I could to prevent him from entering me.

I distantly felt myself moving again to avoid him, but then there were strips of pain down my back. When the shock of that unexpected agony ripped through me, I loosened my grip on myself and he plunged into me.

Gods, it hurt, and I couldn't help but scream.

"That's my good little pet. Scream. Scream and tell everyone how much you love my cock in your tight pussy."

I jerked, and there was another smack against my back in those strips.

He loved my pain. My fight. I willed myself to go still. To stay silent and not react. Willed my mind to go somewhere else. I tried to make myself think of being anywhere other than there.

He pounded into me relentlessly, and that was the one place I couldn't keep from clenching as tight as I could. I didn't want him. I didn't want this.

There was a leather strap around my neck that he used to pull me closer to him with each thrust. It was making it hard for me to breathe.

"You love this, don't you, bitch? You love me taking you like the whore you are," he breathed with each long stroke.

He pulled tight with a final grunt, and I felt him release inside me. It made me want to throw up right there. My stomach rolled repeatedly as he held my throat with that strip of leather. My lungs burned as the air supply was cut off the tighter he pulled me back, and I thrashed, trying to get some air into my lungs.

"That's right, cum for me," he praised, pulling on it tighter.

He thrust into me harder again, and then everything went black.

Chapter 62

Max

"Anything on Hernandez yet, Velarde?" I asked as I stared out the window.

"Nothing. We have a description of him, though."

I looked down at my hands, which were cut and bloodied. The informant we found tonight died way too easily. I hardly got anything from him. Looking back over my shoulder, I saw the blood splattered across the wall and glared at it. It would get worse by the time this was done, but I didn't care. I would find Kelsey, and I would beat and torture this whole town until I did. She would be in my arms, alive and well, soon.

"We will find her, brother." Veldarde's hand was on my shoulder, and it took everything I had not to take him and toss him through the window and watch him fall the seventeen stories to the street. The fact he was my brother likely saved his ass. It may also have to do with the fact that my rage, fueled by fear, was making me unreasonable. "I got information on the nightwhispers from his friend, though."

"Nightwhispers?" I asked.

Velarde was shaking his head and smirking. "You aren't going to believe this."

"I'm not?"

"Remember that white powder that was blown in our face before . . ." He pointed to his neck where his scar still sat after all these years.

I ran my hand along my neck, knowing exactly where that damn scar sat. Only those made by the Dark Witches of Moesia could see it. Velarde's was much the same as mine, but Bella's was a throng of multiple slices. She told us she hadn't been bound like Velarde and I had, and so she fought her captor. It took a while for the witch to kill Bella, so hers were much more violent looking.

"Your point?"

He just raised his eyebrows at me. "You are so distracted and worried about Kelsey that you can't put that together?"

I gritted my teeth and slowly took a deep breath. "Humor me or I'll rethink my decision to not throw you out the window to another death."

He actually winced at that and smiled. "The powder they blew in our face to knock us out? That is what the night-whispers are. We got confirmation that it's being commercially marketed to help with insomnia." As I cocked an eyebrow at him, he took another deep breath and continued, "Only, on the streets, it is being used as a date rape drug. We pulled it from these two trying to sell it and got the names for six more pushing at four of the bars we own. Before you ask, yes, I've already put the word out to Anton, Miguel, Tyron, and Jackson about watching their bars for it. Spoke to the police chief too, who said there have been two rapes reported in the last two weeks, but the victims remember nothing."

"If two have been reported, you know more have occurred and they just aren't coming forward," I growled, balling my hands into fists.

"I have a lead. Want to take some frustration out?" Velarde said, a wicked smile on his face. I raised an eyebrow and looked at the mess behind me. "Okay, more frustration out?"

"You know this is exactly why she hates me, right?" I let a dark laugh huff out. I was itching for a fight, but I also knew that Kelsey was right in this aspect.

"Yeah, well, she will have to get over it, or at least used to it, since she is gonna stick around," Velarde said, laughing.

I just looked at him, shocked. "What makes you think she is going to stick around?"

"Well, according to Isabella, she evoked the old laws of her Earthen Worship, so if she did that, then it sounds to me like she claimed you, brother."

"I let her get captured by Marcus. The Gods only know what he is doing to her."

"Aphrodite really needs to come down here and smack you both! I fucking swear on all that is holy." Velarde groaned with a long, frustrated sigh.

"Why is Caleus calling upon Aphrodite? Please don't. She's a bit of a bitch." Bella practically skipped in, only slowing to a walk when she noticed the mess. She gave me an even look and sighed. She was about to say something when Velarde answered her.

"Kelsey and Max here can't pull their heads out of their asses long enough to realize just how much they love each other," Velarde teased and kissed her on the top of her head as she snuggled next to him.

"Well, that is true, but we have to find her first. Then we can all live happily ever after." Bella nibbled on her lips with worry, but she did her best to make it sound cheerful.

"Yup, definitely rethinking throwing you out the window. Maybe Bella right after." I groaned, stomping out the door and down the hall.

Kelsey was right about one thing she had said. We had loved each other in 79 AD. We did. We both knew that, but Kelsey and Max didn't know each other. How could we possibly love each other?

Kelsey was all I thought about. Not just because Marcus had her and she was enduring the Gods only knew what, but I craved just coming home every night to ask her how her day was, holding her in my arms, and smelling that strawberry scent from her soap. I wanted to go see the world with her. Sure, I'd seen most of it over my last two thousand years, but to be able to experience it with her . . . Gods, there could be no better way to spend eternity.

First, we had to find her.

Bella and Velarde caught up to me, and I hit the button for the private garage on the elevator. I sent a text to one of the cleanup guys to get the guy in the interrogation room and asked Velarde, "So, where are we going?"

"Frenzy," Velarde said.

"Jackson has someone in the basement for us."

CHAPTER 63

MAX

"Downstairs, Max," Jackson said as we entered the club. She was dressed in a tight white dress with cutouts just below the breasts that flattered her fit figure and stood as a stark contrast to her dark skin. Her hair was pulled up onto the top of her head and was braided elegantly. Her hazel eyes were something men had fought each other over, including the two standing at her back. She didn't take any shit, and I fully respected her for it. Jackson had won the rights to Frenzy through blood, sweat, and tears.

The old owner had taken her in after her parents died in a boating accident on the lake. When he died, he had a stipulation in the trust that said Jackson could have the club if she turned a 100K profit in three years. She busted her ass and turned a 300K profit, averaging the minimum per year. His kids were livid when the attorneys handed Frenzy to her. It was a successful club but did nothing for me. It was all techno music and strobe lights, but there was a club for everyone in this town.

I could feel my shoulders tightening as we crossed the floor, and by the time we got to the stairwell at the back, I was rolling my neck and cracking my knuckles.

As I turned to go downstairs, I felt a hand on my shoulder, and when I looked over it, Jackson said, "We have everyone looking out for Marcus, Max. There are two men downstairs. One is rather cranky, and the other says he's met with Marcus a few times but otherwise only dealt with the nightwhispers deliveries. He swears he doesn't know where your woman is."

"Thanks, Jax." She smiled softly before keying in the code to unlock the door.

"Max," she said, and I turned around. "If you find her, me and the boys will go in behind you to do whatever you need. No one fucks with you. If what I'm hearing is right, this could get messy, and I just wanted you to know we got your back."

I nodded, and Vel gave her a smile that had her blushing. It was Bella who said in a tone that was all deathly business, "We will let you know once we have a location."

Two men were tied to chairs at different ends of the room. The one closest had a gag ball in his mouth, and I couldn't help but chuckle. "Seriously? No one could find something other than a ball gag to shut him up?"

"What?" the man in the corner asked, smiling. "Just came from my woman's. It's what I had when Jackson called me in."

I laughed, turning to the man in the chair. His eyes were wide as recognition hit him as to just who was standing in front of him. I reached around and unclasped the back and pulled it off.

"Mr. Vispania," he whispered in horror.

"Oh good. I don't have to introduce myself." I rolled up the sleeves of my shirt, and out of the corner of my eye, I saw Velarde do the same. Slowly, he made his way to stand behind the man. Bella was cleaning her fingernails with a knife next to the stairs like we were waiting for our takeout order. My eyes flicked to the other man, and he was entirely too calm.

Turning to him, I ripped the tape off his mouth and he screamed. I snickered as I saw the strands of his beard pulled out by the root on the sticky side of the tape. "Sorry, your beard is a little thinner now."

"I'm not gonna to tell you anything," he spat, then he hocked a loogie which landed on my shoe. I cringed, and then my eyes flashed in anger. Fueled by the fear I felt, I reached over and snapped one of his fingers. He screamed then hissed at me.

"Where is Marcus?" I said, grabbing another finger and snapping it.

"Please don't make Mr. Vispania repeat himself. I don't want to clean up the blood tonight," Casper, Jackson's bouncer, said. It was a bit of a joke, but he had earned it. Jackson had taken in a lot of kids off the street after she inherited Frenzy. Casper's skin was dark as night, and he could slip in and out of places no one else could, regardless of his size. He was also one of the nicest people in this town, despite his occupation.

"You want his woman?" the man in the chair asked, but it was clear he knew it to be the truth.

The entire room went silent as my fist made contact with his jaw, and I felt bone give way. My hand stung as I shook it out. "Fuck, you have a hard head."

"What do you know of Kelsey?" Velarde demanded.

The man spit blood onto the floor and looked up at me. "I don't know who Kelsey is."

"You just said Marcus has a woman," I said, gritting my teeth. "Describe her."

"Pretty, sexy thing. He's been having fun breaking her in. She's defiant. Red hair, beautiful green eyes, nice, plump, delicious ass. Oh, he loves her ass. She has a tattoo of a moon next to her right tit. Cradles it perfectly," he said, licking his lips hungrily.

Suddenly, there was a knife inches from his dick. My head swung around, and when I saw Bella, she was furious. My eyes flicked to Velarde, and he was instantly in front of Bella, trying to calm her down. I, however, slowly turned my head back to the man in the chair and pulled the knife out of the seat. Bella flung that blade between me and the douche in front of me and still missed his dick by less than a quarter of an inch from across the room. Kelsey and Bella would be a deadly pair for sure.

"Where is Marcus keeping her?" I snarled, turning back to the man in the chair. I was every ounce the terrorizer that Kelsey believed me to be right then.

"Fuck you," he said, and my hand moved, pulling the knife from my back pocket and quickly cutting two fingers off, one after the other.

"Where is Marcus keeping her?" I asked once again when the screaming stopped.

Over and over again, I asked until he didn't have any fingers left. Velarde came over and took the knife from me at that point. The man had passed out, and we would get nothing else from him.

"Deal with him," I said, turning to the other man and kneeling before him. "What is your name?"

"K-kit St. Clair," he stuttered, just above a whisper.

I blinked. I knew that name. "You have an office a few blocks down from here."

"Yes. I specialize in internal medicine."

"Dr. St. Clair." I wiped my hands on my pants. Blood smeared all over them. "I was told that you had dealings with a man named Marcus."

"Y-ye-s . . . Yes, sir. I met with him a few times." His head dropped. "My oldest son had a heroin addiction. Racked up a lot of debt a few years back living in Anaheim. When he overdosed, Marcus' men said I had inherited his debt. I've been running interference to pay it off."

"And lately?"

"He has a new drug."

"Nightwhispers. I'm aware. What have you been doing with it?" I asked, standing up and crossing my arms over my chest as I heard Velarde snap the neck of the guy behind me. St. Clair's eyes widened as he jumped at the sound.

"That's not enough," Bella growled, and out of the corner of my eye, I saw her take a knife from her boot and stab him through his dick. I tried to hide the cringe by taking a deep breath and looked back at St. Clair.

"Look at me, Kit. I'm the one you should be concerned about right now. What has he been doing?" I asked, bringing his attention back to me.

"He just asked me to give it out as a prescription for a sleep aid mostly," he said, his eyes still flicking behind me. "There was a day, though, a week or two ago, that he met with me and he was looking at a picture on his phone. He was running a finger over her face. A redhead. He calls her his pet."

"When are you meeting with him next?" I asked, trying not to grind my teeth. "Or are you only dealing with his men now?"

"I'm not set to meet with him for a few days." His eyes went questioning. "Why? I have nothing to do with this woman you are all so concerned about."

"Do you know where she is being held?"

He shook his head. "No."

"How do you know so much about her then?"

"His men brag about her. They say she's beautiful, and how much they want a piece of her, but Marcus won't let anyone else touch her. He has a woman who works with him, though. She apparently touched this girl one day and Marcus made her pay for it. On more than one occasion actually. I've had to mend the other woman a few times."

"How often?"

"Couple . . . Three times, to be exact, in the last couple weeks," Kit said, his voice shaking.

"Max," Velarde said carefully.

I looked at him, and there was a warning on his face. I paced before the good doctor, thinking things through. Here was a man who at least had some contact with Marcus. He knew Kelsey was with Marcus, but could he get close to her?

"Dr. Kit St. Clair." I turned to face him. All the color drained from his face. "The next time you are called to go in there, get to the redhead. Find out where Marcus is keeping her, how we can get into the building. Find out how many guards there are."

His eyes were wide as I told him what he was going to do for us.

"Mr. Vispania. H-he will kill me if he finds out." St. Clair was stuttering through the fear. "I have a wife, two girls still who have stayed innocent through all of this. My wife knows about the debt, but she doesn't know anything else. The girls are innocent."

"Then let's keep it that way. You get the information I need to get her out of there, and we will ensure they stay happy and healthy. Understand?" My voice was lethal, and I hated myself for it. I had never threatened a man's woman or child. I was not worthy of Kelsey. She was right. I was nothing better than the roaches that went down the dirtiest alleys of Trenton.

But that didn't matter. I had to get her out of Marcus' grip. I had to get her safe, so she could be happy and healthy. Whether that was by my side or not.

The man looked at me for a long moment and just said, "I don't know when I will see her. If I can even get access to her."

I leaned in close, putting both of my hands on the arms of the chair he was sitting on. "You find a way, Kit."

He gulped. "What if she's dead by the time I find her?" he asked, flinching as he said the words.

My hands gripped the chair tight, and I pushed it back so hard, it hit the wall ten feet back. The man's head hit the wall with a thud that had Bella rushing to make sure I hadn't just killed our only way to Kelsey.

"He is bleeding, but he is alive." She glared at me over her shoulder.

We waited ten minutes before he regained consciousness. Vel was making sure he was alright and didn't have any issues other than a mild concussion. When he gave me a small nod, and St. Clair was looking much more coherent, I strode toward him, but Bella's hand was on my chest before I got there. "Max."

Taking a deep breath, I stood before him, legs wide, arms crossed. "Do we have a deal, Dr. Kit St. Clair?"

"We have a deal," he said carefully.

"Casper, let him go home to his family," I ordered. Before they left the room, I said, "Oh, and Kit?"

"Yes, Mr. Vispania," he said, rubbing the back of his head.

"I'll have a tail on you. Get a burner phone or two so you can tell us when you have information."

"Yes, sir." He gulped then slowly went upstairs. It was a long shot. A real long shot, but a shot nevertheless.

"Kit!" Bella shouted after him, meeting them halfway up. She whispered something to him and he nodded. I vaguely heard a, "Yes, ma'am," before they were out of sight again.

"What was that about?" I asked Bella when she got back downstairs.

"If he gets to Kelsey, I told him to deliver a message, one only I would have ever given her," she said. "If Marcus is holding her captive, who knows what else he is doing to her? She needs to know that we are coming."

I nodded and then said, "In the meantime, we continue looking for Kelsey. The clock is ticking. We only have . . ." I couldn't think straight. *How long had it been?*

"We still have two weeks, Max." Bella took my hand. "We will find her."

"It feels like that day I woke up in the boathouse all over again. So close and so far away from her." I barely said the words. "They aren't the same person, and I'm not comparing them. I am, but I'm not. I need Kelsey."

Bella looked at me, then to Velarde, who tried to smile, but his eyes gave off the same worried sense of loss that was flowing through me relentlessly. "I get it, Max. We will find her."

CHAPTER 64

KELSEY

EVERY DAY, IF NOT twice a day, he came into this cell and forced himself into me. Every day, he would come in and beat my body. My ass was so shredded that I couldn't sit on it without resplitting the wounds and bleeding all over the place. He loved the pain, the blood, the torture. The more I fought, winced, and bled, the more turned on Marcus had become.

He had at least brought in a mattress for me to sleep on and one blanket. There had been explicit instructions that it was to be folded in the corner the moment I woke up in the morning, and I was only allowed to touch it when going to sleep for the night.

Someone had even upgraded me to having actual toilet paper in my corner "bathroom." I still hadn't been allowed to clean myself, and as much as Jannessa tried to deny how much she hated washing me, I knew it turned her on. She would always reek of sex when she left. A few minutes later, I would hear her and whatever guard was in the hall fucking each other. There were still no clothes.

When I had asked if I could at least have a shirt, he said, "For you to hang yourself with? No, my Sidonia, you will stay here, ready to do my bidding. I will not have clothing in our way."

I curled up tighter into a ball and groaned. Every inch of me hurt. Every time Marcus left, Jannessa came in. She wasn't a friend. No. Gods, no. She wasn't here to support me or heal any of my wounds. No, she was here to further demoralize me.

She would come in and spread my legs wide, just so she could either collect Marcus' cum dripping out of me, pushing it into herself, or force herself between my legs to drink it up.

I gagged each time she touched me. She would be there for hours, but I couldn't remember what else she would do.

I remembered very little of the last couple of weeks. I knew time passed, and I thought I had been there for about two and a half, maybe three weeks, but time existed somewhere else. Not there.

Was I ever going to get out of here? Why didn't he just kill me already? What was the point? Would I just be a piece of meat to do with what he willed for however long I had left? If I came back again in another life, would it just be Marcus hunting me down and torturing me?

Various images flooded my mind from my time in this cage, but my mind was blocking things out. There were holes, gaps in time. I would wake with parts of my body hurting and couldn't remember what he had done. I would wake up to find new sores, split skin, and one day, I even saw cut marks between my legs. I had no memory of how they had happened. I woke one day last week with my ass bleeding but no memory of having anal penetration with Marcus. My body remembered what was happening, though, because each time he came in, I would shake uncontrollably.

I tried to tap it down, tried to keep my muscles from trembling in unadulterated fear. I had closed my eyes once, and only once, trying to force my muscles to stop shaking, and he forced me to open my eyes with a crop to the cheek. There was a cut near my eye, but ever since, I made sure to keep my eyes on him. He had watched the trembling muscles with such reverence every time.

I heard keys at the door, and when I looked up, I didn't know what to think. It wasn't Marcus or Jannessa before me, but another man. His bright brown eyes widened as he looked me over from head to toe. His hair was your standard men's cut, short on the sides, slightly longer on top. Not long like Tiberius' but just a boring everyday style. This man couldn't have been more than six feet tall, and he was slender in a way that didn't show much shape under his long-sleeve black dress shirt and black jeans. His hands tightened on the handle of the bucket and a first-aid kit in his hands.

"My name is Kit." There was a dark shadow that crossed his face that I could not read. "I'm here to tend to your wounds. Marcus doesn't want you to die of infection."

I blinked at him as he came closer. There was movement by the door, and I curled up in a ball. The near constant guard was watching this man's every move and listening to what he said carefully. I hated that particular guard. Too many times, I had seen him jacking off, watching what Marcus was doing to me.

The man named Kit took slow, controlled steps as I watched him move closer. He ran a hand over his short blond hair and closely shaved beard. He was decent looking, and when my eyes met his, there was sorrow in them.

"Sidonia," he said carefully.

"Kelsey," I croaked. My voice sounded wrong.

"I'm sorry?"

"Please, call me Kelsey," I said hoarsely. My throat was ravaged by the screams I couldn't prevent and from Marcus forcing himself down there. I had once seriously considered just biting his dick off, but he had held a knife to my throat, and there was this small glimmer of me that hoped to see Max just one last time. Only, there were no happy ever after stories for me. I was beginning to realize I would die in this cell. It was just a matter of time. I wanted to die, but each time I thought of letting death consume me, Max's sapphire eyes would flash before me and I would feel that heat in my soul that begged for me not to give up.

His eyes were kind when he responded softly, "Okay, Kelsey."

"*He* calls me Sidonia."

Understanding came upon his face and he nodded. He said nothing else as he tentatively started inspecting each cut and bruise. His fingers were light and gentle. I couldn't help but notice how his mouth would tighten occasionally as he made his way up my body.

"Marcus wanted me to inspect some potential damage to your pelvic area as well."

I glared at him, and my legs shook. Slowly, I tucked my arms around them to hold them still, but it was hard with the restraints. I had some slack, but not enough. Never enough.

His voice was low and soothing as he gulped slowly and said, "Kelsey, I am not here to hurt you. I promise. I am a doctor." Then his voice lowered again, "I promise I am here to help you, not hurt you in any way."

I nodded and moved so that he could look. I tried to stay completely motionless. His hands were ice cold and so gentle that I had to fight back a moan at how soothing they felt. The cold was so good against the heat of the inflammation that I knew was between my legs from one end to the other. He applied a numbing healing cream, and after he was done, he gently turned me over and motioned for me to sit. I winced, and it took a moment before I found a way to sit upright that didn't hurt so much.

His face was hard, and there was a fire in his eyes that betrayed his anger. He leaned closer to me, and I stiffened.

"Sorry, but there is a pretty good gash next to your ear. I need to get closer to stitch it up. Is that okay?" Kit said softly.

I didn't even know there was a gash there. *When did I get that one?* Kit moved closer, and there was a small bite from the needle going in, but I barely registered it. When he was done sewing me up, he made a show of looking for something in his kit but then said, "I need to bite the thread off."

I became a statue. Slowly, Kit leaned forward, and just before he bit the string off, he whispered so lightly I barely heard it, "Hold fast, Kels Bells."

Everything within me stopped. I made a very conscious effort not to look at him as he pulled away from me. He moved back slowly and looked at my lower lip. "There isn't anything I can do for the lip. It's just going to heal on its own."

My eyes slid to his, and there were two quick blinks before he turned from me and left the room like he hadn't just given me both the most confusing message and the most hopeful one in four words.

I didn't dare look back at him. I just curled up tighter into a ball on the floor and stared at nothing.

Hold fast, Kels Bells. There was only one person who had used that phrase with me: Izzy.

Vel didn't know it. He didn't know the meaning behind it. And Max certainly didn't.

Izzy.

It crashed into me like a tidal wave. Izzy was like Vel and Max. It was the only explanation. That night, in the restaurant—the night Izzy died. Max and Vel hadn't freaked out over her death. Neither of them had talked about having a memorial or funeral for her, had even skirted the topic when I brought it up. Vel straight up refused to talk about it, told me he couldn't talk about it. Because I didn't know that Izzy was just like Vel and Max. It was part of this whole secret. Why had she been protecting them?

I internally winced at my own stupidity. After she died and I tried to talk to Vel and Max about Vel's soulmate, he completely ignored the entire discussion and brought it back to Max and me. Just how long had Vel and Izzy been together?

Lifetimes passed before my eyes over the next few hours. Recognition hit as I recalled just how many times Izzy and Vel had been entwined in my lives over the centuries. I could see them all connected so clearly now. I'd been so close to Max and nothing. Not until now.

The shield-maiden, the one I had been so many lifetimes ago, stood before me with her friend Lady Bella now in that cell. They looked down and smiled at me.

"Took you long enough to realize it." Lady Bella smirked as she clasped the shield-maiden on the shoulder.

"Do you really think you weren't meant to be together?" the maiden asked me. *"You are strong. You are a daughter of Gaea. She does not suffer weak women in her line."*

"Your mind has been trying to protect you from the truth. You know you have lived hundreds of lives. Think about the night that I died in that restaurant, Kels Bells," Lady Bella said.

I blinked and they disappeared. Now, I saw us all sitting at the restaurant again, where Marcus had put his hand on Vel's shoulder and talked about killing Lady Bella's husband. Izzy's eyes had narrowed and rage flashed through them. Vel had stiffened and looked at Izzy.

"Sir Lars was Vel," I breathed.

"What was that?" the guard said.

"Water, please?" I croaked. Reluctantly, he handed me a small cup of water. I sipped it slowly as I thought through everything else.

"Though face and form alter with the years, I hold fast to the pearl of my mind." It had been Izzy and my favorite phrase from Hanshan. We learned it in our Chinese history and mythologies class a few years ago, but we had used it as a call to not give up. It was a way for us to know that we would always have each other to get through anything.

Now, knowing that we had been soul sisters for lifetimes, it meant so much more. Even though my face had changed, Izzy had been there. Our minds and souls were one. She and I would hold fast to each other.

Fuck, Izzy! How did you keep this from me over the last few weeks? The man named Kit had blinked twice quickly. There was a meaning to the way he did it. He was conveying Izzy's message.

She was alive, and I was sure that she was with Max and Vel. That was our code phrase that we were on the way to rescue the other. Usually from a creeper or something at a bar, but it was our message. Max, Vel, or this man, Kit, could not know all of that. It was *our* secret code.

I took a long, raspy breath as the guard reached out for the cup, and I handed it back to him. I scooted back toward my spot again and, after a few minutes, found a comfortable position.

Max, Vel, and Izzy were coming. I just had to hold on.

CHAPTER 65

MAX

UNKNOWN:

Jackson and Stillwell. Romano's back door. 10 minutes.

That was all the text message said from the unassigned number. Fifteen fucking minutes ago.

"Where is he?" Vel asked. His gun was in his hand behind his back as he leaned against the wall. He wasn't taking any chances that this was a trap.

"He will be here," I said, trying not to grind my teeth.

It was another ten minutes before the door to Romano's opened and Kit stepped into the alley.

"What was the holdup?" I growled out before Vel could lose his shit.

"I had to make sure that his guys weren't following me. I'm here under the guise of having dinner with my family. Excused myself to go to the bathroom. And after the day I've had today, you can kindly fuck off," Kit said, running his

413

hand through his hair and then scratching the stubble on his cheek. He looked like absolute hell.

"What did you find out, Kit?" Vel asked carefully.

"Mr. Vispania. Do you promise not to kill me for what I'm going to tell you?" His voice wavered. "I have done everything you said. To the letter."

"He may not, but I might," Vel growled, not bothering to hide the gun anymore.

My heart thundered. "Is she alive?"

"Her heart still beats," he said, freezing. I could almost hear the panicked thumping of his heart. "He's . . ."

"Say it," I growled.

"He has beaten and raped her repeatedly. She's a mess. The fact she is still alive is amazing. I don't know what she is holding onto, to not just let him kill her, but it's bad, sir." He said the words so quickly that there was no doubt what he said was the truth.

All sound vanished when the words sank in. He has raped and beaten my Kelsey. We had four days left. Four days. For twenty-six days, he had been brutalizing her.

We had narrowed it down to a four-block area on the west side of town. We thought he was in the pharmacy or financial building, but we couldn't see anything on the floor plans that suggested where he might be holding her.

I ran my hand through my hair, gripping it and grunting in frustration. "Kelsey. Love. Just hold on."

Out of the corner of my eye, I saw Velarde with his forearm to Kit's throat against the wall. Without realizing what I was doing, I walked over and put my hand on Velarde's shoulder and said, "It isn't Kit's fault. He is right. Kit has done everything we told him to do. He wouldn't jeopardize his family. Just as Kelsey is ours, he won't jeopardize his."

Velarde released Kit, and he straightened his jacket, backing away a couple of steps.

"What else?" I said in a voice that threatened to burn the world.

"She's in a cell. In the basement of the Monarch Club." He sighed, looking at me and not Velarde.

"The Monarch Club. He doesn't have any interest in that building." I was confused and looking at Velarde, who had a devastated look on his face. We had almost dismissed it because of that. He had large interests in both the pharmacy and financial buildings, but not the Monarch Club.

"He owns a five percent share of a parent company. There are twenty-five different investors for that building, and each has at least five different subsidiaries. They buried his name way deeper than anyone would care to look," Kit explained. "But he has close ties to the principal owner of the club, Lautaro Amengual, who is active in—"

"Human trafficking. Particularly young girls." I groaned, pinching my nose. "Which is why he has the cells in the basement. Is Kelsey on the first or second level of cells?"

Kit's throat bobbed. "The second in the back. There is a biometric hand pad, and then to get into the back section of cells, there is a retinal scan. From what I could see, there were about six guards in that section. But the entire basement is covered in them."

"Any idea on a total count?" Velarde asked.

"I don't know."

"Anything to help us know what we are walking into?" Velarde asked again.

"You're going to go in there?" Kit shook his head. "Of course you are. I would too, if it were my girls." He looked back through the door to Romano's like he could see his two little girls sitting at the table. He rubbed his cheek and closed his eyes.

"Kit," I said, growling his name.

"I'm thinking, hold on," he said. Then, after a moment, he guessed, "Fifty? I think there were at least fifty in the front level alone, another ten to fifteen in the front part of the second, and then the six where Kelsey is."

"Fuck," I said, running my hand through my hair. "The Chandel event is tonight. Upstairs is going to be flooded with a lot of well-known names. Fuck. Fuck. Fuck."

"There have been rumors of a shipment of girls going through there about every six months, but we stopped the one from three months ago. Must be why they are empty. Is Marcus supplying girls for Lautaro?" Velarde said, now tapping his gun against his thigh. I gave him a pointed look, and he holstered it.

"I really don't give a fuck about the trafficking right now. I want Kelsey back. Alive! Now," I ground out.

"I need to get back inside sir, but I heard on the way out that Marcus was arranging for a large shipment of nightwhispers to hit the streets in about a week, and then he was going to take a long vacation with his new girl," Kit said meaningfully.

"Thanks, Kit."

Kit nodded to both of us, and before he opened the door, he turned to me and said, "Sir?"

"Yeah?" I said, running both hands through my hair.

"She's holding on, but barely. If not tonight, then make your move soon." His voice was so desperate, I could do nothing but stare at him as he slid back in through Romano's door. I would never have hurt his family, but it was the only way to get him to cooperate. My threat had to be more damaging than what Marcus had over his head. He already worked for him and was the only one we had found who would remotely have had a chance of getting to Kelsey.

I kicked the dumpster and my foot crunched. "Fuck!" I cursed.

"Broke at least two of those toes there, brother," Velarde said, raising an eyebrow.

"I don't care. It will be fine in a couple hours." I turned back toward Jackson Street, where the car was parked. "Let's get back to the apartment. Have Bella meet us there."

"The Monarch Club?" Bella asked. "Why the fuck didn't we think about that?"

"We didn't see a connection to Marcus," Vel growled as he clicked away on the computer on the desk. He was trying to bring up the building floor plans on the presentation screen at the end of the room.

There had been a meeting going on in here to expand the museum, but it could wait. When I stormed in, everyone froze, turned to look at me, and then scattered like rats. Apparently, the look on my face was enough to make everyone realize they needed to be somewhere else.

"Don't you growl at me, fucker. You didn't think of it either, and we should have. Saints dick, it was you who headed the team that went in and stopped the last traffic run," Bella said, but there wasn't too much bite in her words. She was just frustrated. We all were.

Finally, Velarde got the floor plans on the screen. The longer I looked at them, the more I realized it would be very bloody getting in. The only way we would get out without innocent lives being taken was if everyone on Marcus' team died.

"When we raided it last time, we went in here," he said, pointing to the west side entrance.

"Max, it's likely he knows that at some point you will figure out where he is and will come to get her. I'm honestly surprised Marcus hasn't baited you about it," Bella said, chewing on her thumb. "We should go in here, on the north side of the building. It will bypass everyone in the club. Less chance of innocents getting shot."

"We?" Velarde's head snapped to Bella's, and there was a hardness in his eyes that I knew meant he didn't want her anywhere near Marcus. She raised an eyebrow at him. "I don't want you anywhere near that building tonight."

"Tonight?" Her gaze swung to me as she continued, "We get one chance at this. I've fought by her side for centuries. How many centuries did she have your back, Caleus? More time than you probably remember right at this moment." It didn't escape my notice his lips thinned and his eyes softened at the point she was making. "Kelsey is your fucking soul, mister. None of us want to see you the way you have been since you lost her. Since you gave up on her. No fucking way am I sitting home like the good little girl we know I'm not. None of us can afford to lose her. There are three days before we lose her forever. Three days to save her, Tiberius Maximus Vispania. We *cannot* afford to fuck this up."

"I'm not letting Marcus have her any longer than he already has. And don't think for a minute I don't realize what is at fucking stake. I should have known that he would . . ." I shook my head. I couldn't say it out loud. "I expected some torture for my benefit, but not to hurt her the way he has. I thought he was more enamored with her than that.

He's been so focused on her, I thought he would have taken better care of her."

Bella nodded, and Vel stared at me. Vel's mouth opened, closed, and then he finally said, "I still don't know why he has it out for you. Centuries of destroying you, and now he uses a woman to do it? Why now?"

"Not just any woman, Velarde." I stood up like the strength of Hercules had just settled within me. "My woman. My soul. My true being."

"But how did he know? It's not like you two have been cozy together. Shit, she hadn't even figured it out until after you stabbed him," Velarde said, his eyes flicking to Bella.

"Does she know I'm alive?" Bella asked carefully.

I shook my head. "No. We hadn't told her."

"She will have figured it out by now. That is if Kit delivered the message." She sighed. "Mother and the Gods, she's going to be pissed."

"What exactly did you tell Kit to tell her?" I asked.

She smirked. "Hold fast, Kels Bells."

I knitted my eyebrows together and looked at Velarde, who had the same questioning look on his face.

"And that right there is why she will know that only I could have sent that message to her." She grinned. "She will know we are coming for her, that I am alive, and she will figure out that I am just like you. She will be rightfully pissed as fuck at you two for not telling her, though. She will be pissed at me, too, but she already knew I was covering something big before Marcus shot me." She rubbed her forehead before mumbling, "I forgot how much that shit hurts."

"Well, it wasn't like we had time to tell her, Isabella," Velarde said, looking away from her. There was a sort of guilt written all over his face.

"How did you choose that message? Why would she know it was only from you?" I asked.

"It was our secret code. When we were in our Chinese history and mythology class a few years back, we came across a quote that hit pretty close to home. *Though face and form alter with the years, I hold fast to the pearl of my mind.* It is attributed to someone named Hanshan. No one knows if he was even a real person, but through all the lives that I've lived with you two, and knowing that the knowledge I've accumulated over the years was going to stay with me, no matter what, it hit home. So, we integrated it. It was our way of saying we were on the way to rescue each other from whatever the problem was: creeps at the bar or come bail me out of jail, bitch." Bella smiled at a memory that she didn't elaborate on.

"You crafty little wench." Velarde smiled at her.

"So, ready to head to the armory?" I was staring at the floor plan and mentally staging out every turn I would need to take to get to her.

Out of the corner of my eye, I saw them stare each other down. Vel let out a heavy sigh in resignation and then looked at me, pulling on all the battlefield experience he had in him as he said, "Let's get Kelsey."

CHAPTER 66

MAX

As I pressed my palm into the biometric lock for the armory, where there was a series of clicking noises from the locking mechanisms moving before the door started to open. I didn't wait for it to finish before sliding in.

Rifles lined the shelves, and drawers and drawers of compact, subcompact and full-sized handguns popped open for us to pick through. I strode straight to the other side of the room and contemplated the different swords I had accumulated over the years. Each one was meticulously cleaned, sharpened, and sure to cut a hair through the air.

Marcus would die tonight. I was taking no chances with Kelsey's safety. I would do whatever I could to protect this family. Either all four of us came out alive or none of us did. I knew there was only one true way for us to end: beheading.

Over the years, we had determined there were about eighty of us made. That number was down to twelve. During those ancient wars, beheading happened by accident or through anger. We had also lived through the age of the guillotine. We were near-immortal, not stupid proof. Many of us got caught by the law, and most of us died during that era.

Marcus, on the other hand, had destroyed many innocent lives throughout the centuries in his quest to tear me apart. He would burn entire cities to the ground, introduce plague, or charge armies through a town. For at least the last 1500 years, Marcus had terrorized *me*. I didn't know where I crossed him initially, but now he would not be walking away. He crossed the line when he took Kelsey. His life became forfeit when he hurt her. This ended tonight.

"Fuck with me all you want, but you have Kelsey. You have the one thing in all of my existence that I need," I muttered under my breath. I reached over and plucked the broadsword that had stood the test of time. It needed some major repairs to the hilt from a few centuries back, but it had always served me well. I twirled it around in my hands. Muscle memory kicked in, and I saw myself on the battlefields of the past. I took a deep breath and grabbed the belt, slung it on, and slid the sword into its sheath.

When I turned to get guns and ammo, Bella and Velarde stopped midmovement to watch me.

"Fuck." Bella's eyes were wide as they flicked to Velarde, who was still staring at me. If they thought for a moment I wasn't going to take Marcus' head tonight, they had another thing coming.

"Anything you want to say?" I asked, staring him down. His eyes went from sadness to questioning before he looked at Bella, who simply nodded her head. When he returned his gaze to me, there was a rage that I had only seen when he became a warrior on the fighting fields.

Bella went to another case across the room and retrieved the sword she had named *Mors Mangone*. I watched as she pulled it from the sheath and ran a hand along the blade. She flipped it in her hands, and when it was vertical in front of her face, she murmured, "Gwaed ein gelynion a rhydd heno." *The blood of our enemies shall run free tonight.*

Vel smiled at her softly before he turned, walked up to me, and we grasped forearms. "To the death, my brother."

"To the death. Though, let's try not to." I smirked, trying to lighten the mood just slightly, and grabbed four handguns, extra magazines, and ammo.

"Tiberius," Bella said, her voice shaky as she looked at me. "I'm only going to say this once. I have been proud to call you my brother. Kelsey is the closest thing I have had in my entire existence to a sister. Knowing now that I have had many lifetimes with her has warmed my heart and proven she is a heart sister, but . . ." She came to stand in front of me and waited for me to look at her. When my gaze met hers, she swallowed thickly. "This *will* be her last incarnation. If she fades to dust, we won't get her back. She invoked the old laws. That has an expiration date. Those three days I mentioned, but's a hard-line expiration date."

My throat bobbed, and I felt my chest cave slightly at the thought.

"I swear, if she dies tonight, I will take your head myself. We all come out of there or none of us." Her eyes blazed with the promise.

I looked down to the black boots I had on and watched as they blurred slightly with tears. "If she dies, I demand you to take my head for losing her. For the shame of it. For the heartbreak of it. I can't continue living without her."

Velarde broke the silence as he stood beside Bella and said, "We all come out of there or none of us. All four of us. I refuse to live my life without either of you. Isabella Edelmann Velarde is my soul, but you, Tiberius Maximus Vispania, are my heart brother. Kelsey is part of that. I promised her on your wedding day that should either of you need me, I would come and help. She needs us. All of us. Now, let's go save our family."

They turned, finished packing, and walked out the door. I stood there wondering what I had ever done to deserve such loyalty from the two of them. They were both so ready to die to save my Kelsey.

They were my family. That wasn't a lie.

"Tiberius, get your ass out here or we leave for Kelsey without you!" Bella yelled back, and a wicked smile crossed my face.

Yes.

Let's go cause some chaos.

CHAPTER 67

KELSEY

MARCUS CLEARED HIS THROAT behind me. I closed my eyes and took a slow breath in through my nose, trying to calm myself.

My hands shook as I turned to face him, but I met his eyes with a new fierceness that had settled within me. For the last few hours, since that man Kit left, I had tried to tell myself that Max, Vel, and Izzy were coming for me. I just had to hold on. Hold it together long enough for them to find me. To get me out of here.

Each moment became harder than the last, though. It hurt to breathe, to move, and I could hardly even crawl to my makeshift bathroom to relieve myself. *It had been days, weeks, a month of this? How much more would my body allow?*

"The doctor says your pussy and ass need to heal for a few days. Such a shame. But I'm sure we can find other

425

ways to enjoy each other. Isn't that right, *my pet?*" he said, running his finger along my throat. He pulled me up so I was standing before him. His head cocked to the side as he smiled. "There is a new fire in you, my Sidonia."

I swallowed as he bent down, holding my chin in his hand to force it up, allowing him access to my throat as he ran his tongue along the length of it. It was always along that same artery. I took a shuddering breath to calm myself and make any fire of hope simmer. I needed it to get me through this. I hadn't realized just how much any hope of surviving had dwindled to an ember.

"You know," Marcus said as he kissed the base of my throat. Then he tapped his throat with his finger right along the main vein there. "If you were to drink from my throat, you could live as long as I will."

I froze at the words but then heard myself say, "Why in the fuck would I want to do that?"

"So we could enjoy each other for centuries. We have had so much fun these past weeks." He smiled, pulling back. As he did, he grabbed my ass and pressed me against him. I whimpered at the pain, and he smiled. "I love those little sounds of yours. The way you play into me. The way you submit to me."

"I do not submit to you," I ground through gritted teeth, finding a bravery within me that surprised not only Marcus, but also myself.

Stepping back, he headed toward the "wall of fun," as he liked to call it. He looked back at me again and said, "You do submit. You submit to me in the most basic of ways, Sidonia. You submit to me each time you break and give in. You submit to me each time I enter you. You submit to me in the little noises you make as I fuck you. It is fucking beautiful."

He walked along the wall, fingering several tools, before taking a knife from its sheath and one of the fingertip vibrators.

I blinked. Marcus hadn't taken one of those before. I braced for the movement as he walked to push the button that would leave me spread eagle and unable to move. When he pushed it, it was all I could do to not scream.

My joints hurt from being in the same position for long periods of time and the beatings that left every muscle in my body in a constant state of agony. Not to mention that the movement had caused some of the scabs to split.

"Stop," I whimpered and felt the tears slide down my cheeks. "Just for one day. Can't you leave me alone? Just for one day?"

As he pushed another button on the wall, a remote popped out on a little shelf, and he slid it into his pants pocket. He turned toward me and took slow, deliberate steps.

"I have two thousand years of playtime to make up for with my Sidonia." He lifted the knife to the spot between my breasts and once again slid it down to my belly button, just as he had done twice before. There were now three lines that ran between my boobs. His eyes never left mine as he did it. It didn't hurt. It was only enough that it split the skin, causing a small amount of blood to well to the surface.

When the knife left my skin, he slowly kissed his way down between my breasts and licked the blood clean as he settled onto his knees. When he was eye level with my center, I tried to knee him in the nose, and my ankle wrenched in the restraints. He hadn't moved, and my knee was still a good inch from his face.

He looked up at me through his lashes and purred, "Oh my sweet Sidonia. I love how you fight."

His hand reached into his pocket, where the remote control was kept, and I was lowered so my feet were flat on the floor. My ankle hurt so much that I couldn't put any weight on it, and frankly, standing hadn't been something I could do since Jannessa took a hammer to it. He lowered and adjusted the restraints more so that I settled on my knees, arms still raised out above me and stretched out in pain. I licked my lips, but they were chapped and cut.

Standing in front of me, he grabbed my hair, and the next thing I knew, his dick was in my mouth. I sputtered and twisted my head, but he didn't relent. He pumped himself in and out as I tried to fight him. He held his hands firm against my head, making it impossible for me to move.

My throat burned and hurt as he hit the back of it. I couldn't do this anymore. It could be weeks or months before Max, Vel, and Izzy would find me. The man, Kit, may tell them where I was, but it could still take them time to find my location in this building. I didn't even know where I was. I could be in a ten-story basement, or on the fortieth floor of one of the many skyscrapers in town, or anywhere in between. Did Kit even know where exactly in this building I was? Marcus wasn't stupid. He would have taken precautions. I felt the cover of darkness settle over me, and I closed my eyes, trying not to move as Marcus kept fucking my mouth.

I'm sorry, Izzy. I can't take weeks of this. I just can't do this anymore, I thought to myself, and I felt more tears slide down my cheeks. I relaxed against the restraints and drew further back into myself.

I was done. I was so done.

I love you, Max, and I'm sorry there wasn't time to try. I'm sorry I never told you just how far down that rabbit hole I had fallen. I love you.

Max wouldn't want me now, even if he had before. I thought maybe he had. That kiss we shared, it held so much promise. I was so damaged now, though. I was the damaged goods the citizens of Herculaneum had claimed I was all those years ago. No one was going to want this tarnished shell of a person. I knew that was what I was turning into—a shell—and I couldn't take the mental and physical assault anymore.

So, in a final act of defiance, I scraped my teeth against him as he pulled out and thrust back in. I was just about to chomp down when there was cold steel at my throat, and my entire body betrayed me as I froze in place.

"Do it, Sidonia, and I will spill your blood right here. You will never see Tiberius Vispania again," he said through his teeth as he thrust himself down my throat, punctuating his words.

I vaguely heard gunshots ring out in the distance, and Marcus' attention went to the door. "Seal it shut. No one gets in or out of this room without my say so."

"What if they breach?" one of the guards asked. I tried to move farther away from him, but he gripped my hair to hold my head in place, forcing himself deep down my throat. He moved, grunted, and released his grip as he came.

Feeling the knife still next to my throat, I moved my head to the right in a quick, precise motion.

I barely felt the sting of the blade cutting through my skin, and Marcus jumped back. His eyes filled with rage, and satisfaction filled me at knowing how angry he was with what I had done. Slapping me across the face, he yelled for a first-aid kit.

I felt hot wetness flow down my throat and across my chest. I looked up at Marcus and smiled. He could never hurt me again. "Never again," I tried to say, but it came out as a whispered croak.

Someone came in and hit the button on my restraints, releasing all four of them from my wrists and ankles. My vision blurred, and there were too many sets of hands on me.

"Don't let the bitch bleed out," Marcus growled. "She won't die today."

Someone was whispering into my ear about how stupid I was, but I could do nothing but smile as my vision tunneled in and out. Somewhere from the recesses of my mind, I started whispering an ancient song.

> *Mother, take me*
> *Mother, heal me*
> *Mother, bind me*
> *Mother, I am yours.*

The words played over and over, but whether they were said just in my mind or out loud, I did not know.

> *Mother, take me*
> *Mother, heal me*
> *Mother, bind me*
> *Mother, I am yours.*

CHAPTER 68

MAX

I LIFTED THE DEAD guard's head up by his hair and held his eyelid open for the retinal scanner. After a little maneuvering, it finally beeped, and the door opened.

Gunshots rang nonstop through the door as I looked over at Bella, who was reloading and rolling her eyes. Velarde, however, crouched down, sighted each of them with his rifle, and with a few twitches of his finger, there was silence.

"Tiberius!" a voice called out a moment later, and I took a quick look around the corner, motioned to Bella and Velarde that there were indeed six other people in the room that I could see, and we turned the corner in unison, shots ringing.

When I swung around to face Marcus, my heart stopped. Fear coursed through my veins, the like I had never felt. Kelsey was lying limp in his left arm as he held a knife to her throat with his right hand. There was already a bleeding cut to her neck that wasn't too deep, but there was a lot of blood.

"Kelsey, love." I looked at her. She was naked, covered in blood from the neck wound, but I saw everything else that had been done to her. Kit had said she was in awful shape, but how had she lived through this? I couldn't even register all the injuries to her. My focus reached back to Marcus' and I said through my teeth, "What did you do to her?"

"We just had a little fun. She's quite the kinky girl, Tiberius." He ran the blade slowly up and down her neck, and she hummed.

"Love, look at me," I begged her without taking my eyes off Marcus. Her eyes fluttered, but that was about it.

"Marcus. Whatever you have done to her, she needs medical attention. She needs help," Bella pleaded behind me. Kelsey twitched then, the blade Marcus was holding pinched her skin, and a small red drop came to the surface. I swallowed hard.

"I told you. We've been having fun." He lifted her, and her head flopped back onto his shoulder. The movement exposed more of her body, and I heard Vel and Bella behind me gasp. My eyes trailed the damage: bite marks, cuts, bruises, both new and old, whipping marks. I then looked at her wrists and ankles.

"You had her chained up," I snarled. "Like an animal."

"Sidonia is my pet. Shouldn't a pet be chained and caged like the animal they are?" he purred, kissing her temple. "She wanted all of this. She submitted to me repeatedly, Tiberius."

"Her name is Kelsey. Not Sidonia," I growled but realized what had been said. "How . . ." My eyes flicked to Velarde, who was trying to figure it out, too.

Marcus smiled. "Oh, Tiberius. I think we both know better than that." He turned back to Kelsey and tried to jostle her awake. "Come on, pet. Time to wake up. Time to tell Tiberius all about us." He sighed dramatically.

"Jannessa!" Marcus yelled, commanding someone to appear. There was a clicking of heels in the hallway behind us, and both Bella and Velarde turned, guns raised.

"Oh, looks like I missed a party," the blonde-haired woman sassed, then she looked at Bella and said, "Isabella Velarde! What a pleasure it is to see you again."

Bella narrowed her eyes at the woman. "Jannessa . . . Delacroix. What in the hell? Ohh, this, this was the man that you have been chasing. You've been chasing him for what, one hundred years? Does he know how much you desire him? Does he know how it was you that killed Milani Vongsay in Turkey? You know who Milani was, right?"

Jannessa's eyes flicked to Kelsey, and Bella smirked. "That's right. Kelsey. The one that Marcus wants so bad."

"Impossible."

"No. See, Milani and I were best friends then. Kelsey remembers her life as Milani. She had a nightmare and told me how you killed her. *That's* how I knew she had been Milani as well. Kelsey has been so many people over the centuries, and the only one that your Marcus has ever craved."

"The question is why?" I growled, my full attention going back to Marcus. Kelsey's breathing was ragged and slow. "And how do you know her by the name of Sidonia?"

Jannessa strode by without a thought or care between us all, and I half-wondered why any of us didn't shoot her as she went by. She stood in front of both of them and asked Marcus, "Yes, master?"

"Wake her," he commanded.

"She has lost too much blood. If I wake her, she may die." But Jannessa just shrugged, reached over, murmured some words, and ran her hand over her brow. It left a dark smudge and faded as Kelsey's eyes fluttered open.

When she saw me, her whole body jerked in my direction, but Marcus held on to her tight. She moaned and winced at the movements.

"Sidonia, my pet. Why don't you tell Tiberius here just who I am to you?" Marcus commanded.

Her eyes swung to me, then to Velarde and Bella. Something akin to hope and sadness swam in those beautiful green eyes, but she kept her mouth shut.

"Tell them, pet." He pressed the knife closer to her throat.

"Do it," Kelsey said through her teeth as she glared at him. "I tried once already. I don't care anymore. Just let me go."

"My sweet Sidonia. You know I can't let you die. You are mine. Now tell Tiberius here just who we are to each other. Who I am to you?"

"You are no one to me but my warden."

"Let's not be liars now, Sidonia," Marcus said, licking up her neck. He winked at me, and I knew he had at least heard rumors of how she could become one of us. "Tell him about Herculaneum," he demanded, forcing her to sit up.

I saw her pull every ounce of strength left in her body as her gaze met mine, and with a lift of her lips, she said, "The truth, Marcus? You want me to state the truth. In front of all here and the Mother?"

"Tell him how you belong to me."

"Marcus, you told me not to lie." Her words were slurring from exhaustion and blood loss.

"Tell him who I am. Why you belong to me," Marcus ordered her again, gritting his teeth. He ran his hand down her stomach and stuck his fingers in her as she winced at the pain of it. I balled my hands up into fists, and I felt Velarde inch closer to me.

"Love. Tell me," I encouraged, giving her whatever strength I could even though my stomach roiled and I was clamping down on every protective instant I had. It was very likely I was going to lose her forever in the next few moments, but then she closed her eyes, took a deep, shuddering breath, and met my eyes with the determination of a goddess.

Her eyes almost glowed with how bright green they turned. The corner of her mouth turned up as she met my gaze. "My name is Sidonia Regillia Vispania and Kelsey Ann Stillthorn. Daughter of the Mother Gaea. Wife to Tiberius Maximus Vispania. My soul is whole, and my husband stands before me alive. He is mine, and I am his. Marcus Dulcitius, you have no hold or claim on me."

A warm wind swept through the room, and I took half a step forward before the words fell from my lips without conscious thought. "My name is Tiberius Maximus Vispania. Husband of Sidonia Regillia Vispania and soul husband of Kelsey Ann Stillthorn. My soul is whole, and my wife is before me alive. She is mine, and I am hers."

I stared into Kelsey's eyes. They were bright green and vibrant. Her eyes filled with tears as her whole body glowed white. Janessa fell to her knees, put her head on the floor, hands facing upwards before her, muttering, "Mother Gaea."

Bella also dropped to her knees, hands stretched out, just as Janessa, and simply bowed her head. "Mother Gaea."

Velarde moved to stand just behind Bella, but when his eyes met mine, they were met with confusion.

The smell of burning flesh filled the room, and Marcus dropped Kelsey onto the mattress. Burn marks appeared where he had been holding onto her and were already blistering. His eyes swung to me, and he twisted the knife in his hands.

Standing, he faced me and growled, "You will not take what was promised to me. Her father arranged for her to be mine. She is mine by right and law."

I blinked, and it took me half a second to recall that conversation with Sidonia all those years ago. "Marcus Dulcitius. You are *that* Marcus? The one who allowed his father to assault a woman who was to be your wife? You left, freeing her and her father of any arrangement that you had made."

"She is mine by right and law," he snapped once more.

"You keep saying that, but does she make you burn like a thousand suns with just her gaze? Does she light a fire in your soul when she touches you? Does the air stir around you as you claim her soul?" I smirked at him as I pulled my sword from its sheath and whirled it in the air, loosening my wrist.

"We feel the heat of no one. It is the nature of who we are," he said, trying to back me up away from Kelsey.

"Oh, how wrong you are." Velarde smirked behind me at Marcus. His hand was now on Bella's neck, and he was running his finger back and forth to either comfort her or calm his own nerves.

"Mother Gaea." Both Jannessa and Bella just kept whispering the words repeatedly. Meanwhile, Kelsey continued to have that soft glow about her. My eyes flicked to hers, and they were shining back at me like wild grass fields.

"Sidonia is mine. You will not have her," he said.

"Marcus—" I started to say, but he charged, and I twirled around, bringing my sword up, willing my muscles to bring strength to the movement. The sword landed on the side of his neck with a wet thud.

Marcus' eyes met mine as I pulled the sword out and whirled in the other direction, willing it to be enough. When it landed this time, it sliced through muscle and sinew before it hit bone. Twisting around to the back of Marcus, I wrapped my hands on both sides of the sword, put my foot on his back, and pulled the sword clean through his neck. I kicked it away from me in disgust.

No one moved as Marcus' head rolled to the other end of the room. Bella and Jannessa didn't even flinch, but Velarde watched as it bounced and hit the wall.

"Good riddance," Velarde said, then he turned to me. "Tiberius."

I looked at him, breathing hard, trying to bring my adrenaline back under control. His eyes flicked behind me, and I turned toward Kelsey. Her eyes were on me, and I went to her. As I placed my hand on her cheek, she sighed and leaned into it. She was so weak.

"She will die if you do not save her." Two female voices came from behind me.

"She must choose it," I whispered, still staring into Kelsey's eyes. She winced as I lifted her up to sit on my lap. I held her against my chest, and her head leaned on my shoulder.

My heart was beating fast, and I was panicking. "Kelsey, my love."

I could feel her. Feel her pulse against me, getting weaker.

"She will die if you do not save her," the genuflecting women said again.

I faced them and said, "I don't know how. Doesn't she have to choose this? I can't force it upon her!"

Janessa and Bella both raised their heads, their eyes glowing green as they said, "*Daughter. If you chose Tiberius Maximus Vispania, drink from his neck vein. You must find the strength within you now and choose a life with him.*" There was an eerie silence when they finished. Their heads tilted to the side, and then they collapsed on the floor.

I looked to Kelsey as she smiled softly and mouthed, "My Tiberius."

CHAPTER 69

KELSEY

HEAT FLOODED EVERY OUNCE of me. Max had come for me. Vel had come for me. Izzy . . . Izzy was alive, and she came for me, too. I lay there seeing Jannessa on the floor, genuflecting toward me, and I huffed a small laugh at the thought. Bella was on her knees, head bowed and refusing to look at me. I tried willing her to, but I couldn't speak.

Max and Marcus were talking, but none of it made a damn bit of sense. I heard the words, but they just didn't compute in my brain. There was so much blood everywhere, all of it mine.

Mother, I had tried to kill myself just as they had arrived to rescue me. They had really come for me.

Daughter.

I blinked. The voice was one of many female voices in my head.

Daughter. You have claimed me as Mother. Now, it is time to claim what is yours, the voice said as I saw Max relieve Marcus of his head. I smiled at the thought that Marcus couldn't hurt me anymore. I could die now. He couldn't hurt me or anyone else again, either in this life or the next.

Not this day, daughter. You don't have to die on this day.

"Good riddance," Velarde said, watching Marcus' head bounce across the floor. Blood splattered everywhere, and I was just relieved it wasn't mine this time.

Max was breathing hard, and when he turned to me, I felt a piece of myself click into place. I felt whole. He crouched before me and placed his hand on my cheek. I sighed and leaned into it. I was so tired.

"*She will die if you do not save her.*" The Mother's voice came from Jannessa's and Bella's mouths, but I heard it in my head as well. I blinked.

"She must choose it," Max said, still staring into my eyes. What was he talking about?

He lifted me, and everything hurt. Max was as gentle as he could be as he moved me to sit on his lap. I leaned against his chest and rested my head on his shoulder. I smiled. I wasn't sure if it showed on my face, but as his arms tightened around me, I felt safe for the first time in weeks.

My hand was resting over the tattoo of that name from so long ago. The one that had started our binding. The name I used when I was selfish and refused to let him go. The one where I had demanded the Mother give me another life with him.

Mother, this isn't what I meant. I wanted to live with him. Have his children. Have a life. I had spent most of the time I'd known him hating his guts. Hating everything he was and stood for. I still didn't like most of that, but there was another side to Max. The one who cherished and was loyal and fierce. Max was someone who matched me. I wanted him. I needed him.

Mother, please don't take him away from me again. I just got things sorted out, and then my past came and destroyed me. Again.

I could almost feel myself detaching from my body. I grabbed onto him tighter, or at least I thought I did. I didn't want to leave him.

"Mother, please," I mouthed against his chest.

His heart was beating fast, and in a voice that showed just how scared he was, he said, "Kelsey, my love."

"*She will die if you do not save her*," that voice said from inside my head.

Max just said, "I don't know how. Doesn't she have to choose this? I can't force it upon her!"

Don't know how to what? What was he talking about?

Janessa and Bella both raised their heads, their eyes glowing bright green as they and that voice in my head said, "*Daughter. If you chose Tiberius Maximus Vispania, drink from his neck vein. He cannot make you. You must find the strength within you now and choose a life with him.*"

My ears hollowed out, and they collapsed on the floor.

Velarde was at Izzy's side, and Max looked at me with a need that I suddenly knew all too well.

"My Tiberius," I mouthed and smiled softly.

"Love. Choose to stay," he said. Then he whispered, his voice thick, "I choose you, Kelsey Ann Stillthorn Vispania."

"Kelsey?" I breathed. "Not Sidonia?"

"Sidonia is only a figment of your strength, courage, and fire. The Mother Gaea knew what she was doing giving you red hair in this life. You have taken what she gave you as Sidonia and over two thousand years have cultivated yourself into a woman who can match me in every way. You have never been afraid to call me out for being an asshole. Sidonia would never have done that. Sure, she would have fought me and demanded to be an equal, but Kelsey?" He smiled at me, and it was the most beautiful sight I had seen in all my lives. His sapphire eyes sparkled with all the love and meaning that he was trying to convey. "Kelsey will dominate me. Kelsey is who I need. So, I say it again. I choose you, Kelsey Ann Stillthorn Vispania."

I searched his eyes, looking for anything to tell me he wasn't telling me the truth, but I felt so faint. My vision was swimming again. I closed my eyes for a moment and prayed for the strength of the Mother to let me live.

When I opened my eyes, there was sheer panic in his. So, I rallied what little strength I had left and said, "I, Kelsey Ann Stillthorn Vispania, daughter of Gaea, choose you, Tiberius Maximus Vispania."

A wave of heat and need burned through me so fast that, without thinking, I grabbed his neck and bit into it. Fire flowed from his neck down my throat. The Mother said if I wanted to stay with Tiberius, with Max, I had to drink from his neck vein, so I would. I swallowed and gulped that fire down until my stomach was a pit of molten lava. I slowly released my teeth and then kissed the spot I had bitten.

Opening my eyes to look at it, I raised my hand and ran my finger over where my teeth somehow broke the skin. With half a thought, white light trailed my fingers, and the mark was gone, except for a small ring of my teeth marks.

His hand was on my cheek, and I barely registered the tears in his eyes or the smile on his face as I took a long, deep breath and my vision went black.

CHAPTER 70

MAX

"It's been two days already," I said, staring at Kelsey. There wasn't much else I had looked at since she bit into my neck. It had felt like that day we died in the boathouse. I felt every fiber in my body melt away as I felt her drink from me. When she was done, my skin was tender and sensitive.

When she passed out, I wrapped her in the blanket folded in the corner, lifted her up, and carried her to the car. I made Velarde drive and just held her the entire way back to the apartment.

When her heart stopped, I clutched her close and panicked. Velarde and Bella had reassured me for hours that she had to die to convert. I didn't take my eyes off her until her heart started beating again six hours later.

When she took that first breath, I sobbed in relief. I hadn't completely lost her. I hadn't realized how tightly that fear had taken hold of me until her chest rose and fell in steady succession.

Now, I wondered if she would ever open her vibrant, loving green eyes and look at me again. We cleaned her up the best we could, but with each cut, she twitched. Once she was clean and in some new clothes, we tucked her into bed, and I slumped to the floor and cried.

"This isn't normal. She didn't convert like we did. Sh-she didn't die like we have," Bella said. "Her heart only stopped for about six hours."

"Where is Velarde?" I asked, sighing through the words. She was trying to comfort me.

"Off doing cleanup." She leaned against the wall and took a long drink of her beer. "We left a bit of a mess in the building. I've paid off most of the police department to keep it under wraps, paid KMTN the usual fee to keep it out of the news, but the *Trenton Times* said they had to run some sort of story about why the building was suddenly closed. There were also reports of gunshots. Convinced them to run a story that there was a storage of fireworks in the basement and they blew up. It's a stretch, but the best we could come up with."

"And Velarde is avoiding you by handling everything himself." I gave her an even look and then called her out on the bullshit as I looked back to Kelsey. "Still pissed at you for not telling him about your previous life?"

She shrugged and then laughed. "Yeah. Guess it's one reason I have always been drawn to her. Mother be! A daughter of Gaea. She was descended from the original deities. Tiberius, do you know what that means? She may be able to use the Mother's power to heal."

"I don't give a shit. I didn't care about her Earth Worship back then either. I sure in the hell don't care about it now."

Then I looked over at Bella. "Do you still follow the old ways? I mean, if you were raised as one, how have you kept that from Velarde and me all this time?"

Bella smirked at me. "I have and I haven't. I don't carry the power anymore, just the knowledge. The power died with me when I converted on that battlefield. The knowledge is still with me, though. Why do you think I still, after all this time, go as holistic as possible, Tiberius? I see the value and need for modern medicine. I know there is no holistic way to cure things like some of the cancers treatable by today's technology. Mother and Gods, just what vaccines have been able to do throughout history."

She shook her head and headed to the kitchen. I stared at Kelsey as I heard Bella rummage through the fridge before coming back in here.

"I'm not going to have the ethical or any other debate as to medical science, though. There is good and bad." She handed me a beer and plopped into the chair next to me. "It was harder to keep it from Velarde than you. I would disappear for years and not see you."

There was a long silence between us. "I kept running from him all those years because of it. He was working with the Templars. Well, what was the start of the Templars before they had a name. We both knew what we were to each other. But him with the Templars? The war they were fighting at the time would never have allowed me to continue existing. I ran to protect him. To protect myself. Over those years, the memory of Earth Worshipers has faded from existence. Even today, there is nothing anywhere about them. It's as though they never existed. Even the Dark Witches of Moesia have faded out. They carry on generationally, still have very long lives, but we both have adapted. I've learned over centuries how to still honor the old ways. During those years running from Caleus, I learned how to hide it."

"Now you both can carry on those traditions," I said, giving her a reassuring smile.

"I'm going to have to teach her what I know. Mother only knows how much she can remember from her days as Sidonia. Does she even want to learn? What does she remember from any of her past lives? Are they just blips on the screen? Are they just one or two memories from here and there?" Bella asked, studying Kelsey.

"I think she remembers a lot more than we know. The morning she . . ." My throat bobbed at the terror that filled me in a moment then released when my eyes fell to her again, knowing she was safe in my home. "The morning she was captured. She told Velarde and me everything. She remembered everything, in detail, of her days in Herculaneum with me."

"Everything?"

"Everything. Things that no one should know. Things that only Sidonia and Tiberius would know about, Isabella." My eyes were wide. Damn, I still couldn't believe it.

I turned to Bella and her face was determined and eyes hard. "And you want Kelsey. It's not the parts of her that are Sidonia, but Kelsey that you want?"

"I am sure I told you this before, but as Sidonia, I thought her the most beautiful woman I had ever seen." I leaned back in the chair and took a long drink from my beer before continuing, "What I haven't told you is I thought the same thing when I first saw you two standing at the entrance at my bar. Before our eyes met, I had looked her over, and it made my cock stir in a way it hadn't since Sidonia. What had really set me off was that I felt that heat once she turned to look at me. Then I was pissed because it had been two thousand years since I had felt that and there was no way it could be her. It just brought all the pain and misery back. It hurt to think of Sidonia."

"Then Velarde and I came and told you of the dreams that she was having," Bella said in understanding.

"You did. It made every memory worse." I took a long drink and said, "And I had nightmares of us in that boathouse again. Of losing her."

"We knew there was something strange going on then. How could she have been dreaming about lives we had centuries ago? No one else had ever had dreams that were so exact in what happened. Even when she was Milani in Turkey a few years back, there were things in her that reminded me of my old friends, but when Jannessa killed her, I didn't look into it more. It hadn't mattered. Milani was gone. By the way, what happened to Jannessa?"

"When Kelsey passed out after drinking from my neck, you and Janessa collapsed to the ground." I took a deep breath. "After Velarde realized you were okay, he went to Jannessa and she was dead. Well, she didn't have a pulse, so just to make sure, he relieved her of her head."

Bella looked off into the distance for a long moment before saying, "Good. Maybe I won't cut his balls off for leaving a month ago then. But you still haven't answered me, Tiberius."

"When you died at the restaurant—" I gulped and then shook my head. "I wanted so badly to just walk away. Marcus was back, and I didn't want to put Kelsey or anyone else in Trenton in danger. After you died, though, I had this uncontrollable need to take care of her. So I did, and she let me. Gods! For days, she let me just take care of her. I felt like I was meeting my purpose. There was just something right about making sure she had pain meds for her throat, had food, made sure she had her water."

"Velarde told me about it. He said he had never seen you like that before." Giggling, she said, "He said you were a downright mother hen."

I half-glared at her and shook my head. "A few days later, I woke up after having a dream about our, well, Sidonia and Tiberius' wedding night. I hated Kelsey at that moment. I bit her head off when she tried to check on me in the bathroom. When Velarde showed up, I ignored all his calls and went to the lake. I tried all day to talk myself into turning my back on her. She wasn't my *her*, and I hated Kelsey for that. I felt like I was betraying Sidonia and what we had."

"She isn't Sidonia, even if they are the same soul," Bella said, jabbing me in the side, making me jump.

"Gods no. I know she isn't. Like I said, I hated her for that, but I also needed her. I still need her. When she was dying, I didn't lie when I said those words to her. I don't regret them, even if she wakes up and decides to walk away. Even if she drank from my vein and it was just a way for her to exercise self-preservation. To make her own choice after the three weeks he had taken any consent or choices from her."

I let out a long breath, touched the spot on my neck that she had bitten into me, and closed my eyes. A wave of certainty went through me at just how right Kelsey was. I looked at her and rubbed my face. "I'm not sure I can let her walk away, but I would try."

"You really did fall in love with Kelsey," she said, surprise on her face. "Velarde told me a lot about what happened when you were hiding at the hotel, but during that week, you really fell in love with *Kelsey*."

I nodded. "You said you don't remember much from when the Mother took you and Jannessa over, but I told her I chose Kelsey. Not the part of her that was Sidonia, but Kelsey. She's a firecracker, and I love that about her."

"Can I ask you something?"

"What is stopping you?" I looked at her like she had grown two heads. "You've never asked for permission to ask me anything."

"It seems weird to . . ." She leaned her head back and sighed. "Tiberius, I've known you for centuries. I've seen you fuck woman just to scratch an itch, but it just left you aggravated. I've seen you try to take pleasure in a man, and it did the same thing. With Sidonia, you two had fooled around but never had penetrative sex until you married. Yet you still chose each other."

"Yes," I said, drawing out the word.

"Yet with Kelsey, you have done nothing. Have you even kissed her?"

I laughed. "It is a bit archaic, isn't it? I've kissed her, but by today's standards, we should have at least fucked each other's brains out, to use your words. Make sure we are compatible, right?"

"I mean, I can vouch for her. She's a great fuck. If you ever want to . . . ," she trailed off when Velarde walked into the room.

"Hey! We have already discussed this, Isabella. I just have to watch next time." He chuckled as he wrapped his hand around her throat, pulling her head back and kissing her. The smile on her face was endearing.

"Next time, huh?" I smiled at her, and she shrugged. I just shook my head.

"Still not awake?" Velarde asked.

"Brother, you are a genius at stating the obvious." I drank down the last of my beer and looked Kelsey up and down. Her physical wounds were healing. Slowly, but they were healing. Those would have healed even if she didn't convert, though. It was the mental damage that Marcus had done that had me petrified.

I saw how the cut was on her neck. Saw how the last thing Marcus wanted to do was kill her. She had even looked at Marcus and dared him to slit her throat because she had already tried to die.

Gods, Kelsey had tried to slice her neck open to kill herself. She had given up. She didn't believe we were coming. Even with the message received, she hadn't believed we would find her before he killed her.

My firecracker had given up. My Kelsey would have rather died than endure anymore of what Marcus had done. The wounds on her had been extensively brutal. He had violated her so severely, yet she survived. *How* had she lived through all that to start with?

I had called Kit after her heart restarted, who, upon hearing that we had gotten her out, came and examined her in the middle of the night. He gave me an overview of what Marcus had done, at least what he suspected based on the injuries.

Bruises had covered her the entirety of her thighs, ass, and were speckled around her shoulders. There was evidence of repeated whippings to her back. Not to mention that her left wrist was majorly sprained, as well as her right ankle. I had no doubt she had gotten those fighting against the bindings he had her in. Her foot was a mess, but I only hoped that her conversion would repair it. Otherwise, I'd have surgeons on-site to fix it as soon as possible. The sores and healing wounds around her wrists and ankles were a clear indication that he had only just taken the restraints off before we arrived. Not to mention, there were cut marks all over her body, including the area between her legs. Those violations made me want to take his head all over again.

I swallowed hard. Gods and the Mother above, if Kelsey even let me kiss her, it would be a miracle.

But she had let me hold her in that cell. She had clutched onto me like a lifeline. She allowed me to hold her in those final moments.

Bella studied me for a long moment before saying, "Get some sleep, Tiberius."

"What if she wakes up? I want to be here when she does," I said, heart racing.

"The Mother always does things in threes. Since she hasn't risen in the two like we usually do, and since the Mother was involved in her conversion, she will probably rise in about ten hours." Smiling, I realized she was trying to comfort me, and it had been almost three days since I got more than about thirty minutes of rest. "Caleus and I will keep watch."

"If anything changes, we will let you know," Velarde said.

I got up and knelt before her. I moved the hair that was lying over her nose. If she couldn't move and it was causing an itch, that would suck. As I laid it next to her ear, I ran my thumb across her cheek, and it was a blaze of fire. I took that as a good sign and then kissed her brow and said against her skin, "I still choose you, Kelsey."

I stood up and looked out of the window on the other side of the bed. Trenton's lights reflected off the Sierras, and for the first time in a very, very long time, I didn't know what the next day was going to bring. Ignoring the stares from Bella and Velarde, who were standing against the dresser, I sighed and went to get some sleep.

CHAPTER 71

KELSEY

"Get some sleep, Tiberius," Bella told Max.

"What if she wakes up? I want to be here when she does," Max had said, but there was fear in his voice, and it made another wave of heat flow through my body.

"The Mother always does things in threes. Since she hasn't risen in the two that we usually do, and since the Mother was involved in her conversion, she will probably rise in about ten hours," Bella said, trying to comfort Max. "Caleus and I will keep watch."

"If anything changes, we will let you know," Vel said.

A moment later, I felt his thumb across my cheek, and it was a blaze of heat that warmed my entire body. I wanted so badly to lean into it, but I still couldn't move. There was a long kiss on my forehead, and he whispered, "I still choose you, Kelsey."

I had been listening to Izzy and Vel for a few hours now, but when I tried to open my eyes, there was nothing I could do. It was as if I were here, but not.

Izzy and Vel started talking about the past and making theories for the future, but I couldn't concentrate on them. It was only Max's voice that had come through crystal clear for me.

My whole body felt feverish. It was a different fire under my skin than when Max looked at or touched me. It was more like if you were laying out in the sun in the valley heat.

Daughter.

I was startled at the sound that reverberated throughout my entire body.

It is time you remember. It is time that you join your soul and live your lives.

Remember? What else was there to remember?

"Please don't make me remember my time with Marcus," I begged into the ether. Before Marcus had taken me, I had recalled every detail of Sidonia and Tiberius' time together, but I was thankful for the protection my brain had given me with all that Marcus had done.

It is time you remember your studies as Sidonia. It is time you remember your lifetimes with Isabella Edelmann Velarde and Caleus Lars Velarde. It is time to live, daughter of Gaea.

The words repeated thrice in my head before I felt every muscle in my body go taut and I was flooded with information.

Memories of my mother and grandmother teaching me about the herbs on Vesuvius, how to prepare them, how to render them to their useful forms, and the deliveries I would make around Herculaneum bombarded me

Memories of a day working hard in the desert, carrying water back to our little shelter, and the way a man, Marcus, had come through the little village and burned everyone and everything to the ground.

There were visions of war, of love, of struggle, and of wealth. There were wars fought with Izzy and Vel at my back or me at theirs. A life of living in the Cambodian temples, ensuring the sanctity of the rituals and texts there. There were lives working as a servant in various royal homes, and lives where I was nothing more than a commoner just trying to survive.

More and more came through, bringing me closer and closer to my current life. Marcus showed up in most of them in one way or another.

There was one constant. There were never any children in any of my lives, even when I had a husband.

"Mother. Will I be able to bear children for Max?" I asked in a child's voice.

Only he has ever been able to create life within you.

"So, I really never had children with any other men in my previous lives?"

No, my daughter. You have never known the joy of children.

"If I choose to stay with him now . . . If I choose to allow him . . . Am able to allow him to touch me in that way? Will I be able to have his children? Even after what Marcus did to me? Did Marcus leave me barren?" I asked, feeling tears slide down my face. I hadn't realized that I would ever want kids. Everything had changed so much in the last two months. The last thing I thought about was a relationship with Max or if kids were something either of us would want. Now it seemed so important to know if I *could* give that to him or not. I felt another tear slide down my cheek as I tried to keep from hiccupping through the tears.

I felt a thumb wipe it off.

Max! My attention was purely on that spot he touched me.

If you so choose to stay with Tiberius Maximus Vispania, you shall be blessed with sons and daughters.

"What of Izzy and Vel? Have they ever had children? Can they?"

My daughter Isabella Edelmann Velarde is unable to bear Caleus Lars Velarde's children. The Dark Witches of Moesia have taken that from her.

"Izzy is a daughter of Gaea as well?"

Yes. Isabella knows of our ways, daughter. While she is not descended from the line who were blessed as you have been, she is the daughter of my grandson Zeus.

I laughed. "Zeus. The Greek God who couldn't keep it in his pants is Izzy's line? Why doesn't that surprise me? Wait. She is Egyptian and German, though."

I could almost feel the Mother laugh and smile.

Many are of Zeus' line. That is true. The line runs wide, daughter. Many are born of my line, just as many are born of the other Primal Gods.

I was quiet for a long time.

It is time for you to return to your soul, daughter. That is, shall you wish it.

I didn't hesitate. "I wish it. I wish to return to Max." But then, a thought occurred. "Mother, I do not hurt here. Will I hurt when I return?"

The mother laughed. There was a joyous ringing throughout my head, and I honestly didn't know what to make of it.

Daughter, you are now as your soul. You are near-immortal and carry the power of me within you. Shall you be mortally wounded, you shall die but rise in three days. Only beheading shall remove you from his side and return you to me. Please do not join me any time soon, daughter. Continue my line. Restore our teachings. Do no harm and help others. Do what Sidonia wanted to spend her life doing.

"And what was that?" I asked shyly.

Helping others.

Then there was a shove, and I was falling fully back into my body.

I felt the bed under my back, Max's hand in mine, the blankets around me, and the warmth of the room. Max ran his thumb across my cheek again and breathed, "Come back to me, Kelsey."

I leaned into his hand and felt him freeze as I continued to move my head into his palm. When my lips reached his it, I kissed it and opened my eyes.

His face filled my vision, and there were tears in his eyes. "Kelsey?"

I smiled at him.

"Love? Is that really you?" he whispered in a broken croak.

My eyes flicked around the room, and I saw Izzy and Vel standing a few feet behind him. He hadn't moved an inch. I turned my head and met those sapphire eyes that had stunned me for as long as my soul could remember. They were warm, and I knew this was where I needed to be.

His eyes narrowed. "Love?"

I slipped my hand from his and brought both of mine to either side of his face. He leaned into my touch, but his eyes still had that questioning look.

I pulled him closer, but he was still hesitant and slowly moved his hands to brace himself next to me. I let a small, wicked smile cross my face.

"Max," I whispered against his lips, as light as a feather.

I felt a shudder rock through him and his muscles tighten as to not fall on top of me.

"Kelsey," he finally breathed.

That was all the confirmation I didn't realize I needed. I reached up and kissed him hard. He was so shocked that he froze for a moment before wrapping his arms around my shoulders, holding me tight to him.

CHAPTER 72

MAX

"TIBERIUS! GET YOUR ASS up. Something is happening to Kelsey," Velarde said. I blinked, and when he repeated himself, he might as well have dumped cold water over me.

"Did she wake?" I asked, already halfway down the hall.

"No."

I stopped and, with a thick throat, asked as I stared toward the doorway, "Did her heart stop?"

Velarde smiled. "No, you stupid fuck. Of course, she still breathes. Come on," he said, taking my arm and forcing me toward the bedroom we had her set up in.

I reached the door, and when I looked at her, her whole body was . . . shimmering. It was the only way to describe it. She wasn't glowing exactly. It was more like a white light passed over her and there was a glimmer to her skin.

"How long has this been happening?" I asked, going to her bedside and taking her hand. Her body was stiff, and when I put her hand in mine, she clenched it tight.

My focus snapped to her face, and the muscles twitched with various emotions. "Kelsey, love. I'm here. I'm waiting for you. I will wait here until you are ready, but please come back to me? Please don't make me wait another two thousand years," I whispered against her hand.

"She's been like this for a few hours, but the shimmering has been getting brighter," Bella said with an odd expression. I was about to ask what she was concerned about, but she said, "She's glowing like she did in that cell."

"It's been what, 70 hours since her heart first stopped?" Velarde said.

A tear slid down her cheek, and I couldn't help but wipe it from her. I thought I felt her face twitch toward me, but I couldn't tell. "Come back to me, Kelsey," I breathed.

I couldn't move. Her face was hot against mine, and I needed her. I sat there for a long time just staring at her. Velarde and Bella both had offered to get me something to eat. I knew I should because Gods only knew when Kelsey would open her eyes again, but I could not take my eyes off her.

My thumb rubbed against the side of her cheek just as a wave of warmth pulsed through both of us, and I froze. After a moment, she leaned into my hand, and when her lips reached my palm, she kissed it and opened her eyes.

I swallowed thickly and said, "Kelsey?"

She smiled at me, and I swore there was a bit of a wicked gleam in her eyes.

"Love? Is that really you?" I whispered in a broken croak.

Her eyes flicked to Bella and Velarde standing a few feet behind me, but I didn't dare move a muscle. Slowly, she turned and met my gaze again. Dear Gods. I was in so much trouble. Her eyes were bright, clear, and more vibrant than I remembered. There was a flash of something behind them, and I narrowed my eyes before I asked, "Love?"

She slipped her hand from mine and cradled my head in her hands. I couldn't help but lean into her. Her thumbs caressed my cheeks, and it took everything in me not to moan at the touch.

She pulled me closer, and I had to move my arms to keep from falling on top of her. I made a very conscious effort to do so slowly, but I balled my hands into fists to keep from pulling her up into my arms.

I wanted to hold her so badly. To tell her everything. To tell her how I felt about her. To use those three words that I hadn't used since the day that we died in the boathouse.

"Max," she whispered against my lips, and I shuddered as the force of my name on her lips fell through me. I strained to keep from collapsing on top of her.

"Kelsey," I breathed.

Her lips crashed onto mine, and I was so shocked that I froze for a moment before my mind cleared enough to realize that she was kissing me. My heart stopped and restarted multiple times in that instant. I reached around her shoulders and wrapped her tight in my arms and kissed her back.

That kiss was my absolute undoing. I would do anything for this woman. If she asked me to remove my head for her, I would do it. There was nothing that didn't feel right and real with Kelsey. I pulled her closer, and she swung herself around on my lap and faced me, wrapping her legs around my waist.

Dear Gods. My cock hardened in that very second, and I slid my hands to her hips to move her back just the slightest bit so she couldn't feel it. She had been through so much. I could wait. I would wait.

When she broke the kiss, she asked, "Why did you move me back?"

I reached up and put a hand on her cheek and said carefully, "Love, you've been through so much. I didn't want to ruin the moment with the instant hard-on you just gave me." I kissed her quickly just so she couldn't retort, and she leaned her forehead on mine and released a shuddering breath.

"Thank you," she said. I couldn't do anything but smile at her.

"Kels?" Bella said behind me, and she gave me a wicked smile, and there was much mischief in her eyes as she slowly climbed off me.

"Izzy." Kelsey stood facing her and crossed her arms. It was all an act, but Bella played into it.

"Kels. I know you are mad. Mother be—"

"Mother be? Oh, so you claim the Mother now?"

"I've always claimed the Mother, even if you three ass-twerps didn't know," Bella growled, but she took a deep breath. "You have every fucking right to be pissed as hell at us after everything. I don't deny that. But when I realized just how many times I've lived a life with my best friend . . . with my soul sister . . ."

Kelsey raised an eyebrow at her, then looked at me, then back at her.

"When I got shot that night, I woke up two days later, just like these fuckers do, and I knew you were safe with them. You were with your soul, Kels. Vel and I had figured it out long before that night, but Tiberius here was too stubborn and too much of a dumb shit to either realize or accept it. So, I went to work looking to find out what Marcus was doing."

I giggled. "Bella. You are rambling."

Bella narrowed her eyes at me, and Kelsey turned around and raised that eyebrow at me, and I winced.

"Isabella Edelmann Velarde," Kelsey said.

Bella blinked. "How do you know that full name?"

"I know a lot more than I did before I died three days ago. I can tell you that," Kelsey said. She turned to me and said, "While . . . resting, the Mother and I had a nice long discussion."

"The Mother?" Bella said carefully.

"Yes. You know, your long-lost ancestor via Zeus, in case you didn't know." Kelsey was enjoying this. The playful nature in her eyes was enticing. "So yes, I know you were raised as an Earth Worshiper, just as I was, Isabella Edelmann Velarde. And by the way, I suggest that you brush up on your pestle and mortar skills. I'm going to need an assistant in the apothecary shop we will be opening. I also saw twelve lifetimes where we were best friends, three of which you, Vel, and I fought back-to-back in wars all over the Asian, African, and European continents."

There was a part of me that was jealous of the lives they had shared.

"Twelve," Bella said, shocked. Kelsey nodded. "Damn. We are going to have to talk about that."

"One of which, I believe, you promised to cut Vel's balls off and"—Kelsey paused for a moment then laughed—"use them in a soup for him to eat.

"I threaten to chop his balls off at least once every thirty years. Vel doesn't even take it as a serious threat anymore." There was confusion, satisfaction, and pride in Bella's eyes as she said, "Wait, we are opening an apothecary shop? What about school?"

"We finish up in a semester and a half, Izzy. Then we can do whatever the fuck we want," she said, throwing her hands up. "The bills ain't just gonna pay themselves. We have to make money."

"No, you don't," I said, coming to stand beside her and taking her hand. I met her gaze for a long, long moment before I continued. "Velarde and Bella have more money than they know what to do with. That is a perk of living for as long as we have."

"Okay, so maybe Izzy doesn't have to work, but I do, Max." She squeezed my hand.

"No, you don't, love. Are you forgetting that I am a mul-ti-billionaire?"

"No," she said and took half of a step back. "I'm not. I don't forget who you are, Max Vispania, much of which we can discuss later, but just because *you* have money doesn't mean that *I* do. I don't accept handouts. I have always worked my ass off for what I have. I have been going to school to get an education off of my inheritance."

I smiled at her. "Kelsey, we haven't had the chance to be a couple yet, but you are my soul. You are my other half. Therefore, everything I have is yours."

She gave me a puzzled look. "Is that your way of asking me to marry your sorry ass?"

I couldn't help but laugh out loud, but when I stopped, she had a smirk on her face and raised an eyebrow. She was indeed waiting for an answer.

I took two steps toward her and got on both of my knees before her. "Kelsey Ann Stillthorn Vispania, everything I have is yours because you are my soul. Period. The fact you are also my wife is completely beside the point."

"Again, is that your way of asking me to marry you, Tiberius Maximus Vispania?" She smirked again at me, and there was a light and question in her eyes.

"You forget, Kelsey, that you already married me in 79 AD. By law, you already own half of my entire life. You have more than that by virtue of being my soul."

"Oh, I haven't forgotten. I still claim you as my husband, but there is nothing . . . anywhere in all of history that proves it. I know of at least four weddings for those two shitheads. I've had one with you." She was fucking with me and enjoying every minute of it.

"Wait here," I told her, and as I walked by Bella and Velarde, who were chuckling, I growled at them, "Fuckers."

I made my way across the floor and into my office. The light reflected off it, making my heart thump so loud, I was sure everyone could hear it. Carefully, I picked up the box and carried it back into the bedroom.

CHAPTER 73

KELSEY

WHEN MAX WALKED INTO the bedroom, he was carrying a box about the size of a shoe box. When his hand moved and I saw what was inside of it, I froze. There was no way. He placed it carefully on the table, and I took a few tentative steps toward it.

I looked at him, then back at the box before me. With tears in my eyes, I looked up at him and said, "Is that?"

"Yes. The very same one. Not a replica, love."

"How?"

"It is the one thing that no matter what happened, how destroyed a village, town, city, or country I was in was, I always made sure this came with me."

"The day we woke in Herculaneum, we went back to your house and he dug through the debris for hours to find it," Velarde said.

"What is the significance other than it was Sidonia's?" Izzy asked. "That was all we have ever known about it."

I stared at it and smiled, tears flowing hard and fast down my face. I swallowed at the lump in my throat as it all played out behind my eyes. Max came over and wiped the tears away.

"I was in the marketplace." I sniffed and wiped my nose. "I saw it in one of the stalls and thought it was beautiful, so I paid too much for it with the money I made from the apothecary shop. I put it on immediately. I went about my business, and when I met up with my father . . ."

"What?" Izzy said. "You still aren't making sense. You are only saying half sentences, Kels."

I looked up at Max. He smiled at me and encouraged me to keep telling the story. I turned my head and leaned into the feel of his hand on my cheek, turned, kissed his palm, then said, "That was when I met Tiberius the first time. If memory serves me right, Tiberius kept me from falling over during an earthquake during that encounter."

"And a few other times before Vesuvius blew," he said, chuckling. "I always loved it on you."

"Well, you asked me to wear it every time we were together. It was one of my favorite pieces because the sapphire in the middle of the lotus reminded me of your eyes." I stepped back from Max and crouched down to look at it. "How has it survived this long?"

"Special boxes, and now in an environmentally controlled one. Which is why I'm not taking it out of its box to put back on your wrist. I want to keep it preserved," Max said.

"Is this your way of asking me to marry you, Max?" I repeated, standing before him.

Slowly, tentatively, he wrapped his arms around my waist. There was a split second of panic before I hitched my breath and stared into his eyes. Those very same sapphires looked back at me and calmed. I felt the restraint in his arms. He understood and was trying.

"Max?"

"Kelsey." He cut me off. His eyes were filled with tears and some emotion that I couldn't place.

I blinked, and another kind of panic tore through me. "I know I said that it was two thousand years ago that Sidonia loved Tiberius, but . . ." Even though it would kill me, I made myself meet his gaze and, in a voice that felt too small, asked, "Do you not want to get married?"

His eyes widened, realizing my fear, and his grip tightened around my waist. "Kelsey Ann Stillthorn Vispania. Marry me. There is nothing that would make me happier than for all the current world to know that you are my wife. That I belong to you." His words came out fast and determined. I blinked at him, and my panic vanished. "Kelsey, will you marry me? Will you allow me to announce to the world that I belong to Kelsey Vispania?"

"Yes," I said and kissed him.

CHAPTER 74

KELSEY

NINE MONTHS LATER

"WHY ARE YOU SO nervous?" Izzy asked as she stood there folding our laundry.

"It's been nine months."

"Yeah, and?" She tipped her head to the side to study me a moment before reaching over and squeezing my hand. "Are you not ready? Don't push yourself. What was done to you is not something that anyone should have had to go through. There are sexual assault survivors who can't physically have sex for years because of the trauma."

"I want this. I want him," I said. "I'm just scared I'll freak out again." Three months ago, even with extensive therapy, I had decided I wanted to move into a physical relationship with Max. He had been wining and dining me since I woke up.

He introduced me as his wife and I introduced him as my husband at every function we attended. The fact that we hadn't actually had a marriage ceremony in two thousand years didn't seem to matter to either of us. However, when I tried to move forward and actually have sex with him, my body froze. I completely froze. He hadn't even penetrated me yet, and I completely disassociated and stopped moving.

Max recognized it immediately, stopped in the next heartbeat, wrapped me in a weighted blanket, and got me some water. I had felt horrible and cried for hours. He just held me the entire time.

I had thought I was ready.

"Max doesn't hold it against you. You know that, right? In fact, he was worried he had done something wrong, maybe pushed you into thinking you were ready," Izzy said carefully.

"I know he doesn't resent me for it." I sighed, throwing down a set of socks. "We have been physical with each other, continue to be, and he hasn't pushed me one step of the way."

"I think he is just happy you are home and back at his side."

"You know, he has never once called me Sidonia." I smiled softly. "Not once."

"He chose you, Kelsey. He has said on multiple occasions that you are what he wants. Don't question it."

"I know that here," I said, pointing to my heart, but then I pointed to my head. "Up here is still a work in progress. I keep waiting for him to slip up and say that other name."

"When you get him in bed, you will know who he is sleeping with. It's much harder for a man to hide it there." Izzy smirked at me. "Don't tell him that I told you this, but he said that once you marry again, he is going to add to his tattoo."

Raising my eyebrows, I was now intrigued. I had spent many hours tracing my fingertips over my old name. "Are you just going to let me stew in that information, or are you going to tell me what he is going to add to it?"

"He plans on changing it so it reads, *Sidonia's flame built over the centuries to Kelsey's inferno.* All still in the same language."

He had, on multiple occasions, said that I was so much more than what I was back then. We talked about his sisters, my brothers and nieces, and all the dreams we had for them before that August summer day. "I would be lying if I hadn't been thinking about getting one that said, *From the ashes, I became the flame.* I guess they represent the same thing, right?"

She winked at me as she pulled me into a close hug and changed the subject. "Do you have a wedding date for me yet?"

I smirked at her. Max and I had a long talk about what kind of wedding we wanted to have. I told him I didn't care if we just had the judge come up to the tower and sign off on the paperwork, but he said he wanted to make it an extravagant affair so the entire world knew who he belonged to, that it had been two thousand years since we were married, and he wanted to do it like it was the first time. I rolled my eyes at him each time. "After we graduate, Iz. There is no rush."

"You keep saying that, but that's in just a couple of months." She threw her hands up in the air.

"I don't mean the actual wedding in a couple months. I mean sometime after we graduate." Giving her an even look, I sighed. "We can't plan an entire wedding in just a couple of months."

"Please, you and Max own this town. You think if I walked into a venue and told them that they were hosting Maximus Vispania and Kelsey Stillthorn Vispania's wedding *this* weekend, they and the entire town of Trenton wouldn't move the Sierras themselves to make the event happen without a glitch?" She laughed.

Folding a towel, I sighed and looked at the ceiling. She had a point. Well, except for the fact that I owned the town. Max did. I didn't. "I'll get you a date. I promise. Speaking of, the last wedding I know of for you and Vel was back in the 1700s."

Now she was the one laughing, throwing some of my underwear at me. "It probably is time to do that again. After ten of them, sometimes they are just tedious. The last one was . . ." She looked up to the ceiling and thought a long moment before saying, "1850 something. One of the local reverends married us up at Jackson Lake. Nowadays, though, it isn't uncommon for people to live unmarried for a long while. So, we can hold off for a few more years. Besides, to the public, we are both still in our 20s. We have time."

My phone buzzed, and I pulled it from my back pocket. There was only a photo of a table set for two with a single candle in the middle of it. A note in a beautiful, elegant script said: *Upstairs. Now.*

I stood there staring at it. It didn't make sense. We were supposed to go to an event tonight, and Max had cooked dinner for us?

"Did you tell him I was going to try again?" I asked Izzy, staring at the phone.

"No. That is your decision. Why would I tell him? What if you changed your mind?"

My heart thudded. I had told myself I needed to do this. I wanted this. I trusted Max. Trusted him wholly. I knew that this was the next step in not only my healing but also in my relationship. I was the person who needed to move into a sexual, physical relationship with him.

"Just wondering is all," I said, answering Izzy.

"Why would you even ask?"

"I thought we were going to the Nerine gala. He has the table set for dinner." I finished folding the towel and putting it on the stack to be put away.

When I reached for another one, she smacked my hand and said, "So why in the fuck are you still standing here?"

I gestured to the laundry and gave her an incredulous look. She stared me down, and I reached for the towel again. She smacked it harder this time.

"Iz!"

"Will you go upstairs, have a great dinner, and then fuck Max senseless?" Izzy said, smiling. "You both could use the railing, for the record."

"You are such a bitch," I said just as Vel just strode into our apartment, in a tux no less.

Sighing, I asked, "Are you planning on fucking all around our apartment tonight?"

"You aren't coming home. Get upstairs now. Max is waiting," Vel said.

I threw a pair of my underwear at him, and he caught them and tossed them back on the table.

"When you didn't text him back, he sent me after you," Vel said, smiling. "For the record, Izzy and I are going to be out tonight."

"We are?" she said, looking at him like he was nuts. "I like Kelsey's idea better. And I *really* enjoy fucking you in a tux. You clean up good, Velarde."

"Too bad. Go get dressed up. Black-tie. We are going in their place. Let's go." Vel smacked her ass as she passed by him. "Taking my wife to dinner first, though. I have reservations at Rataveli's in 45 minutes. So move it."

"A little warning would have been nice." Izzy groaned but headed to the bedroom.

"Watch it, Mrs. Velarde, before I make you marry me in an affair to rival the one Max wants for Kelsey!" he said as she swayed her hips, closing the bedroom door. He turned to face me and smiled. "It's nice to call her Mrs. Velarde in front of you now."

"I'm glad you guys don't have to hide it from me. That night everything went to shit, I wanted to kill you both for hiding so much."

"I'm sorry, Kelsey. We . . . We have had to hide that part from everyone but us, and we needed you to sort it out," he said, pleading for understanding. Then, he smirked and said, "Now seriously, will you go upstairs and fuck that asshat of a brother of mine?"

"How . . ." I glared toward the bedroom and groaned. "You guys are going to be the death of me. He doesn't know I want to try tonight, does he?"

"No. I promise. He won't say no, though, if you just strip and fuck him silly." He smirked at me, gave me a quick kiss on the cheek, and said, "Get upstairs. I'll see you tomorrow."

"Fine," I said, hearing him snicker behind me. Grabbing my keys, I headed upstairs.

CHAPTER 75

KELSEY

I KNEW THE KEY code to Max's apartment and punched it in, not even bothering to knock. Why, when I spent more time in it than the one I technically shared with Izzy downstairs?

When I walked in, it was dark except for the row of candles that lined each side of the hallway toward the main room. I tossed my keys in the bowl and slowly stepped down the hall.

"Max?"

A soft chuckle floated in the air, and I smirked. What was he up to?

When I got to the living room, the whole space glowed with candlelight. The lights of Trenton twinkled out the floor-to-ceiling windows. The sun setting behind us almost gave the Sierras a glowing effect as they rose behind the town.

Max's arms wrapped around my waist from behind, and I leaned back into him. That was one thing that I had never struggled with since coming home. Max touching me wasn't a problem. He could hold me, kiss me, and do a great number of things to me that, according to all the textbooks, he shouldn't be able to do since my ordeal. It threw my therapist for a loop. Well, except for when I tried to have sex with him. My therapist had just tried to remind me that it was a completely normal reaction, and we may have to try a few times before my body would feel safe enough for anything penetrative.

"Hey, love. Welcome home." As I leaned back against him, his head snuck in next to mine as he gave me a kiss on the cheek.

"Hey yourself." I sighed, content. I felt safest here. Once I had gotten over the way he had to live his life, I just accepted the fact that this was the man I loved and nothing else mattered if I was in his arms.

My left hand reached up and cradled his cheek. After a moment, he reached up and held it, his fingers running over the ring I now wore there. Three weeks after I had woken up from my nightmare, Max had brought home a beautiful engagement ring for me. Silver, with a massive diamond in the center, it was wrapped with deep emerald and sapphire stones. It took me a while to be comfortable wearing it. I feared losing it, but Max just assured me that if something happened to it, that he would replace it.

Slowly, I turned to face him. "So, what's with the change of plans tonight?"

He blinked at me, pausing a moment. "What?"

"What's with the change of plans? I thought we were going to the gala?" I asked again, wrapping my arms around his neck and pressing against him.

I swore I heard a moan come from him before he said, "Is it wrong that I want you all to myself tonight?"

"I *am* yours." I gave him a quick kiss. "You don't share me with anyone."

"But there would be other eyes on you tonight. Call me greedy or, wait, I have one better, an overprotective, overbearing asshole." His hands pulled me a little closer, if that was even possible.

I chuckled. I had indeed called him that on multiple occasions since we met. "Whether or not we go out, you are still an overprotective, overbearing asshole. It's just that now I claim you as *my* overprotective, overbearing asshole."

"And don't you forget it," he said, kissing me.

Even after nine months of this, the feeling never ceased to breathe life into me. His very touch lit me up. When he leaned back, my voice was breathless. "Is dinner ready, or what's the plan?"

"Dinner will not be ready for a couple of hours. I just wanted you to get your sexy ass up here so I could hold and kiss you," he said, a blush rising to his cheeks. "Is that such a crime?"

"Perfect," I said, pulling away from him. I tried and failed at steadying my nerves, but when his eyes trailed up and down my body, it gave me the exact shot of courage I needed.

I took a couple of sauntering steps back from him and slowly unbuttoned my shirt. He stood there frozen as he watched me. When I tossed the shirt to the couch, his eyes met mine.

"Kelsey." His voice was thick and questioning.

"Max," I said playfully. I reached down and started unbuttoning my pants. As I slowly slid them off, he took one tentative step toward me.

I stepped out of my pants, tossed them next to my shirt, and took a few more steps back to lean against the floor-to ceiling-windows at the far end of the room.

I swore I heard his heated groan from across the room. His eyes never left mine as his hands trembled while he unbuttoned his. When it landed next to my pants and shirt, he took long determined strides toward me and slammed a hand against the window next to my head to brace himself. My heart raced in fear and anticipation. Not in fear of him, but fear of my inability to follow this through. Looking into his sapphire eyes and seeing all that love and heat for me helped soothe it, and I pinched my bottom lip between my teeth.

His other hand rose to caress my cheek as he said, "Kelsey." His voice was so filled with emotion that I thought I would melt right there.

My fingers rose to trace the lines on his chest, then his abs, idly trailing over my old name before nimbly unbuttoning the button fly of his jeans. It was only seconds before they hit the floor and he sprang free before me. I wrapped my hands around him and his hand tightened on my cheek.

I moved to get to my knees, but his grip on my head tightened, and he growled, "No."

I stopped and looked at him. "What?"

"Are you sure you are ready? I do not want to push you into this." His voice hitched slightly as I stroked him. He could tell tonight was different. Tonight would not be us playing with each other, or me giving him head, or him eating me out.

Oral sex was something I was perfectly comfortable doing and probably the only reason I hadn't gone sex crazed over the last few months. But this? Him? I needed him inside me. Tonight.

I hadn't realized he had loosened his grip, and my head hung a little until he lifted my chin. Still keeping my eyes downcast, he said in a more dominant tone, "Kelsey, look at me."

I smirked because while in our day-to-day life, I would be subservient to him. In the bedroom, he was going to learn just how dominant I could be. My eyes flashed up to his, and a smirk crossed my lips. I looked forward to that discussion, to see just who would fall into what role between us. I was a switch by nature, but could he relinquish that control? It was a discussion we would need to have, if I could just get over my own fucking nerves.

There was a flash of a challenge in his eyes before he reached around, undid my bra, and it fell to the floor. Seconds later, my panties were in pieces next to it.

"You want to fight, Max? Want to have that discussion right here and now?" I said in a tone that dominated even him.

His eyes roamed up and down my body again, and there was a shudder that racked through him. I knew he was mine at that moment, at least for tonight. He looked at me through his lashes and with a smile said, "No, ma'am."

That was all it took for me to push against his chest, and he sat back on the couch. He watched me as I prowled toward him. "We can work out terms and roles later, but right now, you are mine. I am yours."

He nodded his head as I straddled him. His hands rested on my hips, and there was restraint in his fingers as I smiled at him.

I reached down and kissed him hard. One of his hands grazed along my bare skin, leaving ribbons of flame, as he reached up and threaded his fingers through my hair, pulling me closer. His other hand ran along one of the scars that was there and I froze for half a thought, but the feel of his heat reassured me who I was with and that I was in control.

I lowered myself against him and rocked my hips. A smile crossed my lips as he growled deep in his chest and his hands tightened against me.

"Max," I whispered. "Look at me."

His eyes snapped open, and the heat and love almost undid me. Reaching down, I held him, smiling softly as a few short movements of my hips had him resisting the urge to plunge into me. When I had him positioned at my opening, his eyes had half of a question in them before I slowly lowered myself fully onto him.

I moaned as every inch of him filled me. It was like the lava flow of Mount Vesuvius flowing within me. "Gods, you are amazing, Kelsey."

When I was fully seated, my head fell to his shoulder, and my chest constricted as panic threatened to take over. My breaths came in short and quick. Flashes of my time in that cell went through my mind, and I felt each of my muscles tense as the panic rose.

I was with Max.

Slowly, I took a shuddering, deep breath and let it out, willing any panic to release. That was Max's heat against my skin. Max's heat within me.

Max sat there, patient, filling me to the brim, letting his thumb run back and forth against my skin in reassurance. His heat. It was Max's heat I felt. Slowly, I lifted my head and met his gaze.

"I am here. I am yours." With those six words, all the tightness in my chest loosened. I was with Max, and I was safe.

"I am here. I am yours," I repeated back to him and rocked my hips. "I am yours."

His hands tightened against me as he moved with me. Mother be, I had missed this.

No. This was something different. This was fire, heat, and the burning suns. There had never been anyone like Tiberius Maximus Vispania. In all my lives, there hadn't been anyone else who held a candle to him.

We were slow and deliberate in our movements at first, and when his hand gripped my ass, I rocked hard against him.

Throwing my head back, I repeated the movements. His mouth caught my nipple and bit down. I clenched down on him and moaned loudly. I rolled against him, and he wrapped his arms tight around my waist, lifting me, saying, "I want you against that window."

I smirked at him. "What?"

"I have fantasized about taking you against the window for all of Trenton to see for months," he said, nibbling my ear. In what was no effort at all, he stood, me still impaled by him, as he strode to the window. I wrapped my legs tighter around his waist and laughed.

"Seriously?"

"Do you have any idea how fucking sexy you are right now?" He pushed me against the glass and secured his hands on my ass.

He held me against the window and dragged out of me before thrusting back in and rolling against me. Mother, that spot inside me quivered at the motion.

My heart raced at the mere thought of people actually being able to see us fucking in the window, but damn, it was hot. We were on the 16th floor of Vispania Tower. No one would look this far up, but the thought someone could had me rolling against him and moaning.

Stroke for stroke, I met him. Just when I thought he would carry me over the edge, he stopped, and we slid to the floor. There was half of a thought of not being ready to be trapped under him, but he instead rolled so I was still on top.

My heart stopped, started, and then, when he looked up at me, he said, "I am yours."

Emotions so wild and pure flowed through me. He was still giving me all the control. I leaned over, grinding against him, and kissed him deep. His arms wrapped around my waist, and he pounded into me.

A minute later, I was sitting up, undulating against him, his eyes rolling into the back of his head. I couldn't help but smirk at him and ride him hard and fast. His hand moved to between my legs and flicked my clit as he filled me.

"Fuck me, Max." I moaned loud into the apartment. He worked his hips under me in a way that had him creating pressure in all the right places. Meeting him with every thrust just brought me closer and closer to the brink of bliss. Soon, we were both panting and moaning loudly.

"Gods, Kelsey." A few more strong, determined thrusts, and then I was screaming his name. As stars burst before my eyes and the world faded to nothing but that release, I heard him growl my name as he released deep within me.

I collapsed on top of him, my legs trembling, and smiled against his chest. Lying there, covered in sweat, I was feeling the best I had since the morning after I wed this man almost two thousand years ago.

It was easy, like the wind, to say, "I love you, Tiberius Maximus Vispania."

He kissed the top of my head and held me close as he said, "I love you, Kelsey Ann Stillthorn Vispania. Forever."

Books by Kimberly M. Ringer

The Five Angels Series
The Five Angels
The Ash'bani
The Helena Crystal

Duchess' Crown
Duchess' Throne

Ashstrike Sanctorum Series
The Ashstrike Sanctorum:
The origin Story
The Astral's Bonded
The Exorci's Touch
My Kismot Savior
the Kismot's Undesirable
The Therugi's Shiver
The Puroklet's Storm (2024)

The Weekend Series
Weekend with Rylie
Weekend with Malcom
Weekend with Desiree
Weekend with Bethany (2024/25)

Stand Alones
Ashes and Flame
Crafter's Rainbow (2024/25)

About the Author

Kimberly M. Ringer lives in Santa Cruz, California with her husband, little human, and two furballs, Wall-E (a Jack Russell mix) and Pippin (a Pomeranian Terrier mix). When she isn't writing, she is reading, playing with the dogs, playing video games or down at the beach. She's a bit geeky and nerdy, so sci-fi references and other things going on in the science world will often end up in her stories.

Contact Kimberly M. Ringer:
www.kimberlymringer.com
Instagram: @kimberlymringer
Facebook: https://www.facebook.com/kimberlymringer

Sign up for my newsletter on my website and receive freebies, coupon codes, and stay up to date on all things Kimberly M. Ringer and K.M. Ringer
Newsletter Signup

www.ingramcontent.com/pod-product-compliance
Lightning Source LLC
Chambersburg PA
CBHW050947210726
48287CB00004B/1172